Both Hunter

and Hunted

Both Hunter and Hunted

Both Hunter and
Hunted rely on God—Turkish Proverb

Vincent Joyce

Writers Club Press
San Jose New York Lincoln Shanghai

Both Hunter and Hunted

Writers Club Press
an imprint of iUniverse.com, Inc.

For information address:
iUniverse.com, Inc.
5220 S 16th, Ste. 200
Lincoln, NE 68512
www.iuniverse.com

ISBN: 0-595-15619-3

Printed in the United States of America

To past, present and future members of U.S. Foreign Service agencies.

It is the author's intention to donate 10% of his proceeds to cancer research.

Among the people who helped prepare this book for publication are Kathleen Beekley, Jamie Shauvin, Gregg Dillenbeck, James Gaver, and Valerie Haas. My children Cecilia, Romy, Francesca, and Anthony provided abundant encouragement.

Both Hunter and Hunted is a work of fiction, and all characters are products of the author's imagination. On the other hand, some readers may profess to recognize persons and events, and that could make for some amusing conjecture. Have it your way.

Both Hunter and Hunted rely on God—Turkish Proverb.

PROLOGUE

Washington D.C., 2000

Even after nearly a quarter of a century I knew that voice. It was low and throaty and seductive, attributable to too many years of smoking (though she did finally quit) and too many dry martinis when they were deemed to be the best pre-seduction drink. In truth, we didn't need martinis. But it didn't last, the sexual element of our relationship, after I announced that I was getting married. She was angry at first but then her anger turned to scorn when I said who my intended was. "You're reaching too hard and too high, as usual," she said, and she was right.

"When can you come to D.C.?" she asked.

"Why should I?"

"Do you think I would go to the trouble of calling you if it wasn't important? I have something you want."

"Listen, at my age I'm not sure I could get it up, let alone get up to Washington." There was a pained silence while she evaluated my dismal attempt at humor.

"You have ten seconds to fix a date and time or else I destroy it."

"Okay, okay," I said quickly, "I'll fly into National tomorrow morning. Let's meet at the usual at 12:30 p.m." I should have said Reagan Airport instead of National but there was too much running through my mind to correct myself. At least she knew what the usual was when she agreed to my suggestion.

The usual was a little Lebanese restaurant on K Street that had survived the demolition of buildings to its left and right. For years it had been a favorite rendezvous point for agents seeking to find favor with Arab diplomats in the expectation that they would divulge state secrets over a plate of meze. Surprisingly, many did, as the Arabs enjoyed the ability to demonstrate their importance by spilling all, even if much of their information was fabricated and designed to please the host.

She kept me waiting no more than ten minutes, during which I nursed a glass of araq and water, the Arab world's version of ouzo or raki. Laura Ingalls, her real name, not the one she used in McLean, had stood the test of time remarkably well. Her auburn hair was streaked with gray, and wrinkles surrounded her eyes when she smiled, but she avoided the frequent mistake of women of a certain age of slathering on makeup. She was letting nature take its course, and nature was being exceedingly kind.

Laura ordered the obligatory glass of araq and water and we both settled on the house specialty of meze de luxe, a sumptuous mix of specialties from Turkish, Greek and Arab cuisines. From force of habit we carefully evaluated the other clients in the restaurant as we ate, curious to know if any of them would recognize me, as I was the one who had once generated publicity, or, more unlikely, Laura. They would need to be true insiders, as Laura was one of the finest—and least well known—analysts the agency had ever had.

We made small talk while sampling the meze and I tried to discern why she had called. "I have something you want," she had said. What was it? My complete personnel record, including all those items I had not been permitted to see? Or had the agency seen the error of its ways and she carried an offer of employment? Nothing could be more unlikely. Then Laura answered my unanswered question.

"It's in my car, we can pick it up after our meal."

I waited several seconds before saying the words I most wanted to say. "My manuscript?"

"Yes," she replied. "Your manuscript. The one you submitted for clearance and never got back".

I had an immediate flashback to when I had just finished my book. The sense of exultation. The conviction that I was more than just another intelligence agent on the way down. After the business in Istanbul was over I had managed to disguise as a novel an episode that we were certain had altered the course of history. And like a good agent sworn for all time to submit manuscripts for clearance I had submitted mine, passing the only copy to Victor Steir for safekeeping. Then there was that terrible fire in Berkeley, and his home and everything in it had been reduced to ashes. The Steirs escaped but not my manuscript.

Over the years I had written a dozen requests to have my book back. I wanted desperately to publish it. To prove that it wasn't all a waste. No one troubled to reply.

"Why now?" I asked.

"Several reasons. First, I'm taking early retirement to teach at Goucher. I've earned a couple of degrees, you know, and I'll be teaching Southern history. So before I no longer have access to your file—senior analysts can get their hands on almost anything—I asked for your complete file. It's quite thick, and you wouldn't like a lot of its contents."

"What about the good things?" I interrupted. "What about the agents I ran in Bulgaria and Greece and Lebanon? Didn't anyone put something positive in my file about them?"

"I don't want to hurt your feelings," Laura said softly. "I really don't. But you spent a lot of time tooting your own horn; I think that's the expression, always looking for recognition, and you made a lot of enemies in the process. Some of the others were jealous of your career. Some resented that you married a beautiful, rich socialite."

"So they decided to sit on my book. Not to give it back."

I paused to take three shallow breaths.

"You said there were several reasons why you decided to take the manuscript from my file and give it back. What are the others?"

She paused just a fraction. "The word is that you are sick. Very sick."

"Do I look sick?"

"No, you don't. You look well."

"Then they, or you, picked the wrong reason to be kind. I'm just fine."

I felt the meze turning sour in my stomach.

"So they just sat on it. Not give it back. Bust my ego."

Laura nodded her head in silent agreement. "There's a strange footnote to this," she said, finishing her arak and beckoning for the check. "You'll see it when I give you the manuscript. Someone, one of the directors, I think, wrote 'great book' on the top page, 'the fools really did change history; just don't let it get out. Tits and Ass and B.J. won't like it.'"

Those last words sounded strange coming from Laura's lips. But I recognized them and I knew that someone had read my book.

Bastards, I thought, bastards.

The check arrived and Laura insisted on paying. I accompanied her silently to her car where she retrieved a manila folder from the trunk and handed it to me.

"Thank you," I mumbled, and walked away watching to see if someone was behind a tree waiting to grasp my manuscript and take it back.

Then I heard Laura's ignition and the squeal of tires as she pulled angrily away from the curb. It was like me not to have given her a farewell kiss. Again.

Bastards, I thought, bastards.

CHAPTER ONE

Istanbul, August 1975

We came up the Sea of Marmara at about eight knots, hugging the shoreline of Thrace. The breeze felt stiff against my body but it seemed barely to ripple the water. I glanced around the deck. Deserted. Nestled on the narrow patch of deck between the rail and the lifeboat I could escape detection until morning. Morning, when we disembarked in Istanbul and life began again.

I fumbled in my jacket pockets for a cigarette and lit up. The smoke went deep into my lungs, whipped down by the forward movement of the ship. By the light of the half-moon I made out a cluster of orange and blue tents staked out on the shores of the marble sea. German and Swedish tourists, no doubt, eager to soak up the sun in anticipation of the long winter ahead. In a few hours the beach would be thick with flesh and a polyglot din would float like a thin haze over all.

This was my sanctuary, this ship of weathered board hidden from the footfalls of real life. I had come there each morning since the ship quit Venice, and poked around in the crumbs of my thoughts for nourishment, watching the passing ships. That Italian cruise ship nosing into Adriatic ports would be gracious and eager to please; the crew would compete to minister to its passengers, even those obliged to travel steerage due to a temporary shortage of funds. And aboard that British ship British bottoms would be awash in champagne and roast beef served with those tennis balls they dub Yorkshire pudding.

Even that scruffy little Russian freighter beating a southbound course from Venice had looked more hospitable than the S.S. Mediterranean. The crew would eat a typical Russian breakfast of smoked caviar, boiled eggs that burned the fingers, little chilled glasses brimful with vodka. Funny little ship with a funny little name: Tula. Real communist efficiency, picking a short name for a short ship; it made for a short shrift with the paintbrush, painting Tula across the bows and stern. A nation that thinks of efficiencies like that is bound to be great.

That's how it was, those mornings since Venice. I idled away the hours mortaring old concoctions compounded of painful memories and foolish dreams of what it would be like to be back, letting myself forget that the future is simply an extension of the past.

From under the keel of the rowboat dangling in the davits I could make out the low illuminated bulk of the Prince's Islands, and I thought of trellises creaking under the burden of bougainvillea in bloom, their purple flowers so deep in hue that it hurt the eyes to regard them; of great wooden houses, their planks licked clean by the incessant breeze; of wind-swept summits capped with umbrella pines.

Tomorrow, I told myself, tomorrow when the lighters put the passengers on shore and the immigration clerks smiled welcome, I would go to stand in the milling, jostling throng on Galata bridge and watch the turmoil as people raced to catch the boats to the Islands, their urine bubbling inside for fear of being left behind. Then I would descend to the pontoons of the great floating bridge and eat fresh-caught silver palamut and tomatoes as red as a hen's comb at a fish restaurant tucked in the arch.

The S.S. Mediterranean shuddered to the keel as we passed the great gate of the Seven Towers and headed for the inner harbor. The sky was pierced now by the minarets of Istanbul, etched darkly against the moonlit sky, poised like flights of stone arrows. Illuminated by girding floodlights, Seraglio Point lay plump and sprawling, an unkempt and wildly beautiful courtesan of architecture; an odalisque in repose in sensuous embrace with the landscape, its great round breasts of curved stone exposed to the sky.

My body could sense the unheard command from the bridge to reduce speed as the ship rounded the Point and entered the inner harbor. I sat up and gripped the rail like a prisoner gaping from his cell. The city was calling me back.

The S.S. Mediterranean beat a slow course to the roads where freighters dropped anchor. We would be denied access to the harbor docks and obliged to unload by lighter. But then a few formalities and it would be all over.

The anchor chain made a hissing sound as it whipped out through the hawse pipe and the anchor plummeted down to the depths of the harbor. The ship made company with the currents and we stopped, tethered to the bottom, waiting for the dawn.

I looked at my watch: 3:45 a.m. Time to sleep before the sun poked over the hills of Anatolia. One more night and then I would be in Istanbul. One more night, what could it matter?

*   *   *

The immigration clerk let the card slip back into the box and gave me a long, unflinching look of the type usually reserved for Greeks and Armenians. "You may sit over there," he said, gesturing with his shoulder toward a long wooden bench that lined the wall of the Customs and Immigration shed.

I made a feeble attempt to ask a question but bit off the words in mid-verb. The clerk looked the sort who ate immigrants for breakfast, especially seedy-looking ones like me.

Two of my ex-fellow passengers gave me a misery-loves-company nod of recognition as I lurched past a line of sullen, frightened faces. I could imagine the look of cheerless surprise when the time came to poke through my ratty suitcase and its assorted stenches, but beneath the miasma of frayed cuffs, rancid armpits, soiled underpants and wine-blotched pants would be two pairs of clean slacks, two sets of clean underwear, a clean shirt and two pairs of clean socks. These were the clothes of the clean Paul Adams, ready for his triumphant return to Istanbul…when and if they let him in.

I felt in my pants pocket for the slim sheaf of traveler's checks that separated me from total poverty. With thumb and forefinger I counted the six rectangles, savoring their touch. Six times ten dollars is sixty and sixty times…how much could I get on the black market? Eighty-nine was official but perhaps I could get one hundred. That would be six thousand Turkish liras to last me until I got a job.

A half-hour later a voiced barked "Gel!" The imperative in Turkish needs no interpretation, and I jumped to my feet, quickly aware that judgment time was at hand. A different clerk led me to the far end of the shed where a partition of wood and glass separated officials from the incoming herd. The clerk gave a brief but respectful knock and, without waiting for a reply, walked in with a sideways gait that is characteristic of lackeys when they enter the domain of higher authority.

The room was bureaucratic functionalism at its zenith: a scarred wooden desk, bulky over-stuffed chairs, and a bust of Ataturk staring at me with gilded arrogance from atop a bookcase. A lean man with jet-black hair and moustache to match sat behind the desk making a detailed appraisal of his nails. Good looking, early thirties, handsome by some standards. But I didn't like his eyes. They were as black as his hair, and I had the uncomfortable feeling that his gaze could bore right through me if he chose to turn on the juice. He gestured toward a chair and held out his hand.

"Cigarette?"

I swallowed once to make sure that my throat was moist and my voice wouldn't crack. "Thank you." I reached for the brown and white packet that said Bafra and extracted a cigarette. The man opposite leaned across the desk and slowly offered a light, making me work to get it, while his eyes followed my slightest reaction. I inhaled deeply and let the smoke creep out from my lungs. It tasted as good as only a Turkish cigarette can.

"Well, Lieutenant, this is the first nice thing that's happened to me in Turkey." My voice sounded curiously light and distant.

"I am sorry if we have tried your patience," a soft, well-modulated voice purred from behind the smoke, "but there is the little matter of a card with your name on it." He waved an index card between thumb and forefinger. "There are lots of people named Adams," I volunteered. "Quite," he agreed emphatically, "and we are not above mistakes. But how many people are there named Paul Adams who have lived in Istanbul? From 1969 until 1972, to be precise?"

"All right," I interrupted, "my name is Paul Adams. You know that. I have lived in Istanbul. You know that too. So what? Why blackball me?"

"I'm afraid I don't know."

"Then why in the hell am I here?"

He adopted a didactic manner. "Those cards are coded. I can tell at a glance whether the subject has a police record in Turkey or whether he offers, shall I say, political difficulties. Each card also bears a dossier number so that all I need do is ask for the appropriate file next door." He hunched his right shoulder in the direction of a door inscribed in large capital letters PRIVATE.

"Good. Then your dossier can tell you I'm clean."

He appeared to pay no attention to my comment. "However, certain cards bear a symbol that tell me we have no dossier in this office. That I must ask headquarters for instructions."

"And?" I began to get interested myself.

"Nothing."

"Nothing?"

"Exactly. I cannot tell you why we keep a card on you or what you have in your dossier."

"And what am I supposed to do? Sit here the whole goddamn day!"

"That will be enough," he rapped out. Easy does it boy, I told myself. Get smart and they'll have you out of Istanbul in the first freight car. "I'm sorry, lieutenant. I... I"

"I am not a Lieutenant. I am Bey Urfanli. Orhan Urfanli."

"I am sorry, Bey Urfanli," I wheedled, "I've been under a strain. Worry, you know. And I'm hungry."

He spoke rapidly in Turkish to the silent clerk who executed a quick half step out of the door.

"What brings you to Istanbul, Mr. Adams?"

"The fact is, I like it here."

"Ah, the Pearl of the Bosphorus lures you back!"

I smiled. "You've been reading that lousy literature your tourism bureau puts out."

"Then just what does bring you back?"

"I told you I like it here."

"Curious. So many people seek to leave here and you want to enter. There are many frightened people here, you know. Frightened of the violence, of the inflation. Of the immigrants from the villages."

"I know what you mean, Lieutenant. I saw the May Day massacres," and then I had a vision of darting down an alley off Taksim Square just after the shooting had stopped to see a mound of bodies of people who had been trampled to death in the panic. Near them was a pile of shoes of people who sought to run away but hadn't run fast enough

"I must ask again, what draws you back?"

"A job," I interjected.

"What kind and where?"

I bent over to fiddle with my shoelace to give myself a little time. What should I say? Nelson had never answered. I told myself that he would… even that he had answered. But the fact is he never wrote. Oh Christ, when did it pay to lie, when to tell the truth? Why couldn't there be a nice, pleasant in-between?

"I… I expect to be a teacher at the International College."

He made a soft whistling sound and appraised me under those black brows. Teacher at the International College? No wonder the radicals talk of closing it. Paul Adams, B.A. M.H., the H standing for hangover.

"I've not taught lately," I volunteered, "but I did teach some years ago. Summer school. I taught English."

A wizened dwarf entered carrying a tray containing two glasses of tea and a plate of simits, the Turkish bagel covered with sesame seeds. "Please," Orfanli said and shoved a glass of tea and the simits in my direction. He had the grace not to speak for two minutes while I wolfed down three simits.

"That was very kind of you."

Urfanli held out the business half of a telephone. "It is ringing now," he said. "It is ringing the International College."

Oh you smart bastard! Now I didn't have even half a minute, not ten seconds, to get ready, to contrive something to say. A distant-sounding voice uttered indistinct sounds. I cleared my throat, hoping the line would be cut. "Who do you want, please?" the voice insisted.

"I would like to speak to William Nelson. Tell him Paul Adams is on the line."

Two eternities; the creation of six new stars. Finally a voice.

"Hello Paul," it said, just like that. A greeting to warm the heart.

"Hello, Bill, long time no see." Nothing like original conversation to break the ice. "I guess you got my letter. I had to leave France on business before you had a chance to reply."

"Fine," he said, sounding relieved. "Here on business are you?"

"Well, not exactly, Bill. Matter of fact, I've washed my hands of the business world. I can't wait to get back to teaching," my words were little more than a stutter.

I could imagine Nelson smiting his generous brow as he groped for words. "Listen, old man, I... I'm afraid you've got things a little muddled, we've got no job for you here; no job at all."

"I'm delighted to hear that, Bill. That sounds just fine. I couldn't want anything better than twelve hours a week in the English department." He tried to interrupt, but I fought on. "I know it is a heavy schedule but I won't let you down."

"What in the blazes are you talking about?" This time he succeeded.

"Listen, Bill. Something ridiculous has come up...it involves you in a way. Seems the Turkish police have doubts about me. You know. Do I have a job and all that? Fact is, if you don't confirm that I have a job they're apt to chuck me right out of here."

"As bad as that?" Nelson asked plaintively.

"That's right. But it's very simple really. All you have to do is tell them I'm on the college teaching staff. That's all."

"Let me speak to him," he said resignedly. Urfanli gravely took the phone. He spoke rapidly in Turkish to make the proposition very, very official. I caught a few words about qualifications and how long Nelson had known me. I had a good idea of what he would say: fifteen years; we were at Princeton together; met again when he came to Turkey. Character? A little hard to say. We don't know each other all that well.

Urfanli switched to English. "Mr. Adams tells me he will be on the teaching staff at the College. Can you confirm that?" A muscle twitched in my cheek and I felt terribly tired. Urfanli held the speaker away from his ear so that I could hear the reply. Nelson's voice sounded dead and his words came slowly. "Yes. We have employment to offer him". I let out a long sigh.

Urfanli made small talk with Nelson then reverted to Turkish for farewell salutations before placing the phone in its cradle. He picked up my tattered passport, stamped twice on the third from last page and wrote something in longhand. "I'm letting you in provisionally. You can thank Mr. Nelson. Report Monday at eleven to Second Section headquarters for a further interview. The address is written on this card."

"May I go now?" The fabric of my pants, soaked with nervous sweat, had stuck to the artificial leather chair and made a vulgar noise as I rose.

"Adams, I have nothing against you personally. You are just another professional subject. No more, no less. But let me give you a little advice. Be careful. You understand? Be careful." The interview was over. I went back to the customs shed and retrieved my bag. A customs clerk took a quick glance at the stamped page of my passport and waived me on.

A pair of worry beads are as much a part of a Turk's kit as a wallet. Their round smoothness is titillating to the fingertips and they can be snaked around on a desktop in an endless variety of patterns while a particularly difficult decision is weighed and examined with infinite care. Swung on the end of a fingertip they have a hypnotic effect, and it is said that a man can arouse sexual feeling in a woman companion by rubbing a single bead between thumb and forefinger. Urfanli's worry beads were turquoise blue. He kept them in the right top drawer of his desk and never exposed them while interviewing foreigners. He regarded worry beads as somehow quaint and atavistic; a remnant of Turkey's pre-Ataturk days, rather like the veil, the fez and the Arabic alphabet. As a "New Turk" he felt self-conscious about Turkey's past—some of its present, too—and, without quite realizing it, made a symbolic association between his worry beads, cached in the presence of foreigners, and other aspects of his country that disturbed him, like the beggars who clustered near the covered bazaar, shoving their mutilated stumps in the faces of tourists, or the ragged hamals who tottered along under the impossible burdens of crates that no man should be asked to bear. And the aspect of modern Turkey that disturbed him most: the acknowledgment on the part of his countrymen that violence was often a good substitute for reason. But there was no denying that worry beads were helpful when Urfanli wished to reconstruct in his mind a sequence of events that he could not altogether comprehend.

The subject of Paul Adams, for example, bothered him. Why would a man of such apparent meager consequence arouse the attention of his authorities? Did they think his past post at the American Consulate General had been other than what it showed in the records—an ordinary political officer? Or did they suspect that his duties included surveillance, perhaps even contact with some of the dissident political groups that had mushroomed in the universities and the professions.

But surely not even the Americans could not have fallen on such hard times as to recruit a man like that with a veneer of toughness so thin it wouldn't hide a belly dancer's nipple.

Too many questions and too few answers, he thought. That is always the way with me. I must stop trying to get to the bottom of things. Nothing gets an aspiring intelligence officer into more trouble.

That sad effort of Adams to dupe him into thinking he had a job and that pathetic conversation with Nelson! Could it have been a masterful piece of acting? No, not possible. And why had headquarters instructed him to play cat-and-mouse with Adams when it was Colonel Atil himself who approved Adams' entry into Turkey?

Urfanli rubbed energetically on a single blue bead. Tomorrow was Friday and then came the weekend. With any luck he could have Sunday off. A good time to gather a few friends and go out to Sirkeji to see the gypsies dance. Friends claimed they would even strip to the pubic hair if enough money passed. He had an image of jet-black triangles glistening in the oil lamps that cast an uneven illumination on the rites.

Urfanli threw the worry beads into a desk drawer and an involuntary shudder went through his body.

*   *   *

The sun narrowed my eyes as I stepped out of the door and almost stumbled into a blind beggar tapping a white-headed cane in tattoo on the sidewalk. Catchy tune, that. I dug into my pants pocket and felt the reassuring touch of the folder of traveler's checks. One of those Armenian merchants in the bazaar ought to be good for at least one hundred to the dollar. Then I remembered Urfanli's injunction: be careful, he had said, and that would apply to the odd bit of black marketeering. I crossed the cobbled street to something called Yapi ve Kredi Bankasi and went to the window marked "Kambyo." The clerk did not seem staggered by the enormity of the deal when I passed him a ten-dollar check. He held the check gingerly between two fingers, eyeing me warily. "Have you identification?" and it was the first time I realized the word has six syllables. The signature on my passport matched that on the check and he reluctantly passed me a sheaf of bills. I was counting slowly...twice...when I heard a gentle cough of reproof behind me and turned. "I'm sorry," I muttered. "I didn't realize you were standing there."

"Quite all right," the man responded heartily. The accent was English, from Yorkshire probably. "Quite all right," he repeated with fervor. The long equine face seemed fixed in a permanent smile, and his teeth were long and extraordinarily white for an Englishman; their reflection in the afternoon sun would blind an oncoming driver. A kind of permanent high beam. Otherwise he looked an ordinary chap. Medium tall, medium broad, wearing a definitely medium-quality suit that looked too warm for Istanbul in mid-August. His hair was parted low on the side and worn with those outcroppings on the sides that English males cultivate for God knows what reason. But his eyes were good. Blue and friendly, and the flesh around them crinkled from that permanent smile. You could tell he was the sort of person a tourist would seek out to ask directions to Cleopatra's Needle or Trafalgar Square. A schoolmaster or an insurance agent on holiday.

The sun made a mirror of the plate-glass door to the bank and I studied my reflection. A few hours parboiling in a Turkish bath were in order before calling on Bill Nelson. Unkempt faculty might be the mode in the United States but I didn't think the trend had reached Istanbul yet.

CHAPTER TWO

It was noon when I staggered out of the Turkish bath into the blazing sunlight, pausing only long enough before the mirror that distorted my reflection to observe that I made a rather impressive figure, particularly with shoulders that looked six feet across. Perhaps I should pay a call on Urfanli to show him the real Paul Adams. I put the idea aside and walked to the foot of Galata bridge to catch a dolmus, one of those communal taxis that cram in passengers until the door pins snap in the hinges but are favored by the Turks because they are cheap and offer limitless opportunity to caress the thighs of some imprisoned female. My dolmus was a vintage 1950 Plymouth, still going strong after having done enough miles to rival a space probe to Mars, if ever they tried one.

I squeezed into the front seat next to a fat woman who spread over the seat like a great mound of melting ice cream. She fanned herself vigorously with a delicately wrought ivory fan and periodically dabbed at her perspiration-rimmed upper lip with the edge of her handkerchief. The rear seat contained what looked to be five generations of females from a single family who competed simultaneously for attention.

The dolmus driver swallowed his chagrin at the meager number of fares, nursed the car into gear and we were off in a great lurch of bitten tongues and snapped spines.

Nothing appeals to a Turkish taxi driver more than a trip up the coast of the Bosphorus. It is one long sequence of blind turns, seductive views to beguile one's attention, blinding passages from sunshine into limpid shadow, loaded wagons parked in the middle of the road, children darting from between parked vehicles to startle the unwary, policemen's signals delivered when a quick stop is clearly impossible, and approaching cars that play a perennial game of test-your-nerves resulting in God knows how many premature births, heart seizures and wet car seats.

I gripped the car handle until my knuckles were white as we followed the cobbled streets of Besiktas, Kuru Cesme, Ortakoy, Arnavutkoy and the other place names that went through my mind like a litany.

Wooden houses that hadn't known the touch of a paintbrush in a century teetered crazily over the cobbled streets and narrow sidewalks, making it seem that the hurrying pedestrians owed their speed to fear of their imminent collapse. A chorus of agonized screams from the back seat announced that the driver had overshot the stop of the five generations of shrews who had talked incessantly, never pausing for breath all the way from Galata Bridge to Arnavutkoy.

We were nearing Bebek. I thrust my left arm in my pants pocket to search for money and felt something massive slam into my rib cage; it was my companion in the front seat who mistook my quest for change for an amorous adventure in her rolls of fat and had returned my attention with her elbow.

The towers of the Rumeli Hisar castle loomed large before us and I knew that the gates of the International College were just ahead. I signaled the driver to a halt and got out, first remembering to grind my heel on the toes of the melting fat lady. Then I crossed to the college gates and began the long climb up to the campus.

*   *   *

Bill Nelson had changed little. His dark hair was salted with gray; the line between his brows had grown deeper; there was a perceptible elevation to the hairline at the temples, but these few frailties admitted humanity to his patrician good looks that many found tinged with arrogance. He had kept me waiting no more than a busy man normally would, and I couldn't fault him on his greeting. Not effusive, of course, but the handshake was firm and the smile that briefly creased his face was warm. Perhaps I had misjudged the edge in his voice when we spoke over the phone in Urfanli's office, but I remained standing, wanting to be reassured that the gap produced by time was no wider than I hoped.

Nelson stood in front of the big bay window that gave out on the hills of the campus that fell away steeply to the Bosphorus. Over his left shoulder I could see one of the massive towers of Rumeli Hisar; beyond, on the Asian shore, distant but clear, the smaller towers of the Anadolu Hisar. Sultan Fatih Mehmet the Conqueror had ordered the Rumeli Hisar fortress built in three months, and his engineers had completed the job in eighty-nine days rather than face the wrath of their chief. Less than a year after the last stone was mortared into place on Rumeli Hisar, Fatih stormed Constantinople and became the conqueror that launched an empire that was to endure over four hundred years. The view from Nelson's window was calculated to give one a sense of history. I wondered whether he had framed himself there deliberately to establish the context for our conversation. The seconds ticked by as I waited for Nelson to guide me with something more substantial than a smile and a handshake.

"I suppose you think I gave you a rough time this morning."

"I must have caught you by surprise," I murmured.

"Yes and no. I suppose I should have written. In response to your letter," he added, in case the relevance wasn't clear to me.

"Oh, that's all right, Bill. As a matter of fact, I assumed that you had written; that your letter came after I left Paris."

"Would you have come anyway?" I tried to look quizzical, knowing full well what he was driving at. "I mean would you have come anyway, knowing that I had no job to offer you?"

"Yes, yes, I would have come anyway."

"Janice?"

My tongue felt very dry in my mouth. "That would be part of it."

"What do you expect to prove, Paul? That she isn't dead?"

"No I know better than that. It's, well… I guess I'm trying to find out where I go from here."   Nelson occupied himself with filling the bowl of a meerschaum pipe sculpted to resemble a Pasha's head crowned with a turban.

"Sit down, won't you?"

I sat in the deep chair before Nelson's desk, waiting for the little pellet to be dropped in the tank of acid and the lethal fumes to rise. They say it doesn't take long: one or two quick breaths and it's all over.

The voice began anew. "I'm not running a charity institution up here, but a first-class school. And it's not easy. Every time a fuse burns out or a mouse runs across the cafeteria it gets into the radical press as a further proof of declining standards. We can't afford to give our critics too many free opportunities to run us down."

He leaned forward in his chair, his gaze focused on the lump of tobacco smoldering in the bowl of his pipe. "I don't relish saying this, believe me, but hiring a man with your reputation and background could cause us great damage if the press hears of it."

"Then why did you tell Urfanli that you would give me a job?"

"I don't think you gave me much choice."

"I'm sorry. That was a stupid question. Do they still talk about me much around here?"

"No, not much. Sometimes we hear a snatch of news that someone has brought back from Europe."

"Just enough to start the tongues wagging."

How many times had we been dissected at cocktail parties or small dinners here or downtown at the Consulate? Have you ever heard the story of Paul Adams and his beautiful wife, Janice? He used to be a Foreign Service Officer, some say he was really CIA, a promising type, but then he began to drink and whore around. His wife died under mysterious circumstances about three years ago; the rumor was that she committed suicide over Adam's behavior—and then he went to pieces with a crash you could hear all the way to Washington. Got so bad the State Department and the CIA both asked for his resignation just to make sure he got the message, and he's been on a binge ever since. Good riddance to bad rubbish, if you ask me. A friend of ours saw him in Marseilles a few months back and he tried to borrow ten dollars! Claimed he would pay it back in a few days!

I got to my feet and the room began to spin. "I understand, Bill, I understand perfectly."

"Sit down, I'm not finished." Nelson's voice was a command. "I may be of temporary help. The father of one of my teachers has just died, and he may not return to Istanbul until early October. In the meantime I need someone to teach his courses in American literature. It won't be a permanent job, and ends the moment he returns, but it may help you get on your feet."

"That's wonderful, Bill, just wonderful. You know I did my major in American literature at Princeton and old Doc..." He waved me to silence.

"You can use his rooms in Christopher Hall. Small but adequate." He cleared his throat. "You realize that we permit no female visitors in the Hall and no drinking what-so-ever."

"Of course. As a matter of fact, I've sworn off; haven't had a drink in ages."

"You have three weeks to prepare your course material. I suggest you spend most of your time in the library."

"Sure. Sure. You won't be sorry about this, Bill."

"Go to Christopher Hall and ask Bey Turkman to show you Peter Dawson's quarters. By the way, Mary and I are having a few people in tonight. You're welcome to come by about seven." I mumbled my thanks. It could be that I was escaping from purdah already, but it was more likely that Nelson wanted to watch my behavior in front of a tray laden with drinks. But I would be there, ready to pass the challenge.

I got to the door safely and he had not reneged the offer.

"Paul." I held my breath. "I'm doing this for Janice too, you know. She would want you back on your feet."

I thought my heart would stop beating before I reached the staircase. The great, gaping hole that Bill Nelson had made in my chest yawned open and I could feel my lungs, stomach and liver ooze out of my body and slither to the floor before the startled gaze of the janitor who poked his broom along the tiled corridor. I leaned against the wall waiting for my heart to pop out of its cavity.

"I'm doing this for Janice too. She would want you back on your feet." I moaned and the janitor picked up his broom and tottered off in fear. Where was he going? Why didn't he wait to sweep me up off the floor? Didn't the fool realize that it wouldn't be good for the college if the students found a man's innards strewn in their footsteps?

"Doing this for Janice too!" Didn't Nelson know that she was laughing in her grave to see me in this situation?

CHAPTER THREE

William Edward Anthony Blake belched softly against his fingertips and shoved the remnants of the plate of pilaf, tas kebab and green beans in olive oil to one side. Carefully, as though masticating nails, he took small bites of mocha cake and worked them into a salivous gruel before swallowing. Then he peeled a peach from the orchards of Bursa and put it intact into his mouth. He enjoyed the sensation of the whole peach disintegrating in his mouth, knowing that there were few men who could pull off such a trick without making spectacles of themselves. Years ago, while a student in grammar school, he had entertained table-mates and won small bets by putting an entire orange into his mouth and reciting a soliloquy from Hamlet. Once he had been unable to extricate a particularly large example and remembered to this day the bitter taste of acid as he was obliged to chew through the thick skin of the orange in order to work it into manageable size.

Lunch over, Blake rose from the linoleum-topped table that faced the window of the main room of his flat in the center of Galata, just under the great cylindrical fire tower built by the Venetians. He placed the dirty plates in the sink, lit a flame under a blue enameled kettle, put two heaped tablespoons of Ming tea in the acorn shaped tea basket and hung it by an s-hook to the side of a bulbous pot. His cleanup and tea preparations complete, Blake entered the bathroom of his little flat and withdrew a cylinder of dental floss from the cabinet over the wash-basin, drew out a twelve-inch length and wrapped one end twice around his left forefinger. He repeated the process around the right forefinger, and then began to work the floss into the spaces between his teeth, beginning with the upper left side and going as far back as his wide-open mouth would permit. Little bits of tas kebab and rice popped out onto his tongue and these he paused to swallow before proceeding to the next space. Satisfied that the floss had done its work, he squeezed toothpaste to overflowing on a brush of natural bristle and rotated it vigorously for the better part of five minutes. Then he rinsed a ritual ten times and stepped back to appraise his work in the mirror over the washbasin. The smile that perpetually made a gleaming white gash across his lower face seemed especially radiant, even in the indifferent light of the exposed bulb that hung from the ceiling.

"A fellow can't take too good care of his teeth," Blake opined aloud to the mirror.

A jet of steam rose from the spout of the kettle now vibrating on the stove. Blake held the kettle high and poured into the teapot a column of boiling water, which quickly took on the thin tint of Ming tea. While the tea steeped, Blake went to a makeshift bookshelf built of raw bricks and wood and removed three titles: "Constantine, Birth of an Empire," by Harold Lamb; "Gallipoli" by Alan Moorhead and "The Classical Tradition," by Gilbert Highet. These he placed midway on the linoleum-covered table. Beyond, but well within reach, he placed the teapot and a cup and saucer.

Blake took an envelope from the coat hung on the back of the hard wooden chair beside the table and sat down, wincing slightly as he adjusted his spinal column between the slats. He removed four sheets of onionskin from the envelope and placed them one after the other on the table in the blank space between the books and the facing edge. A long one, he thought, and probably nothing whatever to do with me.

The message had been delivered to his apartment well before lunch by the courier assigned to the receiving station at Kandilli. It was ridiculous to put the station on the Asiatic side of the Bosphorus and require each coded message to be sent by ferryboat and then by taxi to Blake's apartment in Istanbul, but the agent who had set up the office before Blake's time had concluded that the Turks would be less apt to discover an illegal radio receiver in an out-of-the-way fishing town like Kandilli.

The four sheets that lay before him were thickly covered with numerical sequences interspersed every six or seven digits by a slash. The code was childishly simple in concept but defied cracking unless one knew the key that unlocked the digits' meaning. The number 127169, the first sequence on page one, meant, for example, that he would refer to book one of the three volumes on the table before him. Twenty-seven indicated page 27; sixteen meant line sixteen; and nine indicated the ninth word in the line. Blake guessed that the first word would be "attention" and set aside the cup of tea to test the hypothesis. He was right, and that deduction told his experienced mind that the subsequent words would say "all points." These catchall words clinched the peripheral value of the entire message and convinced Blake that the hours that lay ahead would be dreary indeed.

"Well," he murmured aloud, "there's nothing for it but to get started." He filled a teacup, put a cozy over the teapot and immediately skipped to the fourth numerical sequence, 345121. His interest quickened as he moved to subsequent sequences and words began to emerge, one courtesy of Harold Lamb, a second from Alan Moorhead, a third from Gilbert Highet. Blake hastily poured another cup of tea; this promised to be an interesting afternoon after all.

CHAPTER FOUR

A man named Turkmen led me up long flights of stairs to two rooms under the eaves and told me they were Peter Dawson's quarters. Then he disappeared and I was left alone to arrange my meager belongings. I lay down—not to sleep, but to seek support on a mattress against the assault of recollections unleashed by my return to Istanbul. Soon I was soaked in perspiration. The room where I lay was a blur of triangles...black and orange, blue and vivid yellow, green and white, crimson and black, dazzling colors that danced before my eyes in a kaleidoscope of constant movement. They were great colored daggers poised to plunge into my body, pinning me to the coverlet like a lepidopteron on a collector's board. Slowly the triangles came into focus and names were spelled out that spoke to me of youth. I wore a mortarboard and robe, looking tall and clear-eyed. The kindly clucks of relatives and friends echoed in my ears; handsome, isn't he; such a bright boy, favors his mother I would say; wants to be a diplomat, well it takes all kinds to make a world; someone at Bryn Mawr seems to have caught his eye; well, much too young for marriage; cum laude! Not one in twenty gets that at Princeton!

The hours passed in sweat and reverie until I heard a distant clock chime six o'clock to remind me of Bill Nelson's invitation.

Peter Dawson could not have been long out of graduate school. The pennants on the walls, the drawers laden with button-down shirts with little useless loops at the back of the collar, the closets filled with sports coats, the striped ties; those were the hallmarks of youth. I tried on Dawson's jackets, searching for one that would make me presentable for the appearance at Nelson's house for cocktails with "a few friends." I picked a dark blue blazer with tarnished silver buttons; it had the stamp of anonymity.

Behind a hatbox in the deep closet I found a half-filled bottle of whiskey that bore one of those contrived in New York labels for Scotch. "Sweat off the Heather," I think it was called, but the name was immaterial. Peter Dawson, absent roommate, was now clothes mate and, most important, whiskey mate, who ignored the College's mandate against drinking in school-supplied apartments. Two long pegs from the bottle glowed warm in my stomach. I fought off the temptation to have a third, remembering the scrutiny that awaited me at the Nelson's house, and brushed my teeth carefully, swishing the toothpaste suds throughout my mouth to damp the smell of whiskey. Then I gargled with mouthwash, holding it deep in my throat and humming musical comedy tunes through the bubbles; several enchanting old favorites behind me, I swallowed some of the mouthwash as further insurance against an alcoholic breath; even an inadvertent belch couldn't betray me now.

I smiled in the mirror and was pleased by the response; there was something warm and essentially likeable about the face that surveyed me. A few weeks of carefully modulated behavior, and the trustees would fire Nelson and hire me in his stead.

I set forth across the campus periodically breathing into my cupped hand to sniff the toothpaste and mouthwash. The imitation gothic buildings grouped around a quadrant scooped out of the hillside looked sturdy and capable of weathering the winter winds that blew with such force out of the Black Sea. Their granite facades were thickly laced with ivy, and an occasional light winked on in the gathering dusk. I asked directions of a group of summer school Turkish students and was guided to a rough road of hand-set stones, barely wide enough for two carts to pass, which led off the campus across the shoulder of the hill behind the more distant of Rumeli Hisar's twin towers. Three tiers of faculty houses were clustered apparently according to rank in a natural amphitheater crowned with cypress trees standing like black and green sentinels against the low clouds that tugged the horizon, their edges now tinted orange by the setting sun. Bill Nelson's house dominated the top-most tier. It had been built at the turn of the century, and the stucco walls, once white and austere, had been weathered gray by the endless winds of winter and their summertime imitations. The house had a resolute air about it; built to last, to stand against adversity, to house solid people intent on performing a solid job. I approached slowly, letting each laggard step give time for the effect of Dawson's whiskey to wear off.

Did I detect a fleeting lapse in Mary Nelson's smile during the moment that it took from opening the door to greet her newest arrival until she recognized me? Her lips pursed as if she meant to kiss me and then thought better of it. "Paul Adams," she said, holding out her hand, "how wonderful to see you. Bill tells me you'll be with us for a little while." I didn't miss the implication of those last words. They said: now don't get nervous, folks, Mr. Adams is only a temporary embarrassment and we'll run him off the campus as soon as humanly, or is it humanely, possible. She gripped me by the hand. "Do come in and have something. You look parched." Little did she know, I thought. Bill Nelson broke away from a little knot gathered on the small terrace that gave off the living room.

"Welcome, Paul. Let's put something in your hand and then I'll make a quick turn around the room. You'll know some of these people, I hazard." He spoke with that slightly arch tone that suggested a superior manner to the uninitiated; not many men would hazard the word hazard. A Turkish waiter, not long out of Anatolia and the color of polished oak, appeared carrying a tray of screwdrivers, small glasses of vermouth glace, and "Perils of the Hill"—tall glasses the color of cherry over white; they could contain homemade vodka, cherry liqueur, cherry juice and soda, and two of them would make the Comintern sing the Star Spangled Banner. The vodka and orange juice of the screwdriver looked inviting, but I sensed Nelson's look of thoughtful attention. "Portakal suyu, lutfen," I said, and the waiter hurried away to get my orange juice.

The names meant nothing to me as Nelson and I waltzed once around the room. I was the chap taking young Dawson's place until he returned. The Turkish male teachers shook my hand gravely and wished me welcome from behind their omnipresent mustaches; the Turkish faculty wives spoke little English and giggled through the introductions; they all looked slightly overweight and to be wearing the same dress. The decibel count had gone up a point or two since I had entered. "Perils of the Hill" were having their renowned effect, and I started to yearn for the moment when I could slip into the kitchen and pour an inch or two of vodka into my orange juice when it finally arrived.

I felt my elbow being moved in the direction of the terrace where a girl was conducting a small group in a spirited rendition of a John Philip Sousa march. No, she was only engaged in conversation, her cigarette describing brisk, baton-like movements in the air. She wore a dark blue jersey dress that outlined a slender but surprisingly voluptuous figure; her hair was dark with a touch of auburn highlighted in the sunset and was drawn back tight from her face and held taut by a white elastic-jersey hair band. She was radiantly attractive.

"Miss Lokman," the other names were lost as Nelson went through the familiar ritual about my fleeting presence. "This is Paul Adams. Paul, this is Suzan Lokman, a member of our English department." Her gaze was intense as she surveyed me in a look of dark warmth.

The waiter slipped something cold and damp into my hand and I sipped noisily to cover my embarrassment.

"I'm interrupting something," I mumbled, "perhaps a discussion of the gold-flow problem."

"Much more serious than that, Mr. Adams. I was telling our friends about new trends in modern Turkish art." How nicely she had embraced me into the group by referring to "our friends." "I was just saying that Turkish art is no longer derivative in character, that people like Kaptan, Bedri Rahmi, Sevim, and Eyuboglu have something uniquely Turkish to express." The names meant nothing to me but the words did. They were expressed in perfectly accented English; one or more of her parents had had a top-level education.

"You're absolutely right, whatever it is." She laughed lightly, just enough to quicken my pulse another fifty beats. "Flattery is the language of fools," she replied. There would be no handouts from this girl. The orange juice suddenly tasted good on my tongue. Bill Nelson coughed softly to remind me of my reputation and moved back into the main room, but I knew without bothering to turn that he would be surveying me with slightly knitted brow.

"The Turks have no sense of public relations," the voice was that of the man who had been playing bass drum in the Souza march; he was young with a dark, unsmiling face and had a beard that enhanced his naturally saturnine countenance. "Why, nineteenth-century Turkish artists turned out masterpieces that would make Dufy wish he had never picked up a brush. But who has ever heard of them? It's the Turks' own damn fault, that's what it is."

"You may be right, Turgut," it was the voice of Suzan Lokman again, "but who in the West would ever believe us? We are nothing to the Western intellectuals but the Terrible Turks, the people who destroyed Byzantium, who massacred the Armenians, who drove the Greeks into the sea at Izmir. Who ever gives us credit for artistic or intellectual attainments?" Attagirl, I thought, you should be stumping Europe and

North America telling people to stop abusing the Turks. Trouble is, no one will believe you. Put you up on a podium in that jersey dress and everyone would regard the lecture as a complete bust. Lord, I could be funny when I wanted to! I reminded myself to tell Miss Lokman of my witticism someday.

The bearded Turgut finally noticed the empty glass in the girl's hand and went off toward the kitchen. Too bad I hadn't thought of that; I could be lacing my orange juice.

"I've heard of you, Mr. Adams." Who said that? Yes, it was the girl, no doubt about it. I looked startled and was happy that the two silent members of our conversational group left for other pursuits.

"It's been a lovely friendship, Miss Lokman. I may do better in my next incarnation."

"You knew my cousin, Raif Lokman. He was my father's brother's son and was a member of the Turkish Foreign Office." I fought my way back through memory; the little scroll that records events in my brain laboriously creaked backwards. There were great, gaping blank spaces and an occasional section filled to the margin with names of people and places. Back and back I went, and there emerged the image of a tall, surprisingly fair boy with large almond eyes who occupied a minor post in the Ministry of Foreign Affairs at Ankara. He had left for Sofia when I had been in Istanbul little more than a year.

"Of course, of course. Where is he now?"

"He's dead. He was a member of a Turkish diplomatic mission on its way to Rome for a NATO meeting and the plane crashed in the fog."

"I had no idea your cousin was on that plane. I'm sorry."

"Mektub, Mr. Adams. It was written on his forehead. A boy so fine and sensitive as Raif had to die before his time."

"Do you mind my asking when he mentioned me?" I didn't truly want to know, but felt I had to.

"Raif kept an album of snapshots of many of the people he met and liked and used to show them to me. He wrote the names of the people and the dates under each one. He loved life so that I think he wanted to build a storehouse of memories for use at some future time."

"And there was a photograph of me?"

"Of you and your wife," she said softly and slowly.

I could see it in my mind's eye: six of us had rented a motorboat from a pier in the Golden Horn and gone out into the Sea of Marmara to picnic and swim off the undiscovered beaches of Silivri. It was a gay, foolish afternoon and we all got slightly tipsy on white wine. After lunch we made schoolboy pyramids on the beach and Raif and I had hoisted Janice to our shoulders where she towered tall and long-limbed, eager for pictures to be taken. That would be the picture in Raif Lokman's book of memories.

"My wife is dead, also." I wanted her to know this.

"I know. I heard about it."

"Paul Adams, I didn't think you'd have the gall ever to show your face in Istanbul again!"

The voice was like a scimitar, slicing through the din of the room, turning everyone silent. Must I turn? Can't someone explain that I am Peter Dawson and that Paul Adams is in the United States looking after his dead father's estate? Surely there must be another Paul Adams in the house. I slowly turned in the direction of the accusing voice and saw the mottled face of a woman I remembered as Emily Cartwright. Her great pigeon breast heaved with emotion and she wore a look of triumph from the joy of having stopped the party in its tracks.

"You may think other people have forgotten, but I haven't. If it weren't for you, dear, dead Janice would be alive today and you know it!" She turned to the assembly, her hands outstretched as though holding a cup of hemlock for the condemned man to drink.

I bolted for the door past the anguished gaze of Suzan Lokman, past the embarrassed guests, and past the towering figure of Emily Cartwright, who impaled me with a look of abiding hatred. She's not dead! I should have known that she couldn't die, wouldn't die. Janice had come back in the person of Emily Cartwright, and I hadn't even seen her enter the party. She had come as in days past, returning to the crowd from a lark behind the hedge, smoothing her skirts, brushing back her hair with her palms, giving me a look of quick contempt.

"Dear, dead Janice" had come back. The name that I had tried so hard to obliterate screamed in my ears. I stumbled through the garden unable to find the gate and fell on the gravel path, tearing a hole in my pants. Blood trickled from my kneecap and Dawson's blazer was filthy with dirt. I dragged myself to my feet and set off across the fields, desperate for the panacea that stood upright on the closet shelf behind Dawson's hatbox.

"If it weren't for you, dear, dead Janice would be alive today." I raced faster across the bramble fields, falling again and again. I knew Emily Cartwright was right.

CHAPTER FIVE

Harold Lamb, Alan Moorhead and Gilbert Highet thumped into place on the shelves of the bookshelf. Someday, Blake thought, I must read those damn books from beginning to end. He stretched vigorously and reached behind to massage the small of his back where it had grown numb under the pressure of the ill-fitting chair.

The four sheets of onionskin had been transformed into three pages of printed words, laboriously set down over endless cups of tea. Each completed word had made him realize the importance of the message now spread out on the table. He chuckled, recalling his prediction that it was just another polemic meant to enlighten the faithful and let the stations know who was boss. Strange that he had heard nothing of this affair before now, but clearly a lot of effort had been made to keep it quiet. He mulled over the contents of the message: Professor V. I. Scherevsky, foremost Soviet authority on ballistic missiles, had, for reasons not explained, traveled without authorization to Albania, where he had claimed asylum. But agents of the Soviet Union had recaptured him, presumably. An automobile accident had occurred during the abduction, which raised the possibility of injury to Scherevsky. Given the rupture in relations between Albania and the Soviet Union, an airlift was out of the question. The Soviet abductors had arrived in Albania on a merchant vessel called Tula and it was assumed that it would now be engaged in returning him to the Soviet Union. To forestall this, it was essential that every effort be made to locate Scherevsky and to release him from Soviet custody, and get him into "friendly" hands; failing this, he should be killed.

"Better dead than a defected Red," Blake mused. Well, it titillated interest all right. A merchant vessel named Tula. There were more than one hundred Soviet ships in the Mediterranean area right now flying the Soviet flag! But it could fly a flag of convenience. One thing was sure-they all had to pass through the Dardanelles and then the Bosphorus in order to reach the Black Sea. That simplified the logistics a bit. Of course, there remained the little matter of boarding a moving ship and kidnapping or killing a man on board. "Details," Blake said airily. "Mere details."

After placing the teapot in the sink, Blake burned the onionskins containing the coded message, folded the transcribed message into a neat square and placed it in the hollow top of the cabinet in his bathroom. Then he quickly undressed, turned out the lights, went into the adjoining room and slipped into bed. He lay there for a few minutes ruminating on the problem, dipping into recesses of memory for bits and pieces of information that would fill in the gaps of the message just decoded, especially the unexplained reasons for Scherevsky having been in Albania in the first place and the motives that obliged the Soviets to abduct one of their own scientists. Then it all came to him in a crisp, clear, plausible picture. Further proof of the importance of knowing history, he congratulated himself on being a cut apart.

Blake's mind now worked rapidly to put a dab here and a line there in a deliberate attempt to blur the crispness and clarity of the picture that had come to him. A good etching, he remembered, was identified by subtle use of light and shadow, not just lines. But something nagged at Blake's brain, some detail left undone. He sat upright in bed.

"Gracious," he said aloud, "I bloody near forgot." Blake got out of bed and padded through the darkened apartment to the bathroom. He opened the cabinet door and extracted his toothbrush and paste; then he brushed vigorously and rinsed his mouth with ritual care, ejaculating the water from his mouth in short, and hard bursts.

Blake bared his teeth wide in the darkness; they glistened like little mystic stars in the mirror, an enameled Milky Way of light to lead a man through uncharted seas. He padded back to his bed and lay down. His last sequence of thoughts before sleeping was: if Scherevsky was injured in the abduction, he will need a doctor; not just any doctor but someone the Soviets can trust; that would mean Italy or Greece; I must contact Rome and Athens tomorrow. Trust the Italians and the Greeks not to keep a secret.

CHAPTER SIX

My previous record for staying in bed without dressing, eating or moving had been thirty-seven hours. It was a record I had established in Istanbul three years before, when the Director General of the Foreign Service and the Director of the Agency, both displaying customary solicitude after Janice's death, invited me to submit my resignation.

Establishment of a new record prompted the sort of carefully controlled examination of behavioral cause and effect of which I am capable when recovering from a bout with a bottle and the subsequent hangover.

The cause in this instance was plural. First, there was Emily Cartwright and her great pigeon breast, a mottled face that glowed with hypertension and bile, and that piercing voice that whipped through a room like a band saw through a log. She had hurled out those words, "If it weren't for you, poor, dead Janice would be alive today." And because I knew she was right I turned and ran for cause two, the only comfort that a grown man can count on: Peter Dawson's bottle.

And the third cause of my prolonged stay in the upper reaches of Christopher Hall was a young woman. Someone I had known no more than ten minutes but who was bright and pretty and talked to me in a way that suggested she didn't expect me to fall on my ear at any minute.

Engraved on the great, big battered tureen of my life will be a new record: To Paul Adams, Who Lay In Bed for Thirty-Eight Hours, Unable to Face Friend or Foe or Self, We Award This Cup. I hoped the crowd at the presentation wouldn't be too big. I hate fuss and attention, and I certainly didn't want Suzan Lokman there to look at me thoughtfully with those big brown eyes that told and hid so much.

A streak of light shone at the gap between the drapes covering the windows, and I knew without drawing them that the day would be bright with sunshine and the sky that special azure blue that only comes when the sky looks down on the sea. It would be Sunday, I concluded, because Bill Nelson's party had been Friday night and I had stumbled back to my apartment in a desperate frenzy to find Peter Dawson's bottle. Now the bottle was empty by the bed and the floor was strewn with clothes and hatboxes, thrown there as I groped about in the darkness.

I sat up tentatively and realized with satisfaction my hangover had dissipated itself through prolonged unconsciousness. I could move my head from side to side without fear that my eyeballs would roll out, and my hands could be held at arm's length without a tremor in my fingers. But the face that greeted me in the mirror over the chest of drawers had seen better days and my body smelled rancid. The college didn't bother to provide hot water on a Sunday morning but it didn't matter. I shaved in the cold water of the shower, letting my left hand trace a path on my face for the razor to follow. I put on my last pair of clean chinos and selected a sports shirt from Peter Dawson's generous selection. The effect was good and I felt almost good enough to seek out Emily Cartwright to tell her she was a retired whore when there was a knock on the door.

"Mr. Dawson is not here," I shouted. "He's in America." There was another rap, rap, rap.

"I said there's no one here."

"Please open the door." The voice was soft but I recognized it as that of Suzan Lokman. I thought of sending her away by maintaining silence; what if Bill Nelson knew she were here? But it might arouse more attention to ignore her than it would to let her in. I opened the door.

"May I come in?"

I stepped back, eyeing her cautiously.

"It's not a very warm welcome," she said.

"You're not supposed to be here. No female visitors allowed."

"I'm a member of the faculty, Mr. Adams," she said.

"That's just the trouble. I'm not."

She advanced into the room, not quite closing the door behind her.

"I was worried about you."

"You needn't have. I'm all right."

"I... I...came by yesterday but there wasn't any answer."

My voice reeked of composure. "I probably went out for a stroll. As a matter of fact I spent most of the day at the library."

"Yes, I know. There's a large key hole in the door."

I felt my face flush. What business was it of hers anyway? Why does this girl I hardly know pry into my life? But I knew I was an ungrateful slob. It had been a long time since someone had worried about me.

"Look, Miss Lokman, I appreciate your interest, but..."

"I've come to ask you to go swimming with me."

"I can't." But I didn't add that Nelson wouldn't approve.

"Why not?"

"I'm going to the library to prepare course material."

"The library's closed until afternoon. It's Sunday." Her voice was politely persistent. "Please. It's a beautiful day and I don't want to go alone."

I turned to the window and drew back the drapes. It was a beautiful day. The campus looked deserted. Everyone would be away at the beaches on the Black Sea or across the Golden Horn at Florya or on the far side of the Bosphorus at the Sweet Waters of Asia. I turned and held the edge of the window for support.

"I can't be seen with you. Don't ask me why."

"But I know why!" She exclaimed. "I know why. That's why I'm here in the first place."

"I don't follow."

"Because it's fun to break the rules, silly."

"That's damned nice of you. If you know so damned much you know that Bill Nelson will kick me off this campus if he sees me with you."

"Bill has taken his family to the Black Sea for a picnic. He'll never know. Look, I'm trying ever so slightly to be nice. I must say it's not everyone who turns me down."

I grew suspicious. "How did you get in here?"

"The kapaci is a friend of mine and gave me a passkey. I come every night and go from room to room pleasing the boys." Her tone was mocking and revealed that she understood my querulous question. "Come on. Borrow one of Peter's swimsuits and let's go. If you're frightened of being seen on campus, I'll meet you below the college wall."

"All right. I'll meet you in ten minutes."

Suzan Lokman slipped through the door and padded softly down the steps. I stood at the window and watched her cross the quadrangle. A small flight bag was slung across her shoulder. She looked tall despite her small stature; she must have known I was watching her... and wondering.

We avoided the macadam driveway that led to the main gate by the Bosphorus and instead followed a path that had been worn amidst the trees and shrub by countless students and lovers. It curved down the hill in broad sweeps and passed the cemetery beside the towers of Rumeli Hisar before sloping down to the highway bordering the Bosphorus. Turkish cemeteries have a naturally unkempt look about them. They are not delicately manicured like cemeteries in America and England, and the memorial stones always seem to be askew as though the persons they guard have turned in their graves and knocked the gravestones out of kilter. Sentry poplars ringed the wall, and the green between the graves was thick with thistle plants and wildflowers. The cemetery had an oddly beckoning quality to it.

I spoke for the first time since we had met beneath the college wall.

"It's too beautiful to be a cemetery."

"It should be. Death is a beautiful thing. That's what Islam teaches, you know, that death is a time of beauty and joy."

"Especially if you've killed a Christian or two." I smiled while saying it.

She smiled back. "Especially Greeks and Armenians…and Americans, now that I think of it."

"What do you have against Americans? You speak their language."

"That's because I'm half American. My mother was a Vice Consul at the American Consulate General here in Istanbul. That's where she met my father when he applied for a visa to visit the U.S. Then about ten years ago she went back, after he died in a car crash near Adana."

"Why are you here instead of the U.S.?"

"Do you think it's so strange that I would rather be here than in America?"

"No, not really. Maybe you're more valuable here."

"What about your mother? What does she think?"

"She remarried and I can't stand the man. So I'm here. And quite content, I might add."

"And so am I. Anyway, do you agree? That bit about death?"

"That death is a thing of beauty? No. Not really. But I know it will come and therefore I prefer to think it may bring beauty." She spoke easily despite the exertion of keeping our balance on the steep slope.

"I know it's fine for the Muslim men. But what about the women?"

"What do you mean?"

"Well, the men live by bubbling brooks and smoke narghiles and have little houris tending to their every need. But what about the women? Do they go into permanent purdah?"

"I assume they are the houris. You seem to know quite a lot about Islam."

"Like everything else in life. Something but not enough."

"It's strange, how few people do. Take the word houri. To Muslims it means someone who has been elected to be an angel and live in heaven in God's gardens. But Christians have corrupted the word and it becomes whore." She shuddered a little.

"I had never thought of that," I said foolishly.

"No one ever does. It just shows how Christians look down on the Muslims."

"Do you really think that?"

She looked at me steadily. "All Turks think that. Even I do. And I'm not a Muslim. It doesn't matter. It's just part of our national inferiority complex." She broke into a run as we neared the level ground by the waterside. "We'll catch a dolmus to Bebek and hire a rowboat."

"Why a rowboat?" I called out, realizing that I was falling behind.

"Because you don't want to be seen with me."

A great black Buick dolmus bucked and shuddered to a halt the moment Suzan raised her hand. We clambered into the front seat, which was already occupied by the driver and a wispy little man whose lap was encumbered by paper bags. I pushed hard against him to make room for Suzan and heard his moan.

"Yumurta, efendim," he said and seemed about to break into tears.

I looked into the open top of the sack. The eggs were intact and I told him so.

"Mashallah,"he said. Thanks be to God.

The man with the sack full of eggs was vastly relieved when we left the dolmus in Bebek. He commended me and my ancestors to Allah for having left his precious burden intact.

We filled a sack with cheese, grapes, hot bread that burned my chest through the sack; bought a bottle of deeply chilled white wine that nestled in the crook of my arm like a cooling poultice, and half-ran, half-walked through the little acacia-filled park that acts as backdrop to Bebek's tidy little mosque adjacent to the ferry boat stop at the far end of the pier. There, perched off shore on a stand of inadequate-looking wooden piles, was the shack of Mehmet Kip, Bebek's most expert lobsterman, whose woven pots were regularly filled with prize specimens of the firm-fleshed lobsters from the somber depths of the Bosphorus. Mehmetcik, as everyone called him, had a sideline of renting rowboats to adventurers avid to row the Bosphorus themselves, to families wanting to tie up to a buoy for a watery picnic, and to lovers eager to row out beyond the view of zealous parents. Business thrived in the early hours of evening, and Mehmet boosted his prices accordingly when dusk fell. He greeted Suzan with a familiar wave and I felt a twinge of jealousy until he said, "Off for another swim honum efendi?" and I concluded that she came often by day and not by night.

We walked the narrow planking that bridged the gap between boat landing and shack and I shook hands gravely with Kip. He was an exception to the Turkish rule that a man is not a man without a mustache. I noted that he had a pronounced gimp in his left leg that made him bob and weave as he walked, like a prizefighter feeling out an opponent.

"Efendim is an American?" He addressed the question to Suzan but I knew enough to reply.

"Yes, I'm an American."

Mehmet balanced himself on one leg and waved his gimp leg back and forth with the help of his left hand. "Turkish Brigade in Korea", he explained. "I had many American friends. Sit down, I'll tell you about the war." He brandished what looked like a gourd. "I play the sweet potato too. Only one in Turkey. I got it from an American."

I looked at Suzan in dismay. The sweet potato had gone out with high-button shoes.

"Sit down and let me handle this," she said softly.

"He'll be terribly hurt if you seem impatient."

I assumed a compromise position, leaning against the rail of the narrow veranda that ran along two sides of the lobsterman's house. Mehmet ducked inside and I could hear sounds of him rustling about.

"Good lobsters today, honum efendi," he called out. "Come look."

We stepped into the shadow of the single room that was Mehmet's quarters. It was simply furnished but neat and clean and smelled of the sea that flowed below in endless course from the Black Sea to the Mediterranean.

Mehmet was standing by a trap door that lay open in the center of this shack.

"You see!" he said proudly.

Six or seven evil-looking lobsters were engaged in battle with a wire netting that formed a cage six feet square below the shack. It was a losing struggle and soon they would wait execution in one of the pavilions that dotted the Bosphorus' shores.

Suzan and Mehmet exchanged superlatives that could hardly have encouraged the lobsters about their life span, and then she crossed to the door. "We can go now. I told him you would like to hear his tales of the Turkish Brigade in Korea one day. He is very pleased."

We stepped onto the narrow causeway and loosed from its moorings a gaily-painted rowboat with a red lobster and the words "Mehmet, Bebek" stenciled across the stern. He maneuvered the long boat from its berth beneath the wooden boardwalk and thrust the nose into the current, where he let the water's strength hold it steady while he looped the leather thongs from the bulbous oars around pegs that jutted up from either side of the boat. A primitive form of oarlock but easier and surer than the metal ones I had known in my youth. Mehmet held a

strong, hairy forearm out for Suzan to grasp and helped her board. He
offered his arm to me, too, but I ostentatiously rejected it.

"Gule, gule," he called out clambering with quick agility from the
boat to the boardwalk. "Yolunuz acik olsun." May your way be clear.
He unleashed the final rope that held us and I felt the boat drift with the
current.

Though my hands hadn't held an oar since I was last in Istanbul, I
did a fair job of clearing the little cove and headed into the deeper
waters. The Bosphorus fell away from the shoreline with alarming
speed and at its maximum is said to be more than nine hundred feet
deep. Geologists say a massive earthquake, possibly the same one that
led to the creation of the Jordan River Valley, the Dead Sea and finally,
the Great Rift of Africa, created it. God, what a sight it would have
been to watch the Black Sea come roaring out of its prison and plunge
into the Marmara!

"Make for the buoy beyond the Chris-Craft. The water is wonderfully clean there."

A film of sweat already moistened my body. I felt my breath come
shorter and shorter and wondered whether I could make the buoy
without calling for help or throwing up or both.

"Just a few more strokes. Pull hard on the right oar...now the
left...easy. A little more and I'll tie up." I heard a slight sawing noise as
the hemp rope passed into the buoy ring and then a tug as the rowboat
reached the end of the tether and found its place in the current. With
what seemed like my last ounce of strength I pulled the oars into the
boat and leaned on them.

"Thank you, Paul," a voice whispered in my ear and I felt strong
fingers massage my neck. I was tempted to reply until it dawned on me
that the girl tenderly ministering to the exhausted rower usually coped
with a boat like this by herself.

"Let me take a quick swim and then I'll feed you."

I turned and watched her doff her blouse and skirt and reveal an orange one-piece suit that dipped deep down her back. She was small, no more than a hundred-and-ten pounds, but an incredible blend of slim strength and voluptuousness, like one of those rare ballet dancers whose body has ripened and hardened like a piece of sculpture, yet whose muscles are invisible. She made an arc in the air and disappeared from the covered prow of the boat into the Bosphorus, emerging twenty feet away, shaking her head like a wet puppy.

I followed suit, awkwardly and with the sort of splash associated with New England millponds and naked boys diving from a rock, their legs bent at the knee, but my breath had returned and the chill waters felt antiseptic on my skin.

"I'll race you to the Chris-Craft."

"No," I called out, "I'll just putter around here…in case the boat slips from the mooring." I watched in admiration as Suzan bucked the swift currents of the Bosphorus with a smooth, flowing crawl. I returned to the shelter of the rowboat; the last thing I wanted was for her to see me flapping around exhausted in the bottom of the rowboat like some landed whale, so I tugged and grunted my way aboard and was enjoying a brisk rub-down when she returned.

I helped her aboard and felt the flesh of her arm brush against me as she passed. Of such things is the life of the senses composed! Suddenly, her fleeting touch took on the quality of a lingering caress and I told myself that it had been deliberate, born of the passion that so often follows a bodily cleansing.

"Please turn while I change my suit, Paul."

I turned facing the shore, knowing that she would be swathed in toweling more concealing than any swimsuit but invoking ritual modesty. Oh, easy, easy, man. Orhan Urfanli, he of the black eyes and black mustaches, had warned, "be careful," and Bill Nelson of patrician brow and manners to match had recalled my "reputation."

"You may turn now," and I knew what to expect. The modern Turkish girl who might have been an American but decided not to be, clad in a bikini and bronzed in every direction. I was right.

Suzan bade me open the wine while she tore our freshly bought bread into manageable chunks and laced it with white cheese.

Omar Khayam probably never tried reciting his quatrain in a rowboat with a girl in a bikini feeding him nibbles of bread and cheese and pouring white wine down his throat, but I am sure he would have conceded that the bow of a boat is almost as good a place to have a picnic as under the bough of a tree. And if Omar Khayam had been a thirty-four year old flunk-out with a grand total of five travelers' checks between him and the poor-house, had an appointment with the head of the Second Section on the next day, and found himself preparing for the interrogation by gazing down the bosom of a ravishingly lovely young woman, he probably would have written an eight-line poem in praise of love in the wilderness instead of settling for a meager four lines. As for Omar Adams, that budding love poet was only slightly high, but happy, deliriously happy; eating, drinking and wondering whether he dared reach out to touch a girl.

"Tell me about Emily Cartwright."

There was a note in her voice that told me it was a long swim to land if I didn't answer.

"She's my dearest friend," I said lightly, "my dearest friend."

"Paul, I'm serious. I want to know."

"You're the distinguished faculty member. You must know about Emily Cartwright."

"Please."

"All right. Emily was a friend of my late wife. Don't ask me what Janice saw in that bag but they were inseparable, constantly clucking in one another's ears. Frankly, I think Emily had a thing for Janice; not that Janice went in for women but she loved attention and welcomed it from any quarter. It made her feel very strong to attract people of both sexes."

Suzan rummaged in the basket and found a pack of Turkish cigarettes. She lit one and handed it to me; an old-fashioned trick out of an old movie but overwhelmingly natural the way she did it.

"Why does she live here? Why is she known and accepted on the campus?" she asked.

"Istanbul is one of the world's last safe havens for oddballs. An aunt died about twenty years ago and left her a small income. It wouldn't amount to much most places, but in Istanbul she's a Grande Dame."

Suzan reached out the fingers of her right hand and touched my forearm, and her voice was suddenly urgent.

"Paul, listen. I know a lot about you. From Raif. I know about you and Janice and what happened to you. I know about her...and the business about the other men."

"Why do you know so much about me? What was I to you that your precious cousin should tell you the sad story of my life?" Suddenly I wished myself off the damn boat, out of the damn Bosphorus, out of the clutches of this girl who knew more of me than I wanted her to know.

"Raif and I were very close. The way cousins sometimes are in Turkey." I looked at her wondering whether she and the dead young diplomat had enjoyed some kind of incestuous relationship. Hell, in this part of the world it still happened that first cousins married. Why not a little...?

The question was cut off in my mind as she read my thoughts.

"No, not that kind of close. I mean, it could have been but before we ever had a chance to think seriously about one another, Raif was dead in that plane crash."

"Then why?'

"Because Raif knew and admired you and was troubled by what happened."

"And maybe because Raif was one of Janice's lovers."

"Yes," she said, "I think so. He was one of Janice's lovers."

"Great. He admired me and my taste in wives so much he decided he would have a bit of it himself."

"I'm sorry, Paul, really I am. But it wasn't his fault."

"I know. He would have needed the strength of ten to fight her off. Well, welcome to the club." I took a long sluice from the wine bottle and shivered in my wet bathing suit.

"Let's change the subject," I said, my voice taking on an edge. "Let's talk about your lovers."

"Paul, Paul. Don't be bitter. Don't you see that I know why you have come back to Istanbul?"

"Tell me why. I don't think I know."

"Because this is the crucible. The crucible where you were burned and seared and terribly tortured and because you have to learn to live with your pain in order to bear it."

"Beautifully put," I said mustering a trace of a smile. "Off to a rousing start, aren't I?"

"Emily Cartwright?"

I nodded in silent agreement.

"You mustn't run from her, Paul. You must stand firm!"

I began to laugh, deep silent laughter that rocked me. Oh, you dear, sweet girl with your elegant accent telling me to stand firm! Didn't you know I hadn't stood firm since I was two years old? Stand firm, stand firm... I gulped for air to fuel my laughter.

She slapped me hard across the face.

"Stop that!"

And I stopped.

"You mustn't run."

"But it's true; it's true."

She looked at me wonderingly, hurt and amazement coming into her eyes.

"It's true. I did kill Janice."

CHAPTER SEVEN

Blake gave a little cluck of satisfaction as he hung up the phone. "We British may be broke," he said, aloud, "but we're not dumb, especially yours truly."

So the ship carrying Scherevsky was definitely Tula. Athens had to repeat the name twice in telephonic code before it sank in, but there was no challenging his subsequent confirmation. Not much of a ship, by all accounts, just a shabby little collector of low-grade intelligence garbage and undoubtedly picked for its inconspicuousness. The Russians had forgone the opportunity to put Scherevsky on shore in Piraeus for fear his presence would be discovered and invite a kidnap attempt by the Yanks or whoever else would want access to his genius. Instead they contracted the help of a talkative Greek doctor to come on board, encase the broken ankles in plaster, and then go ashore to brag about his exploit to his comrades. Bad break for the Russkies, he mused, no pun intended, those busted ankles.

Yes, he concluded, the blokes in Moscow had pondered the intelligence entrails and reached a decision: keep Scherevsky on board Tula and hope for the best. Once the ship cleared the Bosphorus and entered the friendly waters of the Black Sea the job would be all but done.

"Only thing they didn't think of," he confided to the dead phone, "was me."

Blake began to hum. Just a tune at first but then he added lyrics of his own invention. "Better dead than a defected red; better dead than a defected red."

That's very catchy, he mused. Very catchy. Make a good little tune for a London music hall. William Edward Anthony Blake presents his smash musical "Better Dead Than A Defected Red."

Blake laughed aloud and made for the kitchen and reached for the canister of Ming tealeaves. One teaspoon for each cup and one for the teapot. Don't forget first to warm the pot with boiling water and let the tea steep for no more than three or four minutes. And then he remembered his mother's edict, "William Edward Anthony Blake, remember this if you never remember another thing—never warm up yesterday's tea!

"And mind the sugar!"

Two cups later, Blake suddenly sat upright. "Goodness me," he said aloud, "I am getting senile in my old age. Tits and Ass will definitely want to know about this. The idiots in Ankara will never be the wiser and I might cajole a bit more in the bargain."

Tomorrow, he thought, tomorrow I will go to the Grand Bazaar and contact my donme friend and use that little transmitter of his.

CHAPTER EIGHT

I had no choice now. A hasty exchange of banalities at a cocktail party and a few hours spent together sharing wine, bread and the Bosphorus had suddenly stripped me of the shroud of reticence about Janice that I had used to protect myself these last three years. She knew too much, this Suzan Lokman. She and her dead cousin must have filled their hours vicariously living the pock-ridden adventure that had become my life with Janice: Raif savoring the knowledge of my wife's body and the special tastes she cultivated; Suzan trembling with joy at her cousin's conquest, sensing that it was her own body yielding to the young man whom blood had brought so close yet kept so far. Paul Adams would have been a shadow figure; something brought in from one of the Karaguz plays, probably one of those funny Armenians who always provoke Turks into gales of laughter. Yes, Adams would be there. He would escort his wife and one of her lovers to the bedroom door, saying "Apres vous, Gaston," and the audience would howl with delight.

"I'm cold."

"We'll go back soon," she said, turning away, "but not yet. Get out of your swimsuit into something warm and then we'll have a cigarette."

I knew what would follow. More questions. No, questions would be too weak a term, for this girl had advanced beyond that stage of her interrogation. She would simply lead me back to the slap that still smarted on my cheek and she would touch the red marks on my flesh with gentle fingers and I would tell all. The cigarette was waiting for me when I finished changing.

"It was a Sunday morning." There, the first words were out. I had swallowed an oyster on a string and she would slowly reel it up out of my gut bringing with it the refuse of my life.

"Janice woke up early looking radiant and cheerful and we drank tea and ate some simits. Then she proposed that we rent a motor launch and picnic at a secluded little beach near the submarine nets where the Bosphorus joins the Black Sea. I was startled. Janice proposing a lover's picnic. She was really quite enthusiastic, even insistent.

"People wonder how a man can stand to be a cuckold but once you've accepted the idea it's easy, almost fun. I was thrilled by Janice's apparent desire to be with me. I had visions of swimming out from the beach and stripping off our swimsuits and tying them to an inflatable rubber ring, as we had done in the distant past. Before everything went wrong. Out there in the blueness of the sea we would touch one another and return home to be together, or even make love on the beach or in the cabin of the launch. But before that it would be like old times to swim and then lie on the sand and feel the sun warm and excite our flesh.

"So I said, 'Yes, we'll go. We'll have fun!' And she gave me a little grin as if acknowledging my scenario.

"I went out to buy food, all the Turkish delicacies we like so much. It figured to be an expensive picnic. Twenty dollars to rent the launch, another fifteen for some red caviar, shrimp, chunks of lobster and two bottles of the best white wine. But I didn't care. It was cheaper than a night at the Melody Bar."

"You used to go to the Melody Bar?"

"Yes, in my worse moments. It's a vile place and I met some vile women there."

There was a somber pause while Suzan digested that information.

"When I returned Janice was ready. She had a stunning figure but I'm sure Raif told you that, and I'm sure she would regret not having lived long enough to see the bikini come to Turkey. But a white one-piece suit on her was almost like seeing her naked.

"I parked near the dock at Tarrabaya and paid a kid ten lira to wash my car and keep the dolmus drivers from jacking it up and making off with the wheels. I was impatient as hell with the old man who rents the launches and hardly listened to his instructions. The boat had a hull, a motor and a cabin. And that was all I wanted.

"We headed into the strong current that comes down from the Black Sea but the motor responded well. Janice sunbathed on the prow oblivious to the movement of the launch, the passing ships or the bow crest that sometimes spilled over on to the deck. She seemed hypnotized and far away and I was hypnotized by her. We had only been married two years, you know, and in two years you don't discover all the secrets of a woman's body, especially when the secrets have been shared.

"I remember holding the tiller between my knees and bending low behind the wheel to wrench the cork from the wine bottle so I could drink. I didn't want her to see me doing that because she would want to drink too and soon there would be a row and we would wind up the day in a deep sulk as so often happened. So I drank alone. Not a lot, you understand, but enough to feel that little glow in the loins that's so good when you start.

"That's the way it was until we anchored. It was about one-thirty, I remember, and I was famished from the effects of the wine and the sea air but we decided to swim first. I tried to persuade her to swim naked but she wasn't buying it. So we swam quietly for a while and I could feel our rapport slipping away.

"Sometimes when things were going well I would dry her off after a swim and this sometimes triggered something. But not this time. She went inside to change into a dry swimsuit and I could feel my face flush because it was going so badly. She came out and glanced twice at her wristwatch. I was well into the second bottle of wine by now and the cabin on my twenty-dollar launch looked very empty. So I said one of those banalities that are supposed to mean something different like 'Why don't we rest for a while in the cabin?' She knew what I was talking about, of course, for she replied, 'I can't. It's my time.'

"But I knew it wasn't. I, I, used to follow that sort of thing closely. She was lying to me, and I felt a knot of rage and frustration form in my gut. I leaned forward and tried to pull down the top of her bathing suit but she dodged and I fell on my elbow, a little drunk by now.

"Then it came. She looked at her watch again. 'Take me to shore,' she shouted. 'Someone is waiting for me.' I looked up at the bluff above the beach and I saw a tall man in a uniform standing by a large car. She had no intention of making love to me. She was going away. Going away with the man in the uniform.

"I called her a bitch and a whore and other curses in English and Turkish. She turned savage then. She wasn't leaving me, just going away for a few days with someone important. It had happened before, why not again? Anyway, what did I care? I had no right to play the role of virtuous husband, not after what had passed between us. Not after what she knew about my escapades at the Melody Bar. Then came the clincher. It was remarkable she hadn't caught some vile disease from me. I had heard it all before, the litany of my faults recited decade by decade the way a pious nun recites her rosary. But Janice's prayers were born of hate.

"It went on for I don't know how long but I wouldn't budge. I washed down her words with the last of the wine. Then she tried to push her way past me to start the engine. I reached out and felt the straps of her bathing suit in my hand. I pulled and suddenly she was naked to the waist before me.

"It wasn't my wife I saw. Just a half-naked woman. I needed her. Hate, distrust, deception, they vanished in this terrible surge of need I felt. I called to her, 'Janice, Janice, help me.' I reached out and she jumped on to the cabin roof, out of my reach. She stood there on her toes, bobbing up and down like a cheerleader, her breasts bouncing with her movements.

"'Go if you must,' I cried to her. 'Only don't go with hate. Love me first.' She replied by demanding that I take her to shore immediately. Suddenly I felt very tired. I stepped back on a wine bottle that had been rolling on the floor and sprawled backward. Something, my arm I think it was, struck the electric starter button on the diesel and the launch vibrated.

"Janice fell then. She lost her balance and fell on the cabin roof. It wasn't a hard fall, but her head grazed the little wooden safety rail and she had an odd look on her face. She rose to one knee and I thought again of a prizefighter struggling to climb upright after a nine count. Then she rose to her feet and began to curse me and her voice was thick. I was frightened now, frightened to be with her, too frightened not to obey her, so I put the engine into gear to make for the shore.

"But I had forgotten the anchor. Stupid wasn't it? I had forgotten the anchor and the anchor chain and we reached the end of it with a jolt. Janice had been standing, still a little unsteady, but coming back to normal, when the launch tipped down by the bow as the chain went taut. Then she fell in. I saw her look surprised and do a cartwheel from the cabin roof into the sea.

"Why don't strong swimmers come up? Why do people drown when they step into an unexpected hole in the sea floor? I watched and waited for her to rise to the surface but nothing appeared. I dived into the sea, it was no more than ten feet deep there, and saw her drifting off with the current. She saw me too and reached out for me to help, imploring me to come to her. She was half-naked, a kind of sea nymph, beckoning me. Not far off. Just a few yards. Then five became ten and became fifteen.

"I swam but I didn't get any closer. She beckoned and seemed to form my name with her lips but I didn't get any closer. She tried to break for the surface but her system was disoriented now and her struggle only carried her further along in the current. Then I went to the surface to fill my lungs and dived again and watched her shadow writhe against the white sandy bottom of the beach. There's no sea life there, just white sand and water so clear I could make out her nipples.

"Janice went along with the current as I watched, twenty yards, thirty, forty. Her body looked motionless then and moved faster. There was no friction from the struggle of her arms and legs. She just glided and glided and in a little while she was out of sight in the main channel. I swam back to the boat and climbed aboard, expecting to be winded but my chest was barely heaving.

"Then I realized that I had let her die. A little more reach with my arms, more thrust from my legs, more demand on my lungs. I could have gotten to her."

Suzan broke her attentive silence. "It was an accident. A freak of the currents. It's happened before out there."

"No, no. I could have reached her."

"The currents are very tricky in the Bosphorus. The beaches are posted."

"A little more effort, a little more demand on myself, a little more love and caring and forgiveness in my nature. I could have reached her. But I was afraid. Afraid to ask too much of myself and afraid that I might reach her and she would have put a strong hand around my wrist and I would have joined her in that current.

"Fear is natural, Paul."

"I let my wife drift away to her death. When a man lets someone die that he might have saved, because he's afraid, what is he? What would they call him in Turkey?"

"Some people would call him a coward."

I made her utter that word. She was reluctant, but what's an honest girl going to do? Now the oyster of truth she had made me swallow dangled on the end of the string still dripping of my story and I should have felt better for the purge, but poison would seep in again and I would have to swallow the oyster again, sooner or later.

I pulled on my shirt. The late afternoon clouds that appear from beyond the Bosphorus' sheltering green hills began to make their appearance. They moved in fast, bunched together like great, gray grapes. The wind dipped in to ruffle the pennants on the terraces of the restaurants that dotted the shoreline, and the slap, slap, slap of the water against the hull of the rowboat became more insistent.

"What happened to the man Janice was expecting to meet?"

"After I knew that Janice was gone, that the rendezvous would never take place, I looked up on the bluff where he had been standing. He seemed conscious of my regard; he seemed to give a half wave and then I saw him get back in his car and drive away.

Sunday had come and gone.

"We had better go now."

I think we both said it at the same time but there was a terrible ring of finality about it, coming from her.

Suzan rowed us back to Bebek and Mehmet's little pier, never asking for help. Mehmet gave an affectionate cluck of approval as she drew into the pier, spinning the rowboat on one gaudily painted oar, obtaining further movement with the other. He lurched forward on his gimpy leg to retrieve the mooring rope and tied it to the rings that dotted the pier columns that were rooted deep in the firm flooring of the Bosphorus. Suzan sprang up to the pier unassisted and watched impassively as Mehmet offered me a steadying hand.

We retraced our steps up the narrow, winding path that skirted the cemetery in the shadow of the towers of Rumeli Hisar. It would have been a convenient burial place for the condemned men brought up from the dungeons installed by Fatih the Conqueror's engineers. A few steps up to the crenellated summit of the towers, a brief but futile struggle against the inevitable and then a swift, straight drop into the cemetery below. "Death is a beautiful thing,'" she had said earlier. 'Islam teaches that death is followed by a time of beauty and joy." Would she still feel that way after today? Perhaps she would dream my dream tonight. The dream of Janice's long, chest-burning quest for air, the beckoning arms, the mute appeals for help. More likely she would dream of cousin Raif.

I was silent, afraid to speak. "We must leave each other here," she said, "or you'll be seen with me. Goodbye. And thank you." Then she darted up the pathway toward the far side of the campus. I watched her disappear into the dusk and then I climbed the hill to the quadrangle and Peter Dawson's quarters. I rummaged through the shelves, drawers, sneakers, and stacks of old magazines looking for liquid solace without success. I even patted down the pockets of his jackets hoping for a hidden flask. There was nothing left, only the empty glass shell of "Sweat off the Heather" that had comforted me after the encounter with Emily Cartwright.

It promised to be a long night.

Chapter Nine

The old black Buick with the checkerboard pattern stenciled around its upper body drew up in front of Blake's apartment house at 6:00 a.m. A hood was tied over the meter and the signal light that denoted availability was turned off. The man in the driver's seat got out, extricating himself with effort. He had the column-like neck and massive shoulders of a heavyweight Turkish wrestler, albeit past his prime, with a protruding gut of a man who ate mounds of pilaf and baklava three times a day. He walked around the car and kicked savagely at the tires, hoping that a well-placed blow from his heavy, steel-toed boots would puncture them and oblige Blake to buy new ones on the black market.

From behind the curtain of his window, drawn back an inch to permit visibility, Blake watched the spectacle below with satisfaction. "Ahmet will be in a bad mood this morning," he said aloud. "Up so early after a pot full of raki will give him a bad headache and a temper to match."

"Now watch this," he said to himself, as if demonstrating a magic trick to luncheon cronies. He picked up an apple from the fruit plate on his kitchen table, tore off the little stem and thrust the apple whole into his mouth. For a moment it seemed to wedge his jaw permanently open like a suckling pig at a banquet, but his rear incisors found a grip in the flesh and the apple's fate was sealed. Blake bit two matching chunks from opposite sides of the apple, then turned it on its flat side with an upward thrust of his tongue. He bit down again, shearing off additional chunks. Relentlessly, he masticated the core, seeds, skin and flesh into a gruel, letting it slide down his throat until all was finished. "A bloody great food blender, that's what I am," he chirped with satisfaction.

Still chortling, Blake made a familiar path to his modest bathroom for the uplifting task of brushing his teeth. Water, bits of bread crust, a fleck or two of apple skin were ejected in sharp bursts into the sink. Finished, Blake opened wide his massive jaw to examine the beauty within. Mouth still ajar, he eased open the drawer of his cabinet and retrieved a pencil flashlight and played the small beam across every part of the brilliant enamel. Strangled words that sounded like "lovely, lovely" came from his throat.

Ablutions finished, Blake donned a raincoat with frayed sleeves, tapped down a gray felt hat that perched on the two curls of hair that seemed to grow out horizontally over his ears, and descended the five flights of stairs down to Ahmet and the Buick. Ahmet greeted him with a glance that said he knew this trip wasn't necessary, that their mission could be achieved by means other than the lengthy drive through European Thrace to Gelibolu on the Dardanelles. What rankled him most was the taximeter, perched like a hooded falcon beside the driver's window. It would not utter the rhythmic 'putshuk, putshuk, putshuck' that was music to his ears as it meant that the kilometers were rapidly ticking by and money spilling into his purse with parallel speed.

"Gun aydin, Ahmet," Blake greeted the burly driver with forced heartiness. "You big dumb Turk son of a donkey. You'd better greet me with a smile when you see me or I'll take away your plaything." He felt safe in abusing his companion in English for their conversations were normally conducted in Turkish. Three years at government expense at the London School of Oriental Studies had paid rich dividends, and after six years on post in Istanbul, Blake spoke Turkish with no trace of accent.

Blake did not begrudge Ahmet the extra wages he earned as a dolmus driver when the car was not on official business. Augmented income meant augmented availability when circumstances required a man of strength and violence, and there were few men who would not blanch at the prospect of a head-on encounter with the massive wrestler. Blake clambered into the back seat of the car and greeted its second occupant who was nestled in the shadow, barely visible in the dim morning light. This was the man to whom Blake had given the sobriquet "Nuri the Noodle." He was small, no higher than Blake's chest, but there was nothing dwarfish or misshapen in his build.

That sinewy, supple body was capable of extraordinary feats of strength and agility, wriggling through apertures barely large enough to pass a ten-year old child, throwing a knife with uncanny accuracy, or clambering up a sheer wall as if it were no more than a ten percent gradient. He had also heard, though not seen evidence, that Nuri the Noodle was capable of reducing a woman to a lump of fatigued sensation, so great was his sexual appetite.

Ahmet and Nuri were the sum of Blake's small complement of associates, but the combination of their strength, ruthlessness and courage and Blake's brainpower made for an exceptional team. And who could challenge such a conclusion, boastful though it might sound, Blake thought proudly. The big boys pay our salaries with punctuality, have kept me on the job here for six years and enable me to cajole a few lira from Tits and Ass when I have something juicy to report. Best of all, they have displayed the wisdom not to send any of the apes down from Ankara to intrude on the current effort.

Just one message. Nothing more than a few, terse facts were provided as to Tula's route, speed and expected time of arrival at their destination. Blake touched Ahmet on the shoulder. "Hada gidyoruz." Let's go.

The sun had now fully emerged from behind the Anatolian horizon, bathing the city in a sequence of light and shadow. The swarm of cars, trucks, rickety buses, mule-drawn carts and bicycles, which would later turn the Galata and Ataturk bridges that spanned the Golden Horn into choked arteries of noise, anguish and slow movement, were still free of the cholesterol of transport, and Blake elected to postpone his early-morning review of events, intelligence and options until the car cleared the majestic confusion of Istanbul. There was time to think later. This was the time to lean back against the tired springs and savor the stampede of images that thundered into view with turning.

Ahmet swiftly threaded their way across the Galata Bridge, the floating span that connected Galata in the new city with the old metropolis that had known as many names as the conquerors who coveted it. The Dorians had founded the city seven centuries before Christ, naming it Byzantium after Poseidon's son Byzas. The Arabs called it Anthusa, city of bliss, and it was small wonder that travelers drew on the word "enthusiastic," in describing its wonders, unconscious of its Arabic derivation. The Romans, indulging their fondness for variety, called it first Antonia and later Nova Roma, and finally Constantinople, the name that had stayed with it until Sultan Fatih Mehmet drew a noose of men and ships around the city in 1452. Resentful of the fall of Christianity's eastern citadel to Islam, Europeans had sought over the centuries to preserve the name Constantinople, but the Turks were secure in their conquest and imposed the title Istanbul.

Blake enjoyed reciting this little history lesson to himself. It helped refresh his faith in the doctrine of inevitability: history was but a succession of events that operated with ineluctable sureness. Men and societies could struggle against the tide or ordained events but they were so many spiders pitted against the incoming tide. They might float briefly on the surface, seek respite in a calm, but the sea would win out in the end.

Blake's reverie of contentment continued through the car's progress past the Mosque of Sultan Ahmet, the treasure houses of the Topkapi Saray, the vast hippodrome inaugurated by Constantine the Great, the welter of churches turned mosques, mosques turned museums, streets turned alleys, wealth turned poverty. Symbols that nothing is so temporal as what men believe eternal.

They were waved through the flanking towers of the Edirne Gate by an imperious, jut-jawed military policeman and entered the wide highway that led into Thrace. Without consulting his maps Blake knew, even allowing for his favorite detour, that they would arrive in time to have freshly-caught fish for lunch and scan the waters for Tula's arrival. From that moment Sherevsky, Tula and its passengers would not have long to live.

CHAPTER TEN

I awoke at 7:00 to the sound of two birds having a fierce squabble for the favors of a third. How do birds tell one another's sex? With peacocks it was easy enough, what with all the plumage, but there must be many inadvertent homosexual liaisons in bird land before truth outed. Such thoughts, bad grammar and all, were a consequence of not having found a substitute for Peter Dawson's bottle, and I had slept soundly and wakened with a spring in my legs and nothing of substance on my mind. Today I would laze around the library preparing course material. Perhaps Bill Nelson would come by and discover how conscientious I was and start entertaining thoughts about welcoming me permanently to the college staff. Dean of Academic Studies! That would be just right. Throughout my shower and shave I steadily mounted the academic ladder until the University of Chicago beckoned with an offer of an honorary PhD.

Alcohol is not the only means of growing giddy. Successive showers, a swim in the Bosphorus, a gulped-out confession before a bikini-clad priestess in a rented rowboat—absolution without ceremony—-all these produced euphoria faster than a bottle of wine on an empty stomach. Or had they? Suzan Lokman now knew me for a coward and would regret that cousin Raif had selected so weak a man to cuckold, for what joy is there in conquest of the already vanquished? Raif was just a scavenger, picking over another man's garbage.

I pulled on a pair of Dawson's jeans and a T-shirt, breakfasted on the meager remains of our picnic, gathered up pencils and one of Peter Dawson's loose-leaf pads and started for the door. It was then that the early-morning haunts took up their accustomed vigil; it was Monday. At 11:00 a.m. I had an appointment at the Second Section of the Turkish Security Police. Orhan Urfanli, he of the black hair, black mustaches, black eyes and black scowl, had intoned, "Don't fail to keep that appointment."

I undressed and dressed again in the nearest thing to respectability that Peter Dawson's wardrobe still afforded. It was August and I would sweat from the heat, from fear, from trying to divine what lie I could get away with, from seeking to fathom what interior motives lay behind the questions, "What is your name and why are you here?"

If it weren't for the twittering of the birds I might have slept through the ordeal! Better to be thrown out of Turkey than face this. God, there had to be another bottle somewhere; a few jolts of whiskey and my courage would soar. Yank out my fingernails and I wouldn't whimper! No white feather for me; just a little Three Feathers would do fine. A fruitless search. The quest for courage would have to wait until I got off the campus.

If I had a rope I would have tied it around me to keep from falling apart on the walk across the quadrangle to the main gate and the cobbled lane that led down the verdant slope to the Bosphorus road. It was nearing eight. I had three hours left to ease my way into the city, fueled on alcohol, there to collapse in Urfanli's waiting arms.

Fortunately for pious Muslim Turks, the Prophet warned his followers only to be wary of wine, ignoring such refinements as raki, brandy and other elixirs that wise men discovered in order to be drunk and pious simultaneously. A determined man can find a bar open in

Bebek as early as in any other civilized village and I found one a few hundred yards down from the foot of the college hill.

The atmosphere of the bar amused me and I decided to linger for a while to eavesdrop on the conversations. It was only eight-thirty; ample time remained to hail another dolmus for the main event at Beyoglu. The raki bottle was temptingly near.

Some time later, Mehmetcik the lobsterman limped into the bar. I started to descend from the bar stool to greet him, discovered too late that I had not really been seated and collapsed to the floor. I made another great discovery to compare with the one that bars open early worldwide: barroom floors are hard worldwide. Mehmet got to me as fast as his lame leg would permit, but it didn't matter, I was out.

*   *   *

"Paul. Paul."

I was at the bottom of the sea. A talking lobster lay perched on my chest; its claws opened and closed convulsively as the antennae that served as eyes felt their way around my body selecting where and when to begin the attack.

"Paul. Wake up." The lobster spoke again. The savage beak of a mouth gave forth a voice that was urgent but soft. I opened my eyes a slit. The lobster reached out and slapped me briskly. Once, twice. My eyes opened wider. The lobster was still there. It struggled against the string that girdled its green midsection, thrashing wildly with its claws.

"Paul! Dammit, come to."

I turned my head slowly, determined to expose my jugular vein to the lobster's portside claw. "Kill me and get it over with," I cried out.

The green skeleton stuffed with flesh came down hard on me. I let out a cry of fear and struggled to my knees and was halfway erect when I fell again on my rear quarters; but now the lobster was three feet away and the string had grown taut again and I was safe. Cautiously I looked around: if this was the bottom of the sea, why was there no water? Why did the lobster have a string around it? Who taught it to speak English? Why an English speaking lobster in preference to a Turkish-speaking lobster? My head ached with unresolved questions.

The voice spoke again, but this time I could sense that it did not come from the direction of the lobster. This would explain the riddle of who taught the lobster to speak English; the lobster's English teacher was also present! I enlarged my field of vision: this time the voice was coming from a skeleton with flesh on it, not in it. Nicely placed flesh, too. And covered by a snug-fitting green dress with a sash around the waist.

"That was a dirty trick," I growled.

"Mehmet thought of it."

I scowled in the direction of the figure that stood lopsidedly behind the lobster, the end of the string held firmly in his gnarled hands. His charge was a mammoth example of the Bosphorus breed and fully capable of rending me limb from limb if that cord had snapped. I wished it a quick and painful death. The same for its owner.

"Very funny."

"It was the only way to make you come to."

"Why bother?"

"Mehmetcik told me you had collapsed in the bar and that he carried you here. He was terribly worried."

"Afraid I'd die before he could tell me his lousy war stories. He doesn't deserve an audience."

"How many did you have?"

"How many what?" Why didn't she stick to the subject? All this jumping from subject to subject was making me giddy.

"Glasses of raki or whatever else you were drinking."

"Five."

"On an empty stomach!"

"I ate some breakfast. The leftovers from our picnic. I'm very good on leftovers."

"Can you stand up?" She bent down to grasp my forearm and bicep and tugged at me. "Slowly. Slowly." Mehemet stood by the trap door of the lobster cage, lowering my disappointed adversary into the water. He made no effort to help us. "Turks are no gentlemen," I mumbled morosely. That he must have carried me a quarter of a mile from Bebek on his back and then run on a lame leg up the college hill to tell Suzan of my fate didn't excuse things. I mean, what kind of a man encourages lobsters to eat humans?

I was on my feet now, rocking on the balls of my feet, like a punch drunk lightweight waiting for the haymaker. Perhaps I should take a slug at this wisp of a girl in the green dress and let her crippled friend cut me up for lobster bait.

"Let's sit down, I want to hear Mehmet's war stories." The voice I heard was surprisingly crisp considering the condition of its owner.

"No. I have a better idea." She said something quickly to Mehmet who spooned out mounds of firm yogurt onto a plate, and handed it to me.

"Get this down quickly. It will balance your stomach against the raki." The yogurt was slightly sour, the way good yogurt should be, and I gulped down a pint without stopping.

"What time is it?"

"Ten-thirty five."

"Downtown. I've got to get downtown. Fast."

"You're a mess, Paul."

"I can't help that. I've got an urgent appointment at eleven with the Turkish police. If I don't get there on time, it's goodbye Istanbul."

"I'll come with you."

It would have been better without her, to go alone, to return alone, but I quickly surrendered. I tried to thank Mehmet for scraping me off the barroom floor and made the mistake of trying to press money on him for the yogurt. He practically snapped my wrist pushing it away and I reminded myself to thank him properly some day by listening to his war stories.

We left then, my arm over Suzan's shoulder as she nudged me along the pier and up the path that led to Bebek. My head was clearing fast and I could smell the lilacs that grew low on the trellises, thrusting out their perfumed heads for attention; acacias lent us patches of shade against the sun; an occasional lizard scurried across the path. Her shoulder was firm and square against my chest and her hip brushed incessantly against my thigh. I turned to let my lips brush against the crown of her dark brown hair. A girl to lean on. It was so easy to get accustomed to that. A girl to lean on.

I lay back against the seat of the taxi while she washed my face with a saliva-dampened handkerchief, the way a mother does to a child before entering church. The Bosphorus was scudding by rapidly on our left and I closed my eyes against the glare and the insistent panorama of beauty.

"We're here, Paul." This time I wakened easily. I paid the meter, haggled briefly over the size of the tip, bade Suzan good-bye and mounted the steps of the gray ominous-looking but discrete building midway down Istiklal Caddessi. There was no knocker, no doorbell. I turned the big brass handle and the door creaked open. The interior was somber, lit only by a small naked bulb that hung from the ceiling like an undernourished star. Beneath it was a spare desk and behind it was a mean-looking little doorman with a two-day growth of beard.

He didn't even bother to look up at me.

"Oturuz," he said, and beckoned to sit on a bench that emerged from the shadows on the far side of the entrance hall. The minutes ticked by, sometimes slowly, sometimes quickly. The good effects of Mehmet's yogurt were fast wearing off with the elapse of time and the sense of insecurity brought on by the dismal environment.

"This way, Mr. Adams." The voice sounded familiar. I looked up to see Orhan Urfanli standing beside me, looking clean, darkly handsome and superior. This seemed a change for the better from the immigration office where we had first met. I followed him through a plain wooden door at the end of the entrance hall and down a long corridor. At the end we entered a small but modern elevator and rose swiftly to what must have been the fifth floor, though I noted that floor stops were not indicated. Could this be a private elevator to the top? The top man on the top floor?

Urfanli signaled me to precede him and I stepped out into a paneled reception room. It was rich looking without being ostentatious: Turkish carpets on the floors, so thick I could almost hear them go squish-squish as I walked; a few color prints of scenic spots in Turkey; leather furniture several cuts above bureaucratic standard; the inevitable bust of Ataturk atop a bookcase, this time done in alabaster in lieu of gilt. Best of all, a dazzling receptionist with eyes that tilted upward and a bosom to match.

Urfanli's apparent rank and ambition relieved him of the need to adopt the deferential, catered entrance approach that inferiors use in the Middle East when entering the presence of superiors, but he did remember to bring his heels together lightly and nod his chin in the direction of the man who stood beside the massive desk that dominated the middle of the room. Then he advanced swiftly to speak softly to his superior and I glanced around. It might have been the office of the Managing Director of the Ottoman Bank, were it not for the man to whom Urfanli spoke with soft urgency and who responded with the clipped acknowledgment "Hi, hi," which is a Turkish way of indicating that information has been received but a position not yet taken.

He was dressed in military riding clothes, as if he had just cantered up the Istanbul equivalent of the Champs Elysees to dismount in front of his office. The high, spurred boots reflected the care and attention of a loving and tireless batman. He must have been standing all morning;

there was no trace of a wrinkle in the faultlessly tailored uniform that he wore with the sort of elaborate assurance that French officers assume when they ride horseback across the Place du Trocadero, playing at cavaliers in early-morning traffic, suggesting that theirs is the most natural posture in the world while yours is the aberration.

The face was as carefully tailored as the clothes. It was long to match his long body; angular to match the set of his shoulders; puffy under the eyes to correspond to the slight paunch that the tailor had not been entirely able to camouflage. The blue shadows around his eyes could have been laid on by hand but the expression came out of life, not a makeup expert's treasure chest. It was a face that had witnessed and experienced infinity and beyond and, when his eyes flickered across my face and disheveled clothing, my past, present and future were laid naked at a glance. I tried to think of something I had done that was worth confessing.

"So nice to see you again, Mr. Adams."

The voice was soft and melodic with the touch of understatement that brought back the Bank Director image. But what had he said? "So nice to see you again, Mr. Adams!" I tried to plug in on the dormant mechanism that would tell me where and when I had seen this face before.

"I am Colonel Atil. Cemal Atil. Do sit down." The Colonel did not seem perturbed by my failure to acknowledge his greeting. I sensed that Urfanli had pushed a chair in my direction. I sat. Atil and Urfanli remained standing.

"It will come back, I am sure. It was a long time ago in any event and the circumstances were not happy ones."

Could this be the Turkish cop whom I had tried to slug after a fruitless effort to rip the spangled brassiere off a belly dancer? No, he had been just another minion of the law; this was the sort of man who invented words like minion to pin on other people.

"Will you join me in a glass of tea?"

This was the opportunity that I had been waiting for to say something wildly funny, like "No thanks, I don't think there would be room for both of us," but the laggard guardian spirit who keeps fitful watch on my destiny intervened in time.

"No thank you, Colonel. Not right now." The words sounded quite natural and I began to perk up. It had been wise to refuse the tea. A flunky would have come running in carrying a tray with amber glasses and the irregular lumps of sugar and my hands would tremble badly and the glass would shatter on the floor sending shards of gilt-trimmed glass into the tufts of the carpet and drops of tea would land on the Colonel's faultlessly-tailored uniform and the Colonel's receptionist would get bits of glass in her bottom when they enjoyed sport on the carpet and it would be disaster all around.

I waited for the next question, trying to fit Atil into the mosaic of my past in Istanbul.

"It is good to be back, eh."

"Yes, Colonel. It is good to be back."

"And see old friends."

"I have very few of those. Only Bill Nelson out at the International College in Bebek."

"Ah, yes. Mr. Nelson. The man who offered you the temporary job while one of his teachers is away in America."

Atil must have greatly enjoyed the look of stupefaction on my face. My conversation with Bill Nelson had been transparent to the core.

"Then there is no use kidding around, is there, Colonel? What's it to be? Do you let me stay or do I catch the next bus out?"

Atil leaned against the carved edge of the great desk and picked up one of a pair of matched pens in an onyx holder and twirled it slowly between his fingers.

"That depends on the reasons for which you have returned."

"I was happy here once. I want to try to be happy here again." It was true, that lie had just spoken. I had been happy once, back at the beginning.

"But your wife was a part of that happiness. And this time she is not with you."

"No. She is not with me." I felt my tongue cleave to the top of my mouth as I said the words. Would this dreadful man who held me in bondage to his personality see through the fabrication of my oblique response? Would he know that Janice's remains were in a little vial of ashes that had been grafted between my ribs like a planted tumor; that I had come to Istanbul to find a crooked surgeon whom I could lure away from the abortion trade long enough to perform radical surgery in my chest and remove the last vestiges of her memory?

"You still do not recall?"

"No."

"Think back three years. You came to the morgue to identify a body that was found in the sea of Marmara about ten days after your wife's death. Decomposition was well advanced but you recognized her."

It was coming back now, that day when the Consul General came quietly into my office to tell me that a police officer was waiting for me, his tone scarcely concealing disapproval.

I knew without being told that Janice's body had been found. How would I respond? Would I curb the instinct to jump up and shout for joy on seeing the dead proof? Would I cry hysterically? Would I retch at the sight of that decomposed flesh, once so ravishing to the sight and now fearsomely cold after ten days of drifting with the currents?

Death and burial follow hard upon one another in Turkey. A man dies in the morning and is in his grave before sunset. It is a system that the Irish would hardly approve of; there is not time to keen, to weep loudly, and to call in neighbors for commiseration and a last admiring glance at the remnants of a man who had been so good to his wife and children. Depending on station in life, a cortege is quickly assembled, floral wreaths bought and a simple pine box brought to house the last remains that are first wrapped in gauze. If a man is poor his casket is carried into a nearby cemetery, its weight shifted from friend to friend as they compete to show respect for their lost comrade by assisting him on his final journey. The women and children follow at a discreet distance—if they come at all.

Thus the police morgue in Istanbul is small but adequate to the task. There is no need for elaborate refrigeration systems, tiers of drawers, white-gowned attendants showing off cadavers like so many souvenirs up for purchase. Janice was in a low pine box; chunks of ice had been placed around to keep down the odor but the room smelled profoundly of death, and I gagged on entering.

She was still wearing the one-piece swimsuit and the upper half of her body was still exposed. Her breasts were mottled and blue, the flesh that had been such a source of pride and provocation was now ridged and furrowed. There are few sharks in the Marmara so her body was intact but part of her left nostril had fallen off and her lips were slack on her face; I had the feeling that I could reach over and take one between my thumb and forefinger and it would come off to my touch.

"Do you know this woman?"

The voice came in sepulchral tones from somewhere around me.

"Yes."

"Are you positive?"

"It is my wife."

"How do you know?"

"She is recognizable. And there is the swimsuit. I know the swimsuit. And the ring."

"Wedding rings look alike."

I looked around trying to find the source of the voice. Couldn't its owner tell at a glance that this was my wife?

"Our initials are engraved inside the ring."

"Come this way a moment, please."

I was led to the far corner of the morgue, which seemed to have no precise definition. It was at once small and enormous, its walls corresponding to our movement. I heard a low-voiced conversation in Turkish and then a metallic sound that coincided with a sharp grunt.

"What is said inside the ring?"

"From P.A. to J.M. and a date."

"What date?"

"I ... I'm not sure."

"Surely you remember your wedding date."

"September 10, 1968."

A hand led me back toward the box that brimmed with flesh and ice.

"You identify this woman as your wife?"

"I do."

"What do you wish to do with the ring? Keep it?"

"No. Bury it with her."

The ring was thrust into my palm. Without thinking I picked up Janice's cold hand but there was no ring finger on which to put it; just a bloodless joint where the attendant had cut through flesh and bone to help in the identification. Her finger lay nestled against a lump of ice, a patch of red polish still glistened on the nail. I threw the ring onto her stomach and felt my legs lose their strength.

Later in an upstairs office there were questions that I do not now remember clearly; insistent questions about her belongings, effects, disposal of the body, names of relatives. The questions were polite but repeated over and over again until I cried for mercy. The police record attributed death to accidental drowning; whatever bruises Janice had sustained during the fall on the cabin roof had been obliterated by the sea and the decomposition of flesh.

I sent her home in dry ice on a Pan American flight, and I remember the passengers in the transit lounge looking on apprehensively as the box was wheeled out on the tarmac. Almost everyone from the Consulate was there; Bill and Mary Nelson from the International

College and a few people we knew from the Istanbul business community. People from the Agency trying to pretend that they weren't what they were. And Emily Cartwright, ostentatiously weeping, going from person to person to expound her grief; periodically pausing to throw dagger glances in my direction or whisper behind her hand to the Consul General. I thought a grotesque thought about the schoolboy rhyme about the old hermit named Dave who kept a dead whore in his cave and wondered whether the C.G. would want Janice's remains as a memento.

Atil had been my interrogator at the morgue. A man can be excused for not remembering who it was who asked him to identify his wife's body or give him support when he tried to place a ring on a finger that wasn't there. The memory of Janice had stayed with me through the years—she was my one and only cadaver but Atil had progressed from the roll of interrogator in street clothes to Second Section chief and the perquisites of a paneled office, riding clothes in town and a secretary who swept up broken tea glasses from the floor with her bare bottom; so my memory of him was not of a face but of a soft voice that asked and repeated urgent sounding questions.

Now he was asking questions that had been asked years before.

"You recall now."

"Yes." Then I qualified my reply. "I think so."

Atil drew his forefingers across the blue pouches beneath his eyes, as if to smooth away the hours of interrogation and late nights that had contributed to their making. "So why do you return? Because you were happy here? Happy to have your career destroyed, to be cashiered from your service?"

"No! No! That's not it." I looked toward Urfanli, pleading for a signal that he had understood those banal words in the Customs House about rebirth, about beginning again. Words that had stumbled over one another like so many recruit soldiers. But he avoided my eyes, knowing that the right of pardon had been passed to higher authority.

"Then why? To seek out your wife's lovers? Perhaps to kill them? Take revenge?"

"I am trying to drown a memory, Colonel. First to see if I can live with it and then drown it for good."

"You will fail, Adams."

"I must try. I must begin here." It was the best I could offer. It is not such a sin, trying, even when trying seems a forlorn hope.

Atil rose from his leaning position against the desk, caressed the incipient wrinkles from his riding pants and carefully lit a cigarette. Our relationship had been good for one free smoke, no more.

"You may go."

I made to rise, then slumped back. "You mean I can stay in Turkey?"

"That depends. For now, yes. Give me your passport."

I handed him the dog-eared passport that smelled of sweat. He leafed through it quickly to find the page where Urfanli had stamped my entry; he drew two lines through the stamp and wrote a few words down the side of the page.

"This passport has almost expired."

"Yes, I know."

"You must not try to leave without our knowing."

"Colonel. I'm an American citizen. You can't keep me prisoner here!"

The asperity of my words surprised me.

"Indeed not. You are welcome to leave now if you would prefer." He had chosen his words carefully and I got the message. A short leash had been plaited, comprised of not-so-subtle hints, official stamps, words scratched in a passport, qualified phrases saying I could remain, "for now." If I had returned to Istanbul to be born again, Atil intended to function as midwife.

Atil spoke rapidly to Urfanli. I rose and threaded a path across the carpet, careful not to muss the pattern. Urfanli followed.

"Thank you, Colonel Atil," I said as Urfanli opened the door.

"You did well to let her drown, Adams," he called back. The door closed behind me; the hinges of hell were silent and well oiled. The receptionist escorted me to the express elevator and I started down, down, down.

CHAPTER ELEVEN

"You were a little hard on him, Colonel."

"You surprise me, Urfanli. Why?"

"All that about his wife. It was rough."

"Rough but for his own good. Adams is here on some kind of pilgrimage, the kind men make when they think that a few prayers and a kiss on the holy place replace living. Such men need to have their own faith tested or the pilgrimage has no meaning."

"Did he really kill his wife? I mean deliberately let her drown?"

Atil renewed his cigarette from the ember of the previous one. "I don't know, he doesn't know. That's what goads him. Did he let her drown? Did he try to save her? These questions have burrowed into him like pieces of shrapnel that wonder about in the body causing pain long after the scar has healed." He moved to the window and drew back the drapes. "Look."

Adams was in the middle of Mustafa Kemal Caddessi, trapped by conflicting streams of traffic. Suddenly a figure darted out and threw a stern hand up in front of an oncoming dolmus.

Atil chuckled softly. "A child leads him to safety."

"A young woman," corrected Urfanli.

"A young woman who helps a man like him is a child at heart. A child who has not lived to learn that some men are beyond help."

"Why do you let him stay, Colonel, if you hold him in such contempt?"

Atil let the drape fall from his hand. "If we were to banish all men whom we hold in contempt, who would be left? To hold a man in contempt and then to tolerate him is the beginning of love. You will come to discover that. Anyway, he is useful to me."

"Useful?"

Atil beckoned to two leather chairs that flanked a circular tray of beaten copper in the far corner of the office. "Come, let us sit down. There is something I want to tell you. You are new in this office, carefully selected. You must be totally loyal to me and you must understand the nature of our mission."

"Hi, Hi efendim," said Urfanli, almost choking on his words.

"This city of ours," Atil began, "is a legacy entrusted to us to protect. We are bankers to a heritage. A heritage of conspiracy, intrigue, corruption, sudden death, espionage. Name a means that man has found to deceive himself and others around him, and it has flourished in Istanbul. Sin is what has made this city, more so than the churches, the treasuries, the mosques, the aqueducts, the mosaics, the frescoes.

"These other things, what the specialists call our cultural heritage, are easy to protect, and their protection falls to men whose training suits them for that task. But our job is more difficult: it is to protect the sinful side of Istanbul. To be certain that virtue never conquers vice.

"Remember this, Urfanli, there can be no virtue without vice. No beauty without ugliness. No good without evil. Today we are faced with a problem. Istanbul is no longer the espionage center of the world. World War II and nuclear politics ended all that. Now we are in danger of being trapped in a backwater where international intrigue is replaced by smuggling, dope running, theft of antiquities, and the odd act of terrorism.

"Even crime is in danger. We are becoming too efficient. Communications, computers, Interpol, foreign experts: these weapons are too good for our own good. So good that they may seal up our backwater and reduce crime to nothing."

"Excuse me, efendim," interrupted Urfanli. "But that is our job. To reduce crime to nothing."

"You are wrong! Our job is to contain crime, not to eliminate it. Without crime we are nothing. Our city loses its appeal; it becomes just another transit point where the cavalcade makes a brief stop instead of being the goal of a hard journey.

"Think of this, Urfanli! Every year I must prepare a justification for the budget for this office. Do you know what this entails, this justification? It means that I must prove year after year that your job is necessary, that my job is necessary, that the money required to pay the salaries of hundreds of your colleagues is worth spending. There is so much to be done in Turkey: schools to be built, hospitals for the eastern provinces, roads leading to backward villages, and I must compete for public funds against these priorities. Without crime it would be impossible.

"I have tried to persuade our American and British friends to help, but they respond by reducing the number of men in the secure area of the Consulates to three or four. Years ago there were fifteen or twenty CIA men housed in the annex of the American Consulate; now it is a handful. They didn't even replace Adams when he was thrown out. A handful of agents in Istanbul! Do you see what this means? They write us off! On their list of priorities we have dropped from a high place to near the bottom. And why? Because Istanbul is getting a good name!"

"I appreciate your telling me this, Colonel," Urfanli interjected.

"I do not say such things to every man, Urfanli. There are many who would not understand, but you are different. I can confide in you; tell you things, confident that you grasp the motives behind my actions."

"You are right, efendim. I see."

Urfanli did not see, did not begin to comprehend Atil's meaning, but the words came out without references to the thought behind them. Wallahi, he thought, what have I gotten into.

"It is for your own good that I give this advice," Atil resumed. "For Istanbul's good. Engrave it on your heart: there is no virtue without vice."

Atil lapsed into silence and closed his eyes as though in a reverie. He is dreaming, Urfanli thought, of crime to come; of weighted bodies dredged up from the Golden Horn; of midnight raids on crumbling waterfront warehouses and men flitting off into the night like so many wharf rats.

"You may go now." The words were barely audible.

"Yes, sir. But first may I ask a question: you said before that Adams was useful to us. How?"

Atil sat up straighter in his chair, a flash of impatience crossing his face.

"I thought I had explained all that just now, but since you fail to comprehend I will say it again. There is a dossier in our files and it is stamped with the name 'Adams' and the case remains open. There are many such dossiers and they are the statistical support for my presentation to the budget committee of the Grand National Assembly. The more dossiers I can cite, the more unsolved and new crimes, the better are my prospects of obtaining a good appropriation.

"Being an American he is especially useful. And an ex-diplomat, even an intelligence agent, makes it even better. A suspicious person would be forgiven if he is told that an American ex-diplomat arrives broke in Istanbul and then believes him to be back as an agent of the CIA. The CIA is everywhere is it not? The suspicious person might also wonder whether the CIA agent is spying for or against Turkey and would cause questions to be asked of the American Embassy, which, in turn, would levy a report on the CIA station chief who would complain to Washington that he is short-staffed and needs more help. Washington would know that Adams is not spying in its behalf but would wonder whether he had sold out to the Russians -not that the Russians would be such fools- so they would send agents to Istanbul to keep track of Adams and little by little the order of priorities would be revised.

"Absurd? I do not need that startled look in your eyes to tell me it is absurd that is how the system works. Remember, Urfanli, the CIA has the same problem as I have; it cannot exist without espionage, just as this office cannot exist without crime. As Voltaire said of God, if none exists, he must be invented."

Atil paused, savoring the look of incredulity coupled with dismay on Urfanli's face. "That is one way Adams can be useful to me. It is ridiculous to think of Adams involved in anything significant—his fiber is too weak to stand the strain—but with my help he can be given spine enough to help push through an appropriation."

"I thank you very much for your confidence in me, Colonel." Atil did not trouble to respond but watched Urfanli close the door behind him. He smiled.

It had been a good thing, this session with Urfanli, and had relieved his tensions wonderfully. Urfanli had listened with rapt attention, an acolyte at the feet of a master, presumably believing all. This conversation would linger in his memory, like the recollection of first intercourse, and he would test Atil's words against reality. Occasionally he would come back to Atil to ask questions, to see whether his chief truly believed the sermon he preached. But those questions would go unanswered. Urfanli would be obliged to find out for himself what, if anything, Atil held as dogma.

Atil smiled to himself. It was a similar conversation years before that told him that he had been nominated by his superiors to the elite cult of men who would guide Turkey's destinies. Such were the secret uses of mystery.

Atil gathered a handful of paperclips in his hand and began to toss them across the broad expanse of office against a door leading to the reception room. There was a rapid click, click and then another click. Atil was beginning to find his aim. Three more paperclips soared across the room against the door.

Then the door opened and a woman stood beneath the frame. A paperclip caught her on the chest and rolled down into the cleft of her breasts.

"Bull's-eye!" Atil called out jubilantly.

The woman closed the door behind her, and with her hand behind her back, turned the key.

CHAPTER TWELVE

The neat rows started at the brow of the hill and continued in parallel lines across three kilometers of undulating terrain before falling off to the beaches of Gallipoli. The rows were made of crosses and bore names such as Hemsford, Rollingsford, Turner, Blacock, and MacGillvray. The land had been made fertile by the remains of thirty thousand Englishman, New Zealanders, Australians and South Africans who had fallen in a vain effort to wrest Gallipoli from the Turks and their German allies, but the seed that had been planted there was dead seed, buried too deep to break through the covering earth, and the fertility was consumed in the crosses.

Blake threaded his way through the neat rows following a carefully drawn map prepared in the custodian's office at the cemetery six years ago when he made his initial pilgrimage to the cemetery. The coordinates took him toward the sea to a place marked as Grid 10-X. When he arrived there he drew his pocket handkerchief across the nameplate wired to the cross and read, "Edward Maxwell Blake, First Lieutenant, His Majesty's Sixth Hussars, Killed May 23rd, 1915."

He lingered there a while, plunged in thought. It was not the first time he had found an excuse to make the trip to Gelibolu, the Turkish rendering of Gallipoli, ostensibly in pursuit of some official mission, actually to make a pilgrimage to the grave of his mother's dead husband.

The man in the grave was his father, Blake often told himself, despite the fact that Edward Maxwell Blake had died in 1915 and William Anthony Edward Blake was not born until 1923. When he first learned of the eight-year gap between death and birth, he rejoiced in the information, for it set him apart from his fellows.

His mother's explanation for the gap pleased him. "Blake was your father," she told him, "the ones in between after his death and your birth counted for nothing. He was my only real man and I carried his seed eight years until you came along." Her conviction touched him. It was amusing, too, to contemplate having two fathers; one buried beneath a small cross at Gallipoli; the other possibly still living, perhaps a board chairman of a famous company, a member of Parliament, a distinguished theater critic, a patent attorney. The range of possible careers that a son could assign to an unknown father was even greater than that a doting parent might conjure up for a newborn son held in a crook of his arm: fathers are circumscribed in their choice of dreams by knowledge of their own selves; a son need feel no restrictions in contemplating the father he had never known.

Except, perhaps, that there were so few men in England capable of siring a son with such magnificent teeth. In a tattered suitcase beneath the bed in his Galata apartment, Blake kept a scrapbook containing photos of smiling men taken from glossy magazines, advertisements, newspapers, posters, accounts of political rallies, theater marquees—wherever a man might smile on a appreciative public. Many a somber winter night had been spent in coding the photographs—some of which dated back half a century—and developing comparison charts between the subject and Blake himself. Incisors too short; molars slightly angled; canines too long in relation to rest of teeth; lower teeth appear capped; fillings evident in molars; denture…ran some of the notations. None of the comparisons had led him to the identity of his real father and he feared they never would: one could hardly walk up to a perfect stranger, thrust a mouth full of teeth in front of him and shout, "Dad!!" Could one?

The distant blare of a motor horn aroused Blake from his reverie. "Good-bye Dad", he said, caressing the top of the cross as if stroking the head of a faithful setter, "take good care of yourself. I'll be back for a little visit soon as possible." He whistled a tune as he threaded his way between the crosses to the entrance of the cemetery. Nuri gave relevant details as the car bounced along the pocket road leading back to Gelibolu port. Tula had cleared the entrance to the Dardanelles at 12:10 hours and was proceeding at reduced speed up the Straits. There appeared to be no special activity on board, according to a Turkish contact at Canakalle, the entry point to the Straits; if anything, Tula was behaving in the manner of a ship with no place to go. Speed was substantially less than normal for a ship her size.

"How far is she from Gelibolu, Nuri?"

The reply was reassuring. There was still time for lunch. Few things in life compared with a filet cut from a lufer freshly drawn from the sea and baked over a bed of coals. Blake drew his tongue over his teeth in anticipation.

*   *   *

The news got to Orenko as he stood by the deck rail spooling exposed film back into its cassette. He listened silently, afraid to speak, as Captain Vaslov reported that the tremors in Tula's hull had been traced to a faulty cylinder casing that risked shattering with each thrust of the piston into the sheath. It would be necessary, Vaslov said solemnly, to reduce speed even further and make a slow passage across the Marmara.

"Can we make Odessa?" Orenko asked, finally summoning the strength to voice words.

"Perhaps, if we are lucky."

"And if not?"

Vaslov shrugged, "We can try to put in at Istinye on the Bosphorus. The Turks have repair facilities there. Perhaps the clowns can fix the engine. If not?" and he shrugged again.

"But we must make Odessa, Vaslov. We must."

A flicker of a smile crossed the Captain's thin lips. "What's the hurry, Comrade? Someone important is on board?" Then he turned on his heel and strode rapidly toward the bridge.

Orenko stifled the impulse to run after the Captain, to plead for understanding and help. It was too late now: his instructions had been clear: return Scherevsky to Soviet hands. Do not fail. He felt a deep sense of inadequacy. An assignment such as this was not what Tula was intended for. The little ship's ambitions were modest, just as were those of Orenko. Would he fail this test? Must the machine now fail too?

"To fail is to die," he repeated to himself, "to fail is to die. Tula is dying beneath my feet and I will die next."

*　　　*　　　*

Blake snapped off slender bones from the skeleton of the lufer. They were malleable in his fingers. He flexed them the way a fencer tests his sword, then methodically explored the interstices between his teeth. He nodded in acknowledgement as Nuri pointed to the freighter that labored into view, letting a last morsel of lufer rest on his tongue before swallowing.

Tula was not the sort of vessel to stir admiration in Southampton, he thought. Just as well, too, as far as its proprietors were concerned. Inconspicuousness was just the sort of camouflage an intelligence-gatherer wanted; no fancy electronics to arouse attention—that was not Tula's cup of tea. Just a crummy ship that gathered random information about port installations, fleet movements, profiles of likely landing beaches and the like.

Tula, Blake reasoned, was a bit like his radio station over at Kandilli. The nuisance value of being obliged to cross the Bosphorus to pick up radio messages was more than offset by the security of the operation. Twelve years had elapsed since the first BJ operational message had come in, and the Turks were none the wiser about its presence. Tula had probably stumbled its way into every classified port in the Mediterranean without NATO intelligence ever getting a fix on it.

Blake studied the vessel thoughtfully. Was the ship's slow pace a deception maneuver designed to suggest to possible pursuers that Scherevsky would not be aboard a vessel that moved so lackadaisically? Had a submarine drawn alongside of Tula sometime during the sail from Piraeus and Scherevsky been transferred? Was the ship in trouble?

Time to think about these riddles on the drive back to Istanbul. At present speed, he thought, she won't get there until eight o'clock. Ample time for tea and a few preparations to make sure everything goes well tonight. Blake withdrew his wallet, extracted a neatly folded square of onionskin paper on which he had laboriously decoded the most recent message of instructions. He read the words through twice, drawing renewed encouragement from their meaning: take such means as are necessary to achieve your mission.

The sheet of onionskin folded easily into its sheltered square. Nestled in Blake's wallet it constituted one of the bits and pieces of paper that sum up a man's life: identity card, photograph, driver's license, money, a fragment from an old love letter, a card that said "in case of accident or death please advise so-and-so," a tightly folded sheet of onion skin that sanctioned death in the performance of duty.

Blake patted his chest, sensing the reassuring bulk in his jacket pocket.

"Don't worry blokes," he said aloud. "I'll pull this off all right. Someday you'll be bloody glad I didn't join Philby in Moscow."

Ahmet and Nuri regarded him blankly.

CHAPTER THIRTEEN

Dinner was over: grilled swordfish; a platter of baby lamb chops grilled over charcoal, the taste of thyme deep in their flesh; a mound of pilaf, and lastly chunks of yellow melon that tasted of honey and flowers. The houseboat-restaurant with the improbable name of The Six Legged Octopus swayed gently beneath us, and the moon, now three-quarters full, emerged slowly from behind Anatolia. The dome of the world, the Turks call Anatolia, and the stars, the moon and the planets were just beyond our grasp.

Suzan was transfixed by the spectacle, and I had time to study a finely chiseled profile that ended in a determined chin. The moonlight highlighted her cheekbones and I thought of how her people, at least the Turkish half, like the moon, had risen mysteriously from the East to dominate the Bosphorus.

I raised my glass "to Suzan Lokman and her TLC."

She turned to face me and smiled.

"No. Not tender loving care. Turkish loving care."

We drank from the same glass and I let my fingers linger on hers as I passed it.

We had talked of so much and so little all through dinner. It was not the sort of conversation that implanted itself deep into one's memory because it was natural and part of the fabric of everyday living that is hardly noticed but holds life together. I asked why she had never left Turkey to test herself in America and her answer was a mixture of conceit and humility. Turkey was a desperately poor country and needed to guard its resources if it was to survive. Turkey needed her. Beneath that veneer of sophistication and light hearted talk of sex was a desire to serve and helping me an expression of it, even correcting the imbalance between nations. I was an impoverished American seeking help; usually it was the other way around. Now a shapely girl could right the score.

"I'm here to stay, Suzan," I burst out, taking her hands in mine.

"Don't talk about it, Paul. It's too soon."

"Why not? Look at me! I've weathered this day and I hope I never see worse. Do you know what Atil told me? He said, 'You did right to let her drown.' Do you hear that? He said I did right to let her drown!"

"Stop! Stop! I've had enough of Janice today." Her voice showed anguish.

Lord, what an outburst. Glorious hours thinking that I had begun to exorcise the demon from my soul and then this. I looked desperately at Suzan, waiting for her to rise from her chair and declare the evening over; how much time could a volunteer nurse give before tiring of playing at goodness. I was like Richelieu, rotting away inside his purple garments, musk poured on the vestments to hide the stench of decaying flesh. Soon she would tire of the stench that took the form of my words.

She looked at me steadily. "Paul. Janice died in an accident. You tried to save her and failed. That is what happened. That is what you must accept."

"I'm sorry. I didn't intend to start that business all over again."

"Give yourself a chance. You've paid your penalty. You didn't let her drown. It was something to do with the currents. But even if you had, three years has been penalty enough."

"Cowardice is for life," I said, wishing that I had something better to say.

"Then accept you are on parole."

I smiled. It was a good response, far more clever than I deserved. Paroled in custody of a twenty-two-year old girl out to correct the imbalance between nations. Hostage to a young girl's dream. I called the rotund poet who ran the Six Legged Octopus as a hedge against the vagaries of poetry writing, thanked him for his food, promised to return again soon, and paid a bill that equaled three dollars. My traveler's check had lasted four days and four remained.

I helped Suzan into the rowboat, threw off the line and hopped in. There was still hope. At least I would try to enjoy parole as long as judged worthy.

The rowboat labored against the current as we headed out from the houseboat to cross the harbor toward Mehmet's fishing shack. The water that sluices down from the Black Sea beats a fierce course as it flows toward the Marmara. One can feel its strength against the blade of an oar, and I bit deep to make headway. We were just past the lighthouse that divides the harbor and warns of shoal water when Suzan jumped to her feet, the mooring rope in her hand.

"Stop rowing," she instructed. She bent quickly to her knees and looped the rope through an orange buoy that bobbed to the left of the rowboat. I had been too preoccupied with my exertions to see it but Suzan knew the harbor paths so well she sensed the moment when it would pass near our boat. The rowboat drifted backwards to the end of the tether, stopped and began to make gentle pendulum motions in the water.

I shook my head uncertainly.

"Shall we be foolish and swim?"

I looked down at the water. "I...I don't have a swimsuit."

"It's nighttime. No one will see. Of course if you would really rather not..." She let the sentence drift off into the night.

It was a test. She was testing whether I would dare challenge the sea at night.

"Of course, Suzan. I was hoping you would suggest it." My voice sounded tubercular.

She opened the bait box under the prow. "Towels. It will be cold afterward. Look away for a moment." I heard the soft rustle of garments as they fell to the bottom of the rowboat.

"I'm going in," she called. I turned in time to see the pulsing beacon in the lighthouse illuminate an arc of flesh that glowed bronze except for brief white patches. The arc hung suspended for an instant as though on display then it patterned itself in an arrow and breached the water.

Suzan emerged with a characteristic wag of her head that threw tendrils of dark hair back from her face. "Come. Come," she said. "It's cold at night. You must use your strength to keep warm."

Her words quickened my hands. My clothing—Peter Dawson's clothing—fell in a heap to the bottom of the rowboat. A body was beckoning from the sea, and this time I would respond.

"Wait for me, Suzan. Wait for me." The words went unheeded on the water as with sure, swift strokes, she cleaved the stiff current. Five, ten, fifteen yards: the gap between us widened and I felt my breath come faster. The pulsations of the lighthouse showed her path leading to the deeper channel beyond the lighthouse. She was challenging the unknown, daring me to follow.

Trouble. Get into trouble. Lose your strength and call to me. Beckon to me when the light brightens the way and I will come to you. I will find the strength. I will swim to you in long strokes that will close the gap between us. I will reach you and comfort you and put you on your back to give you buoyancy and place my hands under your firm, young breasts and guide you to safety.

"Go back, Paul. Go back!" I looked about, trying to focus on the voice that suddenly showed fear.

"Go back, Paul." She was swimming toward me now with all her speed. The water churned at her feet. A great black shape loomed above us. Then something struck the sea followed by a long, metallic hiss.

*   *   *

Something glistened white in the shallow water near the lighthouse. The fish are running, Vaslov thought, leaning on the bridge rail. Almost as big as a sturgeon. His hand reached for the voice tube, and he snapped out rapid-fire instruction to Radenovitch in the engine room and to the Second Officer beside him. The uneven throb of the engine expired almost as the anchor broke from the hawse pipe to plunge into the sea. Vaslov spread his legs instinctively waiting for the tug of the ship against the chain. It was vigorous. A thin smile crossed his face. Tula will hold.

Vaslov wiped his brow with an oily rag. His forehead was sweaty from the tension of bringing the ship into a tricky anchorage with a faulty motor. He stepped out to the exterior bridge. It was cooler there. He used his thumbs and forefingers to pluck the cloth of his shirt away from his chest. The air flowed in, drying and cooling the warm flesh and mat of chest hair. Refreshed, he looked at his watch: eleven-fifteen. What a trip! Normally Tula would be well into the Black Sea now, the night watch officer imagining already that he saw the lights of Odessa low on the water. Instead they were at Bebek, hoping to find a casing that would make Tula whole again.

"Where is that piss genius?" Vaslov murmured aloud. He searched the deck for Orenko and saw his squat form standing in the narrow triangle of the forepeak, his forearms resting on the wooden molding of the rail.

"You'll suffer, tonight, Orenko. Suffer like the rest of us." Vaslov chortled at the prospect. Tula's crippled engines provided the perfect excuse to reduce electricity consumption and this, in turn, would mean that the luxury of air conditioning would be denied Orenko for the duration of their stay in harbor. Some good had come out of their misfortune. A vision of Orenko sweating and twisting in his berth came to Vaslov's mind. It a cheerful thought, worth lingering over; a few sleepless nights would be a good thing for him. He needed to endure the nightmares that troubled lesser men.

*   *   *

"They had no right to anchor there," Suzan exclaimed.

"Engine trouble. They must have been on slow speed," I gasped, laboring against the oars. "I don't care," she insisted. "They had no right to anchor there."

"Don't be silly. The Captain saw you swimming there and couldn't stop himself. Happens all the time to sailors: a siren appears on the rocks and the ship runs aground. You're what myths are made of. This episode establishes you as myth Turkey."

She giggled happily, drawing protective toweling closer around her shoulders. "Oh, I like that! Paul...careful. We're nearly there."

The familiar rickety outline of Mehmetcik's boat pier straddled by the bulk of his home was closer now. I leaned back on my oars to get a bearing on how to make an approach and to see whether the lobsterman had returned yet from his nightly rounds. Finding a naked girl in his lobster pen might be too much to spring on him.

"He's not there," she called out.

I pushed hard on the right oar, pivoting the boat slightly to make a better approach. We glided the last few yards and then jolted to a stop against the rude pilings. Suzan clutched the towel tightly around her and hopped to the pier. She held the tie line until I could join her and secure the boat.

Mehmet's door was, as always, unlocked. We stepped into the dark interior.

"I'm trembling. I see it all over again—that ship appearing out of the night. I was so frightened."

"You're cold, that's all."

"Yes. You're right." She giggled again. "I wanted to dry my hair on the rowboat but I couldn't think of a way to dry my hair and keep covered all with one towel."

"Let me help you."

I reached out in the darkness toward the rectangle of white toweling that shielded her. It was in my hands and I spread the two ends across my palms and gripped them in my fingers. She was silent.

Her shape was clearer now. My eyes had adjusted to the darkness and the moon was still high. I took her head between my hands and began gently to massage her damp hair.

"Paul." The voice was soft.

I bent her head backwards and drew her to me.

"Paul."

Our bodies touching. The sensation of thigh against thigh, mounds of flesh pressing against my rib cage, lips tasting of salt. Union that precedes union.

Across the water came the distant sound of shrill cadences that were a blend of east and west. Mehmet was returning, piping on his omnipresent sweet potato to celebrate a good night's lobster catch.

"Damn!" I'm not sure which of us said it first.

We dressed quickly and, when finished, lit the wick in a lantern so that Mehmet would think we had been waiting for him sometime.

"Kucuk honum," he shouted gleefully, guiding the rowboat with one oar and brandishing something large and black in his other hand. "It is a monster!"

Mehmetcik bounded from the rowboat to the pier, made secure the tie line with one hand and held aloft his catch. It was a monster lobster, even larger than the English-speaking lobster that had made an attempt on my life in the morning. Nearly three feet from stem to stern.

Mehmet thrust it into my face. "Thirty lira, enfendim. Thirty lira for this. We are rich."

We helped him unload the rest of the catch. Four smaller lobsters and the monster joined the writhing prisoners in the wire cell below the shack. Prison conditions are getting crowded, I thought; a riot, a jail-break, and a few executions—-something had to give in Mehmet's prison. There was hardly room for one more.

Later, when the lobster pots were put away, we drank vodka toasts to the lobster that would fetch thirty lira wholesale, to the joys of living by the side of the sea where the world never stopped living. We told Mehmet of the freighter moored in Bebek harbor and he laughed. "It is an orphan. A Russian orphan. I saw it on the way in from the lobster pots and rowed by to take a look.

"It is called Tula. The homeport is Odessa. That's in Crimea." He volunteered the additional bit of geography to insure that a foreigner would pinpoint the location.

"Yes, I know. They say it's a lovely city. Someday I will go there."

He jerked his chin upwards to show disapproval. "The Crimea is in Russia," the geography lesson continued. "Russia is Turkey's enemy."

"That's done with, Mehmet; that's part of the past."

He nodded in agreement. "Evet, efendim. It is part of the past and now we are at peace. We are at peace because we are strong, we Turks. We know that only the bear that is chained learns to dance."

"A Turkish proverb?" I asked.

"A Russian proverb. The Russians have many proverbs, efendim. Good proverbs."

Mehmetcik wiped his sweet potato flute on his shirtfront. "The vodka has made me a little drunk. I always play better when I am a little drunk."

He played the folk songs of the Laz first, melodies with drive and passion that reflected their origins in the lonely fishing vessels that dared the winter waves of the Black Sea. Then the sweeter, softer songs born in the springs that course down the slopes of the great Uludag Mountain that towers over Bursa. Then we were taken to the jagged peaks along the eastern frontier where soldiers and shepherds shared the solitary night and stood guard, each tending to his respective flock.

Nearly an hour later he stopped, played out. His chest heaved from the exertion. "I used to play that way for my American friends in Korea, efendim. That's where I got this." He brandished the sweet potato. "Someday I will tell you my war stories."

It was the signal to rise. Poor Mehmet. War stories from Korea. But no one to listen anymore. We shook his hand and left.

Only fifteen hours before, I had stumbled up this path on my way to the appointment with Colonel Atil, leaning on Suzan for support and fending off the lilacs that threatened to upset my equilibrium. Now we were hand in hand and I felt the purge of returning to the city beginning to work. And I was being helped.

We emerged into the park. It was two in the morning. About a third of the benches were still occupied; mostly by waiters whose work at the waterside restaurants was now finished and who paused for a cigarette and moments of relaxed conversation before beginning the long walk up the hill to the inland villages. An occasional taxi sounded its horn letting sleeping residents know that someone was still at work. A donkey, left by its owner to graze the lawn, brayed.

Normally I would not remember the face of a man I had encountered only once and then at a bank window, but this was an exceptional face and it belonged to the man whom I had decided was an insurance agent or a schoolmaster on holiday. He smiled at us, and identification was confirmed. I narrowed my eyes to reduce the intensity of that enormous smile. "Hello, there," he said with that television master of ceremonies ability to speak while smiling. "It's good to see a friendly English face at this time of night."

"American," I replied.

"No matter. No matter. Must never forget the famous special relationship." We passed him and I saw again the deep seams born of laughter around his eyes. Yes, it was the man who stood behind me at the Yapi ve Kredi Bankasi when I changed my traveler's check.

When we were enough paces past him to talk without being heard, Suzan spoke. "Who's your friend?"

"I don't know. Sometimes we have friends we don't even know we have."

CHAPTER FOURTEEN

Urfanli slammed the phone in the cradle in exasperation. If this is what it meant to be Special Assistant to Colonel Atil, then promotions he could live without. Special Assistant in charge of fending off cranks would be a more apt description of his responsibilities, he told himself.

Take the phone call just terminated. It was the third time within an hour that the Imam from the Bebek mosque had called, and each time the conversation covered the same ground, though the studied calm that first marked that Imam's voice had now deserted him and was replaced by exasperation with police inefficiency.

"An Imam's life is a hard one, bey efendim," he had said, "but the sacrifice is worth the satisfaction of witnessing the faithful leave their homes and places of business to undertake the ritual cleansing that precedes prayer to Allah. Still it means rousing oneself each morning to greet the rising sun, and you know how early the sun rises in August."

"Evet, efendim."

"There are forty-two steps in the minaret and I must carry a lantern to see on the narrow steps. It is not easy for an old man to climb forty-two steps at five o'clock in the morning, clutching a lantern in one hand and leaning against the curving stone wall of the minaret with the other, but, Allah be praised, I have never fallen, not once in sixteen years of service at this mosque. Sixteen years, bey efendim, sixteen years since I made the haj. It is the pilgrimage that has given me such strength and sureness."

"Evet efendim. Allah be praised."

"This morning, bey efendim, my rheumatism troubled me more than it usually does in the summer. My rheumatism likes warmth but last night a fresh breeze blew for a while and my limbs were stiff on awakening so I climbed the minaret slower than usual to ward off fatigue. When I got to the top I leaned against the stone rail of the parapet to catch my breath so the prayers would not be lost in the dawn. It was then I saw it. There in Bebek Harbor, the hammer and sickle flying in Bebek Harbor!"

"Evet efendim. It was a shock. Where in the harbor is this flag?"

"On a ship. A small, ugly ship."

"Its name. Did you see the name written on the ship's stern?"

"The what?"

"The name written on the back of the ship?"

"My eyes are too poor to read words at that distance. But the flag I saw, I swear to you. I held the lantern high so the light would not blind me."

"Evet."

"Well..."

"Well what, efendim?"

"What are you going to do about it? There are forty million ethnic Turks in Russia denied the right to practice their faith and speak their language. Does that mean nothing to you? You must do something about it. Forty million Turks denied their language and their faith, and you let a communist flag fly in Bebek!"

"I will look into it, bey efendim. You needn't worry."

"But I do worry. It is the mihrab."

The mihrab, Urfanli asked himself, what is the mihrab? It had been so many years since he had entered a mosque to do other than admire a famed example of kufic writing that he had forgotten the terminology. Finally he was obliged to ask, trying to make the question sound more like a comment than a request for information.

The Imam's voice sizzled with exasperation. "The mihrab is the niche in every mosque that faces toward Mecca! Only now there is something between my mihrab and Mecca: a communist flag! It is intolerable, bey efendim. The government must do something about it."

"Evet efendim. But this is the police, not the government."

"The police do not work for the government?"

"Of course. Of course. Only this is a delicate matter."

"It is a delicate matter for me to climb the minaret to call the faithful to prayer before a communist flag. You must understand that, bey efendim. Let the Russians not worship, if that is what they wish, but they cannot plant their flag atop my mosque."

Urfanli had made the mistake of correcting the old man. "It is not on your mosque, it is on a Russian ship."

"It is between the mihrab and Mecca. That is enough for me. Something must be done."

"Evet efendim."

Yes, the third call had been the worst. The facts were the same but the tone of the Imam's voice portended a storm.

There was no choice but to go out to Bebek and make inquiries. Lunchtime was the proper hour to commandeer an official car for the drive along the Bosphorus. A few inquiries, a call on the old Imam for a few placatory words, and then a leisurely lunch, perhaps at the Six-Legged Octopus, to hear Seyfi Munir recite some poetry.

Luncheon at Bebek: the prospect had a calming effect after what had happened these last twenty-four hours. First, the curious conversation with Colonel Atil, who spoke like one of those yezedis in Azerbaijan, practitioners of the religion that believes that evil must be worshipped with equal devotion to good. "There can be no virtue without vice" and "our job is to contain crime not eliminate it" and that funny business about using Paul Adams to obtain an adequate appropriation for the Second Section. Did Atil really expect him to believe all that?

Earlier he had been summoned from duty at the Customs and Immigration service to appear for another interview in a series lasting one week. The news was exciting. A new position was being created in the Second Section: Special Assistant to Colonel Atil, and he, Urhan Urfanli, was first incumbent. He had been surprised but not reluctant; no one argued with an increase in salary, a fancy title and a private office, even if they came to include the need to have an ear talked off by an angry Imam in Bebek. It was better than thumbing through dog-eared passports and watching men mentally urinate in their drawers waiting for the magic words, "You may enter."

There was a knock followed by the cautious opening of the office door.

"Does Bey Efendi still require the dossier he asked for this morning?"

Urfanli returned the file, careful to avoid the receptionist's gaze. Wallahi, he mourned, she will drive me crazy. I try not to look into her eyes and I look into her bosom instead. And that bottom! It shakes like a plate of muhalabi. Patience. Patience, he repeated to himself. The perquisites of office do not include access to all of the Colonel's secrets, especially those known only to the broad couch that sags invitingly against the wall. Not yet at least.

He watched the girl mince her way to the door. She let her hips sway gently as she closed it behind her, advertising the rich line of her body.

It was a new desk and it took some time to find his worry beads. Eventually they were located in the bottom right-hand drawer, coiled in repose. He withdrew them and let the turquoise amulets slip idly over his fingers. Their touch comforted him. Someday, perhaps, the baton of authority would be passed to him and with it opportunities that power provides.

Urfanli thought briefly about reporting the Imam's telephone calls to Colonel Atil, then decided against it. Better to reserve the trip to Bebek to himself, including a good lunch at Second Section expense. The Russian ship and the irritated Imam represented an opportunity too good to share. Atil was right about one thing, at least, he told himself, Istanbul's reputation as an espionage center had declined. Why not invent some tale involving a mysterious Russian ship that suddenly dropped anchor at Bebek? Something contemporary like seeding the bottom with radiation pellets to destroy fish life or dropping spies in plastic capsules who would surface at their leisure. A shrewd man like Atil would recognize the merits of associating espionage with a Russian ship. After all, appropriations hearings were just around the corner.

It was something to think about over lunch.

CHAPTER FIFTEEN

The hamamci purred contentedly as he wadded the abrasive kese and drew it slowly down my back, letting it make the sound of sandpaper drawn across a soft board. I grimaced: Turkish baths are for masochists, for men like me who invite pain because pain has become pleasure. I had awakened early to the cries of the birds that nested outside Peter Dawson's window, and rather than submit again to sleep, which always left me puffy and listless, got out of bed determined to fix an azimuth on the day before reality intruded to change course. Yesterday had begun on a happy note, quickly turned to misery, then to oblivion and finally to ecstasy. Today I would do without misery and oblivion in favor of protracted happiness.

First step had been the Yapi ve Kredi Bankasi, and the whole place seemed more cheerful for my presence. Even the clerk appeared to recognize me as he solemnly passed over one hundred and twenty lira for the traveler's check that I reluctantly passed under the grill. I was down to three checks; if Bill Nelson didn't soon suggest reimbursing me for the magnificent labors I had thus far failed to accomplish I was good for another two weeks in Turkey.

Dolmus rides, chilled white wine and food for picnics on the water, a lantern-lit dinner at the Six-Legged Octopus, two trips to the Turkish baths—these had consumed the first check, but the consequences were worth the price. Consequences like the sound of my name whispered in desire; a sculptured young body pressing close to mine; the smoothness of the female skull when I placed my fingers to her head and drew her to me.

A bucket of ice-cold water sluiced down my back and I howled…the hamamci flashed a smile of delight, grabbed me by the neck, turned me over with a twist of his thick wrist and drew me to a sitting position. I remembered too late his salutation of farewell after my first visit as a massive fist imbedded itself in my gut.

Ritual rinsing, a brisk rubdown and it was all over. I stood naked before the mirror: was it a quirk of reflection or was there really some new definition to my chest muscles? I pressed fingertips together the way they do in the physical culture magazines to make the muscles swell. All I needed was a cache-sex to make all the other boys turn their heads in envy and admiration.

The attendant smiled in my direction and I retreated to the changing room to dress before romance bloomed.

I decided to walk down through Beyoglu to the headquarters of the Second Section. An act of defiance was in order. Nothing serious like spitting on the sidewalk or chalking a slogan on the wall such as "Colonel Atil is a Confirmed Pill"; just a slow pace with narrowed eyes, the sort of gaze that caused plaster to shatter and light bulbs mysteriously to go out. Best to do it from the opposite side of the street. That way I wouldn't have to crane my neck and anyway it was shady there. Not that being seen really mattered any more. Atil had pronounced judgment: I might stay. At least conditionally. That made two people who had paroled me in their custody in one day for the same crime; legal historians take note.

As for Janice, maybe Atil and Suzan were right. They offered convenient options: she deserved to die; it was a freak of the currents: take your choice, every player wins.

In Saudi Arabia they used to stone women to death for adultery, and it had to be admitted that drowning was more humane. A few more days of such reasoning and I would qualify for the Carnegie Award for Heroism. A little awkward, however, to submit one's own name in competition; perhaps I could persuade Atil to write it up for me and then we could split the cash award. The medal, of course, would remain with me.

I arrived at the intersection of Istiklal Caddessi and Mustafa Kemal Caddessi and saw the gray-streaked mass of the headquarters building a hundred yards away. I decided to practice my challenge at a distance on the theory that guerilla warfare is more effective than a frontal assault.

"Colonel Atil is a Confirmed Pill," I said aloud, inscribing my graffiti on the winds. A passerby looked at me in astonishment.

A vintage 1960 Mercedes made the turning onto Mustafa Kemal Cadessi and proceeded at a stately pace to the Second Station Headquarters. The figure of Colonel Atil emerged from the car looking impeccable and horsy.

The son of a bitch must stand up inside that car to keep from wrinkling his breeches. I watched, half expecting his horse to follow.

"Colonel Atil is a Confirmed Pill," I said again. I like novelty. It gave me immense satisfaction to conclude that I was probably the only man on earth who had uttered those words.

*   *   *

Two envelopes had been slid under the door and were waiting for me when I returned to Peter Dawson's quarters at Christopher Hall. I tried to convince myself that if I backed out of the room it would count as not having entered at all; in that way, I could avoid the need to open the envelopes on the grounds that I had never seen them. The logic was flawless, what the French would call Cartesian and my psychiatrist—if I could afford one—fraudulent. I played "eenie-meenie-minie-moe" for

the better part of two minutes in an effort to divine which of the two
envelopes contained a letter saying that Xerox had named me
Chairman of the Board. But it wasn't from Xerox unless Bill Nelson
had switched allegiances:

Paul,

Can you come to my office at noon today?

I have something urgent to discuss with you.

Bill.

The note made up in cogency what it lacked in warmth. Bill's note
reminded me of the effusive greeting he had given me when Urfanli
called from the Immigration Bureau. "Hello, Paul," he had said, and my
whole being quivered at the depth of feeling the words conveyed. I
looked at my watch; eleven-twenty-five a.m.; I reminded myself to
avoid the hour between eleven and twelve the next time the opportunity
presented itself.

Something urgent could mean only one thing. Fellow alumnus
Nelson had bowed to the dictates of good sense, the importuning of
Emily Cartwright, and was about to give me dolmus fare to the nearest
border point. Motive didn't matter. Not when it came to double-
crossing a fellow Princeton man.

I threw the note to the floor and noticed the loser in the "eenie-
meenie-minie-moe" game.

It was from Suzan:

Paul,

I have something urgent to discuss with you.

Please come to Mehmetcik's at one o'clock.

We'll picnic on the boat.

Suzan.

P.S. Don't forget a swimsuit this time.

She must have taken a course in journalism from Bill Nelson. No
superfluous words, no oratorical salutations, such as "Dear Paul" or
"Darling." And couldn't she have wasted the ink and time to write

"Love" or "Your" before writing her name? If she had energy enough to remind me about a swimsuit she had time to drop in a word of affection. Furthermore I didn't really need to be reminded to bring a swimsuit to a picnic on a rowboat even when in company with a girl who habitually swam in the nude with men she had known for only three days.

Everyone had something urgent to discuss with me that always came to the same thing; my walking papers. First Nelson to give me the boot from college; a half-hour or so to take stitches in my pride and then an appointment with Suzan. Over sandwiches and wine she would blush prettily, and look out over the water and say in hushed tones that I shouldn't get any ideas from what passed between us last night. You mustn't think that because I stood naked against you and kissed you hungrily that my behavior denotes love or interest or anything like that.

Two appointments in one day. The agenda of my life hadn't been so crowded in years. I reread the notes; a half-hour left before my appointment with Bill Nelson. I decided that Dawson's quarters needed a bit of tidying up. No telling when that man from Xerox would show up.

*   *   .*

Nelson was framed in the bay window that looked out over the towers of Rumeli Hisar and the shores of Asia on the far shores of the Bosphorus, as the secretary ushered me in. His back was towards me and he made no move to turn around. I made a note to draft a strong letter to the Board of Trustees when this was all over disclosing how much time their Headmaster spent gazing out of the window instead of tending to the educational needs of his charges.

I coughed softly, in case he had missed hearing the squeaking of the office door as I came in.

"I'm just watching Darius. Won't be a moment."

Darius, whoever he was, must have been hanging from a tree outside the window beyond my view.

"He crossed right here, you know." He turned to face me. "In 513 B.C., nearly twenty-five hundred years ago. Darius I, of course. I don't think his successors passed this way. At least not in this precise place."

"That's very interesting. I must have read it someplace but I'd forgotten."

"I hazard he had a rough time of it." There was Nelson's pet verb again.

"Yes. It must have been a hazardous undertaking." Had Bill Nelson brought me in to discuss urgent logistical problems relating to a Persian king who crossed the Bosphorus in whatever passed for a rowboat in those days?

"Sit down, please. I get so wrapped up in the history of this place that I forget my social duties." His line was well phrased, designed to assure me that I wasn't the only person he kept standing knee-deep in historical chitchat while urgent business waited in the wings. I sat in the deep chair before the desk.

"How are things going? You're comfortable over at Christopher Hall?"

"Oh, it's great, just great." I tried to sound properly enthusiastic.

"Always difficult to be in temporary quarters. You never know where to find things." In case you are referring to Peter Dawson's bottle, I said to myself, it was hidden behind a hatbox and is now empty. I had no trouble at all finding it.

"I had a call earlier this morning from a man named Colonel Atil. He said you had paid him a call yesterday."

"Yes, that's right."

"Care to tell me what it was all about?"

"It's…it's all very complicated, Bill. I hardly know where to begin." He didn't accept my implied invitation to let the subject lapse. Headmasters love complicated subjects. "You remember that little fuss about me being qualified for a work permit? Well, it seems this Colonel Atil took a personal interest in my situation and asked me down to talk with him." I groped in my mind for lies; they always came so easily to me; what had happened to that spark of mendacious talent that had seen me through so many tight spots before? "He had been in charge of the investigation when Janice died. I didn't remember him at first...the shock had been too much...but he was the man who helped me identify Janice's body. He gave the order to..." I stopped short. Good God, I had almost said that Atil gave the order to cut off her finger to remove the wedding ring with the engraving inside! "I mean he gave the instructions so that Janice's body could be sent home."

"I'm sorry you had to go through this. Reliving the anguish of her death."

"Yes, it was rough." The lies were flowing now. "Atil meant well, of course. He had never had the chance to express his grief. So when he heard that I was here he arranged for me to come in so he could say how sorry he was about Janice's death and all that."

"Extraordinary. He waited three years for the opportunity to express regrets!"

"Funny people. The Turks." I tried to smile to assure Nelson that I didn't mean anything disrespectful toward his adopted country.

"Yes. Yes." There was a long silence. I had the feeling that it was my cue to say something but there seemed no point in embellishing on a good lie.

Nelson broke the silence. "I was just wondering whether you wanted to ask me why Colonel Atil called."

The mouse population of the world can be grateful to me for my ability as a trap-tester. I can stumble into a trap faster than any mouse alive, thus misleading the manufacturer into thinking that other mice are equally dumb. Now that my contrivance was part of the record, Nelson could check it against what Atil had said; if the stories didn't jibe my fate was sealed.

"Stupid of me not to ask. Is it too late now?"

Nelson frowned to coax back memory.

"I was a bit at sea at first. Atil asked several times how you were; how you were doing out here; and I was obliged to stutter a bit because I didn't honestly know. I mean, I haven't really seen you around the campus since Friday night. Finally he got down to cases and said he knew I would be delighted to learn that he had given you conditional approval to remain in Turkey. You should check in from time to time, of course, but barring unforeseen difficulties you could remain indefinitely."

I tried on my heartiest voice. "That's good news, Bill. I knew it would work out this way all along. But still…"

"I could wish for something better, Paul. Let's not kid around. We're classmates, almost, and almost old friends. I don't like the conditional sound of Atil's approval. I'm frightened of what the board would say if it got wind of my giving refuge to someone the Turkish police regard as a probationary case. You know what I mean…"

"Emily Cartwright," I interjected.

"Yes. And others. But I've decided to take a chance and let you stay on…at least until Peter Dawson returns. After that it's all question marks, and you should make your plans accordingly."

"It's decent of you." I started to rise from my chair.

"No. Not yet. There's something else."

"Yes?"

"The night watchman saw someone come through the college gate with Suzan Lokman last night. It was more like morning, to be exact. He makes routine entries of staff who come in after one." He consulted a sheet of ruled paper on his desk. "2:17 a.m. Miss Lokman in company of an unidentified tall American."

"Let me answer the question before you ask it. I was the man."

"You have a short memory, Paul. You forget that I told you just four days ago that I wanted no monkey business with women here."

"Bill. I'm in no position to argue with you. I'm grateful for your confidence in me, for letting me stay. But this doesn't give you the right to rule my life."

"And I don't want to. But this institution is bigger than your or my private pursuits, including any illusions you may have about Suzan Lokman. She's trouble, Paul. Pure trouble. There's not a student or faculty member on the campus that hasn't fallen for her. She bats a lash and thrusts out a breast and you can hear marriages collapse for miles around.

"Get one thing clear; you're nothing but a novelty to her. A new man to help while away the quiet summer months until school begins."

"If she means trouble, why do you keep her?"

"Because she knows her subject and can think circles around you and me. Because she's the new teacher. Because if we fired her the boys would burn down the campus."

I stole a glance at my watch. The party capable of setting a torch to the college was waiting for me.

"I appreciate your telling me all this, Bill." The words had a stale taste. I made a specialty of telling people that I appreciated what I hated to hear. Like all specialties, mine lost freshness with repetition. First Atil, now Nelson.

"It's for your own good, old man."

My hand lingered on the doorknob. No point telling him. No point telling him that I was on my way to see her. The scenario was already written anyway. A few more weeks of playing nurse to Adams and then back to the old bump and grind when the fall crop of men appeared on campus.

"Thanks again for letting me stay on, Bill. I appreciate your telling me all this."

If the Nobel Prize were awarded for hypocrisy I would be a rich and famous man.

The clunk-clunk-clunk of my footsteps rattled through the deserted stairwells reminding me that aloneness follows you everywhere. Better to live without a calendar than keep appointments like these. Atil had let me know with one brief phone call how completely he held me in his power. Cooperate, behave, do anything I tell you, or the next call will sever the slim thread of Nelson's patience. My job security, actuarially speaking, was about as good as that of a one-legged man walking a tightrope blindfolded over Niagara Falls in a high wind.

CHAPTER SIXTEEN

Everything was working out much better than expected. Much better. Tula's unexpected stop at Bebek was no longer a mystery, thanks to Nuri the Noodle's genius for ferreting out information. Trying to find a replacement cylinder casing in Istanbul for a diesel of Russian manufacture would prove a frustrating task.

William Edward Anthony Blake leaned back contentedly against the park bench, anchoring the heels of his shoes against the rough pebbles that lay scattered on the macadamed surface of the walkway that idled its way through Bebek Park. The sun filtered through the overhanging branches of a horse chestnut tree, dappling him in light and shadow. The park was nearly deserted at this hour, save for a few families taking lunch beyond the lawn on the rocks that bordered the waterside. Their conversation was a breeze born accompaniment to his thoughts; present but unobtrusive.

Only twenty-four hours before, he had been in Gelibolu and had passed a verdict on Tula, but a stay of execution was a by-product of her unexpected arrival in Bebek. Of the two options previously available to him: taking Sherevsky from his captors or destroying Tula, Scherevsky included, only one had first seemed practicable—destruction. Tula's infirmity had changed all that, and Blake instead now maintained surveillance on Tula in a little corner of paradise while the necessary kit for the evening operation was assembled.

A stern-looking young man with black hair and a black moustache emerged from the path leading up from the mosque and walked purposefully in the direction of the houseboat that bobbed at anchor just offshore.

"Laa," Blake said aloud, "very un-Turkish to walk so fast on a hot summer's day. There must be a girl waiting somewhere. I must ask Nuri to find me a bit when this is all over. It's been too long entirely."

Blake slid his hat low on his forehead to shield his eyes against the play of light and shadow. His chest rose and fell steadily and sleep drifted in from the sea. Soon Nuri appeared from beyond a curtain beckoning him with a crooked finger and an eyebrow that arched knowingly. He followed and there, behind the curtain, lay a woman surrounded by fruit. She was bedded down in honeydew peaches, oranges, and chunks of watermelon, red grapes, and all the delicacies that he loved so much. Blake advanced toward her sensing an immense hunger.

*   *   *

Suzan was tapping her right foot impatiently on Mehmetcik's pier when I arrived. The rowboat bobbed alongside and I saw a wicker basket of fruit, bread and small packages surrounding the giraffe neck of a bottle of white wine.

"You're late."

"I'm always late," I replied bleakly.

"Where are your swimming things?"

"I forgot them."

"And I wrote a note to remind you," she sighed.

"You wrote a note to tell me there was something urgent to discuss."

"That can wait," she called, hopping into the boat and casting off the line." I'm hot and hungry. Let's go." I jumped into the rowboat just as she dipped the oars to clear the pier and narrowly avoided a sudden swim. She wore a white cotton shirtdress that accented the tan of her skin. It drew tautly across her breasts as she leaned back against the oars and I thought of Nelson's line about the sound of marriages collapsing when she thrust one out, left or right. Nelson needed a lesson in female anatomy; that was not a chest, it was a bosom, and clearly more durable than the marriages it threatened.

Her skill at the oars made my exertions of the previous night seem like the efforts of a beginner as Mehmet's heavy rowboat skimmed across the water toward the lighthouse.

The Russian ship was still there. It looked less formidable in the daylight; paint had flaked from the black hull near the water line under the incessant impact of the seas; the decks were deserted except for an elderly sailor who spat periodically into the swift currents; a flag hung limply from the mast. The bridge house and the raised poop deck were stained a dull gray from the soot-filled diesel exhaust that usually belched from a single stack. Even the letters "Tula, Odessa" had a forlorn look to them.

Suzan tied up at the orange buoy where we had moored the night before.

"It's gone," she exclaimed, turning to look at Tula's stern.

"What's gone?"

She was suddenly guarded. "I don't know if I should tell you."

"Why not?"

"You'll laugh."

"I could use a good laugh. Tell me."

She stood up in the rowboat and began to unbutton the shirtdress. Underneath it she wore a coral-colored bikini that made my heart skip a beat. She folded the dress neatly, put it into the bait box and sat down again. Then she folded her arms around her calves and rested her chin on her knees in one of those trick poses the glamour photographers use to suggest nakedness.

"I came out earlier today while you were in town to swim and see if the boat that frightened us was still here. It seemed ludicrous when I saw it moored there—scared out of my wits by a ship named Tula—can you imagine? Anyway, I tied up here and swam for a while. I even made a full circle of the ship. A man watched me for a while but he seemed preoccupied, didn't even wave. Wouldn't you wave if you saw me swimming in the water and you were standing on deck?"

"I would jump in. I would jump in and take you back to the Soviet Union as an offering to the First Secretary of the Party."

"This Russian wasn't as imaginative as you. Anyway, when I got back to the rowboat I sunned myself for a while and watched the ship. Then it happened." She paused for dramatic effect. "A hand held a cloth outside the porthole…"

"A waiter shaking out crumbs," I volunteered.

She pulled back her left arm and pointed toward Tula's stern. "There. From the porthole just below that funny little raised deck."

"There's nothing there now."

"I know. I told you. But there was before. A cloth that someone waved back and forth and it seemed to be stained with blood."

"Someone cut his hand and threw the bandage out."

"No!" She said a little crossly. "Someone waved it back and forth, trying to signal."

"Did you see anyone?"

"No. Just a cloth."

"That's that?"

"Yes and no. I watched for about ten minutes. It fascinated me." She fixed me in an even gaze. "Paul, have you ever been to a village wedding?"

"Only when the village idiot got married. Me."

"Be serious. They have funny customs in the villages, customs that haven't changed with the times. When a man marries he expects his wife to be a virgin…"

"What's so funny about that?" I inquired.

"Because it's passé, that's what's funny. And I wish you wouldn't interrupt me."

Bill Nelson's words came back again, "She's the new Turk." The new Turk who thought it was quaint to be a virgin. No wonder the students at the College worshipped her.

"As I said, a villager expects that his wife will be a virgin but it isn't enough to be convinced himself. He must convince his neighbors. So the morning after the wedding he hangs the bridal sheets from the window so that everyone can see the evidence."

"Neat custom. Makes good business for the laundries."

She ignored me. "They can't really be sure, of course; the men, that is. If a girl is in doubt that she will bleed she takes a little vial of mercurochrome mixed with iodine into bed. When her husband is excited and preoccupied she squeals in pain and empties the vial. Even if her husband suspects he doesn't care as long as he can hang his sheet from his window."

"You seem very well informed."

She smiled sweetly. "Don't be a prude, Paul. I'm a grown woman. Anyway, the cloth hanging from the porthole reminded me of the bed sheets stained with medicine. In the village they're a primitive form of advertising. A message."

"The medium is the message. Thank you, Marshal McLokman."

"Dope!"

"So a Russian sailor hangs a stained cloth out of a porthole trying to prove he's a virgin. So what?"

"Sometimes I get so angry with you I could cry! Maybe it was an appeal for help…hasn't that occurred to you?"

"Sure. He doesn't like the cooking."

"Now it's too late. I'm sorry I asked you to come."

"You said it was something urgent," I protested.

"I think it is urgent when someone calls for help." She grabbed for the food basket and extracted bread and packets of meat and cheese. "At least you can open the wine."

She perked up at the sight of the food and the wine and ate ravenously, but I nursed the ominous feeling that making light of her concern for the stained cloth had not been my shrewdest move of the day. I probably wouldn't hold her interest until the end of August, let alone the opening of the fall term. Why hadn't I just kept my mouth shut and nodded my head in admiration at her fanciful story about village virgins, waving cloths and Russian sailors pleading for help? It didn't matter. The cloth was gone.

Or was it? I looked over Suzan's shoulder and saw a rectangle of white and red, about the size of a small pillowcase, flutter from the porthole. My mouth opened in amazement and then I bit down hard into my sandwich. I cursed.

"What's the matter?"

"I bit my finger."

"Oh. You look startled."

"I always look startled when I bite my finger."

Her back was toward the ship's stern. Could I get away with it? Not tell her about the red-stained cloth that waved slowly back and forth from the porthole?

"Suzan. If I tell you something will you promise not to do anything silly?"

"Like what?"

"Like jumping to conclusions about Russian sailors? Most Russians like their country, you know?"

Her face lit up. "Paul," she whooped, turning her head, "when?"

"When I bit my finger." She turned her gaze toward the porthole.

"You see! It is stained red. And it does look like writing."

"Suzan. Slow down. That's a Russian ship over there. It's just some sailor waving around a patriotic quotation."

"Let's go closer," she said, turning back to me, her eyes blazing with excitement.

"No. Let's go farther. Like back to shore."

She began to untie the rope from the buoy. "Put the things back in the basket. Quickly. Before it disappears again." I obeyed, with misgivings. "I'll row closer to the ship so we can get a better look and head out into the main channel so it will appear as if we're just out on a lark."

She bent forward, let the oars find their depth, then bent back. The rowboat hung immobile for a moment then found its way against currents. With coordinated movements she covered the distance between us and Tula until we were no more than fifteen yards from her stern.

"Paul. It is writing. I'm sure of it."

I narrowed my eyes to focus better on the cloth. From our new angle the rectangle appeared flatter and the markings on it more crisp.

"Can you read what it says?" she asked.

"It's meaningless. I can't make anything out."

"Of course! Of course! What fools we are! It's in Russian. The Cyrillic alphabet! Look again. Don't you see?"

I looked again, trying to puzzle out the jumble. "It could be but I got bad Marx in Russian. Get it? That's a visual joke. Maybe I'd better write it down."

"Damn," was her reply. We were past the stern of the ship now, heading out into the channel. She headed the boat upstream in the direction of the Black Sea, her face intent from exertion and thought. "We'll have to get the cloth," she said.

"Are you crazy?"

"We can't just let it hang there, not knowing. It's not reasonable, Paul. I'll let the rowboat drift by and you can reach up and grab the cloth."

"It's too high."

"Then I'll stand on your shoulders!" She exclaimed.

"Stand on my shoulders in a rowboat on the Bosphorus! I can barely sit in a rowboat let alone stand! No dice."

"You're hopeless." She let the oars ride idle for a moment and we began to drift down against toward the ship. "Paul. I'm serious. I'm not going back until we find out what's on that cloth. If you won't help then start back now."

"All right," I surrendered. "So what do we do? If it says anything, it's in Russian. And out of reach. May be we can ask the ship's Captain for a translation." I didn't like the intense look on her face; she really meant to get that cloth.

Odd behavior is accentuated out on the sea according to all the maritime chroniclers. That might explain why Suzan suddenly reached behind her back and unbuckled the cross straps of her bikini top, letting the shoulder straps slip off her shoulders, and sat nine-tenths naked before me in the prow of the rowboat, a curved panel of white flesh dotted with two pinkish -brown nipples having replaced the coral-colored top of her swimsuit.

She folded the top of the bikini, cup into cup, and put it in the bait box. Then she rummaged in the bottom of the food basket and retrieved a small plastic makeup case, just big enough to carry essentials to the beach. She rummaged for a lipstick, took off the cap and screwed out a slender scarlet cone.

"I have an idea," she said, oblivious to her nakedness or my look of stupefaction. "I'll lie face down on the little covered deck while you row near the ship. When we get close enough to see the writing on the pennant try to copy the markings on the cloth onto my back."

"But I can't write Russian," I wailed.

"You don't have to write anything. You just have to copy! Now row!" She lay down on the forepeak, nestled her cheek on her forearms and pretended to be engaged in a leisurely sunbath while I provided motive power for the rowboat.

I put the lipstick on the floor of the boat and took the oars in my hands. They felt slick to my touch. What was she getting us into? If the Russians saw us they would shoot first and ask questions later. I looked over my shoulder at Tula, and then at the slim figure sprawled behind me. Why did it have to be a coral bikini? Why was she so hypnotizing?

"I can almost make out the lettering," she whispered from beneath her crossed arms. "Get ready."

A gust of breeze flattened the cloth against the hull and the long fingers that held it tightened on the edge, wrinkling the cloth, but the red pattern was clear now. I dropped the oars, swung my body around and moved toward Suzan, resting my hip on the edge of the forepeak. The line of my body was perpendicular to the expanse of her back. I reached down to retrieve the lipstick, which slipped from my grasp. Then I held it in trembling fingers and looked up. Slowly, and the rowboat glided silently by, I traced a pattern in red on Suzan's back.

It had only taken twenty seconds but I felt the accumulated exhaustion of a lifetime suddenly perch on my shoulders, and I collapsed backward into the shallow gunwales. We drifted on, past the ship, past the lighthouse, into the channel reserved for the ferryboats. Finally I found the strength to look back at the ship. A man stood on the raised deck and raised his hand in salute.

*   *   *

How he missed the whirring sound of the air conditioner, a mechanical lullaby that had so often brought rest and repose on a sultry afternoon! It was hot in the cabin now. Vaslov had seen to that with his peremptory order to cut all but essential electricity. The developing solutions that sloshed softly in their covered tanks smelled acrid and disagreeable. He looked at his watch and sighed. "Another forty-eight hours and this agony will be over."

What a relief it had been to see the decoded words spill from the cryptographic machine at the Consulate! A sea-going tug was on its way to Istanbul. If Tula was not fit to sail in two days' time the tug would take permission from the Turkish authorities to enter the Bosphorus and tow it away. How right he had been to send that message asking for instructions and how reassuring the reply. It spoke the language of reason, authority, and competence. He could have kissed the surprised code clerk, his delight had been so great.

The heat, the stuffy air of the cabin, the labored breathing of Scherevsky—nothing mattered now. All that counted was the euphoria born of knowing that the end was truly in sight; Odessa was over the horizon, and soon there would be evenings of tea-filled bliss on the hills overlooking the city, patting the grandchildren on their cropped heads, listening to his wife and his daughter Tanya recite the tribulations that had occurred since his absence, slipping off with Leonid to talk of things that men understood.

In the meantime his delicious little joke. He eased his leather belt out a notch to permit full expanse to sudden laughter that seemed to fill the cabin with melody. Poor Captain Vaslov. Poor Vaslov. Out in the city racing from warehouse to warehouse looking for spare parts for Tula unaware that the sea-going tug was already on its way. Withholding the contents of the message had been fit retribution for the Captain's decision to cut off power for his air conditioning unit. Some men could be so petty! Tonight when Vaslov and the First Engineer returned to the ship, coiled with anger and frustration, he would contrive a pretext to take a small boat ashore leaving Vaslov and the old sailor with the leaky bladder to mind Scherevsky. He would take a dolmus to the city to one of the open-air casinos that hung in tiers over the Golden Horn and enjoy a good dinner and the spectacle of Turkish families wading into platters of pilaf and lamb chops so sweet they could have been picked from a tree. Later he would sit patiently through the program of unintelligible Turkish singers and comics waiting for the culmination that came when an oriental dancer appeared from the wings glittering in beaten bronze, swathed in diaphanous cloth that covered and revealed. She would dance to the hoarse melody that cascaded from the throat of a peasant flute, gyrating her hips to the throb, throb, throb of the gourd-shaped drum, and his Leica would capture the climatic moment when the dancer leaned back, her pelvic girdle thrust forward in an attitude of passionate beseechment, her breath coming in sibilant gasps. Yes, it would be something else to put aside for young Leonid.

Orenko swung down from his berth. It was too stuffy inside at two o'clock in the afternoon. "I will go up on deck for a while," he grunted aloud, pulling his belt back to its normal notch, "it may be cooler there."

He slipped on the comfortable slippers that were folded down at the heel to permit quick entry and shuffled out of the cabin. A moment with his ear to the door of the adjacent confirmed that Scherevsky was asleep. It had been a jolt to walk in after breakfast to find the old man wiping a cut on his finger with a napkin. For a moment he thought of a suicide attempt but the cut was little more than a scratch and quickly put right with some tincture and a bandage. Scherevsky complained throughout, and it had been a relief to finish the job and slip the medicine kit back in the drawer.

The old sailor with the weak bladder who had been assigned guard duty was asleep in the shade of a ventilation tube, his hand cupped loosely over his crotch as if to stem the instinct to rise and pad down to the toilet. Between his fingers the cloth of the coarse blue trousers was stained white where countless drops of uric acid had robbed the dyes of their strength.

Bebek was somnolent. A siesta had fallen on the shops, kiosks, street vendors and pedestrians; even the restaurants were nearly empty as noontime diners went home to the luxury of rest between clean sheets.

A ship's horn blared out in the channel, and he crossed the deck to see if he recognized the transient, hoping that it, too, would fly his flag.

He reached the rail just as a girl sitting erect in the forepeak of a rowboat reached behind her back and undid the straps of her swimsuit. She sat straight ahead, the tips of her breasts turned upward in the angle unique to youth, talking in earnest tones to the man opposite who leaned on the oars. Orenko watched in astonishment, fingers tight on the rail. Then he reached instinctively to his chest.

"My cameras," he gasped. "My cameras."

He ran across the deck, kicking off his slippers as he ran.

"My cameras." He burst into his cabin and reached first for the Hasselblad camera in its felt-lined box but quickly recalled that he had not installed a lens after its last use. Next to it was the Dresden-built Zeiss Ikon. It would do. The leather strap firmly in his fingers, he raced back to the deck and saw that the rowboat had crossed Tula's stern and was heading in to shore.

"She has turned on her stomach," groaned Orenko as he unbuttoned the leather case.

He put his eye to the viewfinder and turned the serrated knob. Then he consulted the light meter and his practiced hands made rapid adjustments. A din rating of 15 meant 1/25th of a second at F11. Good resolution; good depth of field.

He held the camera to his eye again and reset the serrated knob again to accommodate the rowboat's movement. A vision came into focus. Once, twice, three times the shutter clicked as Orenko advanced the film without withdrawing the eyepiece from his brow. Then he altered the lens opening to F8 to insure against the fluctuations of sunlight reflected off the sea.

Orenko saw the red marks of sunburn on her back and counseled the man with her not to let her remain too long in the sunshine. "She will be burned. Badly burned," he called, but they were too far now to hear his advice.

He made a visor of his left hand to watch the rowboat drift toward shore. Then he raised the handkerchief in his right hand and waved slowly. Istanbul had been worth a visit after all.

CHAPTER SEVENTEEN

"Some fellows are so violent in their love-making," Blake chortled as the girl walked past. "Of course if I got a grip on that little thing she'd have holes right through her, not just a few scratches." Extraordinary how red showed through the flimsy cloth of that blouse, he thought. Of course, the way they make women's clothes nowadays there's hardly any point in wearing them.

Didn't seem very cheerful for a girl who had just finished a romantic rendezvous. And her boyfriend! One would think he had seen a ghost. Men with such frail constitutions shouldn't take on girls like that. It could be fatal.

That had been a good nap, he mused. Must remind Nuri about that lovely little fruit arrangement he served up. Really not much to do but laze about and wait until it was time to hop a ferryboat over to Kandhilli. Nuri and Ahmet would have everything in order, leaving ample time to review again their plans for the evening.

Bloody Russians would be in for a bit of surprise. He chuckled. The sound pleased him. He laughed a little louder his mouth opened wide. Then he explored the interior with his forefinger, counting as he went. Thirty-two, counting the wisdom teeth.

Those Russians had something to learn about wisdom.

*   *   *

We took a taxi up the college hill, Suzan sitting ramrod straight in back so the lipstick would not be smudged on her dress. She was smiling to herself, one of the little grins that people put on when they cannot hide their excitement or anticipation. This was a game we were engaged in; a treasure hunt after the junior prom.

"Turn right here." Then a few yards later. "Now left." Then "Stop." If I had hoped we were on our way to Christopher Hall to take a shower together and giggle uproariously while I lathered her back and other regions before slipping between the sheets, I was doomed to disappointment. The college library didn't look like quite the place for a communal cleanup.

One or two summer students looked up briefly as we walked through the main reading room and went back to sleep on their books. Suzan paused to exchange a few words with a severe-looking young woman busy at the card index that offered directions with an inflection of her chin and dropped the glasses down her nose to get a better look at me.

The reference room was upstairs at the end of the library where light and ventilation were at a premium. Reference works weren't much in demand in mid-August, I found to my disappointment, and there was no one to disturb us. Suzan quickly found a mammoth tome bound in red, labeled "Russian-English Dictionary." She put the dictionary on the table in the center of the room and stood facing the door. "The window light will fall on my back. You can see better." I watched her elbows work and in seconds her dress had fallen from her shoulders, the loose cloth gathered at her waist. She seemed more revealed than when clad only in half of a bikini.

"Paul. Have you found it?"

Found it? I had not even been looking. Not at the dictionary, that is.

"I don't know where to begin."

"Try to figure out what the first letter is and then find it in the dictionary. Then go on to the second letter."

"Are you sure Russian works that way? I mean isn't it spelled backwards or something?"

She stamped her foot in the familiar signal that said I was out of range with my pot-shot comments. "Look. I'm getting impatient."

I leafed through the pages, first at the front, then at the back, waiting for an index finger to reach out and point "here." Nothing happened. Russian isn't a hard language; there's just too much of it. About 120,000 words too much. I found English definitions of strange-looking words but the Cyrillic letters didn't match those on Suzan's back.

"It's no good. I don't think this is a word at all. Something's missing. The cloth was wrinkled and we missed part of it."

"There we'll have to go back to the boat."

Go back to the boat? I ruffled the pages. "Let's not give up yet." If I ruffled long enough it would be dark and the game over for the day. Tomorrow the ship might sail.

"Didn't I write anything on your bosom?" I asked, trying to sound wildly seductive. "Like maybe the dots on the I's?"

She giggled. "Paul. I think we've been going about this backwards."

"Exactly. That's why I said you should turn around while I look for the rest of the message."

"We'll never find a word at random in a Russian-English dictionary. Go to the shelves and take down the English-Russian one. Then we'll think of English words and see if they correspond to the one on my back."

The English-Russian dictionary was on a different shelf but not so far away that I could drop it out the window unnoticed.

"Let's begin with something easy like 'God Loves Lenin.'"

"Too long."

"Godless atheism will rule the world?"

"Paul…"

I would have preferred not to answer but that wouldn't have made any difference.

"Paul. F for freedom."

F for freedom is on page 408 of Professor V.K. Muller's English-Russian Dictionary, 1973 edition. I held my finger under it and worked right, flicking my eyes from the page to Suzan's back.

I made a sound like a chicken laying an egg.

"Is that it?"

"F for freedom is, or whatever it is I'm saying. It doesn't look like your back."

"Paul. Try H for help."

Harold's Club need not close its doors when I approach. My luck is about as durable as that of a Zionist in Baghdad.

H for help is on page 472 of Professor V.K. Muller's English-Russian Dictionary, 1973 edition. H for help in Russian bore a strong resemblance to the lipstick writing on the back before me. I checked twice to be sure I wasn't at the Cyrillic equivalent of helmet, helot, helter-skelter, Helvetian or hemlock, which was what I felt like drinking a bowl of. No luck.

"Paul?" Her shoulder blades gave a little wriggle.

"H is for help," I sighed.

The door opened and the severe-looking librarian entered.

"Miss Lok..." was as far as she got before she noticed the latest teaching uniform that Suzan was modeling. "Really!"

Suzan turned toward me, her face crimson.

"Really!" It was my turn to say it.

The door to the reference library slammed shut. I could hear the emphatic click-clack of the librarian's heels echo down the corridor.

"H is for help," I said softly. I needed it. When word got around about the extraordinary talents Miss Lokman displayed in her Russian language seminars, there would be a stampede on the registrar's office, with Young Pioneer Adams trampled to a pulp in the process.

*   *   *

The quick pace of the black Ford sedan slowed for the dense traffic near the Dohlmabache Palace. The driver geared down, alternating his right hand between the gear lever and the horn ring in the staccato rhythm dear to Turkish drivers.

Urfanli rested his back and shoulders against the plastic-sheathed seat. Large cars were a luxury in Turkey, reserved for the very important, the very rich, the very crooked and foreigners. That Colonel Atil should have a Mercedes and a Ford, albeit older models, at his disposal was testimony to the importance attached to the Second Section.

What, he wondered, would the Turkish taxpayers think of his recent activities? A man has a right to eat, true, but to eat so well and at government expenses! Seyfi Munir was a better cook than poet. A man with such gargantuan tastes had no business as a poet in the first place; that was a métier that rarely paid its own way. Yes, lunch at the Six-Legged Octopus was the high spot of an excursion that otherwise had some disagreeable aspects.

The Imam at the Bebek mosque had been a surprise. He was a shrewd, intelligent man who advanced the merits of his argument with the vigor of a trained lawyer, and Urfanli had reluctantly agreed that a communist flag on a direct line of sight between the mihrab of the mosque and Mecca posed some delicate procedural problems, and the Imam had been right to make representations. Once this admission was made, the problem mysteriously evaporated. The Imam had wrung an official acknowledgment that the problem existed; an official of the secular state learned that faith is as important as reason. From there on it was tea and friendly exchanges about the timeless beauty of Bebek before Urfanli slipped on his shoes at the entrance to the mosque and walked briskly across the park. Urfanli had looked back only once: the Imam was still watching him, a smile on his face. He had launched a jihad, and a modern Muslim fell as first victim in the holy war.

The Ford accelerated past a line of dolmus taxis that shuffled along hoping to entice passengers inside for a few moments of cut-rate transport. Soon it came to the complex of roadways that led toward the Galata Bridge and the Old City, and the driver turned right in an acute curve to begin the ascent to Beyoglu and Second Section headquarters. He geared down again as the engine pinged from the strain of the steep cobbled roadway.

First the Imam with his smile of satisfaction, and then seeing Paul Adams again: one vexation after another. It wasn't seeing Adams alone that bothered him. It was Adams and the girl, together on a rowboat in Bebek harbor. The same girl he had viewed from the window, stepping out from the shadow to help a crippled soul cross the street.

A lovely girl, too. Not an ugly one, a lovely one. A young girl, at least ten years Adam's junior, graceful, bronzed, possessed of what the Circassians called "the eyes of a doe; the waist of a gazelle." What could a girl see in a half man like Adams when there were so many good-looking Turks to choose from? The thought troubled him. He must find a way to warn the girl of Adams' character. Of the way his wife had died. Of his cowardice. She might not know these things.

*   *   *

The proper way to remove lipstick from a girl's back is not, I learned, in the shower. Lipstick is best removed with face cream. For some unaccountable reason Peter Dawson was not well stocked with any of the name brands, but a jar of Noxzema served just as well. Suzan lay on her stomach on the bed while I finger-painted with Noxzema on her flesh, taking as long in the process as possible. She was half-naked, a condition of dress that seemed to have become quite permanent, and I was entertaining visions of how it would be if the top half were covered and the bottom bare, when she spoke.

"I've been thinking, Paul."

"So have I."

"About the cloth…"

"This stuff is very good for the skin. Wouldn't you like me to give you a rubdown all over? No trouble at all."

She didn't react to my magnificent humor "...and what to do."

"So have I," I replied. "I will now proceed to wipe this gook off your lovely back, make seductive noises and, if they fall on deaf ears, escort you to the police station where we tell the authorities about your discovery. Okay?"

I didn't like the length of silence that followed.

"Turn your head a minute. I want to dress."

"Don't I wipe you off first?" I didn't wait for an answer. She might tell me not to bother and then I would have been denied the pleasure of tracing silly things like hearts with arrows through them on a film of improvised makeup remover.

"It's still early," she purred.

"That's exactly what I've been thinking. Why don't we pillow talk for a while and think about that cloth afterwards?"

"That's not what I meant. I mean that no matter how long it takes you to clean my back there'll still be time to do what we have to do. Now turn your back, please." I turned and spent a long thirty seconds trying to figure out why it was immodest for me to see her bosom in a closed room but permissible out in the middle of the Bosphorus. She finished, kissed me fleetingly on the head, and then sat back against the headboard.

"It's no good, Paul."

"What's no good?" I had lost the thread of our conversation already.

"Going to the police."

"Why?"

"They won't do anything. They'll listen politely, trying not to smile, then when I've finished explaining about the cloth and the message, the man in charge will leer at one of his friends and ask me to undress so they can see the message on my back.

"No, it won't even get that far," she continued. "They'll just tell me to forget about what I saw; that there's nothing to be done. If a Russian sailor wants help, let him jump overboard and swim ashore. It happens all the time in Istanbul; some make it, some don't. This one will just have to take his chances too."

"Very sensible people, the Turkish police," I interjected.

"Then they'll tell me that this is a serious business. That the little ship out there with a hammer and sickle on the flag is a Russian ship; a little piece of Russia out there in Bebek harbor. The police will tell me that there could be ten Russian sailors on board crying for help but that they would be powerless to do anything."

"They're right, Suzan. Boarding a Russian ship without consent would be...I don't know...something like an act of war."

"That's right. That's why the police won't do anything. Nations don't do things like that to other nations unless they're prepared to run the risk of war."

I poked around in my mind trying to find some little gag I could spring to alleviate the growing tension in the room, but no dice.

"But we're not nations, Paul. We're people. People do things their governments won't."

"What are you driving at?"

"Why, I thought you knew!" She exclaimed. "We must try to rescue that Russian sailor ourselves!"

"You're crazy! You want us to tackle what the Turkish government would refuse to do itself? Why? You'll get yourself killed. Not to mention me. Stop the heroics, Suzan, this is serious business."

She stood up. "I know that, Paul. But when I hear a cry for help I don't run away." Her voice was carefully controlled.

"You expect me to cry out in pain, don't you? To jump to my feet and run down to the recruiting office to join Suzan Lokman's private crusade! Well, I am not going to do it. One of the most courageous things a man can do is admit he's a coward. I'm a coward. If the price I have to pay for your company is doing something foolish and unreasonable, then I'll bow out."

I watched her cross the room. "I understand, Paul. Believe me, I understand."

"Suzan, listen. It's fun with you. Great fun. I go back and forth like a guy on a trapeze, silly and happy one minute, morose and kicking myself the next. Sometimes I think the happy minutes will outlast the other ones, but a trapeze makes its own laws. When it goes up it's bound to come down. That's the way it is with me. If you like me because I'm fun and maybe worth saving that's good and I'm grateful. But the thing you want to save is me, and that means accepting me as I am."

"I understand, Paul."

"Stop saying you understand when you don't! If you did you wouldn't ask me to do things I'm not capable of doing."

"That's exactly it, Paul. You count yourself out before you're even asked. It's not being a coward, everyone's a coward; it's being a quitter. I wasn't even thinking of you when I said 'we' must try to rescue the Russian sailor. I was thinking of Mehmet. Good-bye, Paul." She was gone.

*   *   *

Time passes slowly when you have nothing to do but lie on a bed and think of your own inadequacies. I started by telling myself that I was well rid of her. It was inevitable anyway, wasn't it? Bill Nelson had said so and he ought to know. I was a summertime trifle waiting to expire when the first hint of autumn entered the air. She had no right to expect me to kill myself for a Russian sailor trying to prove he was a virgin. The line had been funny the first time I said it; now it tasted like the aftermath of a hangover.

Even my excuses damned themselves: she hadn't expected me to kill myself; she had never even planned to ask me to help her. When a man called for help, it took people of sterner stuff than me to go to the rescue; people like Mehmet. I couldn't reach out to save myself, let alone another human being.

She had said she understood but that wasn't so. How could she understand that a 2,500-year-old man named Colonel Atil held my destiny in the cradle of a telephone? Did she understand, or care, that if I left I would lose more than myself? That I would lose her?

After a time the pennants that hung on Peter Dawson's walls grew hazy. "I will close my eyes," I whispered, "and then I will sleep. When I awaken the ship will be gone and Suzan and I will be young and natural together and never talk again of her childish desire to help others."

CHAPTER EIGHTEEN

I awoke to the sound of the curtains alternately sighing against the window screen and fluttering into the room. The breeze blew strong, and I realized that I was cold, too cold for August. The room was pitch dark. I raised myself on one elbow trying to make out the dial of my wristwatch. No good. I fumbled for the switch of the bedside table. Ten o'clock. I went to the window and the curtain darted in like the tongue of a serpent. I pressed my hand against the screen trying to see out but there was a jumble of darkness. Then a soft pattering sound began and the wind rose out of the branches with a great sigh. Rain fell, light at first but growing in amplitude until the windowpanes above the screen ran with moisture.

I rummaged about in the top drawers of Peter Dawson's bureau until I found a half-filled pack of cigarettes and lit up. It was my first cigarette since the ceremonial smoke Atil had offered me. I went back to the bedside table, turned off the lamp and sat by the window. The tree leaves had quickly turned shiny; there were pocked patches of rainwater in the uneven surface of the macadam roadway that circled the quadrant; the rain fell heavily, hissing softly through the air, pattering on branches, gurgling down the drainpipes that passed near the window.

I drew deeply on the cigarette, coaxing the smoke deep into my system. The stale tobacco burnt quickly.

She was out there somewhere. Somewhere out in that jumble of blackness she was being soaked to the skin in a driving rain. While I gnawed on a stale cigarette, she and a gimpy Turk in a rowboat were preparing to assault a Russian freighter. How could she be so foolish? Why should she reach out in darkness to a hand that waved a red-stained cloth in slow semaphore? It made no sense. Nothing made sense.

The cigarette stub burned into my fingers. I bit off a last puff of smoke and ground out the cigarette with my heel.

Janice and Suzan.

Suzan and Janice.

I couldn't have two of them on my hands.

My knees quivered as I rose to my feet and turned on the lamp, my body resisting what my mind was telling it. I opened the door to the closet and surveyed Peter Dawson's wardrobe. What would he wear on a rescue operation on a night like this? I settled for a pair of worn blue jeans; he wouldn't miss them if they wound up on the bottom of the Bosphorus. Then I slid open the bottom drawer of the bureau. You can't wear a man's cashmere sweater to shinny up an anchor chain even if he does own a dozen of them. At the bottom of the drawer there was a plastic bag with a folded black knit sweater inside. I opened it out and saw an orange "P" on the front inscribed with crossed lacrosse sticks. So my benefactor was a fellow Princeton man and a lacrosse player to boot! Well, the Princeton Tigers had selected their foremost pussycat for this operation. I turned the sweater inside out. No point in giving the crewman on board that ship too good a target.

*   *   *

Orenko looked nervously at the bank of clouds that advanced over the horizon from the direction of the Bosphorus and blotted out the night sky. He consulted his watch impatiently: would these infernal singers never finish their laments about unrequited love? He shifted his bottom on the narrow wooden chair trying to relieve the cramp and sipped tentatively of the glass of lukewarm raw vodka in his hand. It couldn't compare with the stuff at home that danced on the tongue and sang a little tune to the taste buds before rolling down the throat. Moscow would do well to offer a master distiller to the Turks as part of the aid program. What a waste, however, offering help to these countries when there was so much to be done at home. Sweep your own hearth and let your neighbor sweep his own. Good advice, as rich and certain as the soil from which it sprung. Let the Turks make their own vodka.

He looked about. To his left a group of men sat silently rolling blue beads through their fingers. They appeared to be lost in the meaning of the songs; peasants, from their dress, dreaming of distant families who would not be seen again until the summertime construction projects were finished and the men scattered to their isolated villages to live and copulate until spring. At a table on the terrace just below a woman withdrew a moist breast and gave it to a squalling child. A different kind of song. Waiters scampered from table to table-carrying large brown bottles of beer, Coca-Cola, Pepsi-Cola (leave it to the Americans not to miss a trick, he thought), bottles of spring water and an occasional glass of tea. No one ever seemed to write down an order, offer money or consult a menu. It was all very disorderly. Small wonder all the management could afford was wooden chairs that bruised the bottom.

Would this woman ever stop? A wave of applause had been followed by a new burst of words pronounced in a voice that reeked of anguish and despair. How could people smile and display looks of contentment in the face of such din?

A drop of water fell on Orenko's neck and he turned to say something to the clumsy waiter but there was no one near him except a man and a woman who blew cigarette smoke into each other's mouths. Two more drops of water made a plunking sound as they dropped into the glass of vodka still gripped in his soft fist. Then a pattern of drops appeared on the tabletop. He cursed. Softly at first but with growing vehemence. The floorshow would soon be rained out and the belly dancer had not yet appeared.

He covered the leather case of the camera that lay on the table with his handkerchief and looked around. Everywhere waiters and people were scurrying about. The nursing child bawled as his mother withdrew the nipple and made for cover under a tree. There was no pattern to the movement, and Orenko saw the group of men to his left abandon their table and beat a quick retreat to the exits. Soon a waiter appeared from the shelter of the covered service area brandishing a piece of paper after the departing peasants, unable to catch up to his quarry.

The rain was falling hard now, and Orenko heard the bray of horns as the patrons climbed into the waiting taxis before the queue disappeared. They are paying for their disorder now, he thought. Everyone is leaving without settling his account. It is a disaster.

He looped the camera strap around his wrist and started toward the exit that gave out onto the street. His waiter was nowhere about. Another fifteen-lira loss to the management would make no difference. Then he stopped short, turned and walked firmly in the direction of the covered service area. A Russian does not walk out without paying his bill, he said to himself.

After, he had regretted his decision. There had been pandemonium in the service area where an angry man sat behind an antiquated cash register , and by the time the bill was paid the taxis were gone and it was necessary to walk down the hill to the Ataturk Bridge to wait for a taxi willing to drive to Bebek at night. But there had been no turning back. A Russian settles his accounts.

CHAPTER NINETEEN

The rain had let up a little when I slipped out of the door of Christopher Hall and jogged across the quadrant to the distant end of the campus, following the path that Suzan and I had taken together on our first walk together down to the Bosphorus. I ran the half-mile to Bebek wearing a pair of sopping wet jeans, a dripping sweater and a pair of sneakers that gushed water. My chest ached and each breath seemed to ram hot needles down my lungs; my thighs felt spongy under my weight. But I put on a finishing kick that would have sent Ovett and Coe weeping into retirement and streaked down the path to Mehmet's private pier.

Too late. The shack was dark, and the rowboat with the gaily-painted "Mehmetcik" and the red outline of a lobster was gone. I took a step forward toward the pier and my legs went out from under me.

"Damn fool girl," I gasped. "Look what you've done." It was even money, which was wetter, me or the puddle in which I sprawled. I made an effort to get on my feet but rocked back on my haunches. There I stayed, letting my breath come in slightly longer gasps.

"Damn fool girl," I gasped again. Out there with an ice pick trying to poke holes in a Russian freighter. After a while my chest stopped feeling as if someone had dumped a load of hot coals down my throat and my legs regained enough strength to support my body. I stood, teetering back and forth, wondering whether to fall down again or try to return to the college when a familiar voice called out just loud enough to be heard over the sound of the falling rain.

"Mehmet? Mehmet?"

"It's Mehmet's Uncle Paul," I croaked.

"Paul! Where are you?" The door of the shack creaked open slightly.

"Standing in a puddle measuring the rainfall."

A black silhouette emerged from the door and walked noiselessly across the pier to shore.

"Paul, what are you doing here?"

"I heard that the Turkish naturalists club was having a meeting here so I figured I'd find you. Why do you have clothes on? Where are all the nudists?"

"Everybody is me. I'm waiting for Mehmet."

"Does he have any clothes on? I don't want to interrupt anything important."

"You'd better come in for awhile. You look soaked."

I advanced all of two steps before my legs gave way again and I did a slow swan dive into the wet earth. The sight of a man flat on his face in the mud does something to Suzan. In a moment she was at my side stroking her hand over my temples.

"You've hurt yourself," she said concernedly when her fingers touched the bump of my forehead.

"I tried to run through a locked gate at the cemetery. It made quite an impression on me."

She laughed softly.

"I'm sorry it's not worse," I muttered bitterly. "I mean if my skull were fractured you'd have a real good laugh. Help me up, will you?"

She put her right hand into my armpit and tugged. It was just enough to stir the rest of me into action and I was on my feet again. She guided me—steered me was more like it—to the pier and into Mehmet's shack.

"Why were you running?"

"Out of cigarettes. When I run out of cigarettes I run in the rain instead. Well, what do you want me to say? That I came down here to talk you out of this fool venture?" She didn't reply. "I was worried about you."

"All the way from college? You ran all the way from college?"

"When I didn't have my face in a gate or a puddle."

She fumbled on the table for a packet of matches and lit a lamp that smelled of yesterday's fish. Holding the lamp high in one hand she examined my head and pressed softly against the lump.

"It's not serious. Sit down. I'll find a towel and you can dry off." She busied herself in the little alcove that served as Mehmetcik's kitchen and handed me a square of cloth.

"Where's Mehmet?" I asked.

"Out there," she said, pointing in the general direction of the lighthouse. "He's surveying the ship to decide how we should get aboard."

"You've roped him in, eh? He'll wish he hadn't left part of his leg in Korea when those Russians start chasing him. They don't have many lobsters in Siberia you know. I hope you told him that."

"He thinks we can do it."

"He's nuts."

"And you," she said, "what are you doing here?"

I wrung the wrist end of the sweater over the oil lamp, letting the water hiss on the glass. "There was an announcement on the radio that you were organizing a gang of mercenaries to liberate the Turks in Kazakhstan. Big pay, plenty of camp followers. The works. I decided to join up."

"You don't have to, Paul."

"Last Chance Gulch, kid. If I don't tank up this time I'll never make it." Something thudded twice against the pier.

"It must be Mehmetcik," Suzan explained.

The lobsterman clumped into the shack, shaking the water off his clothing like some great sheepdog just in out of a farm pond. He drew a chair up to the table and sat down.

I listened while he gave his report, Suzan providing bits and pieces of translation. I had the uneasy feeling that she was editing out unessential items like the presence of crack units of Russian marines armed with submachine guns spaced two feet apart, or rows of photoelectric cells geared to ring the alarm at the sound of a moth's hiccup.

"Mehmet says there is no one on deck at all. The ship's captain and some other people came back from town and are all in the center part of the ship. You know, in that thing that looks like a house right in the middle. There's a light in the porthole at the ship's back side but no one seems to be moving."

I was vastly encouraged at news of the light in the ship's backside but didn't tell her.

"Mehmet says that the harbor is very quiet. The rain has sent people to bed early."

"What about the lighthouse? Every two seconds and the ship is lit up."

She addressed some rapid-fire Turkish at him and got a fifty-second reply complete with gestures that took about ten seconds to translate. "He says that the stern of the ship is away from the lighthouse because of the currents and that the house in the middle...whatever it's called...blocks most of the light back there."

"Shouldn't we wait a while longer? Say two years?"

She didn't bother to translate my inquiry.

"Mehmet says that the man at the Customs House told him that someone had gone ashore about eight o'clock and took a taxi into the city. He didn't seem to be a crewman. Mehmet thinks we should go now, before the someone returns, and while the crew people are drinking or playing cards."

"Just how does he figure we'll get on board the boat?" Mehmet responded to Suzan's translation of my question by stepping outside onto the pier. I could hear him foraging around in the covered wooden box where he kept his lobster traps, spare anchors, oarlocks, engine cranks and other paraphernalia of his trade. Presently he came in carrying a length of one-inch hemp rope and an anchor. The anchor had a long shank topped with a ring and four curved flukes. It looked light, no more than two pounds, and was designed to hold rowboats and other small craft. He sat at the table and drew one end of the rope through the anchor ring and tied a series of intricate hitches, testing each knot with the pulling strength of his arms. Satisfied with the knot, he picked up the anchor and slammed a fluke into the tabletop.

"Tamam," he said. Tamam is the Turkish word for enough. I had the feeling that I had had enough before even beginning. Then Mehmet addressed another gesture-filled explanation to Sevim that ended with a mime of a man pulling up what I figured was the Turkish flag over the Kremlin.

"Mehmet says that we will row to the stern of the ship and throw the anchor up and hook it over the deck rail. Then I'll climb up hand over hand to the deck." The words took a time to sink in. It wasn't the Turkish flag he was raising; it was the little Turk-American herself.

"You'll climb up to the deck?" I asked, banging hard against my ear to show I hadn't heard well the first time.

"Of course. I can make it easily."

"Of course." I repeated. "Then you'll go to this guy's cabin, haul him up on deck, drop him over the side and sail away into the sunset. Remembering first, of course, to pull the plug in the ship so it will sink fast."

"Don't be funny. I can do it."

"Have you ever tried to climb hand over hand up a wet rope in a rain-storm?"

"No. But I will this time. Anyway, those knots Mehmet tied will help,"

"It'll be like trying to climb up a snake!" I could see from the fierce effort she made to control a smile that the impulse to say that I was the only upright snake she knew had barely been subdued. "All right! All right! You can do it. But what about me? It must be thirty-five feet from the bottom of the rowboat to the deck."

"What about you, Paul?" She inquired.

"I'm coming with you."

"If you're coming with me then you'll climb the rope."

Mehmet had been busying himself with wrapping the flukes and shank of the anchor in strips of cloth and electrician's tape to muffle the noise of the metal as it was thrown over the rail. He gave a grunt of satisfaction and stood up. "Hadi gidiyoruz," he said. Never had let's go sounded more ominous.

Mehmet and Suzan preceded me out of the cabin into the rain; they went directly to the rowboat. I stole a glance toward the shore. A few quick steps down the pier and I could be on wet land, headed for the sanctuary of Peter Dawson's room and a bed with sheets that turned down. But there was nothing left in that bottle marked Sweat of the Heather, and I could never survive the night alone. I followed them and sat in the stern of the rowboat. My legs felt very weak.

Mehmet steered a long course across the harbor in the direction of the Six-Legged Octopus before heading out so we could approach the ship from its stern without passing into the rays that pulsed from the lighthouse. The wooden oars creaked gently against the pins, and the blades made whooshing sounds as he dipped them into the water. I trembled in one long spasm as my muscles contracted from the cold. The rain had dropped to a steady drizzle.

The shore lights of Bebek were behind us now. Ahead was the bulk of the ship. Red and green warning lights were up fore and aft, and the bridge looked like a slab of grayish marble perpendicular to a grave. I could make out the word Tula on the forepeak when the lighthouse went on. Tula. Darkness. Tula. Darkness. Tula. Darkness.

We were within sixty yards of the ship now and I prayed that Suzan would turn her attention from the target ahead and turn and laugh briefly and say that the game was over and we would turn about and go to Mehmet's shack and have a good laugh and drink raki and she would say, "Oh, Paul. You should have seen your face! You really thought I was going to do it." But I only needed to look at that dark-clad body coiled in tension to know that my prayers were in vain.

Mehmet stopped rowing to calculate his approach and sense how the flow of the currents would carry the boat when we drew up to throw the anchor. He frowned in concentration, apparently indifferent to the dangers ahead. Tula was just another lobster to ensnare in the night. He resumed rowing and we made toward the left side of the ship, just below the porthole where Suzan had first spotted the cloth. The light Mehmet had seen before was now extinguished and the cloth was gone.

Mehmet stood up, operating the oars from an upright position so that we could draw in close to the hull. We were alongside now, and he reached out, holding the rowboat steady with the pressure of his palms against the hull. Then he pushed vigorously against the side and the rowboat drew away. He bent down quickly and picked up the anchor; his right hand held it by the shank; the length of rope was loose in the bottom of the rowboat. He drew the anchor over his shoulder and let fly.

The rope uncoiled from the bottom of the boat. There was a dull thunk and then silence. Mehmet grabbed the rope between his palms and pulled. It came taut and the rowboat pulled in close against the hull.

Mehmet has gaffed the biggest lobster of his career. He tested the strength of the anchor's grip with his weight. Then he nodded his head in Suzan's direction. She advanced to the center of the rowboat and leaned forward to whisper into my ear, "I'll go first. I'm lighter." Then she stood on the center seat, took the rope in her hands at the height of her chin, flexed her knees and sprang upward. She climbed quickly, gripping the rope between her ankles to rest her weight, and then thrusting upward with the strength of her arms.

Ten feet from the top of the rope she stopped and seemed to slip but it was only to catch her breath and renew her grip. Then she was even with the guardrail, a hand darted from the rope to the wooden molding, the toes of her right foot reached out to grasp the bottom rail. Her body heaved, all of it at once, and she was over the rail and on board Tula. She smiled down proudly and beckoned. When you are twenty-two and weigh one-hundred-and five pounds and swim or play tennis every day of your life and have muscles disguised under smooth skin that curves but does not ripple, it is easy to smile down from a pinnacle of accomplishment and say "follow me"; but when you are thirty-four and your body and soul are out of condition and the rain is falling into your face and your body is trembling from the cold, where do you find the strength to grasp a hemp rope and command your muscles to climb? I had no strength. I grasped the rope but nothing happened.

A voice trickled down the rope like a drop of rainwater. "Paul, Paul. Help." It said. "I need you."

I recall pushing Mehmet back from the rope and I was standing on the seat. I reached high over my head and jumped. I felt a twinge in my biceps and my fists were even with my eyes. My legs kicked back and forth, searching for the length of sodden rope and then they closed around it. I groped upward again and pulled. This time my body moved more freely. A third time and I began to feel a sense of joy in my strength. My ankles gripped the rope and I heaved again. And again. I looked down: the rowboat was ten feet below me. I heaved again on the rope but now nothing happened.

Mehmet came up the rope. He came up swiftly, his arms plunging down and up like twin pistons. Then I felt the top of his head against my buttocks. He began to push me upwards, using the strength of arms and shoulders to loosen me from my perch. I was being pushed into combat by having my behind butted by another man's head.

The spasms in my muscles relaxed and I reached up again. I put my feet on Mehmet's shoulders and sprang upward. The rhythm had returned and I inched my way up the rope. Soon I realized from the change in tension on the rope that Mehmet had descended. I was on my own again.

A tube of white metal was level with my eyes; the bottom rung of the guardrail. I heaved again against the rope and felt of a hand close on my wrist. "No, no," I called out, forgetting the risk of my voice. The hand let go and the wooden molding was just before me. I hung there a moment, gathering the last energy to pull my legs up to the lip of the deck. Then I was over the rail, leaning for support on a sopping wet creature that might have been a girl.

She let me pant there for fifteen seconds; then her voice spoke urgently into my ear "Paul, we must hurry."

I backed up to the rail to rest a few seconds longer and survey our position. The raised deck of the ship was shaped like the heel of an upturned shoe. Its top was almost flush except for two ventilators about five feet tall and eighteen inches across. The deck rail ran uninterrupted around the curved arc of the stern; forward it jutted out to enclose two small steel accommodation ladders leading to the freight deck below. Forward about thirty yards and running from one side of the ship to the other was the deckhouse. The lights that Mehmet had observed were still burning but the ports were closed against the rain.

I leaned forward to get a better view of the accommodation ladders and felt the chill metal of the anchor against my wrist. The point of the fluke was wedged between the wooden molding and the metal part of the rail. No point in trying to improve on a good thing; if it could support me and Mehmet at the same time it was enough.

"The only way down to the cabin is by those ladders," Suzan whispered, pointing at the accommodation ladders. We'll have to go down there."

"I'll go first," I said. She nodded in agreement and I crossed the deck in soft strides to the platform that gave onto the left side accommodation ladder. I crouched down to peer below the ladder. The bulkhead that ran transverse across the ship was recessed back under the deck; two doors opened off it, giving access to the stern cabins. There were no windows, nothing to tell me who or what was behind those doors. I peered at the illuminated dial of my watch: ten-forty; if there were crewmen in this section of the ship they would not yet be asleep. The question of crewmen nagged at me; how many men were there in the cabin that flew the improvised flag of distress?

My sneakers were silent on the embossed steel rungs of the ladder. I reached bottom and stepped into the little well of dryness provided by the recessed bulkhead. I tried to squint through the door crack but could make out only that it was light within. I listened with my ear to the door. No sounds. Suzan was beside me now. We exchanged glances and I turned the door handle down and waited. I pulled back an inch and peered in. The door opened into what appeared to be a narrow corridor, but the plane of the opening door moved outward, toward the side of the ship, and my range of vision was limited to no more than six feet. I pulled the door back further.

A man lay in jackknife position on a thin pile of folded blankets at the far end of the corridor. His head was toward me, cushioned on a thin shoulder; wisps of white hair fell down from a nearly bald crown. He looked thin and frail, even in the dim light of the small bulb screwed into the ceiling fixture. Was this our man? Was this little bundle of aged flesh capable of dreaming a young man's dream of crying for help and beginning anew? The man stirred and seemed to chew at the air; he twitched and the fingers of his free hand slipped between his thighs in a gesture reminiscent of male childhood. Then I recalled that our quarry was in a cabin with a porthole, not in a corridor. This was not our man. I stepped across him and pressed down the handle; it moved easily in my grasp. Then I leaned against the door with my shoulder, lifting the handle to guard against squeaking hinges. The cabin was dark, lit only by the patch of light that filtered in from the hallway behind us. I felt Suzan press against me from behind. We paused for an instant to adjust to the light.

A voice spoke in Russian, and I felt the hair on my neck rise. We advanced a step and the voice spoke again, more loudly now, and I thought I heard the man in the corridor stir in his sleep. Was the voice calling out instructions?

"Sshh," I whispered. The voice stopped. Silence. No sound of footsteps

I turned to see Suzan fumbling for the light switch in the cabin. She found it and simultaneously turned the switch and closed the door. The room was bathed in light from a wire-covered overhead bulb.

A thin, old man lay in a berth, his hand raised to ward off sudden light and the danger of the unknown. He was covered to his chest by a sheet that seemed strangely voluminous. The raised arm was slender, embossed with blue veins; it appeared to tremble from the exertion of fending off the light. I stepped to the side of the berth and gently withdrew the arm, placing it on top of the sheet. It was like touching a dead stick. The face of the man was sallow and drawn: pinched nostrils, cheeks dotted with the tiny broken capillaries of age, eyes that were a collage of faded blue pasted on a field of mottled yellow.

I glanced about quickly. A metal first aid kit lay on the small chest adjacent to the berth. It was open, filled with tubes, syringes and rolls of gauze; a bottle of mercurochrome stood upright in it. On the floor beside the berth was a stained cloth. I picked it up and showed it to Suzan. The Cyrillic letters were still visible.

The old man in the berth looked at us quietly. Now that his eyes had adjusted to the light he showed no fear, but neither did he show relief nor expectancy. For him we could have been two dark executioners come to exact the penalty paid by those who fly the wrong flag.

Suzan took the stained cloth from my hand, held it aloft, and made a mime of someone rowing. Then she pointed to her eyes and the cloth explaining wordlessly that we had seen the cloth. Then she pointed outward, toward the shore. She looked at him for a moment, probing his reaction for some sign that he had understood. Slowly the man nodded his head.

She rolled down the sheet and we both gasped at the same time. The man's ankles were encased in sheaths of gauze and plaster. He raised his arms a few inches from his chest and made a sign of a man snapping a stick. A fist of panic drove itself into my stomach and I looked to the cabin door, searching for a sign to bolt for the door and run to the deck to slide down the lifeline away from this fetid cabin that smelled of death. We could never make it. An able man might climb the ladder and slide down the rope unaided—but an invalid! I looked at Suzan in desperation; any minute now the sleeping man in the corridor would sense some irregularity within, open the door and sound the alarm.

"We can't do it."

"He's not very heavy, Paul. Together we can get him up to the deck."

"What then? What then? He can't slide down that damned rope. He's too weak."

"Mehmet must have some rope in his boat. He can bring some up and we'll lower him that way."

"The whole goddam Russian navy will be on our necks in no time. No!" I implored. "No. It won't work."

"Oh, Paul. We can't quit now."

"You have no right to say quit," I snarled. "You think that all we have to do is wish this guy off this boat and it's done. Well, it won't work and we'll kill him in the process."

Her face contorted from the impact of my words. Then the old man spoke.

"Please. Please." This time there was no question of comprehension; he spoke in English.

Suzan looked at me in a way that said we were beyond the point where logic or reason worked. She leaned over the berth, put her hands into the old man's armpits and started to work him across the berth.

"Here. Let me do that," I said savagely, pushing her away. I pulled hard and a low groan welled up from the old man's chest. When he was half way clear of the berth I held him half erect with my right hand and pivoted behind him so that I could lift him up with greater leverage, letting his backrest against my chest for support.

"His legs. Take his legs!" I whispered. Between us he was not a heavy burden, just terribly awkward. But spreading his weight between two people didn't solve the problem of how to lower him into the boat.

"Wait. Wait." The voice was that of the old man; its tone equated anguish: those broken legs swinging free in the loop of Suzan's arms must have throbbed with pain. He half pointed, half gestured with his arm to a first aid kit and wallet on the berth side chest. I backed up a step and watched him bring them to his chest slowly, as if they were holy objects withdrawn from some tabernacle.

"We'll have to turn around," I said. "I'll have to go first up the steps." There was something ludicrous in the way we did a slow turn in the cabin; it was like watching a couple trying to make love in a burlap bag: you don't know whether to laugh, applaud or feel sorry.

Almost a minute had passed since we had first lifted the old man from the berth, and I could feel hot flashes pass through my arms from the strain. Soon my fingers would lose their grip in the warm enclosure of his armpits and he would fall. I lifted my knee again to rest his weight and ease the strain and then backed up to the door until I felt its expanse against my shoulder blades. Ages passed while I groped for the door handle, and then it was between my thumb and forefinger and I pressed down and eased inward. The door gave a little and I stepped forward, Suzan carefully following the movement of my body. I passed my fingers into the gap between the door and the frame and pulled again until it came apart enough for me to hold it open with my shoulder.

I craned my neck to look down the corridor and held my breath. The sleeping sailor was rousing from the pallet of blankets. He got to his feet slowly, feeling against the wall for support as his numbed limbs came to life. His face was drugged with sleep and he yawned loudly and rubbed the backs of his hands across his eyes. He was looking my way. Oh Lord, he had seen me! I waited for the inevitable cry of alarm but he yawned again, turned away and began to fumble with the buttons of his fly. Then he reached for the door at the end of the corridor and stepped inside.

"What are you waiting for?" Suzan hissed.

"The sailor in the hall just went to the can. Let's go." I pushed again with my shoulder and backed out. The old man's plaster covered legs thumped against the doorframe as Suzan emerged from the cabin but this time he didn't groan.

We came to the last door, the one that gave out to the accommodation ladder leading to the deck where our lifeline waited.

"I can't open it holding him." I said. "I'll have to put him down. But you hang on to his legs." As gently as I could I lowered the old man's head and shoulders to the floor and opened the door. His face was flushed when I bent to pick him up again and the blood pulsed in the veins of his temples from the sudden change in blood flow. We held him even for a moment to calm the instinct to call out for relief, then I backed through the door into the shelter created by the lip of the overhanging deck. There was a glow of light that I hadn't seen before: the window of the toilet. I hoped that the sleepy sailor had a bad case of prostate trouble and would be obliged to linger for a couple of hours coaxing out the final drops of moisture.

The last moments were agony. The rain was still falling and the steel steps of the ladder were like grease underfoot so I sat on every step, bucking my way up on my bottom. Suzan followed wordlessly, gripping the old man's ankles with one arm while using her free hand to pull against the steel rail, wrestling precious inches of movement from the effort. Then we were on the deck and over to the rail.

I saw a patch of light disappear on the far side of the deck. The old guard had finished his errand at the toilet.

"Call Mehmet," she said.

"Suzan. Over my shoulder. Get him over my shoulder." I wrestled our burden to a standing position and turned to let him fall over my crouched body. His stomach came down hard on my shoulder and he gasped in a cry of anguish that must have stemmed from the deepest fibers of his body. I teetered there in a desperate effort to balance his weight.

A long cry from down in the ship pierced the night.

"Suzan. Over the side. Quick."

"But…"

"You little fool. Go!" She clambered over the ship's rail just as the old sailor came up the ladder. I saw his head emerge above the level of the deck, a look of terror on his face. Not half as frightened as I am, I thought. You're old and weak and I'm young and weak, but I'm carrying someone over my shoulder. I waited for the inevitable moment when he would look my way.

The old sailor cried out as he saw me, clambered to the top of the steps and stopped short, uncertain what to do. He looked in the direction of the deckhouse searching for some sign that his appeals had been heard. There was no sign of activity. A look of resolve came onto his face and he advanced slowly, shuffling across the deck, arms hung low, looking like an aged chimpanzee out to defend his branch of the tree against all comers.

Don't do it, old man, I thought. Don't do it. Let me just slide down this rope and get away. I don't want to hurt you. The voice from the sea spoke again, calling my name in urgent tones. The old sailor advanced, shuffling slowly, looking for the best avenue of attack. He moved sideways to get to the side where the old man lay doubled over my shoulder.

I felt the flukes of the anchor against my hand. I grasped the shank of the anchor in my left hand and pushed down but it didn't give. I pushed harder against it. Still no movement. The sailor advanced again, making wheezing noises. I took a new grip on the shank of the anchor near the ring and pushed back and forth in quick rhythm. There was the sound of wood rending just as the sailor rushed.

He seemed to slip on the wet deck and that may have helped. It gave me time to swing a little to the right and meet the timid onslaught. My left arm drew back, the shank of the anchor cold in my hand, and I swung down into the face of an old sailor who wore a look of pained surprise, his hands raised to ward off the blow.

Then he lay on the deck and blood coursed from the hole in his head where the anchor fluke had dug into his skull. The blood flowed down his forehead into his eyes and then followed the seams of his sea-weathered face into a gaping mouth. It spread on the deck and was diluted by the rain. The old sailor's arms were still raised in an attitude of defense or supplication, I couldn't tell which. Perhaps they are the same thing.

I had killed a man. I looked down at the anchor still clutched in my hand. A little chunk of flesh and a wisp of hair hung from a reddened fluke. A spasm of nausea seized my stomach and I tried to retch but nothing came. Expiation would not be as easy as a pool of vomit.

"Paul. Paul." The sound of my name was followed by a tug at the rope that still led over the side to safety. I turned back to the rail and braced the anchor back into position. It was strangely easy going down. I just climbed over the top rail, the old man still suspended over my shoulder, and lowered both our weights down the rope with the strength of my arms and shoulders.

Suzan and Mehmet were waiting to relieve me of the burden. Together we spread the old man in the bottom of the boat. Mehmet pushed hard against Tula's hull to make clear water to dip the oars. Then we were away.

The rope still dangled down the hull of the ship. It was only right that we leave it there, I thought; the course of freedom runs in strange ways: someone might want to climb that rope, seeking his destiny in a different direction.

Suzan passed me a length of canvas from the bait box forward and I spread it over the old man to keep off the rain. It was falling lighter now—like the mists of spring rather than the torrents of summer—but the canvas would provide some warmth. He looked more dead than alive and I thought at first he was unconscious, but the way he stroked his fingers across the first aid kit and wallet said otherwise.

I looked forward to watch Suzan in the prow. She was in profile again watching the approaching shoreline of Bebek. She hadn't spoken a word since I came down the rope and, except for the action of passing me the canvas, seemed drained of the desire to move as well. What was going on inside that intense young mind now? Was she savoring the triumph born of conquering the unknown—that is what courage is all about, isn't it? Was she brooding over the chain of events her willful-ness had caused? Was she thankful that I had come along on a madcap adventure and not quit—not yet at least? I had the sense of knowing only half a person and for the first time since meeting her wondering whether half wasn't more than one man could comprehend.

"Paul. Look back." I turned. The deckhouse of the ship was ablaze with light now, and the beam of a searchlight played down from the bridge into the sea, but we were well out of reach. We had boarded the ship and disappeared. There was no way for those on board to know who we were or where we had come from.

I decided where we would put the old man for the night. Wrapped in blankets and left with a pot of soup and bread he might live until morning. Then we would find some way to transport him down to the city and, like someone who secretly dumps garbage in the street when his neighbors aren't looking, leave him at the rear entrance to the municipal hospital, a foundling nearer death than birth.

I told Mehmet to go, not bothering to discuss our destination first with Suzan. Mention of a cemetery might not be the word she most wanted to hear.

Chapter Twenty

Blake and his companions had left the ramshackle old wooden house early to convey the impression of a group of friends off to catch the ferryboat back to Istanbul after an outing in the country. Three men carrying suitcases and duffle bags made less of an impression by daylight than at night, when a suspicious policeman might challenge them and probe about, looking for stolen goods. Blake knew that the art of avoiding detection lay in making perfection of the ordinary. Never look back, never step across the street to avoid a policeman, avoid the appurtenances of wealth, cultivate cordial relations with the local authorities, never hurry and, above all, smile, smile, smile. The list of maxims that made up his guidebook on how to be the perfect agent ran on to great lengths and some day, time permitting, he would publish them as a chapter of his memoirs. Blake made a mental note to add another maxim to the lengthy list: never go on mission with a full bowel.

But they deviated from their route before reaching the ferryboat pier. Instead, they enjoyed a pleasant enough wait in the station's boathouse on the Asiatic side of the Bosphorus, near Kandilli. They smoked, nibbled some simits and fruit, and whiled away the time listening to the slap-slap-slap of the water against the pilings, talking about how well

things were going. The food was just enough to quell the pangs of
tension bordering on nausea that always preceded a hazardous venture.
The sound of masticating jaws provided their own special music and
Blake produced the ritual cluck-cluck of approval from Ahmet and
Nuri when he slipped a red and gold peach whole into his mouth and
talked fluent Turkish notwithstanding the impediment.

From time to time Blake had stepped out of the boathouse to survey
Tula at her mooring a mile away. His ten power binoculars drew the
ship close and he could make out occasional signs of movement on the
deck and at one time he watched a small boat pull away toward shore in
Bebek. Then it became too dark to make out anything except the
glowing windows of the deckhouse, pinpoints of light that they would
steer by on their way to the target.

The absurdity of a team of three agents capturing a Russian ship and
making off with Scherevsky fascinated Blake. Who would expect that
an operation like this could be attempted by one Englishman and two
Turks? The negative assumption built into that question was itself an
assurance. They could carry it off. Surprise was the chief element in
their favor. Their launch would draw up to Tula's stern, and an air gun
would propel a rope ladder over the rail. Then the three men would
clamber aboard, each carrying a submachine gun and a sack filled with
grenades. Locating Scherevsky on such a small vessel would take no
time at all. A man of his importance would be kept either in the main
deck house or the cabin in the raised hump at the ship's stern. As for the
crew, Blake reasoned, they represented no problem. When the machine
guns began to chatter they would scurry for cover, or dive over the side
or, as was more likely, they would die in their places, too panic-stricken
to find the means to move. Or they would watch in solemn fascination
as a grenade bounced erratically across a cabin floor before scattering
its lethal shards into their uncomprehending faces.

In just a few minutes it would all be over, Blake surmised, cheered
by the thought of mayhem to come. Then Ahmet would carry

Scherevsky, cupped in one arm, down the rope ladder as easily as a woman carries a sack of groceries, and Nuri and he would follow. The idling engine would come to life, and the launch would hunch backwards as if from surprise before heading out in the friendly blackness of the Bosphorus.

Even the rain that began to fall on the roof of the boathouse would be a blessing, he told himself. If the Russians have guards posted on Tula's deck they will seek shelter rather than risk a soaking. In any case, he had his options. It would be preferable to capture the missile expert alive and exploitable, but the really important point was to prevent his return to Russia, even if it meant destroying the ship.

Having taken account of his latest pre-operational maxim. Blake buttoned his trousers and emerged from the dark recesses of the boathouse. Time to go. Nuri hopped easily into the launch, started the engine and, satisfied that the engine revolutions were at their desired peak, beckoned the others aboard where they huddled under the cockpit cover to avoid the rain, knowing from experience that a warm body functions more efficiently than limbs stiff from cold.

They proceeded at medium speed across the Bosphorus; nothing to suggest that they were other than three friends intent on a nighttime crossing prior to tying up, and going home to bed. They made a course that took them below Tula's stern, on a direct tangent from the boat house at Kandilli toward the somber bulk of the long-abandoned Egyptian Embassy below Bebek, an approach calculated to take them to the offshore side of Tula's stern, thus minimizing exposure to harbor lights or the pulsing beam of the lighthouse near the mosque at Bebek. Blake noted that the rain had subsided to a drizzle and put a foot on the gunwales at the side of the cockpit to get a better view. He signaled to Nuri to slow down and the launch settled into the water before easing forward slowly.

"Something's up, lads," he called, when the launch was two hundred yards from its target. The lenses of his binoculars were damp with rain so he made a visor of his hands and squinted into the drizzle. No doubt about it. There was sudden activity on board Tula. Lights came on throughout the ship, below decks, and above in the deckhouse, and he could make out moving forms on the ship's bridge. Then a beam of light pierced the darkness, probing across the water in the direction of Bebek.

"Hard right, Nuri, and be quick about it." The little helmsman responded without asking for an explanation. The launch heeled on its side and moved away into the Bosphorus, maintaining speed for two hundred yards before Blake signaled that they slow down. They were well below Tula's stern now, out of range of any searchlights, especially in the continuous drizzle. The launch's engine maintained just enough speed to hold them steady against the fast currents.

Blake wiped the moisture from the binoculars and raised them to his eyes. Yes, something was clearly amiss on Tula. Something had gotten their wind up. But what? Had Scherevsky thrown himself overboard rather than be sent back to Russia? Hardly likely that an old man with broken legs could haul himself to the deck. What of the Americans? They had agents throughout Greece. Perhaps they, too, had learned of the visit to Tula on the part of the talkative Greek doctor who had treated Scherevsky. Just like the Americans to try to beat him to it! The only thing special about the special relationship was when it served to benefit the Americans! Blake inwardly fumed, recalling times past when British interests had been torpedoed by the Yanks, like that imbroglio at Suez.

On the other hand, it might just be a bout of panic. Some Russian sailor full of cheap vodka thinking he saw a boat approaching in the harbor and sounding the alarm; now everyone would be scrambling around furiously hoping to win the Order of the Red Star by repelling the non-existent invaders. Whatever it was, he told himself, it spelled the end of any attempt to rescue Scherevsky tonight. Sensible thing to do now is take out their insurance policy, sail away, and then keep tab on the ship's activities.

He spoke rapidly to Nuri and Ahmet and took the tiller of the launch himself. The two Turks started to protest but he cut them off abruptly, holding the launch steady in the water while they extricated gear from the suitcases and duffle bags they had brought on board. First, they stripped off their clothing and put on long underwear, insulated black rubber tights, and long-sleeved jerkins. Then they put on black rubber helmets, and snapped them on to the jerkins to make an effective, if primitive, insulated seal. Once dressed, they assembled lengths of steel pipe into a square about two feet by two feet, with four turn-down handles fixed perpendicular to the plane of the square. In the center, they fitted a square metal box eighteen by eighteen inches capped by a large serrated knob that Blake carefully adjusted. It was heavy and the men grunted as they tested the strength of the fittings by pulling against them from opposite sides. Satisfied with the security of the assembly, Ahmet and Nuri buckled on rubber flippers and helped each other into two sets of underwater breathing gear. They could last under water for at least an hour, sufficient time to carry out their task. Finally, they adjusted the mouth fixtures to assure comfort and good fit.

Blake adjusted the flow of oxygen. It was, he knew, a sensitive business, particularly as their equipment was largely handmade. Too much oxygen could make a man giddy, and produce hallucinations, provoking a desire to discard the intake tube and prompt certain death. Nuri and Ahmet would not travel at great depth-twenty-five feet should suffice—but they would need all their strength and alertness while propelling along a heavy metal object in the darkness. The men confirmed with nods that they were satisfied with the airflow, and bent to pick up the metal frame. Steadying themselves against the cockpit, they waited as Blake increased the throttle and slowly drew nearer to Tula.

Twenty minutes had passed since they had observed the activity on board the ship. Except for one or two brief stabs of light toward the opposite shore, the spotlight's beam played almost exclusively in the direction of Bebek harbor. Whatever had caused their panic had come from that direction. So much the better, thought Blake, they won't see us approaching.

The launch was now no more than one hundred feet out from Tula, abreast with its bow. He took his hand off the throttle, and the launch eased to a stop. The he turned and nodded. In an instant they were gone. He thought he saw a little train of bubbles as they head toward target, two human torpedoes intent on delayed destruction.

Blake chucked. Little Nuri looked trim in that underwater swimming rig. But Ahmet! With that great gut swelling out in front of him he looked like a great distended tire tube that might explode any minute. Blake bit his tongue. Mustn't use that word. Explode. Not old Ahmet! He turned the launch out into the main channel, while noting that his presence apparently had not been noted on board Tula. It would be some time before his companions surfaced again. In the meantime, he would cruise slowly back and forth, imitating a fishing boat, always watchful and waiting.

A good time to remember important duties. He rested his hand on the tiller of the launch and groped in a duffle bag looking for a bottle of mineral water. Finding one, he sluiced the water between his teeth, washing away the last flecks of food that might cause decay. He spat several times into the Bosphorus, knowing that it was richer for his presence.

Too bad that Tits and Ass hadn't bit at his suggestion that they buy a piece of Scherevsky and add him to their missile team down in the Negev. Their reply was succinct, "We have enough home grown rocket experts of our own. Thanks but no thanks. If he doesn't get back to Russia or China that's fine with us." Tits and Ass, he chuckled to himself, he wondered how they would react if they knew the private code phrase for Tel Aviv used by agencies everywhere.

CHAPTER TWENTY-ONE

The fan of the air conditioner picked up speed and clicked uncertainly against the wire screen that protected unwary fingers. A column of cool air felt its way tentatively into Orenko's cabin, as if probing an unknown cave. Within minutes the atmosphere of the cabin had cooled. Orenko placed his body in the flow of the incoming air; it blew against his sweat-soaked shirt, pressing it like a cooling poultice against his chest, and his body trembled as the moisture evaporated in his shirt.

Orenko moaned. How shameful it had been to admit to Vaslov that he had neglected his duty and gone to Istanbul. How he had pleaded for the renewal of the air conditioner so he could cool his chemicals and perhaps decipher the mystery of Scherevsky disappearance. Vaslov had finally agreed, no doubt already preparing a report blaming the entire fiasco on anyone but himself.

Six years away from retirement and this had to happen, Orenko cried to himself. All the old fears welled up again in his chest. There would be no nice little cottage set back in the hills above the seven ports of Odessa to dream of now. No happy hours playing with the grandchildren in the garden. No family and friends to listen in rapture as he recounted the exploits of a grimy little ship that performed great things in behalf of Mother Russia.

Scherevsky was gone. The enormity of the admission overwhelmed him. Scherevsky was gone, spirited away in the night while he waited in the rain to pay a fifteen lira bill. There was no way to disguise the truth: he had gone ashore on an unauthorized mission, intent on savoring the flesh of a Turkish belly dancer, taking photos to add to his collection which surely would be discovered during the investigation. And failing to tell the ship's captain of his absence? What did that signify? A clear indication of dereliction of duty and Vaslov would be the first to confirm it. "Oh God," he moaned aloud. Why me? Why me? I am an honest man. Must I now pay the price of shame for waiting to pay my bill?" The importuning words rang hollow.

There was only one chance. It lay in the chemical powers of the rows of tanks now cooling from the air spinning into the cabin from the whirring air conditioner. When enough time had passed he would remove the Zeiss Ikon camera from its case, extricate the roll of film, and then unfurl it in darkness into the first of the chemical tanks. Now all he could do is sit on the edge of his berth thinking of Odessa, knowing that there is no port of call as distant as the last one of the voyage.

An hour later, beginning to feel numb from the cold, he rose and began the ritual of developing. It would take time, this dipping and transferring, and rinsing, before the images came through. But it was something to do. Something to keep him from worrying about what lay ahead if the chemicals failed.

During the last few minutes of the procedure while the strip of celluloid finally writhed in the rinsing tank, he turned on the red photographer's light. After his eyes adjusted to the new level of illumination, he felt around on the berth until he found the scrap of white cloth that had been retrieved from the floor of Scherevsky's cabin. It was a malediction the old man had scrawled there. It spelled disaster for all who saw it. And someone had seen it! Someone had seen it hanging from the porthole of the cabin that was just within reach of the old man's fingers. Someone had seen it and had come aboard.

Then he remembered the young woman who had bared her breasts, and the painful redness of her back. What was it he had thought? Be careful! You will be badly burned.

He held the end of the filmstrip in a pair of sponge-tipped pincers and let it drip briefly into the tank. Then he took a strip of soft cloth and drew it gently down the length of the film so as not to scratch the delicate surface. It would have been better to let the film dry totally in the cool air but there was not time for such conventional procedures. He snipped off the exposed film at the beginning of the reel from the dark un-exposed portions, leaving five small squares linked together. Then he opened a cabinet beneath the developing trays and withdrew a slide projector and a beaded screen which he fixed to the door of the cabin, letting the weight of the meal cover hold it taut. Then he placed the projector between the developing tanks and turned on the projection lamp. A square of light shone crisply on the screen. His hands trembling, he slipped the film into the aperture that fed the slides, not bothering to waste time on the tedious process of individual film mounts.

The girl was even lovelier than he had remembered. In his haste while taking the photos, there had been no time to appreciate that exquisite body, that finely-chiseled profile, that blend of slenderness and voluptuousness. He averted his glance. This creature, this lovely creature, he thought, she will be hurt.

There could be no doubt. The young man sitting beside her in the rowboat had painted a copy of the word on the square of cloth Scherevsky had dangled from the porthole on to the girl's back. Foolish young people. Foolish girl. You talked yourselves into thinking that his call for help was legitimate, thinking that someone must respond to every call for help. So you came aboard and took him away. Couldn't you see that the act of helping is not important; that what counts is who you help? Would you help a murderer escape? A rapist seek shelter?

Orenko sighed. "This is very sad," he murmured aloud. He adjusted the fine focus knob on the projector bringing various parts of the slide into better definition. Her profile would be easy to identify but the man had slumped forward and his face was not visible. That mattered little. One would lead to the other. The best part was the rowboat; painted across the stern was the name Mehmet; below it was painted Bebek, and the outline of a red lobster.

Foolish young people, leaving a calling card like that.

He clicked off the projector. It didn't seem decent to look at her longer, not considering what he might have to do.

CHAPTER TWENTY-TWO

It had been after midnight when we parted at the entrance to the female staff quarters. The old man had been bedded down in the inside room at the caretaker's shack at the cemetery behind a rough partition of planks, the tops of crates, scraps of canvas—whatever we could find. Suzan made a bed of blankets, obtained during our hasty stop at Mehmet's pier house, and tarpaulins. We worked by the light of a kerosene lantern alternating between moroseness and high spirits, displaying the signs of non-alcoholic drunkenness that comes from fatigue and excitement.

He was very silent as we worked, the old man, and never asked our identities, what we were doing or why. He just lay on the rough concrete floor of the shack and watched us through flickering eyelids, fingers entwined on the first aid kit. If he was grateful for our having responded to his signal from the ship he didn't show it. He seemed to be waiting for us to elect the proper moment to explain ourselves, as though what happened was part of a script and we were the actors following stage directions.

I don't recall our saying goodnight to the old man or uttering harmless clichés that evoked pleasant dreams, reunions on the morrow, God's blessings, or what have you. Our work was finished. Suzan turned down the wick of the lantern and then we stepped outside and waited for the last drops of kerosene on the wick to burn off before leaving; Mehmet on his silent way by the Bosphorus to Bebek; Suzan and I by our silent way up the winding path to the college. The old man was left alone to contemplate what route had taken him to this strange destination.

Now it was morning and I lay on my back in borrowed pajamas in a borrowed bed with my fingers linked under my head and listened to the morning sounds filter through the open window. Was she thinking of me now, over there in the pristine quarters reserved for single female staff? I could see her in my mind's eye, wearing the bottom half of a bikini, sitting Buddha—style on her bed, conjuring up visions of me descending the hemp rope from Tula, the old man slung over my shoulder.

Eight-fifteen. Time to slip out of Peter Dawson's pajamas and think of serious things like food and the man bedded down in the caretaker's shack at the cemetery. Mehmet had assured us that he would go there at the crack of dawn to leave a pot of soup and bread, should the old man want nourishment. Suzan and I were to sleep late, saving our energies for the task of taking him down to Istanbul and a surreptitious dumping at the hospital.

I was in the bathroom, mid-way through shaving, admiring the excellent jaw-line that was revealed as the blade whisked away shaving crème, when there was a knock on the door.

"Kim o?" I shouted in Turkish above the sound of running water.

A muffled voice replied, "It's I".

No one but a girl who had learned impeccable English as a second language would say "It's I" at eight-twenty in the morning. I turned off the faucet, crossed the bedroom and turned the big brass key in its ancient lock.

I opened the door a crack and looked out. "You're early," I said accusingly.

"I know but I couldn't sleep and I'm hungry. Can I come in?" I opened the door to let her enter. She was wearing a lemon-colored blouse and a darker compatible skirt and she looked like something out of one of those magazines that show how young career girls spend their leisure hours between assignations. Her face showed no sign of strain or fatigue. She stood on tiptoe to brush her lips on the shaved side of my face.

"In Turkey," I remonstrated, "the proper greeting is a kiss on both sides."

"Not until you've finished shaving." The prospect perked me up and I went back to the bathroom and turned on the faucet again. She followed me, balancing her body on the edge of the bathtub, and watched quietly while I drew my face into the various ridiculous postures required to remove beard from the jaw-line and the sensitive areas around the lips. I wished she didn't look so damn impassive as I went through this particularly masculine operation. Was watching a man shave such a normal thing for her to do? The question had too many built-in connotations and I nicked myself as penance for thinking it.

"Better?"

She answered by pressing her mouth against my other cheek, holding it there a perceptible moment longer than for the first part of the operation. She smiled, "Smooth as a baby's ass."

"Where did you learn that?

"From my father. He learned it from a visiting American doctor. Whenever he finished an operation he would lift off his gauze mask and tell the nurses that it had gone as 'smooth as a baby's ass.' It used to amuse him."

She stood up from her perch on the bathtub as I spread the wet towel on the rack. "I'm hungry. Let's go."

"Pajamas are not allowed to be worn on campus," I said. "It's a college regulation like not having female visitors in rooms. It's considered damning to have female visitors in rooms while wearing pajamas."

Her heel hit the floor in that now-familiar stamp of impatience. "Oh, hurry!"

Her gaze was curiously indifferent as I dressed; it was fixed through me, not on me. It was as if we were a couple married twenty years for whom the act of dressing had lost its provocative powers.

She preceded me down the steps in the event that Bill Nelson was waiting at the bottom of the stairwell with a shotgun and I watched her start across the quadrant before following. Dressing in front of a beautiful girl can have a disconcerting effect on a man unaccustomed to this sort of thing and I was half way down the stairs before I remembered to go back and put on shoes.

"It's the only thing to do, isn't it?" She was waiting at the wrought iron gate that gave me a hard time the night before and said the words as soon as I came into view.

"There's no choice. In another half-hour we'll have this guy off our hands. The hospital will call the police and that ends it as far as we are concerned. Who knows? Maybe the police will let him stay? The Russian merchant marine can survive without him."

"And you're not angry with me?"

I stopped her progress down the road and spun her to me. "You'd never guess it from modest behavior, but I'm really kind of pleased with myself."

We resumed the familiar trek and crossed the short trail along the inside of the cemetery wall that led to the shack, reasonably confident of not being observed.

Suzan paused at the door.

"Do we have to?" She asked softly.

"Let's go in and get it over with. We tell him quickly, gracefully, honestly, and then we go eat somewhere. Afterwards we'll ask

Mehmetcik to find a cab driver who likes fifty lira notes and can keep
his mouth shut to take us all to the hospital."

She hesitated. "Look," I said a little sharper now. "Last night you
were all ready to dump our prize catch on land and let him look after
himself. A couple of chunks of plaster on his ankles don't make that
much difference."

"Perhaps," she replied, opening the door. "But he looks so frail and
hopeless; like someone who has never had any chance in life."

The interior of the shack was cooler than the outside air. The
looming horse chestnut trees and sentinel cypress which abounded in
the cemetery and set gravestones akimbo from the thrust of their roots
provided generous shade which lent the inside air a cool, unused
quality. It was silent save for the summer sound of droning insects
battering mindlessly against the small four-pane window that let in
sunlight.

I entered the inner room, peered over the barricade and looked down.
It took a moment for my eyes to distinguish the thin face that peered out
over the covering of blanket and tarpaulin; the eyes were open and for a
moment I thought it was the rigid gaze of death but then they blinked
rapidly. I sensed the terror the man must be feeling, unable to see more
than my eyes and forehead over the barrier, not knowing whether I was
friend or a new abductor. I pulled aside a plywood crate top to let us
pass.

He nodded in recognition at us and spoke. "Thank you for the soup."

I looked down and almost kicked the lunch pot that Mehmet had
used to bring food. It was nearly empty. Beside it was a mound of
crusts; Mehmetcik must have removed them to make it easier for the
old man to swallow the heavy brown bread. I smiled fleetingly in salute
to the innate tenderness built into the lobsterman and made a vow to
have a long session of war stories at first opportunity.

"Do you feel better?" It was Suzan who spoke now.

"Much better. I feel much better now." He spoke slowly, forming each word individually as a distinct unit rather than letting them flow together. He seemed to have no trouble with English; perhaps he had learned it during World War II as a sailor on convoy routes where crews of mixed nationalities often occurred.

I bent down to take a closer look. Luster that had not been there the night before now shone in his eyes; his skin, too, was tinged with pink in contrast with the shallow hue we had first observed. With his delicate facial bone structure and thin hair that grew long over his ears he looked more like the popular conception of a Russian poet, not a seaman.

He struggled under the weight of the coverings. "It is too hot now," he said. "Help me." I removed the tarpaulin entirely and folded back the rough wool blanket to the waist; it was olive green and on it were embossed the faded letters AUS—Army of the United States, another of Mehmet's souvenirs from Korea. I was struck by the delicacy of the old man's fingers; they were long and slender, unmarred by the calluses or furrowed flesh that one would expect of a simple sailor; I could see them grasping the fingerboard of a violin, not the valve of a steam pipe. He watched me intently as I examined him and I sensed that he was acute to the questions forming in my mind.

"Who are you?" He asked.

"We are the people who took you off the ship."

"Yes, yes, I know that," he said with some asperity. "But who are you? Who sent you?"

"No one sent us. We just came. We saw the cloth."

He lapsed into silence for a moment, looking back and forth from Suzan to me. "You saw the cloth and came. That is all."

"Yes."

"Just the two of you...and the Turk." He pointed toward the soup pot.

"I'm Turkish too," Suzan volunteered. "Half of me."

He looked at her sharply. "Turkish? American?"

"Why do you need to know who we are?" I interrupted.

"It is important," he said petulantly. "You", he said addressing the words to me, "get something to raise me up. It is fatiguing to talk this way. I need my strength." I got to my feet and began to search for some way to prop him up. Curious way for a rescued sailor to speak; he hadn't even asked me to make him comfortable; he had told me. He was a man accustomed to giving orders. Was it possible that we had made off with the ship's captain? The line of inquiry troubled me too; he was too insistent on finding the motives for our actions. I made up my mind to break the news of the trip downtown as soon as possible. If this was the ship's captain he had probably sold the ship's cargo at a personal profit for the favors of the belle of some French port, which would explain why he needed to get away. But why the broken legs? You don't fracture both ankles jousting in bed with a prostitute, even the best of them. Not unless he had a technique that eluded lesser men.

I found a wooden chair in the main area of the shack and brought it in. I turned it over so the back slats would support the old man in a sitting position and propped the legs against the wall to make it secure. He leaned back, and looked at us again with the intent gaze that I was beginning to find irritating. "Who are you?" He said directly to me, then answered his own question. "You are an American."

"Yes."

"Why am I here?"

"I'll tell you in short simple phrases. This girl and I were out rowing and we saw a cloth hanging from the porthole of that Russian ship in the harbor called Tula. We saw letters written on that cloth and copied them down but they were in Russian so we couldn't understand what they said. We went to a library and got out an English-Russian dictionary and found out that the letters meant help. That's a term that means something to us so we decided we would...help, that is. Last night we rowed out to the ship with our Turkish friend and climbed on board and found you. We thought you were a Russian sailor who didn't want to go back home. It's as simple as that."

"So you saw the cloth…" A long sigh came from his chest. "It was the flag of desperation, you know."

"There are a lot of things I don't understand," I said, "among them being why you used Russian instead of English or something else."

"Yes. You are right to ask. When I wrote that I was very sick and weak. As I said, it was an act of desperation. We revert to first instincts when we are sick and desperate, my young friend. I reverted to my mother tongue, forgetting that Russia and I no longer speak the same language."

"Another thing I don't know," I continued, "is who are you? Russian sailors don't talk like you, even ones who've read Doestoevsky."

"Your experience with Russian sailors is profound?" He asked tartly.

"Look. I'm prepared to believe your country turns out smart sailors, so let's skip the dialectics. Let's just say that I don't think you know one end of an engine room from another."

He regarded me coolly, as though preparing a suitable riposte, and then appeared to change his mind. "Yes, you are right. I know very little about the engine room of a ship. Now that you know so much about me, permit me to ask a question. What do you plan to do with me? Where am I?"

"Exactly where you are is the caretaker's shack of the municipal cemetery of a town called Bebek about fifteen miles from Istanbul." I looked at him carefully, looking for some trace of surprise. "But you knew that already didn't you? I mean you knew Mehmet was a Turk."

"Mehmet? Ah, yes. The man who brought the soup. There are Turks in Yugoslavia, in Greece, in Albania, in Bulgaria. There are nearly forty million ethnic Turks in the Soviet Republics of Azerbaijan, Kazakhistan, Uzebekistan and others. So you see I could not be certain I am in Turkey. I thank you for the information."

The old man had a knack for gracious conversation. Immobile in plaster knee socks, dependent on us for protection, safety, food—name it—this didn't stop him from reaching out for a conversational target like a gifted fencer lunging for the heart. The crew on board that ship was probably swilling vodka in delight over his departure. I looked past the old man's shoulder to focus on Suzan's face; she was smiling contentedly, a charter member of the confraternity of teachers: nothing gives more pleasure than giving an upstart student a solid knee in the groin.

"You have answered my second question," he resumed. "I am in Istanbul. And the first?"

"Refresh my memory."

"What do you plan to do with me?"

"You need medical care. We're going to take you to a hospital so a doctor can look at your legs. You're a sick man. We can't keep you here. You understand that." I mouthed the words without conviction, waiting for him to interrupt, waiting for an outburst of hysteria or anger or relief. His face was impassive. After fifteen seconds he spoke. "There is plenty of sound in an empty barrel."

I think I knew what he meant without asking but Suzan responded instinctively, "What do you mean?"

He turned toward her slowly then back towards me. "It is a Russian proverb. You two...you are an empty barrel. You make much noise because you have nothing in you. You play at being heroes by getting me off that ship and then you turn coward. Do you think I don't know what it means, taking me to the hospital for medical treatment? Do you take me for a simpleton? An unidentified man is brought to the hospital with his legs bound in plaster; he speaks no Turkish; there is no one to say who he is because you...you have gone...you have performed the hero's deed of deserting me." His voice rose steadily as he talked; then he stopped, breathing hoarsely, refilling the well of bitterness that flowed from his lungs and voice box.

"So they call the police and inquiries are made. Ah, yes, the police say. We have been looking for him. The Soviet Consulate has reported that a vicious criminal wanted for child rape and murder escaped. We will take charge."

"That is what will happen isn't it? Taking me to a hospital is just another way of saying that you will put me back on that ship. You are all alike—Turks, Americans, all of you. No staying power. Quitters." He closed his eyes, exhausted by the effort of excoriating us.

"What do you want us to do?" His eyelids darted back. Slowly he turned his head to look at Suzan's downcast face, then he turned to me.

"Young woman," he called over his shoulder, "come where I can look at you. You ask who I am and I will tell you. Then you will help me." Suzan joined me against the wall of the shack and I felt the reassuring presence of her knees against my thigh.

"Who I am is a long story and you must listen carefully. Don't interrupt: just listen. Listen, try to understand, and believe." His voice rose for emphasis on the word believe and he pointed to the leather rectangle just out of reach of his fingers. "Hand me the wallet." Suzan passed it to him. He stroked the alligator skin of the wallet as though the sensation gave him tensile pleasure; it was large and folded like a book. Then he opened it on his outstretched thighs; he was a preacher and had opened the bible on the lectern before him.

"I am Academician V.I. Scherevsky. If you know anything about the history of the development of rocketry, then you know my name. I hold a higher place in scientific history than Konstantin Tsiolkovsky—though he deserved greater recognition—or Goddard or Oberth or Sanger or von Braun. It was I who designed the rocket engines that put Sputnik into orbit. Gagarin, Titov, Valentina Tereshkova, Nokilayev, Bykivsky, all made their trips into space thanks to the principles of rocket design that I perfected." He paused to let the information sink in.

"I hold every decoration the Soviet Union can give to a scientific man. There are Scherevsky Institutes throughout the Soviet Republics.

Everywhere the name V.I. Scherevsky is regarded as synonymous with achievement, with service to the socialist cause.

I am that same man. The man you see before you who pleads for your help.

"In 1955 an agreement was signed with the People's Republic of China for cooperation in the development of atomic weapons. The two great socialist peoples would work together to develop weapons so powerful that the imperialists would abandon their efforts to destroy the growth of socialism; efforts so impressive that other countries would perceive the wisdom of the socialist way to development.

"Two years later I was named a deputy director of the joint Institute for research at Dubna. I am not a nuclear physicist but everyone knew that nuclear weapons required delivery systems, and what could be better than using the rocket engines that I was then developing? I alternated my time between the space center, supervising preparations for Soviet space flights, and working and lecturing at Dubna. It was a good era. People such as Wang Kan-Chang were there. Do you know who he is? He is China's foremost atomic scientist. A great man. A great man. Trained in Germany and then we were colleagues at Dubna in the cause of socialist unity. Chien San-Chiang came also to study and lecture and join us in collective thinking. A gifted man, trained at the Laboratoire Curie at Paris.

"Later, in early 1960, I think, we had long visits from Tsien Hsue-Shen. Ah," he said, lost in his reverie, "what good times they were. He is my special friend, Tsien. You must know his name. He was famous in America until the government hounded him, falsely accused him of sending secret documents out of the country and then deported him. Sending secret documents out of the country! Imagine! A man with a master's degree at the Massachusetts Institute of Technology and a doctorate at the California Institute of Technology accused of pilfering documents." The old man nodded his head sadly. "The only documents he needs are those here…the documents he carries in that magnificent brain," and he tapped his temple for emphasis.

"Tsien and I talked at length of his years in the United States. At first he was trusted, even lionized. He was named director of the rocket section of the National Defense Scientific Advisory Board and he wrote reports that still guide America's views on how war will be fought in the air. Later, at the California Institute of Technology he was Goddard Professor of Jet Propulsion."

We listened in fascination, not daring to challenge or interrupt the flow of words.

"Tsien and I became very good friends. He loves classical music, you know, and his wife is a gifted musician. We sat up late many nights talking, thinking through theories of propulsion, and listening to the sound of fine music. Those were the good years, years of achievement and reward. Years that made me realize that the destiny of the world lay in the cooperation of our two peoples.

"Then that fool, Khrushchev," he fairly spat out the name, "ruined things with his suspicion and bombast. The beautiful edifice of scientific cooperation that we had built was destroyed by a clown posing as a politician. It all came so fast we didn't realize until too late what had happened. Who could believe that all the rhetoric could endanger our basic unity? Leave the talk to the politicians, we said; we are scientists; we have work to do. Then it was over. The Joint Center at Dubna was closed to Chinese scientists. Chien San-Chiang, Wang Kan-Chang, Tsien—all of them—they were hooted out of the country, forced to depart without their documents, wearing only the clothes on their backs, put in dirty trains without heat and sanitation, driven out of the country like so many pestilence-ridden peasants. Soviet Technicians were withdrawn from atomic reactors at Mukden, Ang-ang-chi, Peking, Wuhan, Shensi, Nahkai, from the gaseous diffusion plant at Lanchow that we scientists had begun together. Soon, the withdrawal was finished. Khrushchev had destroyed our dream of a true confraternity of science.

"It was a sad time for me after that. I tried to communicate with Tsien but there were no responses. I wrote letters to the Soviet government protesting its decisions but these went unanswered as well. Then, I was put on forced leave from Dubna and told that further access to Soviet scientific development was to be denied me until my views changed. I was deprived of laboratories, friends, new knowledge." He shook his head, seemingly oblivious to our presence, recalling a bad dream that had never ended.

"I aged ten years in one year. My wife died. Our great nation was in the doldrums. Cuba, bad crops, industrial production down, Russia obliged to import wheat from the Canadian imperialists! Shame! It was a time of shame, I tell you. Then came the second great October revolution; October 15, 1964 when Khrushchev was forced from power. I wept for joy and looked forward to his execution, but the new men proved to be spineless, afraid to execute a national enemy for fear that they will one day meet the same fate.

"A delegation came to see me not long after. Three men with long faces and long coats. They told me that I was to be given a chance for rehabilitation. I would be permitted to return to work at Akademgorodok, the city of science in Siberia. I could have spat at them! Permitted to return to work," he said witheringly. "I knew why they came. They came because the Soviet space program had slowed down since my departure. New dimensions of rocket thrust were required for deeper probes into space, for longer-range missiles, and only my genius could solve the problems they now encountered.

"But there had been a third great October revolution. You remember the day? October 16, 1964, the day that China set off its first atomic bomb at Lop Nor, Sinkiang. It was not much of a bomb, a yield of only twenty kilotons, but it worked. How Chien and Wang must have rejoiced at the reaction on Moscow! Outward calm, but deep in the heart of every man in the Kremlin was panic: seven hundred and fifty million Chinese across a hostile border now armed with atomic weapons.

"Knowledge of China's success guided me. "Yes," I said, I will go back to work; I acknowledge my duty to the Soviet Union: I see now that we are surrounded by enemies." The words grated on my throat but I said them. I went back to work, seemingly all penitent.

"Give me more soup," he commanded. I sat immobile for a moment, not quite grasping the request. "More soup," he said. "I am fatigued." I got up from the cement floor, my legs quivering slightly from the spell in a cramped position, and held the lip of the pot to his lips and let the thick liquid pour down his throat. He finished it and gestured to me to sit down again.

"So I went back to Akademgorodok and pretended to immerse myself in work. When my presence seemed natural again I let people know how distressed I was by the developments in China. Mao was a fool who sought to destroy us all. Russia must prepare for the inevitable. Seven hundred and fifty million Chinese to the east, eager to swarm over sacred Soviet soil. I mouthed all the foolishness expected of me. Word of my conversion reached Moscow and not long after I was invited to sit in on sessions of the Soviet Policy Planning Committee.

"You remember my telling you of panic in Moscow when China exploded its first atomic bomb? Outward calm but inward panic? I underestimated the degree of panic. The Policy Planning Committee was convened to consider the long-term threat posed by the Chinese nuclear weapons development program. Every bit of data available was assembled for consideration: sources in China itself, declarations by American authorities predicting the growth rate of the weapons program and delivery systems, reports from Hong-Kong, data and photos obtained from reconnaissance satellites. There were even photographs taken from American U-2 planes obtained by Soviet intelligence agents from people in the Pentagon, showing ten acres of roof area at the gaseous diffusion plant at Lanchow.

"They worried about everything, these policy planners. China was said to have outstanding claims on 500,000 square kilometers of Soviet territory; China wanted advantageous frontier rectifications in Siberia; control of Mongolia; control of Vladivostok; China maintained that the central Asian republics were more Chinese in character than Russian.

"And behind everything, a backdrop that made the shadow of fear loom larger; seven hundred and fifty million people destined to grow over a billion by the end of the century.

"Fear is the father of politics and our fearful leaders made their decision: they must prepare for preventive war against China and in the meantime make every effort to bring down Mao and his followers. That is the explanation of the troubles in China. Soviet agents. It is Soviet agents who have tried to turn Chinese against Chinese, to undo the great deeds the nation has achieved.

"I found myself almost believing those fools as they deliberated but I knew in my heart of hearts that they were wrong. China is a great nation; a friend to all mankind; an example of righteous and good deeds for all to follow.

"A target plan was drawn up which included elements of the anti-force strategy and the anti-cities strategy. I will explain. Anti-forces target plan include industrial, military and transportation targets such as the Sinkiang missile development center headed by my friend Tsien, the installations at Lop Nor, troop dispersal centers and others. Most important is the anti-cities strategy, since it is through this that the Chinese people and culture can be destroyed at minimum damage to the Soviet Union. Over half a billion Chinese live on one-fifth of the total land area. They live in or near cities such as Canton, Shangai, Nanking, Lanchow, Peking, Mukden, Harbin and Tientsin. Do you recognize these names?"

I nodded in agreement, trying to fix a map of China in my mind.

"These cities are all in the east or central part of China, most are far from the Soviet Union except for those near Vladivostok. The target plan calls for pinpoint bombing of these targets with one-megaton bombs carried by missiles and exploded high enough above the ground to minimize fallout so that radioactive debris would not drift west over the Soviet Union. That is why Vladivostok was considered relatively safe; it is to the east of the targets at Mukden and Harbin.

"One attack with a single launching of one hundred missiles would destroy much of China's population and industry, protecting Soviet security for the indefinite future. No Soviet soldier would invade the land; there would be no war. China would be destroyed and the world, especially the United States, would applaud.

"This is the ultimate plan. But the planners are fearful. What if the great mass of the Chinese people is not destroyed? What if five hundred million vengeful people survive and storm across the long frontier destroying everything in their path? What if the United States uses a Soviet attack as a pretext for an attack of its own? There are many imponderables.

"So they wait, the fearful men in the Kremlin. They wait hoping the United States will strike first; they encourage the Chinese to encourage wars of liberation everywhere, hoping to incite the Americans to preventive war; then the Soviet Union will pose as guardian of mankind to whom all other nations must rely to prevent destruction."

I finally found the courage to speak. "Then why are you here? Why aren't you in Washington or London or somewhere, telling what you know?"

He waved aside my question. "I have not finished. It will not end that way. No nation will destroy China. I will see to that." Suddenly he groaned, the first indication that we had had that he felt renewed pain from his legs.

"Put something under my knees to help the circulation in my legs." Suzan and I got up. She quickly located a pick handle and wrapped it in scraps of cloth; then we raised his knees carefully and slid the bolster beneath them.

"That is better," he said and prepared to resume his story.

"Do you know what Vesak day is? It is the day that half the human race celebrates the birth, enlightenment and death of Buddah, the Prince of Peace. In 1965, it fell on May 14, the same day that China exploded its second atomic bomb. Some people saw that as a crude blackmail threat to the countries of Asia but I know differently. To me, it was a message to the world that the Chinese bomb was an incarnation of Buddah; that it was destined to protect the peace.

"Some months after, a man came to my apartment door and left an envelope. I do not know who he was; I have never seen him since. Inside was a clipping from a Japanese newspaper called SANKEI with an English—not a Russian—translation. The clipping contained a quotation from an interview that Chou-En-lai gave the newspaper. I knew it by heart. 'The objective of China's nuclear tests is the elimination of nuclear weapons. China is striving toward total prohibition and abolition of all nuclear weapons. China will absolutely never be the first to use nuclear weapons under any circumstances or at any time.'

"Under the translation was a phrase. It said, 'The world awaits the new Vishnu and his son Krishna,' and under that the letter T. My heart skipped beats when I saw those few words. They were clearly from my friend Tsien, written in English for he had never bothered to learn Russian.

"And the message, that glorious message! I saw immediately that I was right about Vesak day and its meaning. You must understand the east to understand what I say. There are three names for God: Brahma, Vishnu and Siva. The creator of the world is Brahma, the preserver of the world is Vishnu, and the destroyer of the world is Siva.

"Vishnu, the preserver of the world, sent his will to the world through the words and deeds of mighty heroes. Krishna, the chariot driver of the great Prince was one of them; Buddha, the prophet of eastern Asia was another; he was the last of the heroes but followers of Vishnu believe that another will follow.

"When we were together at Dubna, Tsien called me Vishnu after my initials V.I.S. and said that because of my work in rocketry I was the modern spirit of Krishna the chariot driver. Don't you see? Tsien's note told me that I, the chariot driver, must reappear as Vishnu the preserver. I must come to China to help preserve the nation!"

He lay back again, the pink rims of his nostrils quivering as he sought to inhale energy from the air. His eyes were closed and I could make out the fine fabric of veins that crisscrossed the lids.

"You laugh behind your hands and think that I am mad. I know that even with my eyes closed. But you are wrong; I am quite sane. Only when China has weapons and rockets to match those of Russia and America will she be safe. There will be true peace when her enemies learn that she can respond in kind. Moscow and New York for Beijing; Kiev for Mukden; Chicago for Canton; San Francisco for Tsientsin. That is how peace comes. When your enemies tremble from knowledge of your strength. When a Chinese submarine can penetrate to the very mouth of San Francisco harbor, ready to launch missiles that will exterminate your Omahas and Denvers and Pittsburghs and all the rest. The certainty that China can destroy you too. That is the deterrent."

"And Tel Aviv for Cairo?" I interjected. "New Delhi for Karachi? Paris for Ottawa? Miami for Havana?"

He reopened his eyes to fix me with a hard, disapproving gaze. "That may one day come, but first China. China will protect all of Asia and the Asian people will never know fear again. Chou-en-lai has said it: China will never be the first to use a nuclear weapon. Can America say that, the country that laid waste to Nagasaki and Hiroshima?"

"Look around you! Russia is your proof. When the war was over we could not sleep nights for fear that American planes would come in the night to destroy our land. 'Eliminating potential aggressors,' you would have said. Not until Russia had her own arsenal of weapons and I designed delivery vehicles to carry them—only then did you have some reduction of tensions. Why? Because now we meet as equals on the nuclear chess board: each equal to the other. That is how it must be for China. It is peace I seek, I tell you. Peace."

He fumbled in his wallet that still lay open before him. "Look. I am not alone in this view." He handed me a folded newspaper clipping. It was from the New York Times and dated July 7, 1968:

EXPERTS SAY PEKING'S MISSILES
WILL THREATEN U.S. IN 4 YEARS

Stanford, Calif., July 7 (UPI)

A group of China experts has given the government a report predicting that four years from now China will be near construction of a missile system capable of threatening the United States.

China's attainment of the ability to wage intercontinental nuclear war paradoxically may head off an arms showdown with the United States, the report adds.

A team of researchers at the Hoover Institution on War, Revolution and Peace at Stanford University prepared the "high feasibility" scenario for the U.S Arms Control and Disarmament Agency. A draft of the report has been circulated among government officials.

Dr. Yuan-Li-wu, author of several books on the Chinese economy, headed the research team, which included a dozen other top-ranking authorities.

Taking a long-range look at China, the report also predicts that four years from now Mao Tse-tung will be losing control in China. A new, milder government is expected to be willing to discuss some international peace-keeping steps.

By 1972, the report says, China may be building a fleet of nuclear-armed submarines that could maintain threatening stations near Hawaii.

The power of China to wage nuclear war five to ten years from now, however, will improve the chances of limited arms-control agreements, in the view of the experts who provided the forecast.

Confident of their ability to hit U.S. cities, Chinese leaders will feel secure from U.S. attack, they said.

Their own widespread system of missiles and nuclear warheads will make Chinese leaders aware of the risk of "accidental " war, the experts said, and they will probably be willing to establish a Peking-Washington "hot line" or other measures to reduce the chance of an unintended nuclear encounter.

*   *   *

"You see," shouted Scherevsky at the top of his voice, brandishing the newspaper clipping, "even the imperialist warmongers in America and their tame newspapers know I am right. It is for peace that I work. Only through China's strength will there be arms control agreements. They are right and I intend to help prove them right! But it will come sooner than five or ten years. Soon Tsien and I will work together again as in the old days.

"These past years have been agony for me. I have wakened every day to the hope of some new message from Tsien but none came. I tried to fabricate reasons to leave the Soviet Union to attend international congresses but they always said, 'No you are too valuable at Akademgorodok.' So I languished. Vishnu was chained, waiting for release, and more years passed.

"Then, a month ago, I was finally designated to attend a congress in East Berlin. I slipped away from a plenary session and contacted the Albanian trade representative and told him I needed help. He arranged for me to fly to Albania, the only country to have relations with China. After that it was simple. There was a long, affectionate message from Tsien waiting for me in Tirana saying that a plane was on the way and I was very happy. He wished a pleasant trip to the greatest chariot driver of all. But then I was abducted by Soviet agents. The rest you know."

I think the long discourse drained me of as much energy as it had him. The strength of his convictions was hypnotically evident and I knew that every fiber of his being had been enraged in a long evangelical spasm to persuade us of the rightness of his cause.

"Now," he said. "Now you know all. Now you must help me."

"How?" Suzan asked.

"First you must send a telegram to China, to Tsien. Have you a paper?" I groped in my pants for a scrap of paper but Suzan located a note pad and pencil in her purse. "Dr. Tsien Hsue-Shen, Research Center, Lop Nor, Sinkiang, China. You notice I say only Research Center so the authorities here do not wonder. The text is simple, 'Vishnu is with me and awaits your help.' Sign the telegram with a name –any name—and a post office box. Soon someone will leave a message at the box.

"Until contact is made you must continue to feed and hide me. That is all. I offer you no material reward; only the knowledge that you will have helped the cause of peace by hiding me." He pointed a bony finger at Suzan. "Young woman. Do you agree? Your country had fought the Russians; will you help China resist?"

She didn't reply. "And you," he said, the words clearly intended for me, "will you help?"

"I don't know."

"You must decide. Soon. They are out searching now, I assure you."

"The people on board the ship?" I asked, a touch of disdain in my voice. "They'll never find you."

He shrugged. "If you will not help me you must promise to do something else. Take me out into the harbor and drop me over the side of your rowboat. I either live to complete my mission or I die. You have no right to torture an old man. It is an earnest plea I make; aid me or kill me."

I got slowly to my feet, trying to think of something convincing to say but all I could do was mumble "We'll have to think about it. We'll be back later."

"Soon," he repeated. "You must decide soon." He closed his eyes again and seemed to be about to drift off to sleep. "You agree. You know you agree."

We left, backing out deferentially, as if leaving royalty, and half-ran, half-walked down the slope to the Bosphorus.

"Suzan. I've got to eat." We were abreast of a little teahouse perched on a promontory of land that juts out into the water.

Suzan ordered a samovar of tea and a plate of simits and I ate noisily, using the respite to reminisce. Just five days before I had sat in the Immigration Office with a fast-thinking sleuth named Orhan Urfanli who fed me simits and tea to soften me up for the kill. In the intervening time I had signed on as chief slave to a Turkish-American sultana, been pilloried by Emily Cartwright, and helped rescue a Russian scientist who wanted to enhance the cause of peace by showing Mao and company how to drop hydrogen bombs on Moscow and Washington. Istanbul was turning out to be one long whirl of fun.

Suzan poured another cup of tea for me and held it six inches from my nose.

"What are we to do?" she asked

"You saw the cloth first. You decide."

"No," she said firmly.

"Well, I don't feel like killing anyone today, so that's out. We can't take him to the hospital because the police will come in and then the Russian Consulate will enter the picture. We could go to the American Consulate but they'll deny that the CIA even exists so that's out too. So maybe the only thing to do is send that telegram to Tsien just to see what happens. Besides, I can't wait to get that postcard Scherevsky will send us from Sinkiang."

"Postcard?"

"You know, the one that will say, Having wonderful time. 'Vishnu were here.'"

I did a little buck-and-wing with my feet under the table. Only ten-fifteen and already I was getting off gems like that!

Suzan started to laugh, softly at first then louder and louder. Soon we were both laughing hysterically and the waiter came to take away the samovar for fear we would knock it over or do something else dangerous.

CHAPTER TWENTY-THREE

Trying to decide what to do with a Russian rocket expert who wants you to hide him away for a few days and help get passage to China is no problem at all after simits and a samovar of tea, because they enable your intellect to attain pinnacles of achievement, clarity, and perspicacity beyond the reach of lesser men. Such men cannot define a problem while standing knee-deep in the Bosphorus, on a stone ledge encrusted with mussels that beg to be picked and baked in a wood fire. Or while leaping up to a tree branch to knock down spiky green horse chestnut burrs to throw at the windshield of the next taxi that passes. Or while balancing on one leg on the pyramidal peak of cement stanchion and then trying to tightrope walk the chain links to the next one. Other men can watch a great black-hulled sailing ketch cruise under power in the direction of the Black Sea and know that in six months they will buy one too; or mime in Italian to a passing freighter that has Genoa as home port; or pretend that a girl is in danger when a wake-generated wave breaks against the shoreline and draw her close to feel the response of her body. Yes, other men can do those things, but can they, simultaneously, be thinking deeply about what to do with a brilliant old man who passionately believed that he had a mission to save the world by increasing its capacity to destroy itself?

I doubt it. Even I, who faced the problem in what could be called an immediate way, was having trouble. The best solution was the one that appealed to me least: leave the old man to take over Peter Dawson's classes at the college and send me back to Tula for a stint in a Siberian reform school. I was just explaining this solution to Suzan, when she held up her hand.

"Listen" she stage whispered.

A shrill cascade of musical notes that wondered haphazardly up and down scale like a cat across a piano keyboard came from somewhere near by. The sound of the instrument providing the notes was familiar.

"Mehmet?" I asked.

"It sounds like his sweet potato but not like him."

"Maybe he sold his thirty-lira monster lobster and invested the profits in Turkish vodka."

"Not Mehmet," she corrected me. "Not without us."

The sound suddenly stopped without our having been able to pinpoint its origin.

Then it started again, a series of rambling notes but no music.

"Listen!" I shouted, holding up my hand and cupping it to my ear. "There. Over there in that clump of oleander bushes."

Suzan started in the direction where I pointed. "Mehmet," she called. "Mehmetcik. Where are you?"

A shape suddenly took form in the bushes, remained crouched for an instant and then a young boy darted out of the shadow at full speed. I raced after him; if that kid pinched Mehmet's sweet potato it was the worst mistake of his criminal career. Our mild-mannered lobsterman would cut him up into bait chunks.

The boy was fast and wiry but the end came when he did a two-step prior to darting across the Bosphorus road and a taxi blocked his path. I bent, circled his waist and lifted him up while he flailed with his feet trying to find a vulnerable target. He held his hand above his head to prevent me from reaching the sweet potato held by the mouthpiece in his dirt-brown fingers.

"Give it to me," Suzan ordered sternly in Turkish. She had caught up quickly and seemed not at all out of breath.

"No. It's mine," he yelled back, still kicking with his bare feet against my thighs and knees.

"Then why did you run?"

"I found it. I thought Mehmetcik had thrown it away."

"Put him down, Paul." I let the boy slide to the ground, still keeping a grip on his muscular young arm. With his free hand he passed the sweet potato to Suzan.

"So you knew it belonged to Mehmet the lobsterman," she said, a hint of accusation in her voice.

"Yes, honum efendi, but I thought he threw it away. May I be blinded in both eyes if it isn't true; may both my arms break off if I stole it."

"Then where did you get it?" The foot stomped impatiently.

"In the water, honum efendi. Wallahi, billahi, it's true. In the water."

"Where exactly in the water?" Suzan asked.

"I came to Bebek early, honum efendi. Ever since my father left home I get up early because my mother is irritable in the morning and because I sometimes find odd jobs to do. This morning Yusuf efendi—the man who sells watermelons from the green painted wagon—gave me half a melon to watch his wagon while he carried three melons up to a lady who lives on the fifth floor of the gray apartment house that has no elevator opposite the park." What this added up to was that the kid had a knack for detail and had made off with half a melon while poor Yusuf was saving the arches of the housewife on the fifth floor. I think he read my mind. "Half a melon is cheap for what I did, honum effendi. Otherwise everyone in the neighborhood would have emptied old Yusuf's wagon to the floor-boards while he delivered the melons."

The boy reached up to remove my hand from his arm before I cut off the circulation, endangering the flow of blood and talk. "So," he continued, "I took my half watermelon down to the stone pier near the old hulk they say used to be the Egyptian Embassy and the Six-Legged-Octopus. A friend came and I gave him a piece but I ate most.

"You know how it is with watermelon, honum effendi. A big slice of juicy watermelon and ten minutes later I have to make water. I am very embarrassed to make water in public, even against a wall or behind a bush, so my friend and I undressed and went in swimming in the harbor to make water there.

"I was lying on my back, making a little fountain of it, seeing how high it would go, when something touched me on the arm. First I thought it was a corn cob thrown in by someone who had bought an ear from one of the vendors who sell boiled corn in the big copper vats…"

"Can't you get this kid to hurry up?" I interrupted.

"Be patient. He hasn't had an audience like this in ages."

"So, I paid no attention. The water was warm where I made the fountain so I started to swim away and there it was! Mehmet's shepherd whistle. The magic one that he got in Korea that he used to pipe lobsters into his nets. I brought it back in to the shore. That's the truth, honum effendi, may there be worms in my bread if it isn't."

"If you knew it was Mehmet's why didn't you take it to him?"

"But I did, honum effendi! I went to his shack but there was no answer when I rapped on the door. Then I decided that he had thrown it away so I went up the Bosphorus to the clump of bushes to teach myself to play. If I can learn to play like Mehmetcik then I will be a rich lobsterman." He grinned happily, his story done with.

"Paul, give him fifty kurus." I gave the boy two coins and saw a light come into his eye that said he had decided to change choice of profession once again. We turned to go, puzzled by what the boy had said. Why would Mehmet let the sweet potato fall and drift away unnoticed?

"Oh, honum effendi," the boy called after us as we headed in the direction of Bebek, "I still think Mehmet was there when I rapped on the door to his shack. I heard voices inside."

∗   ∗   ∗

Blake tilted the wicker chair back against the outside deckhouse wall and placed his feet against the deck rail of the ferryboat. The early morning rush hour was passed and he would have a pleasant fifteen minutes to take a glass of tea while the crossing was made from Kandilli to Bebek.

"Cayci," he called to the white-jacketed man with spreading mustaches who stood framed in the entrance to the main cabin. "A glass of tea. A glass of fresh tea, not other people's leftovers. And make sure the glass is clean!"

He reached into his jacket pocket and withdrew a small notebook and a pencil stub. The tea will take a few minutes and there'll be just time to knock off a four-liner, he said to himself. I'll just ignore that bloody view for a few minutes and see if I still have the knack.

Some men use crossword puzzles to demonstrate their facility with words and warm up brain cells prior to arriving at the office for a day of familiar routine; others pit their wits against double crostics, jumbles, or puzzles. Blake rejected these as lacking in originality; one was responding to a device created by someone else; it was being one half of a walnut shell. What provided the real challenge was to create, to put together something that came from within and only from within. His special forte was four-line verse and the little book in his hand held dozens of examples.

He leafed through the pages, chuckling to himself, warming up to the task ahead by reading prize items from the past. Like:

> Old Venus was a gorgeous girl,
> But life for her was tough.

How can an armless sea-borne pearl

Smoke a cigarette puff-by-puff?

He felt ready. The mood was on. He tested the point of his pencil on his eyebrow and wrote:

William Edward Anthony Blake,

Late one night a risk did take.

By George! Not bad. Of course the first two lines were always the easiest. The real test was still to come. He frowned in anxiety, waiting for inspiration to fly in from the sea bringing words in her bent claws. Then he thought of the night before and the odd package borne by Nuri and Ahmet that looked like a mammoth birthday cake. Birthday cake! That was it. He wrote quickly.

He made a special birthday cake.

What rhymes with cake, he thought? Lake? Sake? Make? Let's try to make. The stub flew across the paper.

That would when eaten a great big sound make.

No, too awkward and a little too long. Spake? Shake? Wake? Wake! That was it. He wrote again.

To cause indigestion in Tula's wake.

Not bad, he mused. Let's see how it looks all together. That's the only way to judge a work of art:

William Edward Anthony Blake

Late one night a risk did take.

He made a special birthday cake

To cause indigestion in Tula's wake.

"Bloody good," he said aloud. "Bloody good! Scans like Wordsworth." Too bad there wasn't a bigger market for this sort of thing, he thought. Enough to make a man gnash his teeth, knowing that there's only room enough for one Ogden! He laughed cheerily. "And they say the English are stodgy and dull," he exclaimed. "Ah, if they only knew!"

The cayci arrived, bearing the tea glass with ceremonial dignity. Blake sipped his tea noisily, forming his lips into a funnel, letting the scalding liquid cause pain to his tongue and gums.

Bebek would be at hand in a few minutes and it would soon be time to get answers to some of the questions that had gone unanswered last night: Had something gone wrong on Tula? What caused the panic on deck? Was Scherevsky still on board?

Well, there were worse places to get answers than playing at being a little green lizard, lounging on a bench in Bebek Park. Bloody considerate of the Russkies to drop anchor in such surroundings.

*   *   *

It was just like very day when we drew up breathless at the bottom of the path before Mehmetcik's pier. The long, green rowboat with Mehmet, Bebek, and his special signature of the red lobster inscribed on the stern bobbed lazily in the water. On the far side of the pier three more rowboats were tethered in a row, waiting for customers to grasp the bulbous oars and make for the shallows by the lighthouse.

It was quiet. The door to the shack was closed.

"I'm frightened, Paul."

"Don't worry," I said, searching for words to disguise the fear that welled up like a gusher inside my chest. "He's probably sleeping."

We walked softly down the pier. I started as the door squeaked on its hinges under the pressure of my hand. A shaft of light followed us into the room from the open door. It was somber inside but light enough to see by. I glanced at Mehmet's bed. Empty.

"Look," Suzan said and her hand grasped my wrist.

The trapdoor leading to the lobster cage below was set back. I kicked it back.

The wire cage had never been so full. Great green shapes writhed in the dark water, their claws pushing one another aside; they crawled over a long, still figure who lay face up in the water, neck turned awkwardly, an ear almost touching his shoulder.

"Mehmet," I gasped.

There would be no reply to that cry, now or ever. Only a few days before I had wished him the same fate as the lobster that danced on my chest from a string: a quick and early death. I had my wish. The eyes that stared up were fixed in a look of ineluctable pain that came at the moment when someone had bent that strong, column-like neck to the point of breaking.

"Mehmet," she cried and began to sob. "Mehmetcik, Mehmetcik."

No war stories from Korea now. No more piping on the sweet potato, luring the lobsters into the funneled baskets that lay expectant in the deep channels of the night. No more eager lovers to push into the currents, aiding them on the short voyage to rapture offshore.

And I had never let him tell me his stories. Oh God, Oh God. What had we done to this man who stood straight while lame, who lived to help? I felt my legs start to collapse under me.

The door creaked behind us and I started to turn but strong hands with the strength of steel claws pinned my arms against me. Other hands held Suzan upright, preventing her from dropping to the floor to cry out her grief.

A voice spoke behind me, further back than the body belonging to the living vise that held me.

"Foolish children. You play at games that end in death." The voice spoke again in a language I didn't understand and we were propped up on the wooden chairs that flanked Mehmet's all-purpose table. I looked around; trying to see through the tears of grief, fear and pain that trickled from my eyes. A great, tall man with a barrel chest and arms as thick as a young oak stood above me, looking down from a face that was built of slabs of flesh and bone. Next to Suzan was a smaller man, younger, with pinched cheeks and flared nostrils. His hand was atop her shoulder, pinching the long muscle that grows from the head to the shoulder.

"Foolish children." I looked in the direction where the voice came from and saw a middle-aged man with a round face and a short, blobbed nose beneath a sparse growth of gray hair. His body was of a piece with his face, round and formless, defined only by a white open-necked shirt and the belt that supported his pants. He carried a suit-jacket over his arm.

"It is your fault," he said, "this," and he gestured toward the trapdoor. "All your fault. You meddle in things that are not your concern and now you pay the price."

I felt my jaw wag but words wouldn't come.

"I am sorry about your friend," the voice continued. "It was not my intention to kill him but he wouldn't tell us where you hid our man. We asked him over and over again but he wouldn't tell us. The big man is from Kazakhstan where the people talk Turkish. He tried to persuade him.

"Then your friend did something as foolish as what you did last night. He spat in the face of the man from Kazakhstan and before I could do anything he broke his neck. I am sorry. I truly am. I do not like violence."

Something akin to normalcy began to come back to me. The short round man talked evenly, slowly, with conviction, but he had killed our Mehmet.

"You are a killer," I said.

"No. *You* are the killers. You invite death and when death comes you cry 'murder'. If your friend had only talked there would have been no trouble."

"Who are you?"

"A man doing his duty. My duty is to find the man you took off that ship in the harbor last night."

"I don't know what you are talking about."

He lifted the jacket from his arm and held it by the neck; then he groped in a side pocket and took out a small case of dark plastic or celluloid. He put the jacket on the table and pressed a red button on the side of the case. It opened to form a small tent; then joined the sides with a third plane that was convex and clear.

"I will not waste valuable time persuading you with words," he said. "Look at this." He pressed a white button and a light flashed on in the portable side viewer. I looked sideways at Suzan; she was still weeping softly, seemingly oblivious to our dialogue.

I looked into the viewing lens and saw Suzan prone on the forepeak of Mehmetcik's rowboat. Her naked flesh showed tan and red and even with the minimal magnifying effect of the viewer I could make out the Cyrillic letters on her back and the red lobster painted on the rowboat. My words to Suzan just two hours before stabbed like a needle into my consciousness: 'We got away with it; another hour and we'll have this guy off our hands'.

I handed back the viewer. "Well?"

"Let us not waste time. You know that I know about last night. Now tell me where he is."

"Why? He's an old man. He doesn't want to go back to Russia."

The man before me looked into the faces of his two companions; their faces were impassive.

"The others with me do not speak English. I will speak frankly. The man you took from the boat is a dangerous man, an evil man. He is capable of causing much trouble. He must go back to the Soviet Union where he belongs."

"I don't agree."

"You do not have the right to agree or not agree! What I tell you is so. He is an evil man."

"That depends on your viewpoint," I said. The man's mild manner invited rebuttal.

"I told you before I am a man doing his duty. My duty is to return this man to my ship for transport to the Soviet Union. I will do my duty."

"Duty before life?" I taunted.

"Duty *is* my life."

"No dice." I said.

"No what?"

"Nothing doing. The old man stays here. He doesn't want to go with you. He shouldn't be made to go with you."

"Young man. I did not ask for this assignment. I do not like this assignment. You know the parable of the shepherd and the lost sheep? I was made a shepherd of a certain man who is a danger to the Soviet Union. The man has strayed from my custody and now I must find him. The lost sheep is more important than the flock."

"And if you don't?"

"Then my life is at stake, as well as other lives. Perhaps millions of lives."

I made one more effort. "Why don't you follow his example and stay here too?"

He drew up stiffly and for a moment I thought he would strike me, then he relaxed and a look of melancholy crossed his face. "I am a Russian. Not a traitor."

"He's a Russian and he wants to stay," I argued.

"He is a traitor. A man who betrays his country is a traitor. A man who fails his country is a traitor. I will not fail."

"So you kill us both," I said. "We're dead and you still haven't found him."

"Believe me," he said, placing his palms flat on the tabletop so that he could bend lower and look intently into my eyes, "I do not want to kill you. I have never killed a man. Even in the war when the Germans seized my city of Odessa I never killed. But I must have that man." I stole a glance at Suzan as he spoke; her composure seemed to have returned and she was following the word play intently. I thought I saw her move her head in negation.

"No," I said. "You will have to find him yourself."

The man drew back from his resting stance on the table. "Very well; there are three ways we can solve this. First, you can take me to him and when I have him you will go free unharmed. That is what I implore you to do and quickly. Even now the men with me must be wondering why we talk so long instead of my letting them persuade you differently.

"The second way is for me to tell the big man to kill you slowly, hoping that the girl will talk. But the girl may think you would rather die and she is a Turk and they are tough, so you may be dead before she decides to speak. It is even possible that she would then prefer to die herself, having let you die.

"The third way is the way I will be forced to choose if you do not help. I will tell the big man to wad a cloth into the girl's mouth so that she cannot cry out. Then he will place those great, strong hands around her throat and press hard against her voice box with the tips of his fingers. The pain that will show in her face is incredible. It is a special kind of pain that you have never known. It will continue for as long as necessary because the voice box is strong and will not rupture until I tell him to increase the pressure. She will not be able to call out to tell you to say the truth. That is something you must decide for yourself. And as you watch her, her body rigid with pain, you will talk but she will be crippled for life."

He spoke rapidly to the brute man from Kazakhstan who jumped to his bidding, anticipation written on his face.

"No! I cried. "Wait." Let Suzan suffer for the sake of a desiccated old man who dreamed of being a latter-day deliverer? Watch the anguish jolt her eyes like ten thousand volts of electricity thrust into her body? Sit silent while the voice that had soothed and caressed me was made mute while all I had to do was talk?

"All right," I said wearily. "I'll take you to him."

I looked at Suzan, trying to divine from her expression how she felt. Was she relieved that I had spared her? Disappointed because I had broken before the test of pain began? Her eyes were lowered, fixed on the gaping black hole where Mehmetcik lay. He hadn't spoken and now the lobsters took revenge on their tormentor, clawing at his ears, thrusting antennae into widespread nostrils, probing at the cloth that shielded his body.

"Good. You have decided wisely. Can we walk there?"

"No," I said. "It is quite far." I hadn't the strength to go that last half-mile on foot.

"Then we will take a taxi. The man who speaks Turkish will precede us a few paces and we will follow and get in when he comes with the car. If you say anything or do anything that causes alarm I will shoot the driver also and another innocent life will be on your hands. Remember that."

He ordered us to our feet and we stood, rocking back and forth on the wooden floor of the shack, as if with the movement of the sea. Then we were in a small tight cordon of watchful men who brushed aside the low hanging branches and the sumptuous shrubbery that bordered the path we knew so well to let us pass. The big man hurried ahead to summon a taxi.

*   *   *

"Those blokes are Russkies or I don't know an ill-cut suit when I see one," Blake whispered to himself as the little knot of four men and the girl stepped into the open area of the Bebek Park, heading toward the taxi rank that bordered the road. He held his position of insouciant indifference, careful not to arouse suspicion by a sudden action that would alert the group to his presence.

"Three Russkies in Bebek Park with that nice little Turkish piece I saw yesterday. And the low-class American," he murmured the words softly, his lips barely moving. "I think I'll just mosey over and have a look. Doesn't look like a very cozy group."

He walked parallel and to the rear of them, affecting a casual manner, pausing occasionally to consult a blade of grass or examine the pattern made by a tall shade tree. Soon he was no more than five paces away, leaning against the steel shelter that served the adjacent bus stop. A taxi pulled up to the group paced by an enormous man who he judged was of Central Asian extraction. The youngest of the three men went to the far side of the car and got in. Then the nearside door of the car was opened to let the girl, followed by the American, enter. Finally, a pudgy man forced his way into the back seat, grunting as he went.

Satisfied that all was in order, the giant who stood near the driver crossed in front of the car and got into the front seat.

Blake eased himself away from the shelter and walked slowly to the next cab in the queue and spoke. "Follow that taxi just ahead. Imagine my friends going off and leaving me like that!"

He settled back in the seat. "Something is up all right," he murmured. "The fat one was carrying a gun. I think I'm on to something."

We had bent low to avoid the whiplash of a branch when she whispered, "Paul. Remember Mehmet." Her voice was low, barely audible, but the sound was enough to make the round-faced man turn from his efforts to warn us to be silent.

Then we were in the park with barely fifty yards of macadamed path to traverse to the taxi stand. "Remember Mehmet," she had said. "Remember Mehmet". I needed no admonition to recall those lusterless eyes that could not blink to keep out the salt of the sea; the close-cropped head that bobbed loosely on a neck transformed from muscle and bone and cartilage into a length of rubber. Remember Mehmet! I remembered too much, that was the trouble: the sailor who lay on the ship's deck, blood flowing over his eyes and hollow cheeks into a gaping mouth; an old pain-wrecked man who pleaded—no, ordered— us to help on a mission whose purposes defied understanding; a young girl who whispered words whose meaning I could not entirely comprehend; a Russian who alternated between promises of leniency and threats of pain.

The taxi drew abreast of us and another voice, this time rich with accent and special meaning, spoke into my ear. "The third way, my young friend. Remember the third way." Suzan got into the taxi, seeking to recoil from the enforced touch of the slender man who entered from the other side. I felt the length of her body against mine and a slim hand slip under mine.

Perhaps there were more doors in this secret cavern of destiny that we had never before explored. We could try them; try them all until the final dead end.

I turned to the man beside me. "Do you know where the Covered Bazaar is located in Old Istanbul? We took him there last night to the shop of a friend. He is there, the man you seek." My voice sounded unfamiliar, as if it had been piped into my throat by some external power.

"I do not believe you."

"He is there. In the old bazaar. In the back room of a shop belonging to a man called Abdullah who sells antiquities."

"I hope for your sake...for all our sakes...that you are telling the truth."

I licked my lips. The talent for lies had not atrophied. The facile ability to look humble and solemn and utter preposterous untruths was just beneath the surface waiting for the real Paul Adams to abandon the masquerade of re-birth on which he had embarked. "It is the truth," I repeated. "You promise not to hurt the girl?"

"Young woman," the Russian said quietly. "Give the driver instructions in Turkish. Be careful. You will be understood by the man in the front seat. A false word and the driver dies."

Suzan leaned forward and gave directions in Turkish. Her voice was even and her pace slow so that I would understand also. We were destined for the Nurosmaniye Mosque; just behind the courtyard of the mosque was the upper entrance to the Bazaar. The driver sang out assent, delighted at the prospect of a long run down the Bosphorus road, the cheerful chit-chit-chit of the meter, the prospect of careening around the s-turn at Dohlmabache Palace, turning the car on two wheels.

Deep in the maze of the Bazaar, in that labyrinth of alleys, dead end nooks, festooned shops, teahouses redolent of India and the Archipelago, cajoling hawkers, gawking tourists, fetid toilets and playing fountains we would have to take our chances. Instinct alone would guide us; instinct and the telepathic union that makes it possible for two people to understand one another when nothing is spoken.

The taxi made a U-turn and headed toward Istanbul. The fingers of a slim hand entwined themselves in mine and a message of hope was passed.

The man beside me seemed entranced by the panorama of sight and sound that passed before us. He began to hum softly to himself and a trace of a smile crossed his face as he reached a particularly melodic passage. I studied his profile: nondescript, revealing no special vices except that associated with the inability to balance the intake of food with the outflow of energy. The lines near his eyes spoke of laughter and sunshine; the gray eyes were puffy with fatigue but intelligent and sincere. I had gotten a taste of their sincerity when he spoke with sorrow of Mehmet's death and later when he spoke of what would happen to Suzan if I failed to reveal the old sailor's whereabouts. Old sailor, I thought to myself? It was no longer possible to think of him as that. What was he? Old scientist? Savior? Madman? Possessor of unique wisdom?

"What is your name?" The man next to me asked.

"Adams. Paul Adams."

"I am Leonid Orenko. The girl?"

"Suzan Lokman," I replied.

"A pretty name. I have a daughter her age. Tanya. Tanya is a prettier name than Suzan, but Suzan is a prettier girl than Tanya." He chuckled. "A girl who has a father that looks like me can't expect to be pretty. I have a son, too, but he is younger than you. Leonid, after his father."

"Prettier than me?" I asked.

"He is a good boy," the Russian answered, avoiding a direct response. "He gave me two grandchildren. We understand one another." He eased forward in the cramped seat. "Excuse me," he grunted, reaching into his jacket pocket, "this bruises me." He withdrew the plastic viewer and slipped it into his shirt pocket.

"Where did you get it? The picture?"

"When you are as old as I am you have forgotten that there is such a thing as good luck. Things happen; things don't happen. But good fortune? Never. Good fortune is what you plan for. That is what I always thought. But this," he gestured with the viewer, "this is good fortune."

"I sail and am away from home much. My work is with photography...I won't explain how...and like all work it can be dull so I make the time pass by taking pictures that have nothing to do with my work. Sometimes I stand on the deck of the ship and there comes into view a pretty girl on a beach, or on the deck of a passing ship. Then I take her photo and put it away in a small box in my cabin. Some day I will give the box to my son Leonid. We don't have much to give to our children in the Soviet Union except love and faith and he will know that my box is a way of saying I love him because I am a man and he is a man.

"The young woman will be embarrassed, but I was standing on Tula's deck just as she removed a portion of her swimming suit. I didn't have my cameras so I ran to my cabin and when I returned her back was to me and I took that picture...and others.

"Later, when Scherevsky was abducted, I saw the cloth he had hung from the porthole and thought of a back streaked in red. After that..." he shrugged expressively.

"So you traced us to the cookie who seeks his fortune in China."

"I don't understand," he said, a frown crossing his face. "My English is good but…"

"Don't worry, Mr. Orenko. I don't understand either."

"You acted alone, you two? That is correct isn't it?" His tone seemed to anticipate that we would agree.

"Yes. Only there were three of us, not two."

"Of course. I tell you again I am sorry about your friend. But I am glad it is a matter of people, not governments. People can understand one another when governments cannot. People can do things together that governments cannot." His words brought back Suzan's argument to me: we're not nations; we're people; people do things that governments won't. Could she and the Russians be pressing the same case?

"The man you are hiding," Orenko resumed, "loves knowledge but hates people. He wants to help China build rockets to drop on the Russian people. Do you know what he told me? He said he wanted to build rockets to drop on Moscow! Can you help a man do that?"

"Just a few years ago you built rockets to drop on New York," I rejoined. "What's the difference? Are the Russian people different than other people?"

He paused for a moment before replying. "That is a difficult question. I could say, 'No. The Russian people are just like any other people,' but deep in my heart I know it is not so. The Russian people are *my* people, whatever their follies and sins; I cannot help a man destroy *my* people.

"Listen to me, Adams. Scherevsky tells me…he tells you…that he builds rockets to destroy America too? Do we make a better world by helping everyone to destroy everyone else? Do you Americans put a gun in every citizen's hands thinking that if only there are enough guns all will be afraid to shoot? We must stop somewhere, I tell you! The killing must stop." He leaned his head against the door column and wiped his forehead on his shirtsleeve.

Suzan spoke. "So you stop the killing by breaking Mehmet's neck."

"I told you I regret that. But you must admit he is unimportant. One Turkish lobsterman is not important when millions of lives are at stake."

I knew then that my wavering was over. Scherevsky no longer mattered; in the scales of our personal decision-making, Mehmet outweighed all else. I felt a twinge of pity for the Russian. We were so close, yet so distant.

"Have you ever been to Odessa?" Orenko spoke again but now his tone was lighter.

"No."

"It is not a beautiful city but it has life. You should come there some day. Six years from now, when I am sixty, I will retire there and live in a little cottage above the city that the government will give me as a reward for hard work and many years at sea."

"I understand," I said. "No Scherevsky, no cottage. Is that it?"

"Yes. Yes, that is it. I am a very ordinary man. I want that cottage above all else."

We lapsed into silence. This sincere man, this man who reeked of conviction and simplicity, had let Mehmet die, would maim Suzan, and punish Scherevsky for the sake of his cottage. Was he so wrong? Does a man have the right to do anything in the name of duty?

I had lost all trace of geography during our dialogue; now the shrill whoop-whoop-whoop of the incoming and departing ferry boats told me we were crossing the Galata Bridge, the great floating span that crossed the Golden Horn and debouched into old Istanbul. Just ahead loomed the great New Mosque and from the point where the bridge reaches the peak of its upward arc I felt we would catapult into the mosque's vaulted interior. We made a succession of turns and entered a cobbled road where bumper-to-bumper traffic inched its way upward. Could we make a jump for it here? No, I quickly decided. We were penned in. A false move now would make the Russians suspicious. Our long dialogue had seemed to lull him into a sense of brotherhood. Best to let that last as long as possible.

I looked at my watch. Twelve o'clock. The Bazaar would be swarming with people now, people who might shelter us in a garment of confusion and panic when the time came. The taxi threaded its way down a street lined with tourist buses and halted at a mammoth gate set in a stone arch. Inside was the walled plaza surrounding the Nurosmaniye Mosque and beyond it the entrance to the Bazaar.

We were half way across the plaza, Orenko to my right, the brute from Kazakhistan at Suzan's left, the slimmer man behind us, when Orenko signaled us to stop.

"Before we go in," he said, "I am obliged to show you a curiosity we have brought with us." He talked swiftly in Russian and the men gathered close in the manner of a group of tourists consulting a map. "I must warn you not to do anything foolish in that crowded place. The big man here will now show you something." There was what looked like a piece of ridged metal in his hand, about six inches long with a button on the side at the end of a slot. He pressed the button and the blade appeared, so quickly that I hardly caught the movement. Then he pressed the button back along the slot compressing a spring within until the blade disappeared. "It is not necessary to demonstrate it again," Orenko said. "That is a lethal weapon, so swift it cannot be avoided. It will be held firmly against the young woman's kidney every movement of the time; until we reach the place where Scherevsky is hidden, until you help us remove him from the Bazaar, until we put him in a taxi and take him back to Bebek. One wrong move and the man will press the button. I do not like to kill but he does not mind."

"You needn't worry," I said, trying to reassure him into letting the guard relax one iota, "we'll behave. You won't need that thing."

"The decision is yours," Orenko replied solemnly. "All yours."

We started forward again. I turned my head slightly. The big sailor was keeping careful pace with Suzan's movements to avoid the danger of a sudden dash that could put her out of range of his weapon. He walked very close, his right hand pressed against her body, his left hand firmly enclosing the upper part of her left arm. With the strength at his disposal she would have no chance to wrestle free before that double-edged blade found its mark.

We were in the tunnel of glitter and opulence that is the gold merchants' enclave in the great bazaar. Gold in every form: ingots to hoard under floor boards as counter to the fear of inflation; coins to let dangle from bracelets, and necklaces to cherish in the velvet beds of a numismatist's collection, gold powder to sift into tubes of cloth or plastic and cache beneath the lining of a suitcase or slip into a gasoline tank to cross a suspicious frontier. And jewelry too delicious to describe worked by artisans in the recesses behind the shops. In days past, Janice had often lured me there to cry in ecstasy before each window; sharp, clear cries that brought the shirt-sleeved owners out from shadowy interiors, their eyes as alert and wise as the screech owls that patrol Istanbul's night skies.

I sought to keep a slow pace. When the time came to act I wanted whatever advantage lay in a burst of unaccustomed speed. We passed the last of the gold merchants' shops and made a sharp left turn into the first of the broad, main, covered thoroughfares that constitute the principal routes through the Bazaar. It was years since I had walked these vaulted ways but they had changed little except for a greater abundance of goods. The tiny shops seemed smaller, possibly because of the crush of goods within. A youngster of about ten blocked my path, a leather jacket draped over his arm, and told me in good English that it was just my size. I took a moment to let my fingers linger over the soft leather, wishing there was nothing more serious on my mind than contemplation of a jacket I could not afford.

The brute sailor let go an exclamation of surprise as two hamals passed, bent low under the weight of a pipe load of leather coats that swung pendulum-like on thick wooden hangers. Had he never seen

anything like this before? In all of Tula's travels was this his first exposure to opulence, even on the Turkish scale?

I looked toward Orenko. He was transfixed by the panorama, hardly
looking at me. Soon, I thought. Soon.

"Paul, you missed the turn." She stopped short and quickly repeated
herself in Turkish so the sailor from Kazakhstan would understand and
not press that lethal button. I looked about, not sure of my whereabouts.
Then she pointed to a wooden arrow hanging suspended from the
vaulted ceiling that said in Turkish, French, German and English. "To
the Covered Bazaar."

We turned, our escorts careful not to lose their positions.

"Wouldn't you like to buy some souvenirs?" I said to Orenko.
"Something for Tanya or Leonid?"

"You remember their names!" He exclaimed.

"How about something for the grandchildren?" I pressed. Just
seventy-five yards away was the entrance to the Old Bazaar. Reckoning
time would soon be at hand and I wanted to find some way to delay our
passage; some why to divert attention so that Suzan and I might flee.

"No. I mean I would like to, but no. Some other time. When Tula is
next in Istanbul I will call you and we will come here together." I felt a
new twinge of uneasiness; this man wanted to be my friend; when this
was over he would invite me to Odessa to meet his children and grandchildren. "People can do things together that governments cannot."

Another arrow signaled a turning to the left. I looked at Suzan still
held in the secure grip of the man from Kazakhstan. Would they kill her
immediately, once they found that this was a wild goose chase? Press
the button and let the steel lodge in her kidney? The brute could hold
her erect with one hand while the other hand propelled her body
forward, the blade rooted deep inside, until they found a niche filled
with debris and quickly add her to it. Afterward they would lead me
out, a tame white mouse, and bruise me in exotic ways, not letting me
talk for fear I would interrupt the pleasure.

Thirty yards more to the entrance.

"Have you been here before?" I asked Orenko. Without letting him reply I continued. This is the oldest part of the Bazaar. It was built in 1461 at the order of Mehmet the Conqueror, the man who took Constantinople. It's been ravaged by fire a few times but it's basically the same as five hundred years ago.

"The right hand side—the part over there—is mostly assigned to antiquities shops. You see that one, just beyond the blue and white sign? They make their own antiques but you can't tell them from the real thing."

"I must ask you to hurry," the man beside me said.

"We are almost there," I replied louder than was necessary, hoping that Suzan would understand. "Just ahead, where the copper shop makes a corner. There. That's where he is. On a cot in the owner's office."

We advanced down the crowded passageway and I felt my throat constrict from anxiety. The shop ahead was aglow with a pageant of beaten copper trays; burnished brass horses set on standards of oak; latticed lamps that hung from the cross beams, blue bulbs inside casting a pattern of light; great mangal heaters that sat on fat haunches like indulgent women; swan-necked water pitchers. Three squat brass kettles, their bottoms sheathed in lead, hung from the cross beams on chains of iron links.

Orenko was to my right, Suzan to my left, the brute sailor beside her, his face in profile to me. I stepped up to the raised wooden floor of the shop. Orenko followed but the giant held back to avoid pushing into the crowded quarters.

"Abdullah!" I cried loudly into the surprised face of the man standing aside a hanging water kettle, my hands raised in greeting. Then I pivoted and pushed down against the kettle with all my strength, praying that the sailor would not have time to react. It made a swift pendulum movement and struck him on the temple and Suzan broke from his grasp a second before the blade darted from its metal sheath. I pushed against the chest of the startled Orenko, sending him enough off balance to prevent him from reaching for his gun.

The third sailor grabbed Suzan again by the shoulders but I bent a long pitcher double over his head as the hapless proprietor of the copper shop wailed in protest.

Then we were gone, wriggling down the narrow alleyways, searching for the nearest of the six exits that feed traffic in and out of the Old Bazaar.

"You lead," I cried. "You know this place better than I do." I looked back. Orenko and the two sailors were already only twenty yards behind, the big brute apparently no worse for the encounter with the brass pot. I felt a hot flash of anxiety in my abdomen and the inexplicable calm that had come over me since entering the bazaar dissipated. This was it! This was no child's play. There would be no second chance with the mild-mannered Russian.

You can move just so fast through the jumble of lanes and counter lanes that is the Istanbul Bazaar. Street hawkers, tea vendors, water sellers, pregnant women, mendicants, cameras on tripods—all and more barred our way and we danced and skipped through the maze, seemingly intent on nothing more serious than running from the local truant officer. The yards passed with numbing slowness. I looked back: we were neither gaining nor losing on the determined trio behind us. Orenko's girth might cause him to wilt from the pace but the other men could go on indefinitely and I preferred to be caught in the company of their leader.

A hand reached out to grip my arm and I looked into the stern face of a policeman. He pointed to a sign above that said "Walking, No Running" in Turkish and gestured with his hands to show that I was going too fast. I turned to see Suzan disappear in the crowd ahead. The three Russians were no more than five yards behind me they had witnessed my encounter and had slowed to a walk to avoid a like delay.

The policeman gave me an abrupt salute and waved me on. I glanced back again and fairly howled with joy as a hamal bearing a load of aluminum pipe cried the Turkish version of "Gangway!" And all traffic stopped to let him pass in deference to the great burden he carried. The three men were momentarily penned behind a wall of humanity and I picked up twenty yards on them. But Suzan was nowhere to be seen.

I looked about frantically, trying to discover some familiar store or sign or face in the moving sea of lights and people. Then I looked up; four square rays of sunlight formed their passage through a high, barred window made a pattern on the grimy wall of the passageway; beneath them was an arrow marked exit. I turned and picked up speed again, hoping that there would be no additional policeman to bar my path before I reached the stone archway that delineated the bazaar from the surrounding city.

Four streets branched off in spokes from the exit. Which one had she taken? A voice called my name and I looked about, losing precious time. Then a patch of yellow showed against an unlit street lamp down the second street and I ran again toward her.

"Go. Go." I called. "Don't wait."

She raced down the cobbled street that began to slope steeply in descent. I tried to make a map in my mind that would tell me where she was heading but all I could be certain of was that we were going down, down toward the port, down toward the Golden Horn and the Galata Bridge. My breath was coming hard now and searing pain followed searing pain in my lungs. Don't look back, I told myself; looking back brings fear and loss of balance. Run. Run. Run.

I caught up with her where the cobbled road joined the asphalt thoroughfare that is Istanbul's "Fleet Street", lined with newspaper and publishing offices. We were just two hundred yards from the New Mosque.

"Where are we going?" I cried hoarsely.

"The bridge."

"They'll catch us for sure there". I dared look back on the smooth surface of the asphalt. They had lost on us on the downhill run but were still within fifty yards.

"Paul. Listen," she gasped. "We'll run for the elevated passageway that passes over the traffic to the bridge. Take the left side of the bridge. Then follow me."

I wanted desperately to have details but the exertion of speaking while running seemed to slow her down. We were even with the back of the Mosque now, another hundred yards to the bridge! Then we were starting up the steps to the pedestrian passageway over the snarled traffic below. "What time is it?" she called.

"Twelve-thirty. No. Twenty-eight."

"Hurry. The twelve-thirty boat to Buyukada."

I saw her intention. Island-bound ferryboats leave from the quays made of the floating pontoons that support the Galata Bridge. If we made the imminent sailing and the Russians did not, we could hope for temporary refuge. We were going down the steps that forked left on the far side of the passageway and led to the broad sidewalk flanking the bridge.

"Why this side?" I shouted. "Boat's on other side."

"Follow me." We had advanced up the bridge about forty yards when she suddenly pivoted to the left and appeared to jump over the side. I followed and saw a narrow stairway that led down abruptly to the mammoth pontoon below. A deep-throated "Whoop-whoop-whoop" vibrated in our ears as the ferry signaled for the last of the passengers to board. At the bottom of the stair she turned right to cross under the bridge, hoping by the maneuver to throw our pursuers off and make them lose time, but it was costing us time too.

She was three steps ahead of me. I could make out the figures of the longshoreman undoing the hawsers but the boat was still steady against the dock. We were going to make it! I saw a yellow figure slip sideways through the mammoth gates of the entranceway that had begun to slide inexorably on their rollers across the greased belt of steel. My legs felt like jelly under me. No, I couldn't make it! I couldn't make it! The gates slammed shut before me. I grasped the iron bars trying to shake them open. It was over.

I looked back. The Russians had only briefly been thrown off by our ruse and were closing hard. The ferry gave another "whoop-whoop-WHOOP" and the pontoon creaked under my feet as the bow drifted out and the stern ricocheted against the quay. I looked around. A man was coming down the quay parallel to the barrier, leading a donkey hauling enormous wicker baskets filled with watermelons. With one last convulsive burst of effort I jumped onto the donkey's back and vaulted upward to grasp the spiked perpendicular bars; the same momentum carried my body high enough so that I could reach a horizontal cross bar with my right foot. I hung there a moment, unable to move, then hurled myself up and over the bars and plummeted down the other side, landing on all fours.

The attendant inside the gate shouted his outrage as I shook off the effects of the ten-foot fall to the pier. The ferry was two feet from the dock now and out over the white, bubbling water the gap grew with every second. I sprinted down the pier and jumped. I won't make it. I won't make it; the words beat a staccato refrain in my mind.

Then I was down in a great coil made of inch-think hemp that bruised my shins as I landed. Someone was caressing my forehead and murmuring and there were distant cries of "Cay, Cay", and the caw-caw of sea larks and a triumphant blast of the ship's horn as the waters passed beneath the bow. A stranger patted my shoulder in admiration of my exploit; other hands raised me to my feet and I leaned against a girl in a sheer lemon-colored blouse whose hair smelled sweet and whose voice said, "Paul. Paul. My Paul."

CHAPTER TWENTY-FOUR

We were seated in wicker chairs on the broad, empty expanse of the open top deck of the ferryboat. The sea was white and frothy behind us as the wake emerged in a shaft of turbulence from the churning screws then slowly dissipated into the vastness surrounding it. The profile of Istanbul loomed lower now on the horizon; the domes, towers and minarets lost definition and began to blend into a single unit of darkness silhouetted against the blue sky.

I felt an involuntary shudder pass through my body and I reached out to take Suzan's hand. Lord, how I loved that view: flights of stone arrows called minarets pointing to the ramparts of God, the stone breasts of the seraglio that lay naked and exposed to the gaping sky, the soaring domes of the mosques that mocked their weight, the panoply of old and new that fought for space on the crowded hills, the sense of time. Time of the moment, time of the past, time of the future. And the present moment, what special flavor it had: the smell of burning fuel that wafted to us from the smokestack, the quiver of the planks over the stern-mounted screws, the just discernable movement of the chairs as they vibrated in sympathy to the movement around them, the hot touch of the tea glass against my palm, the sour pungency of the remaining tomato and goat cheese sandwich that lay half eaten in the shelter of my crotch, the wind that whipped a yellow skirt up sculptured thighs, the welcoming sea that parted to speed us to shelter from fear and danger.

There had been no need, no desire to speak those first few minutes. Our bodies and spirits begged for repose so we had climbed the stairs to the open deck, populated only by a cayci and a few young tourists who sang unintelligible songs while a bearded youth picked chords on a battered guitar. Then we drank three cups of tea and ate nearly two sandwiches each, savoring the crude lunch as if it had been a catered feast from Maxim's. We smiled and broke into spontaneous laughter, recalling the headlong race through the twisting, contradictory streets of the Bazaar and Old Istanbul before the last frantic dash to the ferry-boat. Sometimes we shouted above the noise of the wind and the engines but our words were swept away into oblivion and we contented ourselves in knowing that time equated distance and safety and that the sun was a balm.

She cupped her hands to my ear and told me our destination. "My uncle has a cottage on a deserted point of land. We'll go there. I have a key."

"On your father's side?" I shouted.

"You mean my uncle?" She whispered.

"Yes." I shouted.

"My father's brother." She whispered.

"I just wanted to know whom to thank." Half my words were lost in the roar of the wind and the exhaust stack but I think she understood my meaning.

Soon the express ferry gave forth its familiar whooping sound and we knew that the long, projecting quay of Buyukada was near. The Turkish penchant for poetry failed when someone attached the name Buyukada, the Big Island, to the largest of the Prince's islands, the group name for the flotilla of three patches of land that sprung up from the Marmara; still it is no more banal than Long Island, I suppose, and the name would outlive me. The brief vacation was over; our escape route took us to an island that had a single exit—the ferryboat back. Unless the Russians had tired of the chase, an unlikely prospect, they would be on the one o'clock express to Buyukada, leaving us only a half-hour lead.

Suzan led the way and we jostled our way through the throng of vacationers. For them, Buyukada would be a careless, car less, tension-free retreat where fruit hung low from the trees and nights were made for food and tender caresses; for us it would be a kind of prison. We trod on city-dwellers corns and tired arches, but were in the gaping exit door before the boat drew fully abreast of the dock. She jumped lightly over the gap, eager to add precious seconds to our measure of safety. I followed reluctantly; the dock at Buyukada had a reputation for having been a scene of the deaths of several temerarious travelers who had jumped too soon and been crushed between the hull of the incoming boat and the pilings of the dock.

She gave the stubs of our tickets to the attendant at the end of the pier and we entered the small square that is the economic pulse of the island. A row of ten or more restaurants veered off the left following the shoreline. The tables were crowded with people lunching on silver palamut, caught that morning in the azure waters of the Marmara, on succulent shrimp that reached the proportions of small lobsters, on chunks of young lamb skewered on shafts of steel, the meat inter-spersed with bay leaves, slices of onion and pale green peppers. I looked at the diners hungrily; the sandwiches we had eaten on the ferry now felt sodden in my stomach. Oh, if only we could forget this crazy pace and join the throng, forgetting Scherevsky, Orenko, Atil, Janice,— all the names that brought anxiety and danger into our lives!

"Have you money?" Suzan asked.

"Yes. Nearly a hundred lira."

"Good. We'll need food." We crossed the square to a grocery store and filled a string bag with bread, yogurts, vegetables, a shoulder of lamb, a tin of olive oil and a bottle of wine. Suzan carried a sack of eggs crooked in her arm. "This will last us until tomorrow," she promised. "If not we'll be eating caviar and shaslik anyway."

I laughed shortly; more likely we would be skewered ourselves. She gripped my arm eagerly. "Paul. Look!" I turned, expecting to see Orenko approaching, but instead it was a long two-wheeled cart drawn by two men, their foreheads glistening from perspiration. On the cart was an enormous swordfish, at least ten feet long from the tip of its sword to the end of its flared tail.

"How big?" She called to the sweating fisherman.

"We caught it this morning, honum effendi, did you ever see such a fish? One hundred and sixty kilos. It makes your friend look like a midget." Suzan laughed as she translated their comment and I tried to look as if I enjoyed the joke too, hoping they weren't prescient, and wouldn't be pressed into service again to haul me onto the pier to be packed in ice for transport to the Istanbul morgue. Tonight that great fish would be parceled out to restaurants and housewives to be marinated, skewered, and cooked over beds of glowing coals. Swordfish on a sword; there was a moral to be drawn from that but it seemed too ominous to reflect on. The fisherman pressed on with their prize followed by a crowd of the curious and I saw an old man touch his head in salute, a gesture that acknowledged that death was not long distant for him too.

At the top of the square, where it begins to slope upward toward the low hills that dominate the island, is a small mosque built to remind men of the omnipresence of Allah. It is usually empty; even the pious old men who still guard old traditions of white beards, close-fitting caps and black flowing bloomer pants, find that all of the island is imbued with God's spirit and the mosque seems irrelevant on a summer day. But the fountain that feeds the row of spigots where ceremonial ablutions take place also provides water for the tired horses that pull high-wheeled carriages to the villages nestled on the slopes above. They come down the hill at the end of a long journey, their eyes wild with fatigue and the fear born of the way hoofs slide on the slope, chests heaving to magnify ribs that try to burst through foam-flecked hide, tendons quivering between joints, and they stop by the fountain to drink gratefully of the cool liquid that flows from the faucets into the deep troughs. When their thirst is sated they nuzzle in a sack of oats until the next weary traveler steps on the footrest and heaves himself into the worn leather seats of the carriage.

Deliverers, all, I thought. They, Scherevsky the latter day Vishnu, Orenko, Suzan and I; each under the command of a master stronger than himself; each acting out a role whose dimensions he could not control.

"No carriage today, Paul. The others may ask whether we have taken one." It didn't matter; I wouldn't have wanted to ride.

I glanced down the square to the clock tower at the entrance to the pier. One forty-five. In fifteen minutes the next boat would dock. Time was running short. We left the square by the westernmost of the four roadways that fed in from different areas of the island and mounted steadily past the tourist hotels, souvenir stores, bakery shops and assorted markets that pressed down on the port until we entered a long lane barely wide enough for a horse carriage to pass. Behind natural walls of bougainvillea, oleander, hazelnut and fig trees, and lush lawns dotted with ponds, were the great wooden gingerbread houses of Buyukada, garlanded with trellises, lacy rails, teetering balconies, and ivy that provided haven for nightingales, starlings and summer insects.

Then the houses began to thin out and we passed through a long stand of umbrella pine growing in a shallow crater of natural sand. The road curved to follow the undulations of the shoreline then dipped sharply and I felt the muscles in the back of my legs tense from the change of direction. To our right we could see a short arch of beach and a small float where bathers sunned themselves.

"When I was a child, my uncle invited us out every summer. I used to swim there often and catch crabs with my bare hands." We used to swim there, too, I recalled to myself, Janice and I, and once, on a moon-light night before our life together went sour, when we were new to Istanbul and every new sight was an enchantment, we had made love on the sand on a far corner of the beach.

"Another ten minutes," she cried joyfully and reached over to pat the string bag that I carried over my shoulder, letting the weight press against my back. "Is it heavy?"

"I'll manage," I puffed, "just don't drop those eggs. Say, don't you think we should have picked up a boat schedule?"

"I know it by heart," she promised. "Every fifteen minutes from six until ten; every half hour thereafter."

"Couldn't we hire a fishing boat and sneak away by night?"

"I thought of that, too, but it can't work. All the boats are clustered around the port. They'll surely stay in the port area, hoping to catch us when we leave. I think we have a better chance on a crowded ferry than if we get caught on a small boat. Don't you?"

I thought of the swordfish that glittered gray and sliver on the cart. "Yes," I replied. "I agree."

The road was ascending again to cross the hump of a promontory that jutted out in a triangle of green into the sea. "We're almost there," she cried. We quit the macadamed road and entered a path just wide enough for two people to walk side by side and wound through a grove of cypress and sentinel pines. The trees were spaced wide apart and the ground between was loose and reddish in tint and soon our feet were of the same hue. We crossed a low knoll and just beyond, perched on a rocky ledge a hundred yards above the sea, was a small two-storied cottage built in the manner of an Alpine chalet.

"Oh Lord," I exclaimed. "Let's stay forever."

We ran the last few yards to the entrance. Suzan explored in her purse.

"My uncle gave me my father's key to the cottage when father died. He's an old man now, a widower, and he doesn't come here often." She withdrew a loop of string from which a key dangled. "Sometimes I come here weekends or when I have a special reason."

"A married lover? An impoverished boyfriend who cannot afford a hotel?" I tried to sound light, but the words were as crooked as the smile that twisted my face.

She looked up at me levelly. "For special reasons, Paul. For my special reasons." She turned the key in the tumblers and the door creaked open on disused hinges. I hung back, fearful and ashamed. The dreadful scar of the past suppurated still in my soul.

*   *   *

Captain Vaslov drummed nervously with the fingers of his left hand on the cabin desk; with his right hand he lifted a tumbler of clear liquid to his lips and sipped slowly, breathing through his mouth after each sip to cool the vodka as it pleasurably seared his throat.

Three in the afternoon and still no sign of Orenko and the two sailors. The numbskull would be lodged in a Turkish jail by now telling his story to the roaches while precious time passed. Radenovitch, too, where was he? Yesterday's search for a replacement cylinder casing had ended in failure; why waste time and money on another aimless pursuit, through the offal-ridden streets of Istanbul, of something that didn't exist?

What a mess! And all because of Leonid Orenko, converted Ukrainian peasant who played at being an intelligence agent but lacked the brains to tell meat from manure! If Orenko had remained on board to guard his precious prisoner this would never had happened. Instead he had gone into that vile city in search of prostitutes while others were left on board to do the work. And if the old man in the cabin was so important why put the sailor from Minsk as guard? Everyone knew his affliction, how he made water more often than a chain-smoker lit cigarettes, half the time in his pants.

Vaslov searched his brain for other faults to lay at Orenko's doorstep and poured more vodka into the tumbler. Orenko! Orenko! I didn't like the man from the moment I saw him. That round face, that smile disguising a black heart, that unruffled calm, that blasted air conditioner to cool his nights while I, Pavel N. Vaslov, Captain of this ship, sleep with nothing but a noisy electric fan to cool my brow. And that perennial talk of Odessa and retirement! A Soviet man was made to work, not to dream of sitting on his fat ass in a teahouse. If Orenko wanted that he should have been born a Turk!

Turk! The thought made him raise his glass to his lips again. In a city of three million people that professed to be a port there was not one cylinder casing to fit Tula's engine. All day that had gone from shabby store to rat-infested warehouse with the specifications book in hand and always the same reply, "Yok, efendim", accompanied by a raise of the chin, and a look that suggested that he and Radenovitch smelled of dead fish.

There was a slow, respectful rap on the doorframe and Vaslov looked up to see the radio operator standing before him, a message in his hand. "Excuse me, Comrade Captain. I think you will want to see this." He handed the white sheet to Vaslov and stood waiting for permission to depart.

"Thank you. You may go." Vaslov held the message in his fingers as if holding a dirty handkerchief. It is bound to be bad news, he thought; there is nothing but bad news because of that wretch Orenko. He placed the paper on the desk, weighting the top with the half-empty vodka bottle. Ah! The letters were hard to read; having an illiterate radio operator was a real burden. He fumbled in a niche of the desk and withdrew a pair of steel-rimmed spectacles with long springy temples that looped around the ears. The writing was clearer now and he read slowly, forming the words with his lips:

CONFIRMING EARLIER MESSAGE TO ORENKO, SEAGOING TUG EN ROUTE ISTANBUL FROM SEBASTOPOL. ANTICIPATE

ARRIVAL ISTANBUL AUGUST 24 REPEAT TWENTY-FOUR 1800 HOURS REPEAT EIGHTEEN HUNDRED HOURS LOCAL TIME. YOU SHOULD READY TULA FOR DEPARTURE AS SOON AS FORMALITIES PERMIT. EFFECTIVE ON ARRIVAL, CAPTAIN SEAGOING TUG WILL ASSUME COMMAND YOUR SHIP. ADVISE TURKISH AUTHORITIES YOUR DEPARTURE PLANS. CONFIRM RECEIPT THIS MESSAGE. CONFIRM ARRIVAL OF TUG. CONFIRM DEPARTURE TULA.

Vaslov read through the message again hardly daring to believe his eyes. Then he uttered a stream of oaths. "He knew," he croaked hoarsely, "he knew. He knew all along. The bastard knew all along a tug was coming. He knew but he didn't tell me. He let me wander all day in that dismal city and never told me a tug was coming. That fat Ukrainian pig! That offal!" Vaslov's voice rose in a steady crescendo until thick veins stood out on his neck and forehead and patches of color mottled his face. He brought his hand down hard on the desk and the tumbler in his clenched fist shattered. A spear of pain went up his forearm and he looked down dully to see that his hand was bleeding. He poured vodka over the wound and let the bloody liquid run across the top of the desk and drip on the worn carpet of the cabin.

"The bastard." He said again and again. "He knew. Well, he'll pay for doing this to Pavel Vaslov." The captain looped a handkerchief around his hand and drew the knot taut with his teeth. So this was why Orenko had gone off early in the morning, pleading that there was no time to encode a message telling Moscow of the prisoner's disappearance. What a subterfuge, he thought, and I, Pavel Vaslov was dumb enough to be taken in. But no more. No more. Orenko had been afraid to tell Moscow that the man was gone. Afraid to reveal how he had abused his trust. Afraid to divulge how he had preferred the company of belly dancers to duty. Well Moscow would know now!

Vaslov ripped the case from the pillow of his berth and wiped the blood and vodka off the desk. Then he crossed to the other wall of the cabin and dialed a number on the ship's intercom. "Comrade radio operator," he shrieked when the buzzer signaled that someone was on the line, "bring me a book of telegram forms and sharp pencils and hurry!"

He sat down hard in the chair and flexed his cut hand. It was stiffening. No matter, he thought. It will be hard but I will manage. They will know everything. Every detail!

*   *   *

Urfanli whistled jauntily as the elevator hummed on its private trajectory to the fifth floor of Second Section headquarters. Burnished concave strips of aluminum massaged his back and he found that when leaning his elbows on the little rail that ran around the cube of the elevator he could reach out with his feet and touch the opposite wall. Where but in a private elevator reserved for a special few could a man do that? Indulge in little fantasies denied to others? Listen to the electronic hum that told a man he was going up, up, UP!

What a lunch, he thought, belching slightly. I will have a behind like an Anatolian fat-tailed sheep if I eat many like that. Two bottles of raki for three of them had been a bit much but his friends had been so insistent, so proud to celebrate his new eminence. Those looks of admiration tinged with envy when they came to fetch him and were ushered past the door freshly inscribed in gilt letters "Orhan Urfanli, Special Assistant." What a delicious title! It revealed so little yet told so much. He could sense them trying to rub their toes through thick shoes in the deep piling of the carpet, watch them make fists of their fingers to stifle the impulse to pick up one of the green dossiers that lay in studied disarray on his desk, see them lick their lips as he told the receptionist in authoritative tones that he was leaving for an important luncheon and instructed her not to make appointments until three-thirty, at least.

Their faces blanched a little when he had suggested lunch at Hasan Efenfi's in response to their casual inquiry "where to?" The food would be magnificent—the meze an endless parade of delicacies brought past in slow defile, the interstices between dishes just enough to renew the appetite, the raki drawn from special vats, the peaches and Bursa grapes so sweet you could make them ooze just by looking at them hard—but the price would equal a week's salary for a low-level functionary of the Second Section. Urfanli knew that the ritual clamor associated with reaching for the check would end in the cost of his lunch being parceled between the two men who saw in the title "Special Assistant," a visa to greater hopes for themselves.

How deferential they had been; how eager to compete for the privilege of tipping the clear glass pitcher of raki, letting the long neck tinkle against the rim of the glass, adding a few drops of water to turn it the color of a summer cloud; how carefully they insured that the portions of shrimp and red caviar were divided inequitably with deference to rank. When other patrons had left Urfanli lowered his voice and told them of the secrets set forth in the green dossier of a dead American woman who served up her body for eager partakers and the men chewed vigorously and wished her back to life in their consciousness and sipped at the cloudy liquid feeling it distill anew in the cauldron of desire.

The waiters were coughing vigorously behind their hands and had swept the table free of crumbs for the twentieth time before the meal ended and the two men paid the price for second-hand occupancy of the pinnacle now occupied by Orhan Urfanli. They parted loudly amid expressions of mutual affection and kisses on the cheek on the sun-swept sidewalk before the restaurant; the un-anointed to the familiar routine of scrutinizing passports at the Immigration Office; Urfanli to the tall square building on Mustaffa Kemal Caddessi where the porter stood when he entered and a private elevator responded to the command of a privileged few.

Urfanli steadied himself against the rail as the elevator bounced gently before coming to a stop. Ahh, he thought, a little too much raki; they poured too much raki. The reception room was empty and a small red cone of light burned over the door to Colonel Atil's office, the signal that the Colonel was giving dictation and was not to be disturbed. Urfanli knew otherwise; when told that he was never to seek to enter the office when the lamp was lit he recognized it as a glowing phallus symbol denoting desire within. Its presence meant Atil had returned from lunch and was enjoying the supreme prerequisite of rank.

Quietly and carefully he removed and hung up his jacket and sat down at the desk. The absence of the receptionist meant that he could not have immediate access to the dossiers; there was time to rest his head on the blotter to sleep for a few minutes and let those distended little veins that throbbed in his temples return to normal. Then he saw with annoyance the four small rectangles of paper fanned out on the desk pad; the word urgent was printed in block letters at the top of the one last pierced. Reluctantly he took them in his fingers and reversed their order. The first note was stamped 1:10pm and said "The Imam from the Bebek Mosque called. I told him you were in a meeting." The second was stamped 2:05pm and said "The Imam called again and insists you call back immediately." The third note was timed at 3:10pm and read "The Imam from Bebek called. He is very angry. If you do not call soon he will write to the Prime Minister. He says that if you spent as much time in prayers as you do in meetings you would be the most pious man in Istanbul." The fourth note was stamped 3:45pm "You-know-who called and insulted me at great length. He says the thieves of Istanbul must have danced with joy when they learned you had joined the police department. He asked me how to spell your name so when the Prime Minister reads his letter he can take action." There was a postscript below the main body of the message. "Colonel Atil returned from lunch a few minutes ago and asked where you were. He has called me in for dictation so I cannot take any more phone calls."

Urfanli read the notes, his dark features growing more petulant. Brainless woman, he thought. I hope she's more efficient on that couch than she is a secretary! She doesn't even leave me a number to call

back. He beat a swift tattoo on his desk and chewed the ends of his
mustache. The Imam meant business about that letter to the Prime
Minister, he was sure of it. Atil would not be pleased if his receptionist
were called out from under her duties to place a phone call. Urfanli
frowned at the array of switches on the phone before him; it had been a
mistake not to pay more attention when the receptionist showed him
how to recognize an intercom call, how to get an outside line, how to
monitor a call placed elsewhere in the building but passed to him for
surveillance. But who can pay attention to such things when a woman's
nipple is practically in your ear canal and your nostrils twitch at the
heady mélange of perfume and a female body?

Perhaps he could go down to one of the lower floors and seek help
but the clerks would simper and smile behind their hands at the spectacle of a Special Assistant so special he could not fathom how to make
a phone work. There was a sharp, insistent buzz from the outside office
and looked down to see a white patch appear over one of the switches.
Should he rap on the door, using the incoming call as a pretext to seek
help? No. The receptionist could not emerge half naked from the inner
office, a skirt held over her loins, for such a purpose.

He mustered his courage, lifted the phone from the receiver, pressed
a switch down and listened.

"Has that idiot Urfanli returned from his meeting yet? A familiar
voice shouted.

"This is that idiot Urfanli speaking," he said sharply. That idiot
Imam might talk that way to a receptionist but he would change his
tone when the conversation became exclusively masculine.

"I am happy you admit it!" The voice rejoiced. "Bey efendim, if you
spent as much time in prayer as you do in meetings you would…"

"Be the most pious man in Istanbul," Urfanli interrupted. "You left
that message once already."

"Do we pay the police to sit in meetings or catch criminals? Every time a man turns around there are new taxes. Do we pay taxes so you can talk all day long?"

The little veins in Urfanli's temples throbbed unevenly. Patience, he told himself. Patience. Mail service between Istanbul and Ankara is very fast.

"It was urgent police business, bey efendim. I am sorry you were obliged to wait. What can I do for you? The ship in Bebek harbor?" His tone was solicitous, recalling the magical effect that a similar tone had produced during an earlier conversation with the Imam.

"No. No. There is no breeze today and the flag hangs limply so I cannot see it well. Besides, it is red and if I close my eyes I let myself imagine that the hammer and sickle turn into a white crescent and then it is the Turkish flag. No, today it is something worse."

"Evet efendim, something worse."

The Imam let his voice drop in a conspiratorial tone. "Bey efendim, there is a dead man in the Bebek cemetery."

Urfanli looked at the earpiece of the phone in stupefaction; was it the effects of the raki or had the Imam actually said what he thought he had said? The doubt was erased when the voice at the other end said again, "There is a dead man in the Bebek cemetery."

"In the name of Allah, what is so unusual about that?" Urfanli exclaimed.

"Efendim?"

"I mean what are cemeteries for?"

"You mock me," came the agitated reply. "You mock me at a time like this? A man more dead than alive in the caretaker's shack at the Bebek cemetery and you make jokes?"

Urfanli sucked in his breath. "More dead than alive," the Imam had said. This put a different complexion on things. "Who is he?"

"I do not know. The caretaker found him in the shack at the cemetery and came running to me with the news. He thinks he is a gavur, a foreigner."

"A foreigner? Is he sure?"

"Almost sure. He does not speak Turkish. He does not speak anything."

"Have you told this to anyone?"

"Do you think I climb my minaret to announce to the faithful that there is a half dead gavur in the Bebek cemetery? Do you take me for a fool, bey efendim? No. I have told no one. Only I have been trying for over three hours to tell the honorable Special Assistant who passes his time in chit-chat."

Urfanli resisted the temptation to snap back. "Where is he now, this man?"

"Still in the caretaker's shack."

"Send the caretaker back to look after him. I will come as soon as possible."

There was a whispered conversation on the other end of the phone.

"No, bey efendim. He won't go until you come."

"Why not?"

"He moans. The man in the shack moans. It is considered a bad omen for a man to moan in a cemetery.

"All right. All right. I will come as soon as possible."

Urfanli put the phone in its cradle and leaned back, pressing the heels of his hands against throbbing temples. Ohh, that raki. It would be a long time before he let those friends buy him another meal. He rose from the chair, put on his suit jacket and stepped into the reception office. The red light still burned over the door to Atil's office. Where does he get the energy, he thought peevishly, he has the gonads of a twenty-year old.

He quickly scrawled a note and left it on the receptionist's desk to establish that he had been in the office and summoned away on urgent business. Should he risk disturbing his chief? No, there were risks that prudent men didn't take; nothing must be done that would cause a man to come and carefully scrape away that new gilt lettering on the door that read "Orhan Urfanli, Special Assistant".

The elevator took an interminable time to mount to the fifth floor and seemed to vibrate in its long, black shaft in time with the pulse in Urfanli's temple.

*   *   *

We ate dinner on the small terrace hewn out of the rocky ledge that served as foundation for the cottage. "I have a peasant's tastes," she explained as she put the steaming main dish on the crude table fashioned of trunks of young pine trees and topped with unpainted planks. "We call it 'ekmek yogurtlu kebab'...meat on a bed of bread and yogurt. You spread the bread on the platter and cover it with yogurt that has been gently warmed but not boiled. Then you add lamb that has been broken from the shoulder bone into little chunks and simmered with tomatoes and herbs."

"Where did you learn how to cook?"

"In a village in eastern Anatolia. Two summers ago, my last year at the university, I spent my vacation at a village near Lake Van near Iranian Azerbaijan."

"Why?" I asked. "I mean why go to a village when you can spend a summer in Istanbul?"

"Because so few Turks know their own country. Because most city people hold the villagers in contempt. They see them in their baggy trousers and patched jackets, caps with the visor pulled to one side, unshaven , wandering around the city searching for work, looking hurt or confused or hungry or sullen, and instead of reaching out to help the city people mock them, give wrong directions, pretend not to hear when a question is asked—do all the things people do to demean one another."

"So you organized the Turkish Peace Corps."

"Why not?" She shrugged. "Must we import the love of our land, the way we import our cars? Turkey will never be a strong country again until we hitch the energy of the peasants to something other than their plows; until we realize that our true roots are in the hard soil of Anatolia. I learned a great deal out there in the village: how to cook good food; the meaning of heat and hardship; how to recognize honesty; that the peasants are clean and that the women shave the private parts of their bodies. Things that city Turks never learn or knew existed in their own nation."

"Suzan Lokman, midwife to the birth of an Anatolian village." I tried to say the words so that she would know they were meant in admiration.

"That too. I watched the peasant women give birth to children. In those places women retain the instincts of a bitch dog that bites through the umbilical cords of her puppies and eats the afterbirth. They give birth without help."

"Listen," I said, adopting a plaintive tone. "I get faint when I see a bruise or a bleeding finger. Can't we talk about something else at mealtime."

"You can admire my cooking." She spatuled out an enormous portion from the platter onto my plate.

I began without waiting for her to serve herself. "Magnificent." I meant it.

There are meals you eat because they meet a biological necessity. The body craves for food and you shovel things down until your gut begins to bloat and already you have forgotten what you have eaten or with whom. This was a meal prolonged, sipping slowly of the pink wine that kept its chill in a copper ice bucket, savoring the tender chunks of meat, soaking the coarse bread in the mixture of yogurt and sauce until every wide pore dripped and then letting it dissolve on the palate.

The sun sets earlier in the waning days of August and it was nearly dark before the moon appeared over the low hills that undulate up from the sea in long, curving swells to the bare plateau of Anatolia. It came orange at first, tinged by the last rays of the sun and the lights from the resorts that line the Sea of Marmara, and then became that iridescent mixture of blue and white for which no proper descriptive word has yet been invented. Behind us the little cottage was dark, partially because we didn't want anything man made to intrude on this spectacle, partly because we felt more secure if no lights signaled a human presence to the watchers in the port that lay over the hill to our right.

She entertained me through dinner with stories of her first year of college teaching telling me, without false modesty, of the stir she had created on the campus when she wore a mini-skirt to class and a plunging décolleté dress to a faculty cocktail party. And of comments of shock and outrage when she did a belly dance at a charity bazaar. I recalled Bill Nelson's observations about the roar of collapsing marriages when she batted an eyelash; mostly I remembered the statement that I was a summer interlude, a way to while away a dull summer until the fall term began. Could the girl who spent months in an Anatolian village be the same one who reveled in the reaction of the older faculty? Could she find me a worthy substitute for a peasant who sharpened his plow with a rock and cut acres of wheat with a hand-held scythe?

Suzan and the elders. The way she told it was so different than the not-so-subtle condemnation built into Nelson's tone. A bright, young girl, half liberal, half conservative, invading the temple of orthodoxy, spreading admiration and resentment wherever she moved.

The fruit had been reduced to little mounds of seeds covered with a thin film of pulp, corrugated peach pits scattered like moist wooden eggs on the plate, gondola-shaped lengths of melon rind floating on a white china sea, and we smoked stale cigarettes found in a seldom-opened desk drawer, the dried leaf burning bright in the night air. We were on a peak of nowhere watching the stars burst into view beyond the cone of a bright moon and below the sea was its own life of movement flecked with sinuosities of light that responded to the breeze.

"You're certain" she said, "all three?"

"All three. No question about it. The slender one on a bench by the fisherman's wharf; the brute at the top of the square up near the mosque, talking sometimes to the carriage drivers as they brought horses to drink; Orenko at the entrance to the pier where the boats leave."

"They'll have to sleep."

"Yes, but not until the midnight boat leaves and there's no service until dawn. They'll sleep in shifts and watch the fishing boats go out."

"Yes. That's what they'll do," she agreed.

"We could just stay here, you know. Outwait them."

She shook her head slowly. "And the old man...do we let him starve? There's no Mehmetcik now to take him soup and rice. We can't let him starve to death."

"No. I suppose not."

It was like a dialogue that we had recorded and were now playing back. We had nothing new to offer one another on this subject since I had come back from reconnoitering the port. It had taken me a long time, the descent through unknown paths and the return uphill journey in the afternoon sun, but it had confirmed what we already knew in our hearts: that Orenko and his men had taken the following boat to the island and were guarding its exits.

Down there near the port, watching from an alley between a row of stores, I had thought how simple it would be, how good for all concerned, if I walked forward and accosted Orenko, ready to tell him Scherevsky hiding place. My stupid outburst when Suzan had mentioned her using the cottage for "special reasons" still rankled despite her quiet "I understand, Paul" when I blurted out an apology. Some gesture of atonement—even to a Russian confessor, seemed necessary. But I held back. Fear laid a restraining hand on my shoulder but something else, too; the knowledge that Scherevsky's destiny was far more Suzan's right to decide than mine. I was a conscript in this struggle, too minor a player to make decisions alone.

"Tomorrow we'll be brilliant," she said lightly and the tape in the mental play back machine spun onto the reel. She stood up. "Let's gather the dishes and stack them in the sink. Then we'll walk down to the sea and watch the crabs burrow up out of the sand."

Minutes later I was following her down a steep path that made two S-curves on the slope before ending in a flight of steps cut from great boulders that shouldered their way out from the hills to guard a crescent of beach.

I looked at her standing just ahead of me, feet apart, heels dug into the sand, diamond-shaped patches of sea glistening between elbows and body, a mane of dark hair flowing down her back and I waited for words that I longed for but didn't deserve.

She turned to face me and her hands moved from her hips to the buttons of her blouse. "We'll swim. We'll swim out and find a sword-fish and he'll carry us over to Istanbul."

"Yes. Let's ride tandem on a swordfish all the way to Bebek."

Her blouse was open now and I stepped forward and slipped it from her shoulders. Then I folded it and placed it on the sand. I took off my shirt and she folded it beside hers. We undressed slowly, handing one another our garments as if they were an exchange of vows, folding them in two neat piles that touched.

Our feet dimpled the sand and then the water lapped at our ankles, our knees, our groins, and the whole flesh of our bodies. No night monsters disguised as ships emerging from the darkness to disturb us; just long, sure strokes through a sea that seemed grateful for our pres-ence. No visions of a beckoning body trapped in a private current leading to death; but a strong, slim girl who sucked in air from the side of her mouth as she sped across the water powered by churning arms. No private torture inflicted by a man who thought himself a coward; the sea was a therapy that told me I could be a man again.

Afterwards I dried her with my shirt and we trembled slightly as our muscles contracted to make blood run faster and ward off cold. She bent to pick up our clothing and then we walked naked up the slope, hand in hand at first, reluctantly parting as the trail narrowed, looking at the secrets of our bodies with candid hunger.

Inside the cottage we climbed in darkness up the stairs to the bedroom under the eaves. Two long rectangles of white-sheeted beds faced the window and we lay together on one and her hair flowed across my arm. Then we kissed and her lips tasted of the sea and her body tasted of the sea and soon the things that I had forgotten could happen happened again.

*   *   *

It would have been possible to watch the fisherman's wharf and the pier from the window of the hotel that looked down on the square but he couldn't stand the thought of staying in the same room with the giant from Kazakhstan who began to snore almost as soon as he placed his head on the rough pillow. Leonid Orenko preferred to sit on an empty bench by the pier, hoping that the hours until he could rouse someone to take his place would pass quickly but knowing that the time spent in waiting is the longest time of all. The midnight ferry had departed fifteen minutes late to accommodate a wedding party returning to the mainland. The revelers spent long minutes saying farewell and the older woman whispered to a younger woman who had a frightened expression on her face and clung to the sleeve of a young man whose hair fell over his forehead, and who teetered on the balls of his feet as he clutched at the air in a series of salutes to his male companions. The young couple crossed the square unsteadily after the boat had signaled its final good-bye and the man stopped to bathe his head in the horse trough before they mounted a cobbled lane to a distant hotel.

It is like in Odessa, he thought. The groom drinks too much vodka and desire mounts to the head but no place else. Well, there was always tomorrow but it was a bad start to a marriage when a new bride must sit by a window and cry instead of enjoying the good rest that follows fulfillment.

He had gone to the hotel room but the sound of snoring and the stench of unwashed feet drove him to the bench by the pier. Waiters at restaurants waited impatiently for the last diners to leave, rolling up canvas awnings to encourage departure and prevent night moisture from forming on the fabric; the creak and clop-clop of carriages was gone; the ticket seller for the ferryboat drew the gates to bar entry to the pier. Life had filtered out of the top of the hourglass, building up for the morrow. Only on the small fisherman's wharf was there movement and the sight of quiet men furling nets and going out to sea alone or in pairs in long, graceful boats kept Orenko there, straining tired eyes to see whether a man and a woman approached.

Now he sat alone without even a cigarette for company, a crumpled ball of paper and cellophane at his feet, waiting for the hours to pass. Waiting until he could shake a man into wakefulness and stretch out on a bed that swayed and creaked, and place his head on a pillow wet from another man's saliva.

"Everything I do turns against me," he whispered. "Everything I do turns against me." How would it sound in a People's Court when Tula returned to Odessa? Comrade judge, it happened because I placed a bandage on an old man's finger, because I yearned to see the flesh of a woman's stomach gyrate to strange music, because I lingered to pay my bill, because I was lulled into thinking that two young people wished me no ill, because…because. Because, Comrade judge, because it was not right to give me the responsibility of escorting Academician V.I. Scherevsky back to the Soviet Union. One measures a load by the strength of the donkey, and I should not have been asked to bear what I could not carry. It is the State that failed, not I, for it was the State that had me submit to its will and bear a load beyond my strength. The State knows my strength, Comrade judge; it has measured and graded my ordinariness. It has recorded every facet of my weakness.

But it would make no difference, the impassioned appeals, the pleas for mercy, and the cries of repentance. Even if Scherevsky came within grasp it was already too late. The damage was done. There would be no one to testify in his behalf.

Even those young people had turned against him. He had wanted to like them, that young girl, that young man. The girl was prettier than the profile in the colored slide revealed, even in grief when sitting silent in the taxi, thinking of the dead man who kept company with the lobsters. Some day she would come to forgive him, Orenko told himself. When the grief had receded into acceptance and she would admit that it was as much her own fault as his. But could he really claim that, he asked himself? Wasn't it the certainty that death was one of the instruments he needed to find Scherevsky, the reason that he had selected the brute from Kazakhstan and the young man with pinched cheeks as helpers? Didn't he know that killing was no stranger to them? That stories circulated on board Tula about barkeepers in Piraeus with crushed skulls, prostitutes in Venice who joined the rubble in the canals? No, he was forced to admit, to have selected such men to help in the search made him party to murder.

The young man would have been easier, if left alone. It had been pleasant to talk to him on that ride to the Grand Bazaar; he would have liked to prolong the conversation over tea when Scherevsky was safely on board Tula. But it was too late for all that now; now he must be tracked down and forced to talk under the duress of great pain until there was no shred of doubt of the truth of his words. The lump he had put on the great skull of the Kazakhstani would be paid for many times over.

Sad, sad, sad, he repeated over and again to himself. We should be friends, not pitted against one another. I, Leonid Orenko, act in the name of duty; he, Paul Adams, in the name of something called freedom. Need we be so far apart? And the girl, Suzan Lokman, in the name of what did she act? The heroic image? Yes, that was it. The girl was the strange force that obliged men to attempt things beyond their capacities.

His thoughts kept him uncertain company as Leonid Orenko sat on the bench, watching the clock above the entrance to the pier, wishing the hours away, fearing the dawn.

After a long while the clock struck two and he rose to his feet in anticipation of the short walk to the hotel where he would shake the sailor from Kazakhstan into wakefulness. He mounted the creaky stairs of the hotel and fatigue seemed to join him in the dark stairwell. Yes, I am tired, he said to himself. Tired. Now I will sleep and tomorrow I will find the young couple and do what I must do. Sad, sad, he thought, but it is not revenge I seek—only justice.

CHAPTER TWENTY-FIVE

After love had exacted its toll of energy we lay on the bed and watched the moon rise and disappear above the field of vision afforded by the tall windows. We talked in low whispers until the little tremors that ran through our bodies ran their course and then we enjoyed the communion when two people sleep as if one.

I wakened once during the night when an owl screeched its presence and flew near the cottage, its great wings making soughing sounds in the air. It was gone when I reached the balcony but I stood there a few minutes listening to other night sounds that came from the sea below and the forest behind. I made a note not to tell Suzan of the owl that flew near our window. In Turkey the screech of an owl is regarded as a harbinger of death and we had had our share of that.

The seven o'clock sun poured through the windows. I leaned on one elbow and looked down at Suzan. Her forearm was across her eyes to ward off the sunshine and there seemed to be the flicker of a smile on her face. I leaned down to kiss the side of her breast where the flesh begins to swell out from the ribcage and she stirred. Her lips parted to form my name, soundlessly.

"To hell with Scherevsky," I said. "Let's stay here."

"Don't tempt me, Paul. We'll come back. Later."

She sat up in bed and, suddenly modest, drew the sheet to her shoulders.

"Go fix us breakfast, darling. There's something I have to do."

I gathered my clothing and went to the landing where the stairs curved and entered the bathroom. I showered slowly and shaved under the cold needles of water, using a razor from the medicine chest. Down in the kitchen I rummaged in the cabinets until I found a canister of tea, cups, plates and knives and forks, which I set on the linoleum-topped table. Then I boiled a pot of water, toasted bread under the grill in the oven, mixed eggs in a china bowl and waited until the sound of the water overhead in the bathroom stopped and I knew that Suzan had finished with her shower.

I mounted the steps to the bathroom but she had already gone up the stairs to our bedroom. She was on the balcony, draped in a towel that was furled above her breast and ended at her thighs. There was a length of cord drawn across the balcony and on it hung a single sheet that was freshly washed and dripped water on the floor. She smoothed the sheet on the rope, drawing the corners taut, oblivious to my presence.

"An old village custom?" I asked softly. "I thought it was the man who hung out the sheet, not the woman. Only it was hung before it was washed."

"There are no neighbors to impress here," she replied, her back still to me.

"But the meaning is the same?"

She turned toward me. "Does it matter, Paul? Does it matter that much?"

"No. It doesn't matter. It doesn't matter at all." Then she was in my arms and the towel that enveloped her fell to the floor. I carried her to the bed that had gone unused during the night and now she smelled of the lingering fragrance of soap and her flesh was clean to my taste and the union born of two eager bodies was more special by the light of day than even it had been by night.

It was ten o'clock when breakfast was done and we stood side by side washing and drying the dishes, talking of the day that awaited us.

"The early morning crowds will have gone by now," she said.

"And they'll see us crossing the square," I continued, "and we'll be finished before we've begun. Isn't there any other way to get to the pier? Can't we swim or something?"

"And get on the ferry boat in bathing suits? They won't let us past the gate. No, we'll go down to the square by the back paths that you took yesterday when you went scouting. We can hide in the alley until just before a boat is due to leave and then make a dash for it. If we're lucky they'll be caught by surprise and can get on board before they react."

"With one or two tiny bullet holes in our backs," I said with a semblance of a smile.

"No. That's just it. They can't use guns on the island! They need us alive, at least until we take them to Scherevsky."

I wiped the last cup slowly, wishing I could agree. The ritual of drawing an absorbent cloth across the dishes had kept me occupied and tamped down fear, but now there was no escaping the necessity to lock the door of the cottage behind us and strike out for the port. While Suzan went upstairs to take in the sheet that she has dried on the terrace and close the window latches I drew a heart on the dusty kitchen window pane and inscribed our initials inside. One day we would return and I would draw cupid's arrow through this childish acknowledgment of love.

A few minutes later we started up the path through the sentinel pines and turned left on the macadamed road that led down to the port trusting that Orenko would maintain vigil below and not spread his limited manpower away from the pier. Soon we reached the upper reaches of the old villas and we could hear the strident cries of children playing in the sheltered gardens, the bray of donkeys registering displeasure at being made to deliver loads of groceries up the slopes, the rustle of lizards in the vine-covered walls adjoining the narrow road.

"Suzan," I said hesitantly. "When we get to Istanbul…if we get to Istanbul…what then?"

"Yes? What then?"

"We can't send that telegram, you know. We can play at kids but we can't play at God. I mean we can't decide that Scherevsky is right about how to make peace and send him off to China."

"I agree."

"And we can't let the Russians take him back either."

"No. I mean, yes. We can't."

"So what then?"

She stopped to look at me. "Shall we go to the American Consulate try to find someone to tell this to?" Her tone showed that she knew what I would reply.

"No. They'd chuckle and make wise sounds and hint that I was drunk again. Maybe reach into a desk drawer and take out a bottle to test my will. Old Adams has the drunkies-drunkies for sure. Imagine coming here with a story like that! No. Not the American Consulate."

"So?"

"I was thinking. Years ago the British had a chap here who knew his stuff. His calling cards said "Commercial Officer" but he had other interests, like keeping tabs on the bloc countries. We'll go to them? The British?" It was a statement framed as a question.

"All right. We'll go to them. They'll listen."

Suddenly we were smiling, knowing that a good decision had been made. We skipped down the path; Istanbul suddenly seemed just at the end of the path.

Ahead of us a man staggered down the slope carrying an enormous wicker basket as large as a barrel strapped to his back. It was filled with grapes that pressed upwards against the wicker top and spilled out over its sides.

"Poor devil," I said. "That load must weigh one hundred and fifty pounds."

"Be thankful it isn't tomatoes. Those men carry tomatoes down from the hills all the way to the pier then ride the ferryboats into town to deliver them to the market. A load in a basket that big weighs nearly one hundred kilos."

We drew abreast of the man and I looked at apprehensively. One hundred kilos weighed two hundred and twenty pounds and I gave him one hundred and fifty at most. That meant he was capable of transporting a load half again his weight.

"You see how the straps are arranged? The third one...the one that goes from the basket and passes over his forehead...is the one that really does the work. Most of the load is passed down his spine and not against his shoulders." Her explanation was concise and told of the summer spent in the Anatolian village.

"And that's why they say strong as a Turk."

"I wish it were for better reasons," she replied.

We passed the man and I noticed how lightly he breathed but it was sad to see a man doing an animal's work. The road curved sharply and then we could see the port below and the square looked empty except for occasional shoppers. People would be off at the beach by now, working up an appetite for a long pre-siesta lunch. The time had come for us to quit the road to follow the paths that led down to the built up area behind the stores, the section where the island's year round residents lived.

"Suzan," I cried. "Wait!"

"Do you see them?"

"No. Something else. That little light bulb called inspiration. The man toting the grapes—he's the answer to our prayers."

"What do you mean?"

"Think, child, think. We buy his grape basket, his cap, anything he'll part with and then you will take the place of the grapes in the basket.

Paul Adams, the poor man's porter carries you onto the boat along with the rest of the produce sellers while Orenko gets sunstroke on the island waiting for us to appear."

"Oh, Paul! That's wonderful. But can you do it?"

"Carry you!" I said in mock horror. "I carried old Scherevsky didn't I?"

The porter was even with us now and she called him over and negotiations began. I averted my face so he wouldn't spot me for a foreigner and up the price, and my flesh began to itch in anticipation of climbing into his patched pants. Their voices rose in counter-pointed anger followed by soothing words and invocations of Allah. Finally it sounded as if a bargain had been struck, and the porter leaned his basket against the wall and slowly did a deep knee bend until its bottom touched the ground. Then he slid out of the straps and turned the basket on its side to empty out the contents.

"Can I talk now?" I said in my best Turkish.

"Yes. He knows you're a foreigner."

"How?"

"I tried to get him to give up his pants and shirt but he refused because he could recognize the smell of a foreigner. He said you might be dirty and have body lice." She clearly thought that we had latched on to the wittiest porter on Buyukada.

"Tell him I return the compliment . How about his cap? I need something to cover my face."

"He's going down to town to buy one for you. I'll make you up in the meantime." The porter shuffled off, upright now without his burden, clutching fifty lira of my money.

"How do you know he'll come back?"

"I didn't give him money for the hat but I said that we would give twice the price shown on the bill. He'll come back."

I stood still while she scooped up hands full of dirt from the path and rubbed them on my face and arms and rumpled my hair. Then she crushed a bunch of grapes in her hands and let the juice trickle down my shirt and trousers until I thought I would drift away to the port. This was followed by more dirt spread carefully over the wet areas until I looked like the sort of mud cake that kids hurl at one another when school is over.

"You are enjoying this a bit too much," I complained. "I'm supposed to look like a porter not something that got lodged in the sewer."

"Verisimilitude. I use that word in English classes to impress the students. You have to look like the real thing."

The porter returned in ten minutes with the cap and took obvious exception to my condition. "Wallahi, hunum effendi," he cried, raising the palms of his hands upward in the familiar invocation of God's witness to events. "If I thought I looked like that I would find another job. It is bad enough to be a porter without being mocked. Give me back my basket! I will not let a man who looks like that carry my basket which is accustomed to honorable loads and an honorable owner."

Suzan recognized the symptoms of a renewal of negotiations on the ground of unforeseen contract conditions and interviewed before he left us to find the local representative of the legal aid society. "I know that money cannot buy a man's pride, efendim," she said earnestly, "and we do not mean to offend, but remember you can sell the grapes again and we will pay sixty lira as agreed."

The porter wrinkled the sheaf of bills in his hand and counted them between thumb and forefinger, "Peki, honum effendi. Ten more lira for the basket and ten lira for the cap and your friend can be as dirty as a pig's behind, not that I ever hope to see one."

We soiled the cap and adjusted the visor so that it hung down over my right eye. Suzan and the porter fitted the straps on my shoulders and I felt their edges dig into my flesh just from the weight of the empty basket. The strap that passed over my forehead was too short and the porter quickly dug another notch to accommodate my height. Then he coaxed me down to a squatting position, the way a man encourages a donkey, and I leaned against the wall waiting for one hundred and five pounds of girl to break my spine. The porter clearly relished the opportunity to clasp Suzan's thigh and place a helping hand under her buttocks as she clamored up on my shoulder and settled down into the basket, her face forward; but this took second place to the special delight of raining down bunches of grapes on her shoulders and head.

"It must look right," he chortled.

"Tell him the word is verisimilitude," I muttered, regretting the extra weight of the grapes. The porter laced the top of the basket and we were ready, except for one small detail; my inability to move. I tried to heave myself upright from my position against the wall but the weight bound me to the ground.

"Tell this clown he's just given me a double rupture with those grapes," I whispered.

"Wallahi, your friend is a weakling, honum effendi. I could lift you up balancing on one leg." He bent double and put his hands under the basket and lifted. Slowly and with ominous crackling sounds my legs stretched until I was upright but still leaning against the wall for support.

"Lean forward," she admonished. "It will balance the weight." I obeyed and felt the slats of the basket emboss my back. I staggered forward a few steps to test my balance. "I can manage now," I grunted. "What time is it?"

"I don't know. I can't see my watch in here," came the muffled reply.

I held my wrist before me and saw the flesh beneath the hair glisten with sweat. "It's ten twenty-five," I said. "Almost time for the ten-thirty boat. Let's go. And tell the comedian not to follow us holding his sides with laughter."

Suzan whispered through the slats and the porter settled down beside the pile of grapes and brandished a cluster over his head. "They have never tasted so sweet, honum effendi. May you be as fertile as the vines on which they grow."

It was two hundred long yards down the last stretch of road to the square and the dock beyond and each step sent pains shooting up my legs but we seemed to look natural to the passing carriages and occasional strolling shoppers. I saw the little mosque to the right and poked up the front of the cap visor to look ahead. The big man from Kazakhstan was standing with one foot on the watering trough and looked over the top basket as we passed. I fell in beside another porter carrying a load of lettuce who grunted a greeting at me but I kept silent. A familiar face loomed somewhere off in the shadows against a store front but I didn't dare turn to look. The gates to the pier were only twenty yards ahead and there was still no sign of Orenko or the slim sailor but my heart beat faster when I saw the white ferryboat that loomed at the end of the pier.

Then a medium-sized man with a round face and gray hair stepped out from behind a cluster of pilings a few yards before the ticket booth and I held my breath. He seemed to be looking directly at me. I hiked my thumbs under the straps of the basket hoping that my spread fingers would shield my face and walked past him. There was a look of sadness and confusion on his face and I felt a twinge of pity.

A voice spoke in Turkish beside me, and repeated itself. Oh Lord, we had no tickets! I dropped my left hand to dip into my pockets and saw the glint of my wristwatch in the sunshine. Did porters wear wristwatches? Try as I might I couldn't spread the strap with one hand to let it nestle in my pocket. I withdrew my left hand and handed the ticket taker some coins and he passed back a ticket. Then we were through the gates.

Had Orenko seen me? Turning, even a little, was impossible with the load that pressed against my head and neck muscles. I felt the hot sweat of exertion and the cold sweat of fear run in rivulets down my chest. The boat whooped twice to announce its imminent departure and the pier was shorter by thirty yards leaving twenty to go. Traffic on the pier had thickened now as passengers and other porters jostled one another for position at the gangplank.

"Did he see us?" a small voice inquired from behind my ear.

I grunted in what I hoped was a way that indicated I didn't know. The rope-carpeted surface of the gangplank was just ahead and I started up the final few yards to the boat. Another voice said something I didn't understand in Turkish and a hand gripped my shoulder. I stood still waiting for Orenko to speak, certain that we had been seen, when the hand propelled me forward along the narrow deck that girdled the boat beside the passenger cabins. "Go to the rear of the main deck. That's where the porters are sent," Suzan whispered. I gripped the rail and inched along while waves of pain shot up my back and into the base of my skull.

The open passageway fed into the triangular-shaped main deck under the upper first-class passenger cabin. Six or eight porters had placed their baskets in the center of the deck and were lounging against them, unwrapping sandwiches or lighting cheap cigarettes.

"You'll have to put me down," the voice said again into my ear.

"I can't. If I try to sit I'll collapse and you'll roll out. I'll have to rest the basket on top of the rail."

"Suppose I fall in?" Came the muffled inquiry.

"Ssshh. My colleagues are looking at me." I used the rail as a lever to work back along the deck until the hull began to curve sharply at the stern. The deck quivered under my feet as the ferryboat captain revved the engines before engaging the propeller shaft and I reached out to steady myself by grasping a perpendicular pipe that ran between decks. Then I pivoted slowly on the pipe and bent forward until I could sense that the bottom of the basket was athwart the rail. After that it was simple: I stood upright and the weight transferred from my spine to the rail; all my body did was steady the load.

The pain that followed exemption from the load was even greater than when the straps pressed against my head and shoulders. Sharp needles worked their way upward from the soles of my feet to the pit of my groin while others followed a trajectory that began with the long muscles of the neck then descended. The mixture of juice and earth that Suzan had plastered my shirt with joined sweat to sluice down my body.

Free now from the restraining harness of the head strap I could look down the deck toward the gangplank. There was no sign of Orenko and his colleagues. I breathed a deep sigh of relief. Our ruse had worked.

"I think we've made it kid," I grunted, using my hand as a voice baffle.

"Insallah," she murmured in reply.

On the gangplank I saw longshoreman slip the great hemp nooses of the hawsers from the cast iron pilings and the ferry whooped urgently to summon a fat old woman who waddled down the pier waving a cane and summoning divine intercession to prevent the boat from leaving. Ferryboat captains, unlike bus drivers, have a sense of chivalry and the boat quivered against the pier while passengers and crew cheered her valiant approach. Then she was on board, gasping against a bulkhead, fanning herself with a scarf, singing the praises of Allah, captain, crew and passengers, gathering energy to enter the comfortable cabin for a glass of steaming tea.

The pilings groaned in protest as the impulse of the boat's screws drove the hull in before it caromed out into open water. A path of turbulence emerged between us and the pier and grew until the water turned blue again and we were en route to Istanbul.

"Any sign of them?" The voice inside the basket seemed more chipper now.

"No. But remember they could have come on board without my seeing them while I was carrying this soggy load."

"The soggy load you speak of is supposed to be the woman you love."

"Well, it's awkward in this position!" I felt a fingernail slip between an interstice of the slats and dig into my back and I let out a yelp of protest.

"Don't do that. The others are looking at us...me."

"Can't I get out now? It's cramped in here."

I looked around the deck and as far forward as possible before replying. "I don't think so. We can't be certain Orenko and his boys aren't on board so you have to remain hidden. Anyway, I only bought one ticket. You're a kind of stowaway."

"You can buy another ticket on board," she argued.

"Money, honum effendi. You gave the guy who produced the grapest show on earth my sixty lira plus ten for the cap. The money I gave for my ticket cleaned me out."

The porters leaning against the baskets in the center of the deck were clearly interested in my conversation with myself and whispered excitedly to one another. Then one of them got to his feet and came warily toward me and I had the feeling he planned to exorcise demons by beating my head against the deck. I smiled weakly as he approached and pointed my right forefinger to my temple making small circles in the air. The other porter nodded gravely by way of acknowledging my infirmity; then he wished me better days and went back to his fellows.

Two minutes out and still no evidence that the Russians were on board. I smiled broadly. Poor Orenko! Every time he stepped out the door someone dropped a bag of water on his head. I wished him well, dead Mehmet and all, and hoped his masters would take into account that he wasn't a poet and didn't warrant severe punishment.

We rode along in silence until I noticed that the load of grapes in the wicker basket was getting increasingly restive. "What's the matter in there?" I whispered.

"I've got a splinter where I can't reach it."

"Then suffer in silence."

"Where this splinter is, it's you who will be sorry."

"I'm sorry already. What am I supposed to do, ask one of the porters to reach through the bottom of the basket with a tweezers?"

"You and your brilliant ideas," the voice answered in exasperation.

"A grape idea." I chuckled.

"That's twice you've tried to make a joke on grape and both times they went sour."

"Well, they got us out of the 'arbor, didn't they?" The fingernail raised a new welt on my back and I decided that conditions in the basket were worse than I had supposed.

"Patience, sweetie. Another twenty minutes and we're there."

I looked around again but without budging from the post at the rail. Except for the six porters there was no one else in sight. Even the ticket taker had not made his appearance.

"A progress report from your captain," I whispered. "We are now passing the big barn of a railway station on the Asiatic side and if I look hard I can make out the navels of the bathing beauties at the Yacht Club. Please pass this notice on to the passenger behind you."

I felt movement and heard rustling behind me. Then a hand dangled a bunch of grapes before my eyes. "Hungry?" A familiar voice said. I reached up and broke off a cluster of green beauties lightly flecked with dark sugar spots.

"Put 'em away, dope. Someone will see you."

My warning was too late. Behind the green cascade that dangled from Suzan's hand I had failed to see the approach of the ticket taker. He stood before me now and the bristles of his mustache danced a jig of anxiety on his lip. I waited for him to say something but his Adam's apple bobbed up and down in a futile effort to make words. Something hummed in my ear and tried to be a voice; a voice that sought to make the word "ticket, ticket" with jaws shut tight. I dug in my trousers pocket and removed the cardboard rectangle and handed it to the open-mouthed ticket taker. He punched it instinctively and his eyes carried a look that told me he had seen something but couldn't quite believe what he saw.

I reached high over my head and shoved back the top of the wicker basket and fished around trying to find a stem to grasp. "Uzum, effendi," I said in my best Turkish. "Uzum?" Damn that girl! Why didn't she get the message? Then I felt something thin and strong clip between my fingers and I pulled out an enormous bunch of green fruit and offered it to the ticket taker. He looked blank for a moment and then the sight of those tender baubles of sweetness restored consciousness. The mustache bristles spread wide to accommodate a smile and the ticket was thrust back in my hand along with fervent expressions of thanks and admiration for the quality of my grapes. I nodded in agreement, waiting for my breakfast eggs to decide that the moment had come to make for daylight.

Then the ticket-taker crossed the deck and was gone beyond the far side of the passenger cabin, juicily shouting a demand for tickets.

"Idiot," I said through clenched teeth. Then my heart stopped beating. Two men were approaching down the narrow strip of deck that led to the gangplank: Orenko and the slender sailor. I pulled the visor lower on my forehead and tried to bend forward under the load to reduce my bodyline. They advanced slowly, glancing through the windows of the passenger cabin as if in search of someone. Then on the far side of the boat the brute appeared, a scowl and a lump on his forehead. Orenko entered the broad expanse of the rear deck and walked toward the knot of six porters. He made a slow, elaborate circle around them studying their faces. Then he came toward us and I prayed that Suzan's application of dirt and juice would disguise my features. It was evident from their manner that they were still in search of their quarry. If they could be fooled into moving on to probe other parts of the ship we stood a chance of slipping ashore unobserved.

I held my breath as Orenko surveyed me and moved on, back toward the direction from which he had come.

"They're going," Suzan's voice whispered. "I can see them through the slats. Oh, no! They're coming back. Ohh!" Her voice drifted away into mute terror and I saw the three men come back our way and form a rough triangle around us, Orenko just ahead, a sailor flanking either side.

"The game is over, Mr. Adams," Orenko said. I didn't look up and didn't speak.

"The game is over Mr. Adams," he repeated and a voice inside me agreed. I looked up into his round face and gray eyes.

"How did you know?" I asked.

He poked at my shirt collar with a pudgy finger. "Turkish porters do not wear little buttons on the collar. I saw them and saw an American."

"Very good," I said. "But how did you know we came on this ferry?"

"I didn't until the very last minute, until I remembered how the porters carried loads down the pier. They walked as if their burdens were filled with air. Then I remembered a tall porter who staggered as he walked and thought of you. It was a chance."

"You go to the head of the class. If you knew all along we were here, why didn't you move in sooner?"

"So that you would know how it feels to think that you have something within your grasp and then lose it at the last minute. Because of yesterday."

I tried to shrug under the straps. "That was for Mehmet." He shrugged in his turn. "Now we are even and now we begin again, only this time there can be doubts. Have you ever heard of the Mad Sultan Ibrahim, Mr. Adams? There is a legend that he ordered that one hundred and fifty of his favorite concubines be sewn in sacks and dropped into the Bosphorus. He did that to insure obedience from those who remained in the seraglio.

"I am going to do the same thing to your favorite concubine. Even now the sailors are drawing tight the strings that secure the top of the basket and in a moment the man from Kazakhstan will cut the straps from your shoulders and Miss Lokman will drop into the sea."

"You can't be serious Orenko. You're not that kind of man."

"That is correct. I am not that kind of man. I despise violence; but you have made this necessary. You and your foolishness. When you see that basket disappear into the water and realize that her death is only a lungful of air away you will understand what harm you have done—to her, to me, to everyone. When that moment comes you will plead to take me to Scherevsky."

I tried to reach back to dig my fingers into the wicker slats so that when the knife cut the leather straps I would fall back with her, but strong hands gripped my wrists. "No, Adams. You will stay. For her it will be easy and swift. Not for you."

"Orenko." I cried out. Listen. You say you hate violence and I believe you. You say you must kill her because you can't trust me. All right, that part's true! You trusted me and I tricked you. But where does it all lead you? You kill the girl and I take you to Scherevsky. You kill me, you go back to Odessa. So? Where are you then? Is this the sort of memory you want to live with in that cottage you dream about? Is this the sort of story you'll tell your grandchildren? The brave intelligence officer who murdered a girl the way people drown unwanted dogs? Ibrahim—that Sultan—he was mad. But you're not mad Orenko.

"Listen. I have something better for you. I'll take you to Scherevsky. I promise. But when you go back on that ship I'll go with you. All the way to Odessa. All the way to Moscow or Siberia or wherever you want. I go back as your prisoner, the man who tried to abduct a scientist of the Soviet Union. I'm CIA, I'm Chinese, I'm a Nazi. Call me anything you like and I'll agree. And I'll get up in the prisoner's dock and I'll tell the judges how Leonid Orenko thwarted my plans; how he fought for the interests of Mother Russia; how he outwitted the agents of imperialism.

"I'll do that, Orenko, if you'll let her go when I take you to Scherevsky. That's better than another killing isn't it? Better than a lifetime of nightmares? You're not a killer, Leonid, don't let yourself be one." I stopped. My breath was gone and my voice quavered.

"You promise? You will come with me?"

"I promise."

Orenko spoke rapidly in Russian to the two men beside us and they replied angrily. Then talked at great length and I hoped in my heart that he was telling them of the glory that would be theirs for assisting in the capture of an American spy.

"Thank you, Paul" said a voice in my ear. "Even if he doesn't accept."

"It was the grapes. I didn't want to lose those grapes."

"We can still try to escape… when we get on shore."

"Not me, child, I promised." I heard her start to sob and the basket vibrated on my back.

"Don't cry. I'll have lots of company out there in Siberia. Just think of the education I'll get with all those writers and poets and teachers." The sobbing grew in volume. "Please," I said.

"It's the splinter," she choked out. "I want to lie down and let you take out my splinter."

The whoop-whoop-whoop of the whistle sounded in our ears and the ferry slowed to make its entry into the dock beside the Galata Bridge. Not quite twenty-four hours had elapsed since I vaulted the fence the day before on our outward voyage. Now it was all over; the next fence I tried to climb would be charged with electricity.

The argument between Orenko and the sailors continued through the last approach to the city; then he turned to me. "They think me a fool for believing you."

"Nine times out of ten they'd be right," I replied. "This time you're right."

"Adams," he said, suddenly pensive, "don't you think it was just the idea that you would make me a hero that persuaded me. I admit I would rather be seen as a hero than a simpleton. But it was something else. We Russians are a sentimental people. You listen to our music, you read our poetry, you study our books and you know that we are all soul, all sentiment. That is something no system can change. When you called me 'Leonid' and told me I was not a killer- those were the words that made the difference."

My reply was drowned out by the blast of the whistle that told us the pier was at hand. Orenko took my ticket from me and formed us into a tight a phalanx. He held back from moving until the porters on the deck helped one another adjust their burdens and shuffled toward the gangplank. They had watched our discussion uncomprehendingly, partially blocked by the bulk of Orenko's back; it was just as well: any intercession on their part would have led to a swift slicing of the straps on my shoulders.

The ferry was almost cleared of passengers as we edged up the narrow strip of deck adjoining the passenger cabins. The load seemed lighter now and I realized that the Kazakhistani had put his hand, palm upward, under the basket and was propelling me forward on the strength of his forearm. Helplessness closed in but I told myself that it didn't matter: I had promised.

A quick passage of ticket stubs from hand to hand and we were in the familiar tumult of the pontoon-supported boardwalk under the Galata Bridge. They were all there—the sights and sounds I loved so well, but now they blended into one conglomerate image as though pressing for attention in my consciousness, knowing that this would be my last opportunity to savor them before the long voyage north. I thought of the unfinished image etched in the dirt of the windowpane of the cottage on the island. Before I parted I would tell Suzan to go there for a special reason: to draw the arrow through the heart and then climb the stairs to the room under the eaves to look out on the terrain where love had flourished.

"Walk under that bridge," Orenko said quietly. "Miss Lokman can get out of the basket there." I walked under the bridge to a dark niche made by the overhanging arc of the girders as they rose from the pontoon to support the causeway above.

"You'll have to help me put the basket down," I said. Orenko and the slim sailor steadied me as my legs bent at the knee until the wicker bottom touched the pontoon. Then they cut through the cord binding the top as I slipped out of the harness. Patches of sweat marked where the straps had been and I thought of lathered horses just in from a long gallop.

Carefully, as if they were treasures, I lifted out the remaining bunches of grapes and removed sprigs from Suzan's hair.

"I can't move, Paul. Help me." I reached down to put my hands under her arms when the Kazakhistani pushed me aside. Without thinking I struck him in the gut but my blow only glanced off. I thought he would crush my skull against the girder but Orenko called out sharply and the giant backed off.

"Once more like that Mr. Adams and I may not be able to control him."

I didn't answer but went back again to helping Suzan rise from her cramped position. She stood, rocking back and forth on the uneven surface of the basket until muscles adjusted to the new position; then she climbed out and stood on the pier and I could see thighs quiver spasmodically beneath the thin cloth of her skirt. "Walk a few steps, slowly, and lean on my arm." We walked back and forth on the pontoon, Orenko and the Kazakhistani dogging our heels. "I'm alright now." Her voice dropped. "Don't do it, Paul. Take them to Scherevsky and then run!" There was no time to reply before Orenko barked out a terse "We will go now."

The Kazakhistani gripped my arm firmly in his massive hand while the slender sailor held Suzan's wrist. Then we followed Orenko up the steel stairway that led to the bridge above and the taxi ranks. Hurrying passengers coming downwards jostled us on the stairway, intent on reaching the iron gates of the pier before they rolled shut and the outgoing ferry departed. Orenko turned left at the top of the stairway and we started down the broad sidewalk in the direction of the New Mosque where the taxi drivers competed for fares.

I was just beginning to enjoy the sensation of walking upright again, free of the great basket and the wrench of the straps, when an old Buick dolmus approached honking wildly. A man shouted, "Taxi, Taxi" from the window of the front seat, ignoring the regulation that passenger pick-ups are forbidden on the bridge, and the ancient car slammed to a stop beside us. The two doors facing the sidewalk opened simultaneously and two men emerged. From the back seat a man as big and burly as the brute Kazakhistani; from the front a slim, wire-thin man who popped out as if on a coil. The big man reached out a massive hand to push Orenko across the sidewalk into the cast-iron safety rail and almost simultaneously brought down a tire iron across the wrist of the Kazakhistani who howled in pain and released me. At the same moment the small man brought down another tire iron across the neck of the slender Russian sailor who fell soundlessly to the sidewalk.

I looked about wildly trying to fathom what had happened, who the men were, when a voice called from the taxi "Get in. Get in." The panic level was rising on the sidewalk and I thought I heard a distant whistle. Without waiting further I took Suzan's arm and we jumped through the open road door followed by the big man. The tiny man vaulted back into the front seat and the Buick engaged gears and roared forward. I turned to look back at the sidewalk. Orenko was on his feet, shaking his head wearily. The brute sailor danced a jig of pain on the sidewalk.

I settled back against the seats, trying to fathom what had happened, who had called in English from the taxi. I looked at the head of the driver and saw a thick head of hair parted low on the side with tufts that grew out over the ears, the collar of a suit that looked too warm for August, a shirt that showed frayed threads at the collar. I leaned forward to get a better view and a reflection blinded me from the rear view mirror. Squinting my eyes to see better I looked again and saw that the mirror had turned into a single, broad majestic smile that glittered and danced before my eyes.

The wonderful, delicious humor of it struck me. The school teacher on vacation, the man at the Yapi ve Kredi Bankasi whose smile burned through the cashier's protective grill, the lounging vacationer who greeted me at Bebek park, the familiar face on the island. Oh Lord, I cried out to myself—those smart British, cloaking their agents in nothingness, painting them to blend with the woodwork of life. We hadn't gone to them; they had come to us!

I leaned farther forward and grasped the back of the seat. I began to laugh and the words choked against my chest as they sputtered out. "You…you…you smiling fox, you! You're a British agent! You're on to everything!" Then I collapsed back against the seat and Suzan started to laugh too from relief and joy. In seconds we were all laughing: the hearty, crinkle-eyed Englishman in the front seat who drove swiftly up the winding streets of Beyoglu; the little man beside him whose head was barely visible above the back of the seat; the giant with the massive gut who filled half of the rear of the car; Suzan Lokman, brave, beautiful teacher of college English and I, Paul Adams, recent retread on the wheel of life. We laughed and laughed until our sides hurt.

Poor Orenko, I thought, my sides convulsing and the muscles of my stomach aching from the strain of joy, he didn't deserve it, poor devil; but it wasn't my fault this time; I hadn't tried to escape—I had been made to escape. Some day I would write him a letter explaining everything and assure him that I had meant to take my word.

Each effort to speak to Suzan produced the same result: a flow of meaningless words like a blast from a blowtorch, fed on hysteria, fanned by relief. The old Buick stopped in front of a narrow, gray building and I thought I recognized the grimy neighborhood near the Galata Fire tower. We all got out and the Englishman led us to a weathered door, the magnificent high-beam smile never leaving his face. "You'll have to walk a few steps, I'm afraid. My digs are not very luxurious, you know."

"That's all right," I replied. "We understand." What I was thinking of was the memory of luxury apartments habited by CIA men I had known in days gone by, their broad balconies, luxury furnishings and white-coated servants belying fronts as manufacturer agents, book distributors or visiting researchers. The British knew how to do it, I told myself. Would the Englishman understand it if I told him I always did revere the British despite Paul? No, that was too arcane a gag when serious business remained to be done, like telling him of Scherevsky whereabouts.

We went up five flights before stopping at a narrow unpainted door. Our guide fished in his pockets for a ring of keys and preceded us into a small room that seemed to double as both living room and dining room judging from the table and straight-backed chairs drawn up near the window. The apartment was non descript, the sort of thing that it would be difficult to describe after a visit; it fitted perfectly the agent's need for anonymity.

The Englishman turned and beamed a welcome. "It's not much but it's home. Good view, though. Can see all the harbor from here right over to Seraglio Point. Now let's get acquainted. I'm William Edward Anthony Blake, your host, rescuer, and friend."

"I'm Paul Adams. And this is Suzan Lokman." I noticed that Blake didn't shake hands, something that underscored his nationality.

"Let's get right down to cases," Blake continued. "We know a good deal about one another already so there's no point wasting a lot of time in detail. The Russkies have been chasing you because you know the

whereabouts of a man named Scherevsky and they want him back.
Right."

"Yes. That's right. We helped him get off a ship out at Bebek,
thinking he was just a seaman. Then we found out he's some kind of
rocket expert."

"The best. A very valuable man in the right hands; very dangerous in
the wrong ones."

"He wants to go to China," I said, eager to convey our knowledge.
"He tried to persuade us to send a telegram to a man named Tsien at the
Chinese Missile Development Center."

Blake arched an eyebrow. "Said that, did he? Did you send it...the
telegram?"

"No. The man you saw us with...his name is Leonid Orenko and
he's a Russian agent of some sort, not very important I gather...he got
to us first. But we weren't going to send the telegram anyway. We
decided to take Scherevsky to the British."

Blake beamed genially. "Very wise. We British have a way of
handling these things. No bad publicity, no magazine articles, and that
sort of thing. Just quick, quiet action. You and this charming young lady
need only tell me Scherevsky whereabouts and I'll take over from
there. We'll hide you out from the bad nasties for a few days and then
you can go on your merry ways."

I turned to Suzan for conformation that the time had come to divest
ourselves of responsibility as Scherevsky guardians. She nodded in
agreement, reading the inquiry in my eyes.

"He's in the back room of the caretaker's shack at the cemetery just
past Bebek."

"Alone?"

"Yes. The man who helped us get him was killed. He's sick, you
know...Scherevsky...his ankles are broken. He needs medical attention."

Blake was all resolve and decision. "Fine. Fine. I'll tend to everything. You can just stay here and enjoy the view over by the window

and Ahmet and I, he's the big fellow, will go and fetch the old man while Nuri stays to keep you company."

He strode to the sidewall of the room and disappeared into an alcove that looked to be a kitchen. He talked over his shoulder and I saw a flash of light and heard the thump of a door. "You can have a wash up if you want, eat a bit of fruit," he reappeared bearing a bowl heaped with crimson yellow peaches, "but don't try to go out. Might be dangerous." He placed the bowl on the table and beckoned us to sit. Then he picked up the topmost peach, opened his great mouth and popped the peach inside the way a man eats peanuts with his martini. His jaw worked vigorously while he spoke. "Lucky thing for you that we spotted you, what? Those Russkies can be mean when they've a mind to." Bits of peach flesh rained down from above as he spoke and I felt like an Ophelia to a sibilant actor's Hamlet. The peach was done in seconds and he removed the fleshless pit. "Watch this," he said and placed the pit between the molars of his right jaw. His facial muscles contorted briefly and I heard a sound like the breaking of a log; then he spat into his hand and displayed the crumbled fragments of the peach pit.

"Bloody good, eh?" He laughed shortly. "Well, I'm off. Don't move, mind!"

CHAPTER TWENTY-SIX

Orhan Urfanli stood rigidly at attention, waiting for the next assault. The momentary lull in the Colonel's wrath was like standing in the eye of a hurricane waiting for the storm to unleash its fury again.

"Son of a dead body washer," the ultimate epithet was like a flagellation chain whipped across his face. "Species of a donkey! Brother to a goat!" Atil's brow was mottled red under his tanned skin and his eyed flamed with rage as he stood erect three feet before Urfanli's immobile form. He clawed the air with his riding crop, searching for additional words of abuse. Then he dropped the whip and went limp, personal energy drained from the exertion of deep anger.

They stood in a white cubicle of a room on the third floor of Second Section Headquarters. A porcelain globe burned over their heads and cast shadows on the men below. There were three of them. Urfanli, not daring to move; Atil, now pacing the floor of the room, executing sharp military turns when he encountered an obstacle; an old man who lay on a narrow white bed, his ankles bound in plaster, his chest heaving in short sequence.

Atil stopped his pacing to survey for the hundredth time the figure on the white bed and thought of all the times in his career that he had witnessed death and death in the making. It was there in the room with them waiting behind the tall three-sectioned screen that towered over the foot of the bed, waiting to put in its appearance for the act that required no encore.

"So you brought him here last night," he said as if repeating a lesson.

"Evet, efendim. At seven o'clock."

"And you looked at the wallet then?"

"Evet, efendim."

"And you did nothing about it?"

"The cards were in Russian, bey efendim, I didn't understand them I thought he was a sailor, just a sailor."

"Just a sailor," Atil repeated acidly. "A sailor who carries an alligator wallet trimmed in gold that would cost you a month's pay to buy. You are so impressed with Russian propaganda that you think that Russian sailors own alligator wallets?"

"No, efendim."

"A sailor with no calluses on his hands, with arms so thin he could not raise a mop above his head, let alone clean a deck?"

"I am sorry, Colonel."

"Idiot! That's what they all say, the idiots who act without thinking. I am sorry I put the knife in my wife's gut; I am sorry I strangled the old woman who resisted my advances; I am sorry I stole that gold watch. And you! I am sorry, Colonel, that I am such an idiot."

"It won't happen again, efendim. I promise you."

The tall figure in riding clothes snorted derisively, "Indeed!" He kneaded his hands as though wiping dirt from them. "You went to Bebek at four yesterday afternoon?"

"Evet efendim. After the Imam had called for the fourth time about this man in the cemetery."

"And instead of telling your superior in the next office you go off on your own to play the distinguished Special Assistant. A foreigner is found half dead in the Bebek cemetery and you decide you know better what to do than your superior."

"You, you…were giving…dictation, bey efendim," Urfanli stuttered, "the red light burned over the door. You told me never to disturb you when the receptionist was in the office with you." He felt his face turn red, recalling his mental image of the Colonel and the receptionist in embrace on the leather couch.

"Fool! You could have interrupted!"

"But…but…I thought…" Urfanli's jaw wagged aimlessly.

"I know what you thought. You thought I was inside polishing the seat of the couch with the woman's bottom! Dirty minded idiot! I was working inside, working to save your job and the jobs of other idiots like you who should be street sweepers, not policemen. Appropriations hearings are only a week away and while I work, pouring over justifications, revising statistics, bolstering my arguments, you sit on your hot crotch and imagine that your superior wastes his time in frivolity."

Urfanli ground his teeth together not daring to speak. It was the fault of the raki at lunch, he moaned to himself. They got me drunk deliberately so I would show bad judgment and be fired from my job. Jealous bastards! I'll pay them back someday.

"What did you think we would do with a Russian rocket expert? Shoot a box of baklava to the moon? Send Orhan Urfanli and his dirty mind into orbit the better to peer into people's bedrooms?"

"But Colonel. You told me yourself that Istanbul was becoming a backwater; that the city was getting a good name; that this endangered our jobs. A Soviet missile expert caught in Istanbul will make wonderful publicity. The city's reputation will be restored; the CIA will come back in numbers."

Atil looked hard at his colleague. "The Soviet Union also has an aid program to our country. Is one missile expert worth glass factories, steel mills and petroleum products? When a painter does a portrait he weighs the strength of the colors to be used. We must do likewise with the image of the city that we create. Some colors are too strong…like red. Red is too strong a color right now. Do you follow me? I tried to be subtle with you the other day, thinking that you had a supple mind and understood my words. But I was wrong. It is the image of crime and espionage that we must create, not the actuality. I do not care two kurus if there is ever a spy in Istanbul again as long as people and governments think there are.

"But this man! What is his name...Scherevsky...he is not a spy; he is a scientist and scientists arouse sympathy and respect whatever their inventions. Therefore he is no good for our purposes," he wagged a finger didactically, "as long as he remains in Istanbul. Once gone, gone where he can no longer endanger us, he will be a fit subject for myth making. Then will come the whispering in the corridors, the backhanded confidences exchanged with susceptible journalists, the planted questions in Parliament, the rumors that fit about the diplomatic circuit."

"I understand, Colonel," Urfanli said admiringly. "You are so right."

Atil fixed him with a withering stare. "I am touched by the wisdom of your judgment, though it is somewhat tardy."

"I am sorry, bey efendim. It won't happen again." Urfanli began to relax, sensing that his superior's anger had begun to ebb. The time had come to make practical amends or the gilt lettering on the door would be flaked off by morning. "What can I do to show how sorry I am, bey efendim?"

"You know the story of the wise fisherman, Urfanli? The one who throws back a part of his catch so that the fish will multiply? Scherevsky is a fish. He came in from the sea and he will go back to the sea where he will spawn for us. When he is gone, thousands of little fish will show themselves and I will see to it that all the world learns of the mysterious doings in Istanbul."

"Evet efendim."

"Evet efendim what?" Atil asked sharply.

"Evet efendim to what you say, efendim."

"And what did I say?"

"You said I must throw Scherevsky into the sea."

"Idiot! I said no such thing. Do you take me for a murderer? If you had any sense you would realize I said that Scherevsky must be returned to where you found him: to the caretaker's shack at the Bebek cemetery. When that is done you will take a rowboat out to the ship called Tula and let them know that a strange man who murmurs in Russian awaits them"?

"Evet efendim. I understand. Without saying that I am a policeman."

"Idiot. You never were." Atil glanced at the heavy chronograph on his arm. "It is now five o'clock. Wait until dusk and then take the old man out in an unmarked car. Put him where you found him and then go. Go to your home, go to a house of ill repute, go to a mayhane, I don't care. Just go someplace where you can forget this man, this conversation. Even try to forget that you are such an idiot."

"Evet efendim."

"You may go now. I will stay with the old man for a few minutes."

Urfanli backed out of the room, bumping the doorframe as he went. A loud 'thwack' echoed in the small white room as Atil brought down the riding crop hard against the burnished surface of his boot. Then he laughed softly to himself. Poor Urfanli would not soon forget this episode. It had been a mistake—assuming that Urfanli was a worthy successor—at least going by the evidence at hand. He was much too literal, too direct, lacking that quintessential quality of being able to look beyond the stars and see the universe.

Atil turned an enameled chair and out its back toward the bed; then he straddled it and folded his arms across the top. Genius hides out in unlikely places, he thought, staring at the inert figure on the bed. Imagine a bag of bones like this capable of disguising an intellect so powerful it could devise a way to send a rocket as heavy as the heaviest minaret into the heavens. It will flicker out soon, that spark called genius; the old man is too spent; the plaster on his legs is like an anchor that will drag him to a grave.

It had not been easy to decide that Scherevsky should be returned to Russian custody. The Americans, the Chinese, the Egyptians, the Israelis; others would welcome a man like that in their hands; but Turkey came first and Turkey's needs dictated that Scherevsky not become an embarrassment, despite friends, allies, would-be allies, enemies, or what have you. Decision-making is like art: simplicity is dangerous in the wrong hand; there is nothing more difficult to draw than a straight line.

"I heard," a voice croaked from the bed.

"Then you know."

"Kill me. Don't send me back."

"I don't send you back. I send you to the cemetery still living. It will be your own people who take you back."

"Let me die! The voice cried. "Let me die."

Atil rose to his feet and smoothed down his breeches. "No, old man. It is not yet time to die. Later you may die anyplace you please. But not here."

"Oh God," the man wailed. Then he lapsed into silence, the bellows of chest rising and falling swiftly.

Atil closed the door behind him and walked softly down the hall, careful not to let the heels of his boots strike against the floor.

*   *   *

Vaslov waved the sheet of paper jubilantly before throwing it in the air and watching it flutter to the floor of the cabin. Then he kissed the tips of his half clenched fingers and threw his hands outward like an opera singer saluting a rapturous audience beyond the footlights. His feet danced on the steel floor of the cabin in a little jig that belied his years.

"Such news!" He cried out exultantly to the walls of the cabin. "Such news."

The jig stopped and he stooped to retrieve the paper. The words glowed on the page and seemed to assume a life of their own to equate the potency of their meaning. "Such news," he cried again.

He looked at the brass clock above his desk: fifteen hours seventeen Moscow time; seventeen hours seventeen in Istanbul. Within two hours the snub nose of the tug would round the point just past the towers of Mehmet the Conqueror's fortress and sidle up to Tula, ready to fix the hawsers to the dead ship and transfuse new life from the massive power of its engines. Then they would weigh anchor and head north to the Black Sea and the familiar sea roads that led to Odessa.

Thirty-six hours since Orenko and the two sailors had left the ship; another four and they would be obliged to remain for good. Better that they should return, Vaslov decided, so that Orenko can face the retribution that awaits. If a life of exile awaited him, how preferable that it be one imposed by justice, not accidental or induced by the man's craven will.

Vaslov turned to look at the mirror on the side of the cabin. A two-day growth of beard showed white and black on his face; his shirt was gray inside the collar. He slipped his fingertips inside the shirt, touched the warm, damp hollow under his armpit, and sniffed. I must wash and change clothes, he said to himself, a Captain in the Soviet merchant fleet cannot greet a fellow officer looking and smelling a goat from the Caucasus. Not at a time like this.

*   *   *

"He's taking his time about it," I said for what must have been the twentieth time. "It's after six."

"It must be the traffic," came Suzan's reassuring reply. "The traffic jams at Arnavutkoy are terrible at this hour. Really."

"Maybe he's dead. Maybe he starved to death."

She stood up to study again the view from Blake's apartment window. Every detail of old wooden houses tumbling down toward the sea; new stucco buildings waiting like vultures for fire, earthquake, and age to provide new skeletons of the past on which to feed; the distant yellow outline of Agia Sophia; the parade of ferries carrying homeward bound commuters, scudding like insects across the Golden Horn and the lower reaches of the Bosphorus—all would be engraved in her mind by now like a Roberts etching.

I had washed slowly to help pass the time but still felt dirty; the fruit Blake had left us tasted alien. Our adventure with Scherevsky was drawing to an end but we felt no sense of achievement; by now the old scientist would be safe in British hands but we had deprived him of what for him was a dream, for others a nightmare.

The cluttered sound of men running up steps came from below. I looked at Suzan in expectation and smiled. "They're coming."

A key rattled in the door and Blake stepped in. His face was mottled and unsmiling and his breath came fast from the rapid ascent up five floors of steep steps. I started to rise from my chair by the window when the edge of an open hand sliced down from above and smashed into my cheekbone. My head hit the floor as I fell and waves of darkness ebbed and flowed through my brain.

"My patience has ended, children," a voice said, but this time there was no hint of a smile lurking behind the innocent words.

"Very funny, you two."

"Yes," I replied, trying to fathom what Blake meant. "Sometimes I am very funny."

The sharp toe of a shoe gouged into my shin and I howled and slumped back on the floor.

"Shut up, you bloody fool." I stopped, letting the pain find another exit than through my cries. "Now get up!" I don't think I would have made it but giant hands dug thumbs into my arms and I was dragged to my feet then shoved down on the chair again. I tried to speak but my jaw muscles rebelled against moving in the snarl of pain that was my jaw.

"Now where is he?"

"I told you," I said, barely moving my lips. Blake nodded to Nuri who out a hand on the top of my skull and another under my jaw and pressed them together like a vise.

"When was the last time someone kicked you in the kidneys?" Blake asked, almost casually. "Suppose I just put two inches of toe into your kidney for fun. You know, the sort of fun that makes your eyes pop out from pain. You won't be able to scream, just tell me how it hurts with your eyes." I tried to shake my head but the massive hands held my head immobile. Suddenly the pressure was released.

"Please," I gulped out. "Please. Why are you doing this? We're allies."

Blake spat. "Allies? Very amusing. My allies are eight hundred million Chinese. Are they yours?"

"But you said you were a British agent."

"My dear boy," Blake twitted. "I said no such thing. You said that and all I did was laugh at the joke. Truth is, of course, I was a British agent but that was a long time ago, before I saw the great yellow light that illuminates the world. Now about that little kick in the kidney."

"Blake, Blake whoever you are. I told you where he is." The face before me was wreathed momentarily in the familiar smile then reverted to fury.

"Listen to me, young fellow. Those Russkies are pikers compared to us. They actually think they have something to live for; we Chinese have something we're willing to die for. The Russkies went soft and didn't rough you up enough. That won't happen with me and my pranksome friends here."

"But you're not Chinese. They're not Chinese."

"We are what we think we are. And I am Chinese. And the Chinese people want and need V.I. Scherevsky who is also Chinese."

I swallowed hard, trying to think through the maze of words and pain. Surely this must be some kind of a gag. An Englishman and two Turks playing Chinese but no one had taped up the corners of their eyes or drawn drooping mustaches on their lips.

"Blake," I finally gulped out. "Why?"

"What do you want, Adams? A little reading from the little red book? All power comes from the barrel of a gun—that sort of thing? Scherevsky helps us build nice long rockets that can pulverize your fat, stupid cities. Then you Americans and all the rest roll over and play dead while Chinese use the ancient arts of persuasion wherever necessary. It's all written out, you know. All you have to do is read the scenario to know the ending."

"Scherevsky doesn't see it that way," I said. "He thinks that helping you build rockets is a way of guaranteeing peace; that if everyone is armed to the hilt no nation will risk war."

Blake snorted. "Bloody theoreticians! You can't scare almost eight hundred million Chinese with a threat of war! It's like the Friday salts I used to take as a child: a little nuclear war is good for you, gets the poisons out of your system."

"Scherevsky helps you and then finds out the truth…what then?" I asked.

"Are you bloody serious? Are you really serious? Do you think that makes a bloody bit of difference? What Scherevsky thinks? Let him think we want rockets to send up fireworks to celebrate the Fourth of July, the Assumption of the Virgin Mary, the Queen's Birthday! Who cares? What men think is meaningless. It's what they do that counts."

"I think your crazy."

"Exactly. Only what you think is not important either. It's what you do! Like telling me quickly where Scherevsky is hidden."

I sighed, knowing that my words would earn that kick in the kidney that Blake yearned to give me. "I've told you." The blow didn't come;

in its stead I saw the great beam of a smile suddenly stretch across his face.

"Very funny. Just like in the adventure books isn't it? The brave hero suffers unspeakable tortures but refuses to speak. Touching but very untrue."

"I told you…"

"Be quiet," he interrupted. "But since you like adventure and games we'll play games. When I was a boy up in Yorkshire some of the boys used to tease me because I had no proper father and called me bastard. I rather liked being a bastard but I didn't like anyone to call me one, if you see the difference. So I would figure out little ways to take revenge, like peeing in their thermos jugs, tripping them on a flight of steps, pouring ink on a fresh text—all manner of little things.

It was rather Biblical, you know. An eye for an eye, a tooth for a tooth. I called it tit-for-tat. Someone does you a bad turn that's 'tat', so you give them 'tit' in return. Got it?

"That's what we're going to play now. A little game of tit-for-tat. You have been naughty and done me a bad turn by not telling me where Scherevsky is hidden. You did tat. So I am obliged to retaliate."

"Tit for tat?" I inquired numbly, waiting for that toe to start in the direction of my kidney.

"Exactly. I am now going to bite the young lady's breast off."

Tit for tat. Something whirred inside my head and I felt myself falling forward off the chair. I tried to look at Suzan but all I could see were white lids drawn tight over eyes; even through the opaque flesh I could see terror and anguish. There was a sharp, splintering sound as I hit the floor and I remember asking myself why the floor should break into little pieces from my fall and thinking that old apartments are dangerous places to live in. The floorboards heaved and bucked under my body and I reached out in a frantic effort to steady them. Something mercilessly hard ground down on my left wrist then moved off and I looked up to see a great, tall body with an assembly of slabs for a face locked in wild embrace with another great tall body that grunted and snorted. I shook my head and looked toward the window where two smaller men gouged at one another's eyes and drove sharp knees upwards seeking places of soft vulnerability that makes men howl and go sick when hit. They looked like a couple on a dance floor, holding one another close, moving as one. I blinked and saw the smooth contorted face of the little man called Nuri suddenly go white and cry out. His knees flailed at the air and the two men spun about in front of the window, the one motivated by the frenzy of the other, their arms linked, and I had trouble distinguishing where one man began and the other one left off. Then Nuri howled again and his body coiled. When the coil was compressed to the limit he shot up and the top of his head struck the sharp point of the chin of the man above him. They staggered in mutual unconsciousness against the tall windows. I thought I could stop them, they seemed to move so slowly, but their linked bodies pressed against the glass and it gave and burst outward and shards of glass and two silent men showered down onto the street below.

Where was she? Where was Suzan? I looked along the floorboards and saw her slumped against the wall beyond the window. She must have been thrown there by Nuri when the door was kicked open with that splintering sound I heard when I struck the floor. Her hands were spread wide on her face but between the interstices of her fingers I saw that her eyes were round with fascination as she watched the grim struggle that continued over my head. Ahmet, the powerful Turk with biceps as thick as a man's thigh was slowly strangling the huge Kazakhistani whose left arm hung useless at his side while his right hand beat helplessly on the cropped head of his opponent. The Russian's face went from scarlet to crimson and his body sagged against the wall; his tongue popped from his mouth and I could see a pattern of ruptured veins suddenly emerge in his eyes. His good right arm dropped down to his side and I saw his knees buckle as that massive body drained of life. Then the light shimmered on something

silver as the blade flashed from the steel tube in the sailor's hand. His
arm drove upward into the lower half of the Turk's protruding gut and
liquid spurted out from it, like wine when the cork is pulled from the
bung. Everything happens in pairs, I thought, as the inert weight of the
two men supported one another. They leaned that way for what seemed
an eternity—for them the beginning of one—their arms dangling
loosely at their sides; then they toppled over and the floor of the apartment bucked and heaved again and dust rose from the cracks in the
boards.

Four men dead in thirty seconds: how quickly it comes when the
moment arrives.

I rolled away from the two still giants, fearful of some final convulsive burst of movement—a fist smashing against my temple, a knife
driven into my liver as a coiled muscle straightened itself, a forearm as
hard as a plow hacking against my throat—and got to my hands and
knees.

Blake, Blake, where was Blake? And Orenko. Where was he? I stood
up and remembered the pain in my bruised leg and I reached out to
support myself against the window frame and felt an edge of glass bite
into my palm. It was my day: a bruised cheekbone, kicked shin, trampled wrist, a lacerated hand; nothing serious, of course, just the sort of
thing to make you wish the day had never begun.

Someone had dropped his pearls, I thought. One of these men has
broken a string of pearls during the argument. No, of course not, they
weren't pearls. They were a witchdoctor's professional credentials in
disarray. But how they did shine, except they're at the jagged ends
where they showed pink! And there was other pink on the floor; not
pink really, more a deep red and it made a broad, unevenly shaped
pattern on the boards like color passed through a serigraph.

Trust it to Blake to smile right through to the end. He would have
been a good Englishman if only he hadn't been born in Yorkshire that
gave automatic entitlement to Chinese citizenship. Only the smile

lacked something; it was vacant, empty. Yes, that was it. An empty smile. Empty of teeth. Just a black-red expanse of emptiness and gums where once those pearls on the floor had shined.

Orenko had certainly kept his composure. He had slept through the whole thing on a deep chair, his chin on his chest, his breath coming with comforting regularity. I walked over to him and realized that he had not really been indifferent to the recent events. There was a purple lump on his forehead that swelled up under his sparse gray hair and he held what looked like the leg of a splintered chair in his hand.

A siren and a voice sounded in my ear. Sometimes in storybooks they are the same thing but for sake of argument I admit that this siren was the sort that police cars used to herald their presence.

"Paul. Are you all right?" Suzan spoke now.

"They play a rough game of bridge around here. Did you see that guy who broke his pearls on the floor?"

"Yes. Poor Blake. Those magnificent teeth. But think of all the peach pits that have been spared."

"Not to mention those peachy ti…"

"Paul!"

"It's been a long day, kid."

"Then let's go."

I bent down and lifted Orenko's head from his chest. "Get me a glass of water, please." She went to the alcove. "Leonid, wake up. It's Young Pioneer Adams here." I slapped him gently on the cheek. "Orenko. Wake up. The party's over and it's time to go home." Suzan returned with a glass of water and I let half the glass trickle down his head. "Orenko. The other guests are staring at you." I slapped his cheeks again and he opened his eyes and looked at me without recognition.

I held the glass to his lips and he sipped automatically, letting water spill over the side of the glass and trickle down his rough chin. "Orenko" I repeated. "It's me. Adams." Something clicked behind those vacant eyes.

"Adams," he said. "Adams."

"Time to go, Leonid. The police are coming." I put my hands around one chubby arm. "Upsy daisy!" He got unsteadily to his feet.

"Where are my men?"

"They got tired and left early. Come on. We've got to hurry."

It was a coltish thing to do, picking up a man's teeth, so large and splendid they would have gone well on a horse, but think of the use I could make of them: replacing piano keys, an ivory ice cream scoop, charms for a bracelet, a Chinese back scratcher; it would have been wasteful to leave Blake's teeth on the floor so I put a handful in each pants pocket and they clicked there making the sound of billiard balls.

We went down the five flights of stairs as quickly as three cripples can, Suzan in the lead. She peered out the front door and announced that a crowd was gathering around the corner of the building where Nuri and the slender Russian had tested the durability of a cobbled street but that the front was clear.

We walked up the slope toward Beyoglu, listening to the mounting wail of the siren behind us and then its quick silence as if it were astonished by the spectacle. One street short of Istikial Caddessi we hailed a cab after Orenko assured me that he had money to pay the fare.

"Where are we going?" He said.

"To Bebek."

"You could have left me."

"We Americans are a sentimental people, Orenko. All soul, all sentiment. You listen to our music, read our poetry and you realize that. When you said that you weren't going to drown this girl I made you a promise. Now I keep it."

He smiled. "I deserved that. You can't claim to be a poet because you didn't kill someone."

We rode on in silence for a while. The lights of the city snapped on as we went, Taksim Square was in the transition period between the departure of the home going commuters and the arrival of the night people. We rumbled down the long hill past the tiered gardens of the Park Hotel, past the great German Embassy that Kaiser Wilhelm had built to celebrate his approach to the east, past the oval stadium where weekend crowds consider a game without mayhem in the grandstand a disappointment, and we were down to the Bosphorus Road. An air of unreality overcame me: it had all happened, this wild sequence of people and events, we were on the last leg of our journey to nowhere and back, but I couldn't believe it. A girl had saved my life and I had saved hers; together we had scraped together enough savings for me to buy a one-way ticket to Siberia. I may be the only living American who decided that going to Siberia was the appropriate way to celebrate becoming a new man.

"How did you do it?" I asked. "Find us."

"It was the license number on the taxi they took you in. I took it down and ownership was traced to a man named Ahmet. After that it was not difficult but it took some time."

"And you arrived in the nick of it!"

"The what?"

"It's a colloquialism. You don't hear it often anymore."

"Who were they?" He asked.

"An Englishman and two Turks who ate a box of poisoned fortune cookies. They wanted to take your friend Scherevsky to China. I thought the Englishman was a British agent at first so I told him where Scherevsky was."

"You what?"

"Only he wasn't there. Either he wasn't there or they went to the wrong cemetery."

"I don't understand."

"It's a new gimmick we're trying out here before Forest Lawn. It's a cemetery where you go before you die, just to get the feel of the place. We hid Scherevsky in this cemetery and Blake, the Chinese Englishman, went to get him only he he we gone. So I may not be able to serve you up Scherevsky after all."

Orenko laughed softly, just loud enough for us to hear. "It's not a bad idea you know, a cemetery you try out before dying,"

"It's a very commercial proposition," I agreed. "Maybe I can get you the concession in the Soviet Union. You can bring capitalism back the hard way."

He laughed again. I love a good audience.

"Orenko," I said. "Excuse me. Leonid, I mean. I'll let you have the theme song I use for the commercials free of charge. It's called 'The Ghoul of my dreams tried to look like you.' Listen I'll hum it for you."

Even the taxi driver joined in the laughter.

Some lines are great no matter what the language barrier.

CHAPTER TWENTY-SEVEN

Night had gathered in from the hills of the Bosphorus and the road was dark except for brief patches of light that identified the little towns leading out to Bebek; traffic was sparse as if cars and people had elected to stop to tank up on fuel and energy for the night ahead. Orenko asked questions about life in Istanbul as our ancient taxi shuddered along. Commonplace questions about the price of eggs, how much a construction laborer earned, what it took to rent an apartment. I waited for him to say he wanted to remain in Turkey, but it never came; the magnet called a retirement cottage in Odessa drew him north still.

We slowed down for the passage through Bebek as white-coated waiters tried to importune us to enter restaurants for an evening of music, wine and good food. I invited him to invite us to dinner, explaining that I had no money, but he laughed and said "Next time. Next time." I didn't remind him that the 'next time' was a long way away for me.

I told the taxi to stop at the foot of the hill that led up to the cemetery and from there we walked up the narrow lane to the gates. The night was still save for the rasp of insects and the rustle of night animals that scurried among the gravestones.

Scherevsky was gone; Blake had said so. We were on a pilgrimage to an empty shrine but we had to share the knowledge—all of us, Suzan, Orenko, myself—that the long journey had been in vain. I led the way down the path bordering the fence and entered the door of the shack. It was jet black within and I felt my way along the wall to the second door that led to Scherevsky refuge. I opened it and smelled the unique aroma of Turkish tobacco.

The voice that said "Enter" was familiar. A beam of light flashed in our faces and turned to illuminate the darkly handsome face of Orhan Urfanli.

"Adams!" He exclaimed in a tone of pained surprise. "What are you doing here?"

"Just following your advice about staying out of trouble, Lieutenant."

He frowned and seemed about to close-question me but thought better of it. "Come in," he ordered. "All of you. I am armed." The light flashed again over our faces and seemed to linger for a moment on Suzan. Then he passed the beam over a still shape that lay on a palate on the rough floor of the shack.

"Scherevsky?" I asked

"Yes."

"It was you who took him from here?" I said, recalling Blake's rage at finding his quarry gone.

There was no answer to my question, just a pause as Urfanli surveyed us all again, flicking the shaft of light from face to face.

"Who are the others? He asked.

"The girl is Suzan Lokman; she's a teacher at the International College up on the hill. The man is a countryman of Scherevsky"

"He is from the Russian ship in the harbor?"

"Yes," I replied, wondering again what Urfnali's role had been in the events following our abduction of the old scientist.

"He wants to take Scherevsky back to the ship?"

"Very much."

Urfanli pursed together the black darts of mustache on his upper lip. There was another long pause before he uttered the single word, "Good."

"He is still living?" It was Orenko's turn to speak.

"Yes. Are you ready to take him with you now?"

Orenko looked at me hesitantly. "Yes. But we have no boat."

"I have one tied up down below."

We improvised a stretcher from the palette and two sheets of plywood and put Scherevsky on them. He was conscious but didn't speak; he just moaned softly as we lifted the palette onto the plywood. Urfanli took the front, I took the rear, and we backed out of the shack. Once outside, Orenko and Suzan stood to either side to balance the load. Then we went up the path to the entrance gate and cautiously descended the cobbled road to the shore of the Bosphorus.

It was brighter down there and I could see Scherevsky eyes studying me intently. "Remember your promise, Adams. Aid me or kill me. Tip me over out on the deep water and let me die. You promised."

I blinked, groping for some way to tell him that I couldn't do it. The words that finally came were no comfort, "I'm sorry. You must go back to the boat, back the way it was before the girl and I found you. We didn't know what we were doing."

"Only a few do. And you were too weak-willed to understand what I had to do. All I wanted was peace. Peace for all of us."

Should I tell him of Blake? Of his shrill disdain for Scherevsky's credo? Of 'a little nuclear war is good for you'? No, it was too late for that; let him clutch that misguided dream to his chest like a holy medal. It was too late to tell him. I looked at Orenko to see if he comprehended the old man's words but all I could see was that he looked very sad.

Urfanli let Orenko take his place at the head of the stretcher and untied the long rowboat. Suzan gasped as she saw the red outline of a lobster painted on the stern. "It's Mehmet's boat!" She gripped my arm and Scherevsky rocked on the improvised stretcher. Mehmet's boat but no strong, sure arms to guide it; no lilting melodies to echo over the black waters; no clear eyes to mirror intelligence and loyalty.

We put the stretcher between the forepeak and the center seat and it was time to go.

How to make a final farewell appear sweet and yearned for? How to accept the good-bye without reprise? There was no time to weave a fabric that could conceal what I felt inside. I kissed her on the lips: salt of the sea; the perfume of sweet-smelling soap; they came back to me in alternating waves of desire and sadness.

"I kiss your eyes," she whispered, not seeking to argue me out of what I had to do. I repeated the phrase in Turkish; it seemed less maudlin, more natural in its native tongue. It is an expression of love that can serve a lifetime while the words 'I love you' are fragile and die an early death.

We parted. Nelson had been right. The coming of autumn heralded the end. It wasn't exactly as planned or foreseen but which ending is? I would go as I had arrived; on a boat, coming from nowhere, going to nowhere. She would return to classes and autumn winds would whip the leaves down from the trees, and soon the rain and the sleet would fall for days on end and all the transient summer things would be made mulch of to feed the summers ahead. And her memories would take on the patina of time that enriches in depth as it robs in luster.

I shook hands with a solemn Urfanli. There were lots of questions I should have asked: how he figured in all this? Was Colonel Atil somewhere offstage pulling the strings that make mere mortals dance? Where had Scherevsky been during his absence from the graveyard? I decided to let the questions form on the gray slate of my mind but go unsaid. Answering one's own questions is a wonderful time killer and speculation is always more fun than truth.

"Good-bye, Urfanli. I think you can tell your headquarters to burn that little card down at the Immigration Office."

He drew his brows together in that characteristic frown and looked from Suzan to me. "Why you, Adams? Why you?"

There were at least fifty other questions built into those two words and I didn't feel up to the answers. I nodded in Suzan's direction, "The girl can explain everything," I said with something akin to a smile. "She knows better than me anyway."

Orenko sat in the rear of the rowboat while I took the oars. He was entitled to return to Tula in style, playing coxswain to a one-man crew. Anyway, I needed the exercise and I think that Mehmet would have preferred to have me at the oars of his boat rather than one of the chained bears that had learned to dance. I headed straight out from shore planning to pick up the currents to half-row, half-drift the last half-mile down to Bebek. Suzan was standing on the shore waving soundlessly and I permitted myself the luxury of thinking that perhaps she didn't cry out for fear of betraying her feelings, and mine in the bargain. Damn, I had forgotten to tell her about the unfinished heart on the kitchen window; some day she would see it, perhaps with another special reason at her side, and smile in mock embarrassment and wipe it off with a quick swipe of a dish towel.

I drew hard on the right oar and braked with the left; the rowboat pivoted on its shallow keel and I could feel the currents accept our presence and we were soon drifting fast. I let the oars go slack to serve as a primitive rudder and felt my shoulders go slack, as well.

"You promised, Adams. You promised." The voice behind me had the sound of a rasp drawn over steel. What could it matter, he was imploring, one more death? One more intellectual concubine on the bottom of the Bosphorus?

Suddenly I was angry at the whining man who insisted I take his life with my hands. "You want to die! Do it yourself," I shouted over my shoulder. "Ask Orenko to kill you. He'll do it and mutter that he's sorry, as he did with Mehmet."

"That's not fair, Adams," the man before me interjected. "You killed Mehmet just as much as I did. Meddling in an affair that was not your own. I did not kill that man myself. I was only doing my duty."

"You're too easy on yourself. The crimes you commit in the name of duty!"

"And those you commit in the name of freedom," he shot back. "Why are they different? Our score is settled now—we can be friends. You, an American, you acted foolishly and I, a Russian, acted in the line of duty. You are a prisoner of a tradition of foolishness that says that all men are different; I am a prisoner of a system that says that all men are bound to one another; that each is part of the other. Can't you see that? We are both prisoners reaching out from our separate cells and therefore we can be friends!"

I lowered my hand into the black waters that carried us along toward the flashing light of the electric sentry that stands guard over Bebek harbor. Can something as weak and infinitesimal as the pulse of a man's wrist matter in the vastness of an ocean current? Can the depths respond to something as meaningless as one individual?

"Leonid. I like you, Mehmet and all. I mean it. I really do. I like your children and try to remember their names. I like your dream cottage above Odessa and hope you will invite me there one day. I like the fact that you are asking questions that nibble away at the hard crust of the obedience you call duty—duty to a system. But you'll never really make it until you, Leonid Orenko, come to recognize that it's men who make systems. If you are a prisoner to a system, then change the system. Men should not be made by systems; systems should be made by men."

He turned his hands upward in the act of a priest summoning blessing on a sinful congregation. "Ah, boy, man, whatever you are. You do not understand. You think it is easy to talk abstractions like freedom and conscience to people who have known suffering and fear, but believe me, the man who has never felt the surgeon's knife cannot appreciate the blessings of anesthesia. We Russians—we have felt the bare blade deep in our beings and we fear—we fear that the blade will strike again. Perhaps from the east next time."

I picked up the bulbous ends of the oars and dug them deep to accelerate our pace. "So you let fear be your guide."

"That surprises you? I am no fool, Adams; I read your newspapers; I listen to your radio stations. What is this talk of 'assured destruction capability' and 'second strike potential' if not the language of fear? Why do you lavish billions on anti-missile defense and rockets that carry multiple weapons if not from fear? We have a saying in Russian—a saying for every occasion and this one suits you: if everyone washed his own doorstep how clean the town would be."

I laughed. Laughed heartily. "Leonid. If ever I get back to America I'm going to set up a business inventing Native American proverbs. We need some. Like 'if every state washed its own superhighway how clean the country would be' and 'there's plenty of sound in an empty ghetto.' It could be a big thing, especially at election times."

"I don't follow you sometimes."

I looked over my shoulder. Bebek was just ahead.

"Looks like they have the reception committee out for you. The ship's all lit up."

"I understand," he said tensely. "I understand." He leaned forward to touch my knee. "Adams. A sea-going tug has come down from Costanza to take Tula in tow. Look over your shoulder and you can see it off Tula's bow. Already its hawsers have been fixed to Tula and her anchor is up. You know what that means?"

I looked back to confirm his words. "Yes. It means she's ready to set sail."

"And you…you are ready to set sail as well?"

"Don't make it more difficult than it has to be. I promised. That's that."

His hand squeezed my knee. "No. I won't let you come with me. The others who heard that promise: they are dead. There is no need now."

"What about the trouble you'll be in when you get back to Russia?"

He shrugged philosophically. "Ah. At my age, at my age you stop worrying so much about things like trouble. I will look after myself."

"And your cottage?"

"If I am to have a cottage it must be because I am worthy of it. Not because you lied and said I was a hero when I know here," and he thumped a hand on his chest, "that I am not. I want a Russian cottage, not an American one. You understand that?"

We were almost abreast of the squat tug that throbbed in the water, its low gray hull redolent of power and tenacity. A searchlight played from the tug's command bridge onto Tula's bow and the black hawsers were already taut from the strain. Sailors in white uniforms with round, tasseled caps stood tensely on the deck.

"Yes. I hope you get it, your Russian cottage."

"They see us from Tula, Adams. I see Captain Vaslov pointing down from the Bridge. Now listen closely. Row over to the ladder and hold us steady while the men come down and take Scherevsky from the prow. I will follow them and push the rowboat out from the ship with my leg. Row. Row away fast and if anything happens dive into the sea. The shore is not far. Do you hear?"

"Yes. Yes. Thank you. Guide me in."

"Hard on your left oar and brake with the right. Now brake with both. Adams. There will be no time to say good-by…left oar again…so I will say it now. Good-bye. And thank you. I don't know why I thank you, but thank you."

Tula's mottled hull was just a few feet from my right side and I could make out the rivets on the steel plates. It was bright out there: the searchlight, the pulsing lighthouse, ship's lamps; all combined to turn the early night into early dusk.

"The ladder! Take the ladder." I turned my body to the right and held on to the steel and wood platform at the foot of the steps which bounced under the impact of descending men. Let them get Scherevsky first, I told myself, that was important; then Orenko and then away. God, what a stroke of good fortune! And Bebek beaming welcome two hundred yards away! My shoulder muscles rebelled as I started to ease backward again to make it easier to reach Scherevsky. The rowboat wouldn't budge. I heaved again against the platform without success. There was a clamor of voices shouting in Russian above me. Why wasn't anyone helping? Why leave it all to me?

The clamor got louder and I turned my aching neck to look upward to the ladder. Something long and metallic with a black hole in one end was pointed at me between the steps of the ladder. I shook my head and looked forward to Orenko. He was standing in the rear of the rowboat, his face an ashy gray, and a burly white-uniformed man shook an imperious finger at him. The accommodation ladder was crowded with young men in white uniforms and among them I saw the peaked visors and gold braid of rank. Then another great hand grabbed me by the collar and I was on my feet. The rifle between the steps was succeeded by a military pistol that was held even with my stomach in the hand of a very tense, very nervous young man who wore the thin braid of an ensign on his epaulets.

"Orenko," I called out. "What's going on?"

He looked at me. "Too late, Adams. An optimist is a wise man turned fool. We are under arrest. They say I am a traitor."

"And me?"

"You are in the traitor's company. That is enough."

The nervous young man beckoned with the pistol in a way that required no interpretation; a gesture with a pointed gun is as meaningful when executed by a Russian as when done by an American, perhaps more so. Orenko was already on his way up the ladder and I followed, thinking fleetingly that now was the moment to vault dramatically over the rail but knowing that I would be dead before I hit the water.

Orenko stood on the freight deck near the rail under watchful surveillance of two seamen and a tough and efficient-looking young officer who seemed to be the senior man in sight. His head was down-cast and he spoke without looking up. "You should not have spoken in English. Until then there was some hope I could tell them you were a Turkish fisherman I hired to row us to the boat. Now…"

He didn't need to finish the sentence. I looked over the side of the ship. One of the white-uniformed young men had cradled Scherevsky in his arms and was carrying him easily up the steep ladder followed by another sailor bearing the plywood stretcher over his head. The Russian navy was not lacking for brawny types. First the brute from Kazakhstan and now a blond giant who carried a man up a flight of steps with casual indifference to his weight.

I couldn't fathom the animated conversation in Russian that followed Scherevsky arrival and even Orenko didn't seem to be paying much attention; but the subject matter became clear when the uniformed sailors passed their weapons to other men whom I took to be members of Tula's crew. Someone blew shrilly on a boatswains pipe and a few minutes later a gray tender appeared from the patch of shadow between the tug and the ship and drew alongside the accommo-dation ladder. Then the men in white descended quickly, causing the ladder to buck and sway from their weight and hurried movement.

Everyone looked to be eager to go except Leonid Orenko and Paul Adams who, by a stroke of misadventure, had been branded with some kind of guilt by association. You have to be careful about your choice of enemies in these troubled times; one or another of them might turn out to be a friend. I wondered whether Orenko and I would wind up sharing a cell.

I looked again over the side. A sailor pushed against the platform of the accommodation ladder with a boathook; the tender pulled away and headed toward the squat shape of the tug which trembled on the water waiting for the signal to send a surge of power to the screws and pull away. Mehmet's rowboat was gone; I searched the darkness behind us but there was no trace of that gaily painted stern. It was out of sight, guided now by the currents of darkness to a destination that could not be predicted. I wished that Mehmet's body had been on board. It would be more appropriate for him to have been borne out to sea on the shield of his rowboat than be buried in the earth.

It was happening so quickly and quietly I was not aware that the ship was moving until it came abreast of the lighthouse. Then I sensed a slight tremor in the deck plates as the energy of the wake transmitted itself to Tula's hull. There were no signals of farewell; no waving of hands to admirers who grew increasingly blurred on the shoreline; no garlands of flowers strewn on the water; just astringent commands called out in the terse vocabulary of authority and two ships, one tethered to the other, moved off into the deep channels of the Bosphorus.

I looked at Orenko, trying to divine his thoughts. How forlorn he looked: the breeze whipping through thinning hair; broad trousers pasted tight against a protruding stomach and stubby legs; hands, unshackled still, but held behind his back passively waiting for the moment when someone would step forward and girdle them in steel circles; eyes fixed on the plating of the deck.

"Leonid," I called just above a whisper. "Leonid." There was no reply. He would have been right to turn and say, "All this is your fault, Adams. The fault of you and the girl. Look where adventure has led us." He would have been right: Mehmet dead, Scherevsky back on board Tula, Blake's smile in smithereens, assorted dead men littering apartments and streets, Orenko and Adams under arrest; everyone a loser.

Soon we passed the promontory that juts into the water just past the Bebek cemetery and I strained to make out familiar figures on the shore. She would be someplace with Urfanli now, telling him in breathless tones of what had transpired leaving out only a few essential details.

We made an odd, neglected group on that deck. Orenko and I stood near one another but uncommunicative; Scherevsky lay on the deck on his crude stretcher covered only by a sheet of tarpaulin that one of the sailors had thought to put over him; two sailors stood on either side of us holding guns that looked heavy and foreign in their hands. I began to muse that perhaps they meant to have us remain together all the way to Odessa when a distant voice called out from the direction of the bridge and Orenko raised his head to follow the words.

"They order us forward," he said to me. "Help me with the stretcher." We bent and renewed the procession that had begun at the Bebek cemetery. It was awkward crossing the deck; even in the wave less waters of the Bosphorus Tula swayed and lurched as ships do when they lack their own motive power. It would have been simple to stumble against the rail and let Scherevsky slide into the sea; would satisfaction match surprise when he sensed the inevitability of the plunge, the finality of the water's chill? Even suicides must feel surprise when the time comes.

Two men came down from the bridge to help us keep the stretcher steady as we mounted the steep ladder that led from the deck to the upper tiers of the center deckhouse. Funny, I thought, how no one greets Orenko; these men have sailed this ship with him for years and yet no one speaks; he is as much a stranger here as I. The tribe has turned spears of silence against the outcast.

We reached the open bridge and put the stretcher down to catch our breath. The ship had drawn even with Tarabaya and over to the left the new resort hotel was a rectangle of white light against a backdrop of black hills. How quickly time and distance pass when we want it the least! Ten minutes more and the sea tug and Tula would pass over the submarine nets erected by the Turkish navy to prevent encroachment by Soviet submarines and enter the Black Sea. I tried to summon to my memory the names of the little fishing villages along the coast, the restaurants where I had eaten, the beaches where I had fished and swum, but nothing came, not even the memory of where Janice had drowned. A great eraser had drawn itself across my mind wiping out recollections: sweet, bitter, half way between that had been so much of my life.

I waited on the outside bridge for instructions, resting my knees against the round rings of the life preservers that hung from metal hooks along the bridge rail, feeling very old and tired; but the men in the bridge command area were too intent on guiding their inert ship to pay us heed. Except for the guns held by the sailors before us, it was as if we didn't exist; the great Soviet scientist, Academician V.I. Scherevsky, lay on cold plating like a forgotten piece of freight.

A thin middle-aged man wearing a crisp uniform emerged from the bridge and issued what sounded like a long sermon in Russian. He addressed his words to Orenko and his features exuded triumph and hate.

"I didn't know your best friend was on board," I whispered in Orenko's ear when the man paused to answer a question asked by a subordinate inside.

"He is Tula's captain. I see now what had happened. Vaslov, that is his name, told Moscow his version of what has happened here. Now I am charged with dereliction of duty, traitorous actions, and complicity in the murder of two of the ship's crew."

"Murder! But..."

"The Istanbul police find the bodies of two Russians who carry the identification cards of Soviet sailors. They notify the Soviet Consulate that notifies the only Soviet ship at anchor here: Tula. From there it follows that I conspired in their deaths because there is no one else to blame."

"Me? What about me?"

"Perhaps. Yes. You will be blamed too. But it is the system again. For them I have become a heretic and heretics always fare worse than men who never believed in the first place."

I nodded in agreement at the accuracy of his words.

"But there will be punishment for you, Adams. The system demands that also. A trial to exact the last measure of shame."

"Fine," I declared. And in the process I tell the truth. How this whole business began with something as inconceivable as a girl who sees a cloth hanging from a porthole and thinks of a village wedding. How a man figures he can find redemption climbing up a rope from hell.

"They may not believe it but they'll have to listen, Leonid. I'll tell them how two men get involved in making decisions about things they know nothing about, like whether nations should be strong or weak; whether systems are just or unjust; whether men have the instincts of cowards or whether they're willing to sacrifice themselves for others.

"So they don't believe me! Who cares? That's what it's all about, isn't it, what we've been doing? It's simple, Leonid, simple. We'll make them listen to us."

Orenko shook his head, "They won't believe you, Adams. The revolution has destroyed simplicity. They won't believe you."

It came from the stern of the ship, that mammoth sound that tore at my eardrums, pushed the flesh of my face hard against my cheekbones and rammed up my nostrils popping little blood vessels. I cried out with pain as concussion forced the air from my lungs. With the sound came a convulsive movement and Tula's stern reared out of the water. I was thrown hard across the narrow bridge deck against the rail and felt the bones breaking in my left arm. Then I was flat on the deck and the ship was tilting to its portside. I gripped the bottom rung of the rail with my right hand to keep from falling onto the freight deck below.

A great tongue of fire soared into the night from the stern of the ship and voices cried out in anguish and panic. Inside the bridge cabin a man hung suspended over the broken glass of a window that had been blown outward by the blast. The two sailors who brandished the guns were gone.

"Orenko. Orenko!" I cried out but there was no answer. Then I heard a rustling sound. No, it was louder, like the sound of a child's sled being drawn across cement, the steel runners grating against the unyielding surface. I hooked my knee around the rail and drew up on one elbow. Just below me Scherevsky's wooden stretcher had lodged in the angle formed when the bridge swept backward to accommodate the ladder leading up from the deck below. Now it was sliding free, heading for the open space before the ladder. I watched in helpless fascination as the stretcher slid. It was just four short feet but the friction of the wood on metal stretched the distance. He was smiling, Scherevsky was, knowing that things had finally come his way.

He crossed his hands on his chest and made no effort to brake his slow descent. Just then the ship lurched further to port and was now at a 45-degree angle. The stretcher teetered on the edge of the stairwell. Then a thin arm reached out and pushed against the railing. In a flash both the stretcher and the man were gone. I couldn't see them fall but I knew the trajectory led to the sea; two seconds later there was a splashing sound that told me that Scherevsky the Chariot Driver was near the end of his last, mortal voyage.

Fire fed on diesel fuel burns with a roaring sound; there is none of the comforting crackle associated with wood or even coal; only the terror that comes when fuel, men and things are consumed in a holocaust of flame and sound. Tula's stern was nearly clear of the water now and glowed like a mammoth torch thrust out of the deep. I craned my neck forward and saw the tug standing well away from the flames; it must have cut the hawsers when the explosion hit to avoid being sucked under when the nose of the ship went down.

"Orenko! Orenko!" I cried out. "Where are you?"

A voice replied from somewhere below. "Adams! Are you alright?"

"Scherevsky gone," I shouted. "Over the side when the ship tipped."

"I know, I saw." Orenko called above the roar of the flames. "Are you all right?"

"My arm's broken." A stab of pain in my elbow confirmed the diagnosis.

"You must jump! You must jump!"

"No good. I'm stuck." I tried to wrench my body upward with my good arm but the pitch of the deck voided my efforts. I looked down the slope of the bridge: if I let go, I thought, I'll slide down the way Scherevsky did. Could I make it through the gap over the ladder or would I be wedged under the railing and lie helpless until the ship plunged down? And if I fell into the Bosphorus, what then? With one arm broken I could hope to swim no more than fifty yards before pain and exhaustion overcame me.

"Adams." I recognized Orenko's voice, nearer now. "I am coming." There was a sound of shoes clomping on metal and Orenko's head appeared at the top of the ladder below me. "Let go, Adams. Slide down to me."

"I'll be stuck under the rail."

"No. No. I will stop you." He raised himself up over the top step of the ladder and threw his wide body down in the angle made by the steep pitch of the deck and the rail. "Hurry."

I unhooked my knee from the stanchion and let go of the pipe. It is not long, the bridge of a small ship like Tula, but the descent was an eternity. The corrugated metal surface of the bridge bit into my flesh and my limp left arm sent waves of pain throughout my body. Then my feet struck hard against Orenko's body and he gasped in pain.

"Adams. Listen," he called, and his voice sounded unfamiliar now. "Go quickly before the oil spreads on the water. It will kill you from fire or suffocation."

"I won't be able to swim."

"It's a chance. Go. Go. Go quickly!"

"What about you?"

"I will follow. Quickly! I feel the hull moving under us!"

I relaxed the joints of my knees to let the weight of my upper body cause them to flex; then I pushed against the deck with my right hand and raised my back up so that I was poised almost perpendicular to the water; my feet still dug into Orenko's side. "Almost," I grunted and pushed harder against the deck. I felt my body held in balance, ready to follow whatever impulse my waning strength provided.

"Go," a muffled voice cried.

I sprang up on my knees, reached over with my right arm in a futile effort to restrain my useless left arm, and fell forward into nothingness. There was a great roar of fire in my ears and then liquid silence as my body crashed through the tensile barrier of the water's surface. How deep and black the water is, like looking down into pits of eternity; how it beckons with unharnessed strength; how the sound of fire was replaced by the roar of prolonged thunder in my ears! How Janice beckoned from below in wanton gestures that I never knew in life; how the water pleaded to enter my lungs and bring eternal comfort and strength! How odd to look up and see great red towers dancing beyond the opalescent surface, coming nearer and nearer. How strange the sensation of air filling the orifice called the mouth to enter eager lungs as I bobbed on the water.

A great hulk loomed above and I realized that I was less than five yards from Tula's overhanging sides. If she suddenly pitched down I would be trapped beneath. I turned on my right side and stroked out, away from the ship, waiting for the splash or other sound that told of Orenko's departure.

I turned on my back to rest; already I was gasping from fatigue and my arm throbbed all along its length.

"Orenko!" I called out feebly but my voice was lost in the roaring of the fire and the tumult on board the ship.

Then I saw him rise above the rail of the bridge deck. He was almost a comic figure standing there, gripping the rail to keep his balance, his shirt awry, his face smeared, his body oozing fatigue and defeat. I lifted my good arm to wave a brief signal. He turned his back to me and I thought he was summoning energy to throw himself over the side into the sea.

"Hurry, man; hurry," I shouted to myself. "That ship is going down!"

He turned back toward me, raised an arm in salutation and then cupped his hand to his mouth to magnify the voice that cried out, "Goodbye, Adams. Goodbye."

Something round and white soared out from his other arm and made shimmering circles in the air before it splashed down in the water a few yards away. I let it drift to me and looped my arm over the reassuring bulk. The fire was waning now, the fuel tanks must have been low, but even in the declining glow I could see the neatly stenciled letters on the life preserver that said, "Tula, Odessa."

My legs churned water and the gap between me and the ship lengthened as I clutched the life preserver tight in my good arm and drifted in the current, watching Tula's final agony and thinking of Leonid Orenko, wishing that it could have been different.

CHAPTER TWENTY-EIGHT

The man at the wheel of the vintage black Buick waved a chorus of angry drivers past on the wide stretch of road just before the resort town of Buyukdere. Such a hurry on a summer's night, he thought; bloody people always in a hurry to get somewhere where they can sit and talk the evening away. It was a bit awkward, he admitted, trying to keep pace with a slow moving ship while at the wheel of a car, even allowing for the sinuosities and grades of the Bosphorus road which made the car cover three kilometers for every one traversed by the ship.

The road turned from macadam into cobblestone and narrowed to accommodate the tumult of Buyukdere where pastry shops, restaurants, balloon sellers, sidewalk photographers, vendors of boiled corn, and people bearing plastic jerry cans filled with the town's prized spring water threatened to put the cork in the bottleneck and stop traffic completely. Blake geared down, letting the engine maintain its own pace with the traffic. He felt uneasy, locked up in the gay atmosphere of the town; the buildings that lined the coastal side of the road blocked his view of the procession that moved north toward the Black Sea. He sounded the horn impatiently as a family group made a leisurely return to a double-parked car, immersed in the joys of eating sheets of helva stuffed with ice cream. Bloody fools, he said to himself, that's how to get cavities. Human nature is so perverse; people always doing what they want to do instead of what they should do.

Another family spotted the checkerboard pattern that circled the Buick's body and tried to enter the car but Blake hiked his chin in the Turkish manner that means, "No. Not under any circumstances. Positively not." It is the most consummately negative gesture ever invented. The abrupt movement of his jaw made a spasm of pain. He looked in the car mirror at a particularly bright spot in the road and winced at what he saw. Sad. Sad. Gums, nothing but gums.

He let out a sigh of relief as the lights and confusion of Buyukdere faded away and the road broadened again. His eyes strained against the night trying to pick up the moving cube of light that would be Tula's deck house. Could it…?" No. Yes. There it was, not a hundred yards offshore, borrowing movement from the squat shape that plowed imperturbably through the water. Blake looked at his watch; nine o'clock. Another five minutes and the ship would draw even with the military area at Sariyer; that would be the end of the road for Blake; a military policeman would wave him back with peremptory arrogance and there would be written in his gesture the fact that civil mortals might not pass.

It is just like in the textbooks: at one hundred yards the speed of light is perceptibly faster than the speed of sound. The stern of a ship bucks up and a pillar of orange flame shoots skyward before the sound of the blast reaches the ears and rattles the windows in shoreline homes. Then it all becomes one, when sight and sound are indistinguishable: the surrounding sea turns into a pattern of black with flame-colored high-lights; oxygen whooshes as it is sucked into the flame to give it strength and character; the prow of the ship dips beneath the water; the great brass screws rise with the stern and hang shimmering in the night like immobile golden butterflies.

Blake jammed on the brakes simultaneously with the first visual stimulus that reached his eye and the car stopped before the sound of the explosion had finished repeating itself concentrically against the receding hills of Thrace and Anatolia. He watched in rapture, peering through the window opposite the driver's side, then realized that the view would be better if he descended and joined the curious knot of people that had gathered to watch the spectacle.

He looked again at his watch. Nuri and Ahmet had done their work well, poor devils. Thirty-three hours since they had slipped over the side of the launch and secured the mine against the ship's hull. It had been timed to explode somewhere between thirty and thirty-six hours—it was so hard to pinpoint these things with a homemade timing device—but precision was unimportant so long as it worked. A bloody shame, Blake mused, that Nuri and Ahmet aren't here to enjoy this too; it wouldn't be easy, recruiting two new men of their caliber.

The crowd had thickened now as additional cars and a bus loaded with German tourists stopped to witness and photograph the unequal struggle of ship against fire. Blake was seized with the temptation to accost them and point proudly to the pyre and declare, "That's my doing. William Edward Anthony Blake did that, and let it be a lesson to the rest of you, too," but he contented himself to mutter a phrase aloud, a phrase that had crossed his lips often since the terrible struggle in his apartment just a few hours before, "Ruthian thonsza bit-thez."

Instinctively he spread his fingers before his mouth the way a man does who is called to the door in the middle of the night and remembers too late that his dental plate is in the glass tumbler on the bedside table. The gesture made him recall the loss he had suffered and he called out again, this time with a special subdued fury, "Ruthian thonsza bit-thez! Ruthian thonsza bit-thez." The words sounded good, albeit unusual, to his ears but no epithet could compensate for the anguish he felt each time he drew the tip of an index finger gently across the succession of pink humps where once his teeth had been rooted. Twelve monuments to a beneficent nature, careful diet, dental floss and infinite care were gone, gone with a finality that had made Blake's heart throb unevenly when he awoke to the discovery. What a blow it must have been to make twelve teeth of such unique caliber simply disintegrate, disappear. Gone...gone from his mouth, gone from the room, perhaps gone to the hidden resting place where aged bull elephants go to die...the mysterious treasure house of ivory deep in the jungle of eternity.

Now, watching the ship burn in the harbor, he was glad he had resisted the temptation to join his teeth; that he had had the wit to descend the outside staircase of the apartment building before the police arrived and started asking the messy questions they always asked on discovering a room full of bodies. Headquarters would never approve a voucher for "one set of false teeth..." so it would be necessary to devise other ways to extract the necessary sums without the wizards of the abacus ever being the wiser. It would take time, however, much time and the wait would be a lengthy mixture of gruel and pain. The worst of it, he knew, was that headquarters would probably not trouble to congratulate him on a mission achieved; there might even be a reprimand for having failed to assure Scherevsky's services for the Chinese missile development program.

The flames had begun to subside and small boats had headed out from the shore to gather survivors. Here's wishing you bad luck, blokes, he said to himself, meaning the words for the rescuers. Then aloud, "Ruthian thonsza bit-thez."

A successful mission. He knew it if no one else did. There was only that little four-line poem in the little red notebook for some startled biographer to fall upon someday; would he see the meaning behind those innocent words? Trouble to probe deeper and learn the entire story of how one man had served his cause and country?

A successful mission...! Service to cause and country...! Blake drew his tongue lingeringly across the hillocks of pain that traversed his mouth. A successful mission. Service to cause and country...Yes, he told himself, he would do it again. But oh, what a terrible price to pay!

CHAPTER TWENTY-NINE

How light and bright and white it was in that room. My lids were heavy but they couldn't resist the infusion of brightness that made me acknowledge wakefulness. The first thing I saw was my arm hanging from the ceiling and, terrified, I began to search for the rest of me. An arm hanging from the ceiling meant that I had been sliced to bits by the ship's screws; there must be bits and pieces of me elsewhere in the room. But suppose they hadn't found anything but my arm? People would frown and not want to associate with me-say I was a no body. The accuracy of the accusation was very upsetting: it was bad enough to be a nobody without being a no body.

A nurse entered the room and poured a glass of water from a metal canister on the table beside me.

"Where's the rest of me?" I asked.

She ignored my inquiry. "Time to take your temperature."

I looked at her suspiciously. "How?"

"Rectally."

I breathed a sigh of relief; there was more to me than an arm. Perhaps if I phrased the question differently I could learn more. "Where am I?"

"The Admiral Bristol Hospital," she smiled. "You were admitted last night with a broken arm, assorted bruises, quite a lot of water in your system and …turn a little on your side please…be careful of your arm…suffering shock. Is that all right? How do you feel? I'll be back in a moment."

She was gone and all my answers and questions crumpled together in my mind like a ten car accident on the Los Angeles Thruway.

There is more to me than meets the eye, I reasoned, looking at the oddly-shaped arm that hung from the ceiling on ropes and pulleys. The little vial of mercury suggested warmth in the old body, at least a portion of it. The acid test would come when someone walked into the room carrying a tray covered with those tricky dishes hospitals use to keep food cold and tasteless. No, breakfast had been served while I was still asleep; there was an enormous sugar covered doughnut leaning against the wall. They must expect it to last a week or more, a doughnut that big. And who ever heard of writing "Tula, Odessa" on the side of a doughnut.

Poor Orenko. I hoped those last few moments were not too long.

A hand reached under the sheets and then a voice said "Thirty-seven point one. Normal." Fahrenheit I would be dead; centigrade I was normal; everything depends on how you look at things.

I didn't like the sound of the word 'normal'. It suggested an early discharge from the antiseptic refuge of the hospital to the world outside; a world already girding itself for the dulcet sound of fall and the grayness of winter.

"May I come in? I won't take but a minute." I turned to see Bill Nelson standing in the doorway, a sheaf of tired looking gladiolas in his hand, looking like Tennessee Williams' gentleman caller. He didn't need to open his mouth again for me to know the message he brought; I was tempted to recite the lines for him but that would have been making it too easy.

"Come in, Bill." I said, feigning warmth and enthusiasm. "Darn nice of you to come by. How are things at the college? Mary?"

"Just swell, Paul. What's more important is how are you? I just learned this morning."

"It just happened last night. I gather I got hit by a truck or something. It's nothing serious though. The nurse said I was normal but frankly I don't trust centigrade thermometers. Won't you sit down?"

He looked uncertain. "Where can I put the flowers?"

"Oh, just pop them in that vase on the bureau. I'll ask the nurse to bring water later. Sit down." It was mischievous repeating the invitation to sit, knowing that he wanted desperately to convey the bad news and leave.

"This is just a quick visit Paul; to tell you that I got a letter from Peter Dawson saying that he's coming back—coming back very soon." He paused as if ill at ease in these chaste surroundings that lacked the context of history he enjoyed in his office at the International College. "You know what that means, of course; there won't be a teaching post to offer you this fall." I nodded my head, reluctant to summon up words of my own, letting him continue. "I'm sorry but you can understand how it is. I mean I can't just dream up a position that doesn't exist. It's a question of funds and..."

"Don't worry, Bill," I interrupted, "you can't have mice and me running across the cafeteria. Think of what the press would say 'Giant White Mouse Terrorizes International College' and a sub-head 'Investigation Demanded.'"

He tried to force his mouth into a smile but nothing of substance appeared on those patrician features. "Well, I'll be off now. Oh, I almost forgot. The college will pay your hospital expenses...five more days. That's the least we can do."

"Thanks very much, Bill. I have a little favor to ask." He frowned, as if anticipating a request for cash in addition to the institutional generosity just offered. "Next time you see Emily Cartwright tell her that I'm my own man again. She won't know what your talking about but say it anyway: I'm my own man again."

He put on a different version of the perplexed headmaster furrowed brow, as if to say that he, too, didn't know what I meant. "Why…why…Yes. I'll tell her. She'll be glad to hear that. You know how she loved Janice…and you."

A little comedy relief is essential at the end of a scene like that and it came when Nelson backed out the room and hit his head on the door-frame in the process. I tried not to laugh until he was far enough down the corridor not to hear but I don't think I succeeded. Laughter should not be suppressed for long; it's bad for the blood pressure.

I had barely begun the serious business of contemplating Nelson's announcement and feeling sorry for myself when the nurse arrived to tell me that two people wanted to see me and was I too tired? I admitted to being a pillar of strength and a few seconds later Suzan stood in the door followed by a lean young man with black hair, a black mustache, black eyes and, I suspected, a black heart to boot.

Was it only a week ago that I had stood on the terrace of Bill Nelson's house and seen this girl, this fragile creature made of steel; this radiant face crowned by dark hair and auburn highlights; this image of slender voluptuousness that made the color rise in my cheeks as memory flooded my brain? Only a week?

How long would I be obliged to wait to hear her speak and know from the timbre of those first few words the direction of our relation-ship? Was it already too late to hope that she would spring forward and cup my face in slim hands, and kiss my lips in a way that spoke of the future?

"We can't stay but a minute," she said, advancing two steps and I knew that it was too late. "We're on our way to Mehmet's funeral at the Bebek cemetery." My hopes rose again. "And after that Orhan asked me to have lunch so I can finish telling him the story of what happened."

There was a crashing sound as hope broke through the surface of the earth and disappeared into the molten core below.

"How are you?" She finally got around to saying.

"Fine. Just fine. And you?"

"Oh, wonderful. It's like waking up after a bad dream. Orhan thinks we were very foolish to do what we did. He says that it could have developed into an international incident."

"Really?" I murmured, trying to remember that my arm was in traction.

"Indeed," Urfanli's urbane voice purred through. "Colonel Atil was very upset when he learned that you were involved. He gave me a message for you. He said that if ever you try to tell this story he will deny everything vigorously. He also asked me to remind you about certain suspicions he has about you. He also said that you should pass to see him before you leave Turkey."

I looked at Suzan, trying to puzzle out whether she was tuned in but she was busy admiring Bill Nelson's limp bouquet.

"That's three."

"Three?"

"Three messages. The Colonel is full of friendly messages. Didn't he send a message wishing me a speedy recovery the better to get me out of here fast?"

Urfanli failed to see the brisk humor of my inquiry. "The Colonel is riding this morning," he said obliquely.

Suzan stepped in to separate the antagonists before they elected to do something brutal, like utter a harsh word. "I'll be back as soon as I can. Perhaps tomorrow or the day after. We get course assignments tomorrow for the fall term and I'll be terribly busy. As soon as possible...I promise!"

I managed to muster a smile. "No hurry. I'll be here a few more days. Five to be exact. It's kind of pleasant only I can't smoke with my left hand. If I had any cigarettes."

She bent down and brushed her lips on my forehead. "Bye for now."

"Oh Suzan!" She paused half way to the door in one of the fastest getaways since Man 'O War. "I hope you have a good enrollment in Beginning Russian."

She prolonged the pause and smiled. It was a good smile. "There are some things that have to be forgotten, Paul, before they become memories. I gave a lot for you; as much as I could. Perhaps as much as I ever can. I think it was worth it, don't you?"

Something hurt badly inside and I wanted to cry out with pain. It had been a mistake to wave goodbye with an arm bound in plaster that was suspended from the ceiling, so I closed my eyes for a while to let the hurt go away. The nurse said later that I had slept and that it was a natural reaction to the morphine they had given me when my arm was set, but for me it recalled my childhood when I cloaked disappointment and defeat in sleep.

Later I tried to pick my way through lunch and was asking the nurse when I would be able to play left field for the San Francisco Giants when a second nurse arrived and announced that a young man wanted to see me.

It should have been no surprise, seeing my ratty suitcase and the green duffle bag in the hands of a young man whose angry face disclosed a depressing absence of sense of humor, but I have an infinite capacity to be surprised so when the angry young man spoke and said, "I'm Peter Dawson", I gulped air and thought of an empty whiskey bottle, dirty sheets, filthy clothing, and other little mementos that I had left as signs of my tenancy in the apartment in Christopher Hall. He dropped my things on the floor the way a man does who is obliged to pick up a dead rat by the tail and deposit it in a garbage pail. Too bad, I thought, I would have liked to like this young man; anyone with a drawer full—no, two drawers full—of cashmere sweaters can't be all bad, especially with winter approaching. But he didn't look in the mood to grasp the proffered hand of friendship and since I had only one good hand left I held back.

"The Dawsons travel fast," I said. "A half-hour ago you were in the 'he's coming back soon' category and now you're here with a load of my dirty laundry."

"I've just come back from my apartment," he began acidly.

"Yes…"

"And seen the mess."

"Yes…"

"I'm very put out."

"So am I," I commented truthfully. "I'm put right out of your apartment."

"And I expect reimbursement for the following." He thrust a sheet of paper into my hand on which were symbols that looked like words and numbers:

1 bottle of Sweat off the Heather	$ 8.00
1 pair of blue dungarees	$ 6.00
Cleaning bill for assorted slacks and a blazer jacket	$ 3.50
Miscellaneous laundry	$ 3.00
Replacements of soap, shaving cream, razor blades	$ 1.00
Cleaning woman 1 ½ days at $5.00	*$ 7.50*
	$ 29.00

I read the sheet three times before daring to speak. "Look, friend, I admit to being a dirty old man but there's just not enough of me to mess up a little apartment a whole day and a half's worth."

"It's disgusting," he answered, pulling down the corners of his mouth and giving each syllable full value, "simply disgusting." I began to see the merit of not having Peter Dawson as a roommate. He took a pen and something shiny and rectangular from his jacket pocket. "This," he said, brandishing my thin sheaf of traveler's checks in his outstretched hand, seems to be yours. And this, he waved the pen ceremonially in the air, "is mine. I will now hold one while you hold the other and write your signature on three ten dollar travelers checks."

How can a man resist a request put as nicely as that? He unfolded the plastic cover to smooth the pleat out of the checks and I looked at the signature scrawled in the upper left hand corner. Paul Adams, it said, pride of the world wide network of executives, writers, artists, rich widows, government officials—the everywhere people who never carry cash. I signed my name three times, trying to make the operation appear nonchalant. Dawson gripped the little book of checks and made that tingling brrdt, brrdt, brrdt sound that happens when a travelers check is torn loose from its mooring and after a long sequence of brrdts passed the book back to me. Without another word he turned and was gone.

I caressed the richly-textured paper of the remaining check between thumb and forefinger; then I remembered the vexed young man who had stomped from the room. My change, I thought. My one dollar change! It was outrageous, lying there in a hospital full of people, being robbed in broad daylight, but all I could do was howl at the top of my voice, "You short-changed me, Dawson. Come back, dammit, you short-changed me!"

They discharged me from the hospital four days later without even suggesting that I accept a cash reimbursement for the unused day the college was paying for. My arm was neatly supported in a blue denim sling and the bruises acquired during our encounters with Blake, Orenko, and assorted scoundrels hurt only when I made a special effort to reach out.

I didn't have anything to give to the personnel except a winning smile, the remnants of Nelson's tired gladiolas, and a bouquet of roses sent by Suzan that still retained traces of its original beauty. No one seemed to mind; in fact, no one seemed to notice my departure except the little man who polished the hospital floors and who looked vexed as he watched my duffle bag etch a path through a freshly waxed corridor.

It took a long time to walk down the hill from Nisantas to the Bosphorus encumbered with luggage, a life preserver looped over my neck, and my left arm in a sling, and I found that I tired easily, but by noontime I was in hailing distance of the dolmus taxis that cruise the route from Istanbul to Bebek. My ratty suitcase, duffle bag and life preserver were thrown atop a heap of watermelon rinds and I recognized the car and driver who had hauled me out to Bebek the day of my arrival. I looked apprehensively for the old crone and her retinue of daughters, daughters-in-law, granddaughters and great granddaughters, just to be certain that the whole mad sequence wasn't beginning again, but a different batch of tired and harassed travelers waited impatiently for the blissful moment when the motor kicked over and death waited at every turn.

Seyfi Munir recognized me when I arrived at the Six-Legged Octopus and readily agreed to lend me a rowboat with an outboard engine. After a few ungainly efforts to operate the engine with one hand I pulled away from the Six-Legged Octopus and promised to be back soon. I thought of everything and nothing on the trip to Buyukdere, trying to concentrate on nothing to the exclusion of everything, but bits of the latter slipped around the barrier of nothingness and I knew that though Janice was out of my system someone new had entered and the process of dislodging her memory would be slow and costly.

The black and red stern jutting out of the water and the great brass screws that glittered in the mid-day sun had already become a tourist attraction and small boats cruised around Tula's remains, their occupants gaping and exchanging worried looks. I slowed the engine and cruised through the circling boats until I was over the after part of the deckhouse visible just three feet below the water. Every detail was clear and I went slowly past: the row of portholes, the gray and white painted bulkheads, the rectangular brass plate that said "Tula, Odessa". It was the place I wanted. I turned the rowboat sharply around, cut the engine and drifted back over the submerged deckhouse. I cupped my right

hand and dipped it into the water to slow my passage over the remains
below; then I reached down into the gunwales and lifted up the life
preserver and placed it gently on the water, just over the brass plate, and
said something silly and sentimental that was meant to tell Leonid
Orenko that if ever he got out of his half of the prison I wanted to help
too.

The rowboat drifted some time before I pulled the starting cord and
coaxed the old engine back to life. Fierce concentration on unimportant
details in a way of controlling big problems, at least that's what the
guidance columns say, and I lavished care and attention on the tiller of
the rowboat trying to forget that I had no job and one travelers check to
my name, trying to forget Atil's message that I see him before leaving,
remembering a young girl who had become a woman to make me a man.

After a long while of remembering everything I wanted to forget, the
familiar shape of the Bebek lighthouse loomed out of the water and
beyond, on the far side of the harbor, was the boxy outline of the Six-
Legged Octopus.

Seyfi Munir stood on the near side of the houseboat's little terrace
and beside him stood someone smaller who waved a hand in greeting.
A man can't live without hope but there comes a day when hope must
be carefully rationed and husbanded for the uncertainties ahead. So I
tried not to notice the sudden rapid thumping I felt in my chest and I
was careful not to open up the throttle of the old outboard as its
propeller churned in the water and powered the rowboat back to its
moorings.

Epilogue

When Paul Adams returned from his trip to Tula to pay tribute to Orenko, a familiar figure stood on the dock—Suzan Lokman. His hopes for a long-term relationship were quickly dashed as she rightly reasoned that when you have completed the adventure of a lifetime there is little hope for another to top it. Knowing that Adams had only one ten-dollar traveler's check left, she lent him her entire savings thus enabling him to return to Paris. Except for one brief infraction at an overnight stop in Bulgaria (and who wouldn't get drunk in Bulgaria), he stayed sober. Suzan returned to her teaching at the International College. She had to fend off the attentions of Orhan Urfanli for several months but he finally came to understand that he was not the man for her. Ten years after the adventure that may have changed the course of history, she was elected to the Turkish Parliament.

As for Adams, he visited Col. Atil again to pay his respects and farewells, but primarily to ask the question that had nagged at him since their first meeting, "Colonel Atil," he inquired, "were you the man in uniform who was waiting for Janice just before she drowned? The one she was going off with? The one who gave me a half-wave?" Atil's jaw muscles twitched and he gave a flicker of a smile, turning his face halfway away from his interrogator, but did not speak words. But

Adams sensed the truth. And why Atil had said, "Adams, you did well
to let her drown."

On his return to Paris and thanks to another alumnus of Princeton,
Paul Adams got a job with an American bank with sumptuous facilities
on the Champs Elysees. He gradually prospered there and eventually
returned to the United States to open a small investment firm, the kind
that specialists call a "boutique." A couple of disastrous marriages
followed. He kept postponing the repayment of the loan that Suzan had
made him, hoping that she would make contact and thus provide an
opportunity to rekindle a friendship and possibly their love. But that
didn't happen and he finally paid her a decade later with ample interest.
She used these funds to help print posters during her election
campaign. More than once they reminded her of the scrap of cloth that
V.I. Scherevsky had hung from the porthole of Tula.

Colonel Atil was on the wrong side of the draw when a military-led
revolution overthrew the Turkish government and was obligated to
retire. He still wears his impeccable uniform almost daily and that gives
him a certain cachet in his career as an antique dealer specializing in
Hittite artifacts that are much cherished by collectors.

Sadly, Vaslov and others besmirched Orenko's name in every way
possible and this led to cancellation of his wife's right to a widow's
pension and the family's eventual eviction from their cottage in Odessa.

GLOSSARY

Most of the Turkish words and phrases in "Both Hunter & Hunted" are understandable in the context presented. When you next visit Istanbul, you will hear them often, especially the word "Welcome." One word that merits special attention is "donme" when Blake refers to his "donme" friend in the Grand Bazaar, the Kapali Carsi, as a means of contacting Tits and Ass.

Centuries ago, when the Sephardic Jews were driven out of Spain, they found refuge in the Ottoman Empire, thus contradicting the notion that Muslims are automatically hostile to Jews. In truth, Sephardic Jews prospered in the Ottoman Empire, and many converted to Islam, thus becoming "donme", a word that takes its origins from the Turkish verb "donner", to turn. In modern Turkey, "donme" continue to play an active role in the country's cultural, artistic, and business life. After the establishment of Israel some "donme" migrated there. Interestingly, many returned to Turkey.

A few words about some other simple codes:

Tits and Ass—as you have discovered, this refers to Tel Aviv, for which Blake did some occasional freelance work. Tits and Ass was often used in the intelligence community as a tongue in cheek reference to Israel, partially out of respect, partially in derision.

B.J.—When an ex-director of the CIA wrote on Adams' manuscript, "Great book. But don't let it get out. Tits and Ass and B.J. won't like it," the B.J. was a reference to Beijing.

ABOUT THE AUTHOR

A former U.S. Foreign Service officer who has lived in Europe, The Middle East and Asia, Vincent Joyce is a novelist, dramatist, and lecturer, and when not following creative pursuits, has been an executive of a major international bank.